Prologue

Staten Island, New York
October 22, 1767

"I'm not afraid if you're not! Are you?"

"A little, but I want to do it anyway. Quiet now, and stay close behind me."

It was growing dark, but the two girls left their sway-backed nag tied in a thicket just off the Bay Road and darted through the blowing trees toward the lighted manor house. Libby, the leader, was twelve that year, her curls as flame-hued as the maples. Ash-blond Merry was only ten and adored her elder sister, despite Libby's usually brooding, bookish ways which their mother said were most unladylike. But, right now, the long, quiet days helping Mother at their cottage was forgotten in the rush of adventure. Poor, ill Widow Fencer, to whom the girls had just delivered honey syrup for the easing of her lung cough, was forgotten, too. They were going to look up close at Melrose Manor, the largest Tory home on the island!

They halted, breathing hard, on the far side of the vast vegetable garden, which was now cleared by early frost. All bounteous, beautiful and forbidden Melrose lay

stretched before them, as if they—outsiders and daughters of a staunch Whig family—had a right to be here. Just for now, what did it matter that the Tories were ever loyal to the English king, while the Whigs were for colonial independence? Tonight, they were only going to peek into that other world before hurrying back to their own, even if things were getting worse every day and some said war would come for sure.

Libby's eyes widened, and she bit her lower lip in awe. The many windows of the main house sparkled like jewels dangled before candle flames. This late in the day and year, no one worked the geometric flower gardens, clipped the boxwood hedges or strolled the lush bowling green. The girls had never before been closer to Melrose than the edge of the circular drive, where they had peered past the iron gate and stone walls at its rose-brick triple-storied magnificence. From here, it seemed a fantasy of fireflies gilded the house, just as the glow of wealth and mystery gilded the lives of the Gant family, who lived within.

"No wonder Father wants to build us a place just like this!" Merry exclaimed. "Wait till we tell him we saw it up close, too."

"Don't be a noodlehead." Libby tossed her blowing crimson curls. "He would tell Mother we've been here, and we'd get trounced. This is just our secret, whatever we see inside."

"Inside?" Merry's voice trembled like the leaves. "But they might see us. They say the Gants never want anyone unbidden on the grounds. Libby, I don't—"

"Shhh!" The older girl pressed a finger to pouted lips. "We will never be this close again until Father builds us our own Melrose and the Gants invite us to a party some night. If they don't become enemies we have to fight with powder and shot, that is," she added. "Besides, I want to see all the things I've read about! Stay here if you like, and I'll return soon enough."

But Merry was not about to be deserted while Libby charged ahead without her. And if Libby ever did tell Father about this, Merry intended to be able to put in her shilling's worth, too, so Libby didn't get all his time, as usual. They bent low and darted through the small orchard, heading for the covered walkway that linked the kitchen to the main house.

When they came to the edifice itself, it loomed larger than it ever had from a distance or in Father's grand tales of how he delivered the mill's best vellum paper here. Cool, clean candlelight poured out into the dark to cast long golden rectangles on the grass. But even standing on tiptoe, hands on cool brick, the girls could not jump high enough to glimpse what was inside.

So near and yet so far, Libby fumed silently as she crumpled a fistful of snuff-hued wool skirt. She was ordinarily a proper, circumspect girl, but some deep-buried wild and willful streak had surfaced in her tonight. She *had* to see into Father's dream house. She *had* to see how these others lived, rich folk, King George III's royalists, as real as those elegant beings who strode the pages of the English books her godfather Atwood Simpson gave her to read. She *had* to know how she herself would be expected to look and act when Father finally had enough money and land for their own Whig version of Tory Melrose Manor!

And then Libby spotted the ladder, propped against an apple tree on the edge of the orchard they had just run through. She motioned Merry after her, and they carted the spindly thing back to the house. She tried to ignore Merry's tragic face and the warning shake of her corn-shock hair.

"Mother will skin us alive!"

"Just one peek and we'll be gone!"

The ladder scraped the brick, and they froze. Finally they leaned it next to a lofty first-floor window. Her heart bumping like wheels on cobbles, Libby climbed it, rung by rung.

She leaned out slowly and squinted into the glare of interior light. Her lower lip dropped in wonderment.

It was a story of faraway, wondrous, noble England come to life from the printed page! Painted paper on the top half of the walls and wainscoting colored green as grass below! Glittering mirrors reflecting light from costly spermaceti candles in polished brass wall sconces! A table as long as the Morgans' whole parlor, spread with delicate porcelain and shiny silver, not dull, sturdy pewter! And three beautifully arrayed people attended by six crimson-coated, bewigged servants. Two servants for each person!

She knew the man with the stern-visaged face was Charles Gant, the eldest son and heir. He looked like a handsome, stern tutor. He seemed to be lecturing the other two: a woman with auburn tresses piled high and looped with pearls as big as cherries and a young man whose hair glinted silver-blond. But the backs of those two were turned to her. For some reason she could not fathom, Libby was determined to get a glimpse of those other two faces. She scampered down.

"All three of the Gant children at supper, but they look quite grown-up!" she told the nervous Merry. "Just one more peek from that next window, unless you want a glimpse. It's not so awfully high, you know."

Merry shook her head, for the ladder seemed both tall and precarious. She plucked at Libby's sleeve to ask, "What are they eating? I'm ever so hungry. We have to get home, Lib!"

"One more look." Libby grunted as she tried to lift the ladder and position it a bit closer to the next window without scraping it on the rough bricks.

Merry chattered on. "Mother says eldest sons are the only kind to wed. But he's really old, the Gant heir, isn't he? Father says he is four and twenty and might inherit soon, since his father is still ill in London. Well, I want to wed an heir, of course, but—"

"Merry, hush and help me before—"

But it was already too late. The ladder seemed to totter, then leap of its own accord right for the sparkling window-panes. Glass shattered, then tinkled forlornly. The quiet night seemed to shriek with the brittle breaking of their fine fantasies.

Within, a man shouted and a woman screamed. Horror-struck, Libby leaned the ladder on the brick wall and stood rooted to the grass, still gazing up. Then Merry yanked her hand and they ran.

Libby knew she should go back to apologize even as her feet pumped faster, faster. She stopped once, leaning her shoulder against a tree, gasping for breath to tell Merry they must return to face the Gants. Father would be appalled, Mother mortified to her grave, but they must face up to what they had done.

But then they heard pursuing shouts. And barking!

"Lib, guard dogs!" Merry cried, making no attempt at silence now. "Come on!"

Libby let her younger sister pull her along until they both stumbled over a downed tree limb and sprawled on damp garden soil and slippery leaves. Libby glanced back as they scrambled to their feet. Lighted, luring Melrose seemed to slip away through the trees as they ran again. They turned in the wrong direction somehow, then tried to double back toward their horse. There was a shoulder-high stone fence here along the road. They had missed the gate! The dogs yapped closer. Horse's hooves pounded amidst shouts as the girls fled desperately along the wall.

"This way," Libby threw back over her shoulder at her panting sister. "I'm sure of it!" But the dogs seemed so close. Her heart clattered in her throat. "Merry," she gasped, and pulled her sister to a halt. "This is all my fault! Here, quick, I'll boost you over and you run!"

But then they saw the first dog. A blur of dark hair, white teeth. Panicked, Libby yanked Merry on, but the dog

lunged. Libby felt it rip at her ankle. She kicked it off. She ran on, her ankle both hot and cold, like her churning emotions.

"Halt! Halt there, I say!" a man's voice commanded. A ring of horses and torches and baying dogs suddenly had them hemmed in against the fence. Merry broke into sobs, and Libby pressed her behind her and spun to face their pursuers.

"Law, ragamuffin girls, Master Charles!" another voice boomed. "And I thought sure 'twas Whigs breaking windows in protest over the Townshend Glass Tax you Gants been proud to pay Mother England! I'll call the pack, sir."

"No, wait, Barney. They deserve to be chewed up and spat out, the dirty hoyden scum!"

Libby cowered at first. This one who spoke was Charles Gant himself. The torch he held distorted his fine features as he glared down at the terrorized girls. Growling, the dogs crowded closer, but then they backed off at a crisp command from someone else. Libby's ankle was throbbing. She could feel the inside of her shoe slippery with blood.

"Look, brother, the dogs ran them ragged! Don't terrorize them further. Let's take them to the house and send for their people. Make them pay for the windows!" the voice that had called off the dogs resounded as its owner dismounted.

Libby gawked as Merry gripped her elbow like a vise. It was the younger son, the silver-haired Gant. He looked to be at least sixteen. Quite tall and lanky, he stood proudly, like some young conquering Roman Libby had read of in Plutarch's *Lives*.

He glared at them, too, squinting into the leaping torchlight. "Out running free at all hours? Your names, mistress?" he demanded of Libby.

"They ought to be lashed!" Charles Gant interrupted. "I recognize them now. Silas Morgan's spawn! Damned ne'er-do-well Whigs like that bastard should be gelded so's

not to whelp more of his kind, like these dirty bitches from his litter! I'll not have them in my house!''

Libby gasped as if she'd been struck. Father was none of those foul things he said, and she and Merry not—not what he had called them. She wanted to tell them that one day her father would be as grand as they were, with a house as fine as theirs, but when she opened her mouth to talk back, her trust in Father's grand designs faltered for the first time in her young life, and she merely stammered.

And in that moment, the awe Elizabeth Constance Morgan had long tended for Melrose and its seldom-seen inhabitants solidified to stony resentment against the Gants. This was all their fault! She and Merry were trapped like prey, standing dirtied, downtrodden and degraded, while the Gants remained clean and calm and controlled. Her shame magnified as the silver-haired Gant glared at them. She wished more than ever she were a bold Son of Liberty like her godfather Atwood. She'd show these royal boot-lickers then!

Pride and hatred stiffened her childish features and hardened her embarrassed gaze. She squared her thin shoulders and lifted her chin to speak, but Charles Gant cut in again.

''I say, these chits and their sire aren't worth enough to even get the window price. Come on, Cameron. I've not the time to haul them in for either a beating or a fine, not when I'm leaving tomorrow. Catherine will scold if we miss the trifle and sherry our last night together. Throw the filthy little rebels off the grounds, Barney!'' he ordered. ''Here, boys, to me!'' he called to the dogs. His horse's hooves flung clods of mud at the stunned and frightened Morgan girls as he wheeled and thundered away.

Cameron, whose young face already hinted at the stamp of Gant disdain and inherent superiority, remained one moment more. He looked as if he would speak. His eyes, glowing in the torchlight, met Libby's defiant stare. Then he frowned and remounted his big black horse to follow

his brother and the others off into the darkness. The girls stood facing only the gruff-looking Barney.

"Off the grounds, you two! You heard Master Charles." When Libby stood her ground, he tapped her shoulder with the butt end of his whip. She jumped back as if he'd used the lash. That was the way she felt, as if the despicable Gants had actually whipped them like the bitches they thought them to be.

Barney hesitated at her harsh glare. "Out, then, or I'll tell your sire you been a-throwin' stones at your betters' windows," he said, with a wave of his torch toward the gate.

Libby's entire body shook now, but she kept a tight hold on Merry's hand to steady her. She had never felt brought so low, and all because her dear, deluded father thought the Gants were to be admired and emulated, even with their Tory blood. If it weren't for Father, she never would have trespassed, never would have believed she could somehow imagine a life so fine.

But she saw things clearly now. Aye, she would get off these grounds, for she had henceforth new grounds for resentment and revenge. Let the Gants call the Whig Morgans filthy rebels! If war ever started, she'd show them what a proud rebel could do! She found her voice at last, for this servant was not one of the Gants, he was only paid to do their will.

"The window...'twas an accident. We intended no harm. But I insist we make reparations for it."

"You heard the master. Laws, it don't mean a fig to him, one more window. He and Mistress Cath'rine be off by packet for London on the morrow and Master Cameron to Virginia to school anyway. So go on now, and don't never come back!"

Libby realized for the first time just how rich the Gants must be. She pulled at Merry's hand, and they started away. To have a house that looked like *that* inside! To pay scant

heed to the cost of fine broken glass...to actually want to pay the King's cruel taxes! A sharp fear stabbed her that Father could never be that rich. Perhaps, just perhaps, everything he had promised might not quite come true. But no! She believed Father, not these high-and-mighty Gants!

Barney noted that, though she limped as she led her shaken sister away, the thin, tattered girl held herself as erect and proud as Mistress Catherine. Frowning, he followed a few steps farther. Too late, he saw that the girl trailed a path of blood outside the gate. He hunched his old, gouty shoulders in a shrug. A sad little incident, he mused, but naught else would come of it.

One

❧⚬⚬⚬❧

April 24, 1775, the City of New York
Publick Proclamation
To be post'd on sundry Premises forthwith:

Printing of the *Liberal Gazette*
hereby suspend'd
due to the sudden Death of
its Printer
in a tragic Ferry Accident

Brady's Pond Cottage
Staten Island, New York
April 24, 1775

"I know you'll miss him terribly...."

"Our deepest sympathies, Mrs. Morgan...."

"Nice little speech the pastor gave, not a bit too long...."

Silas Morgan, aged forty-three years, three months and seventeen days, was buried on a bright, warm spring morning. Georgina, his widow, still pretty in a faded way her two daughters' vibrant beauty recalled, was dazed by her sudden bereavement. And, although she was taking comfort from the outpouring of condolences and visitors, she knew

all too well she had greatly overextended herself to provide a fine funeral feast this afternoon.

"If there's anything we can do, Georgina, just anything..."

But Georgina Morgan also took comfort in the knowledge that her beloved, if spendthrift, husband would have felt great pride in the outlay of hospitality and the handsome mourning rings that went to each guest. And Mr. Larchmont, who owned the mill for which Silas had delivered linen rag paper for years, had sent over two firkins of ale and one of fine Madeira for the occasion. The new widow had sent him a note of thanks that also requested a reckoning of the worth of Silas's shares in the mill. She had no doubt that, when Mr. Larchmont himself arrived, his news would buck them up. She would offer to sell him the Morgan shares. She needed the money desperately to tide the family over until the girls were wed and she could live with them.

"His troubles are over now, my dear, and ours yet to come...."

Georgina fanned herself harder as she moved among her guests, nodding, commenting. She could see Libby presiding over the spread of food under the front windows. Georgina knew that Libby was taking her father's tragic loss the hardest, but her elder daughter had been stoic, as solid as a rock. What good were women's tears, she had declared to her mother, when they would not bring her father back or fulfill any of his plans?

But still waters ran deep, as Silas and Atwood had often said of Libby, and Georgina knew it to be true. Her eldest child was made of stronger stuff than even the metal stays Georgina insisted the girls wear under their gowns each day. Something Georgina did not quite understand had put both fire and steel in Libby's character seven or eight years ago. Georgina might never ascertain exactly what that was, but she was thankful for it now.

"I just hope he didn't suffer, dear Georgina, you know what I mean...."

Libby had comforted her mother and Merry, had in fact been a pillar of strength, ever since the news had come last week that the Gant ferry that linked Staten Island to Manhattan had foundered in a sudden storm, with both Silas and his best friend, Atwood Simpson, aboard. It was Libby who had gone down with the minister to the shore to identify and bring back poor Silas when the bodies had been recovered after four days in the bay. She had solemnly agreed they should provide this fine feast. She had helped the servant girl to prepare it, although Libby's loves were far from domestic pursuits. But, unfortunately, and here Georgina's musings took an unhappy turn, it was also Libby who had balked at encouraging Eddie Tiler's wooing when here she was, a twenty-year-old stubborn spinster who should long ago have been wed!

Libby interrupted Georgina's thoughts. "Mother, you'd best sit a while." She neatly extricated the older woman from the chatting group where she stood. Mother had obviously not been listening one bit. Libby had seen her eyes roaming the parlor, as if she were searching for Father among the guests. "People understand. They will come to speak to you today if you will but sit."

She led her mother across the room toward the best hoopbacked chair before the hearth, catching snatches of random conversation as they passed. Everyone was abuzz with the news that mere farmers and tradesmen calling themselves Minute Men had stood up to armed British might at Lexington and Concord, near Boston, five days ago, and paid for it with their lives. It was sure to be the spark that set off the powder keg, everyone agreed on that.

Though His Majesty's troops had been garrisoned for years in New York City, just over the bay from Staten Island, all were agreed that the city might be spared occupation for at least a while. Britain's attention seemed

focused on the present unrest in Massachusetts. New England militia were gathering to besiege the British in Boston, and most of the New York-based Royal Navy had been sent north to help. So, in fact, the British presence in New York was actually less than it had been for many years, and mostly seemed content to stay aboard the two warships anchored in the bay at the bottom of the East River. Nobody was quite sure what was going to happen with the colonial unrest, for there was still no American army—just scattered local regiments—and no commander-in-chief had been named by Congress yet. Still, most committed Whigs felt that it was a war in all but name, and that a full-fledged conflict would eventually result.

"Bonfires and fireworks in Manhattan tonight to celebrate the stand at Lexington and Concord," Faith Mc-Dougal was saying. "Imagine, the Minute Men taking on those ranks of English firepower with old hunting muskets!"

"That big, proud city over the bay from us had best be careful," the Anglican minister said, in a ringing doomsday voice, as he popped another hunk of cheese in his mouth. "The entire fleet's likely to come sailing back from Boston to whip them like schoolboys for celebrating tonight! God forbid," he added, his mouth full, "but rabblerousers 'gainst the public peace deserve severe chastisement.

"Nosiree!" he added. "It'll never come to a real war, taxes or not! Besides, Staten Island's firmly royalist Tory, but for forty some souls!"

Heads turned now. Conversation lagged. Everyone here—Tory, Whig, or uncommitted—knew the Morgans were Atwood Simpson's friends, and that his recalcitrant newspaper had been worse than mere Whig—it had been out-and-out revolutionary! Atwood was a boyhood friend of Silas's who had prospered in the city with the *Gazette* and his stationery shop, so the loss was doubly tragic for the Morgan family. Over the years, Atwood had poured his

benevolence on the Morgans, with gifts for the ladies, books for his godchild and continued friendship for a man long ago dubbed a worthless woolgatherer even by those who liked him.

"Anyhow," another voice put in, "nothing will happen here on Staten Island, even if the English and Governor Tryon do come back, bet my last shilling!"

Georgina shook her head, and her blue eyes met Libby's hazel ones. "Such terrible talk on this day!" she muttered, sinking into the chair that had been her husband's favorite. "How can they gossip and argue, even laugh, on a day like this!"

"Because life goes on, Mother, as unfair as it seems to us now," Libby said quietly, touching her mother's shoulder. "Besides, at a funeral feast everyone senses how dear life is because someone else has lost his. They are still alive, so they are feeling relieved, whether they know it or not."

"Stuff and nonsense!" Georgina fanned her face again. She had no intention of talking about fancy, high-flown ideas that probably came from some old Greek philosophy book. Why, the Greeks that wrote all that drivel were long dead! Such pursuits did nothing to teach a young woman how to keep house or get a good husband in these modern times!

Georgina's eyes darted about the room again. Yes, the servant girl, Sally, was keeping the serving board well stocked with platters of sliced corned beef, woodcock and quail. What a pity they could not afford to keep the girl anymore, even if Mr. Larchmont bought Silas's shares in the mill. When Merry and Libby wed, there must be some dowry money. Silas had wanted large dowries. With their last servant gone, the girls would just have to prepare meals, but without a man about to feed now...

Georgina Morgan's thoughts rambled off again. How proud Silas would have been to see so many here. And yet,

bold as brass, he would be telling everyone in this little house about the big house he would build someday over-looking the bay, finer even than Melrose Manor. My, my, how she had loved that man. Even when he had brought her extravagant gifts he could ill afford and they had argued over his high-flying fantasies, how she had loved that man! Georgina cleared her throat and looked up into Libby's watchful, concerned face.

"I hardly meant to scold, Elizabeth. Not today. You've been such a pillar of support, my dear." Georgina patted the hand Libby had laid on her shoulder. "But I do not want your new burdens in the family to affect the time you have for Eddie. If he would simply just request a be-trothal," she said with a sigh, looking across the room at Eddie. "You could both live here, you know, even if he does take bricklaying jobs building those new houses on lower Broad Way Street in Manhattan. My, how your father admired that neighborhood."

"Mother," Libby said, choosing her words carefully, "Eddie has not exactly asked me to wed. And if he did, I would not jump at the chance now simply because we need a man who has a paying trade in the family. Besides, I don't love Eddie."

"Love, pooh! Respect and duty first. Love will come!" she insisted behind her fluttering fan.

"You mustn't say such things about love, Mother, not today. You cannot deny that you and Father were in love from the first, despite some differences along the way," Libby insisted. "And I intend to have the same!"

That rejoinder silenced Georgina. She had never quite known how to handle her eldest when she balked. From the time Merry had been born and Silas had heard there could be no more children but the two girls, he had reared Libby almost like a boy. He had taken her on his delivery rounds, both on the island and in the city. She had been taught to swim, to ride—pillion, sidesaddle and astride—

and to shoot. Georgina never would have known all that if Merry hadn't tattled once, but she had immediately put her foot down on the shooting and riding astride.

Their eldest daughter had learned more than to read, write and cipher; she had devoured all the books her father had given her from Atwood's vast library in town. The last few years, she had even spent numerous days at the so-called "liberal gazette" Atwood owned in Manhattan. The girl had even come back with ink all over her. From setting type, of all things! Suddenly Georgina felt estranged from Libby, as she so often had over the years.

She glanced over at the eighteen-year-old Meredith, called Merry. In her salmon tabby velvet gown, the blond, pretty girl circulated in the crowded parlor with the mourning rings on their best tooled leather tray. Merry's generous nature and her tendency to wish for things she would never have were her only legacies from her father. Perhaps partly in regret for that, Merry had wept bitterly since the news had come last week.

Meredith Prudence Morgan, at least, Georgina thought smugly, had been reared to be a good housewife. She hadn't had her nose poked in a book all these years. Her fine embroidery samplers spangled the walls; her creative handwork spoke from family garments, from the linen cabinet, from the treasures stored away for both girls' hope chests. Of course, Georgina had to admit she greatly disapproved of the girl's tendency to go about in curl papers and her dressing gown till all hours of the morning. And Merry had a wretched habit of slouching or leaning. Why, you'd think the backboards and harnesses she'd laced the girls into for years to give them ladylike posture had been mere wet noodles! Still Merry was her mother's girl.

With a flip of her fan, she summoned Merry over to join them. Merry put her ring tray down on the gateleg table and bent to kiss her mother's cheek.

"It looks as though everyone has a ring now," Georgina said.

"Just a few left, Mother. And one to be saved for Mr. Larchmont. Oh, there he is, just come in!"

Merry darted off, and the other two Morgan women followed her to the door to greet the wealthy, portly owner of the paper mill. The buzz behind them in the parlor quieted.

"How do you do, Mr. Larchmont," Georgina said with a taut smile. "Please come in."

"I hope the rum and ale my man fetched over went far enough," he told them brusquely, not budging a step inside.

"So very kind of you. I hope you received the note of thanks I had Elizabeth write. You…you did not happen to bring the papers I asked for, did you?" Georgina toyed with the fan.

"No, no. Frankly, Mrs. Morgan, if you're concerned about Silas's salary, you have three days' wages due you, but that's about it. I'll have it delivered promptly tomorrow, if that will help."

Georgina almost swayed on her feet. Libby felt as if she'd eaten a bellyful of sour green apples. Other guests were drifting toward the front door. When one called out a cheery hello to Mr. Larchmont and he pointedly ignored it, Libby suggested they step outside a moment. Georgina sent Merry back inside to get some of his own Madeira for him, then gripped Libby's hand hard. Libby held tightly to her mother's arm to prop her up.

"Were there no shares, then, in the mill itself?" Libby asked, to spare her mother the shame of the answer she knew was coming. Silas Morgan had had so many plans, so many desires, that had somehow mingled fantasy with reality.

"Shares?" he repeated, and his old-fashioned periwig bounced as he shook his head. "Surely, you must be confusing that with shares he owned at Simpson's gazette in the city, ladies. Great loss, Atwood—for those few of us

who can't abide bending knee to the Brits, at least. And Atwood's poor son will be in more dire straits without him. Great pity.''

"A great pity," Libby echoed as Merry bustled up with a pewter cup of Madeira on a tray. Libby knew her father had held no shares in the *Liberal Gazette*, however close he had been to Mister Simpson. But he had evidently boasted to Mr. Larchmont that he had. The heavy man gulped the Madeira straight down and banged the cup on Merry's tray in his haste.

"So pleased the ale and Madeira are good," he said to the silent, embarrassed women. "My most heartfelt condolences to you all. The three days' salary will be sent over straightaway on the morrow. And some writing paper for you, Mistress Libby. Silas was always proud of your, well…masculine intellect, as it were. I really must be off, ladies. My condolences again.''

The three Morgan women stood as still as stones in the warm April sun as the man mounted and urged his horse away.

"Mother," Libby asked quietly, "do we have deeds to the plots of land Father said he bought from the Gants over the years?''

"Deeds?" Georgina repeated, and blinked dazedly at her. "Your father's deeds? I just don't know. Why don't you and Merry look for them tomorrow, after Sally heads back home?" she said, turning to speak to her friend Mistress Edgmont, who had followed them to the door. The two women went into the stone cottage together, while Merry and Libby just stood on the threshold, staring across the newly plowed Gant fields and woodlots that marched nearly to their door.

"Our father's deeds—" Libby said aloud. Her voice broke. Her insides felt like a runaway carriage bumping downhill toward the rocks and the sea. Silas Morgan's heritage for his family, whom she knew beyond a doubt he

had loved most dearly, would be nothing but penury and hollow dreams. And yet, she missed him terribly. She had always looked up to him and adored his flair and bravado, but now her love and loss were mixed with bitter disappointment in him, even anger, anger that shamed her for its sharp bite.

"No shares in the paper mill," Merry muttered, and took Libby's hand. "Only Mr. Simpson owned the gazette, and he's gone, too."

"Father was always so proud the Gants sold him some of their land," Libby added forlornly. "But now, I even doubt—"

Merry hugged her tight, and Libby choked back a sob.

"Whatever are we going to do, Lib?" Merry asked shakily as they stared down at their clasped hands with their foreheads pressed together. "The beehives out back are something, but with both of us so sensitive about bee stings, Mother can't work them alone! And the hives are probably all sitting on Gant land!" she wailed.

Libby almost admitted she could marry Eddie, but the words stuck in her throat. And then, as if her refusal to take the obvious path had summoned him, Eddie Tiler appeared in the doorway behind Merry.

"Oh, sorry," he murmured when he saw their emotions so plainly displayed. "Too much talk inside for me, I guess." He shuffled slowly, shyly, closer as the girls stepped apart.

Edward Tiler was two years older than Libby, and everything about him was stocky and sturdy. He was large boned and muscular, with a barrel chest. His eyes and hair—and sometimes, Libby thought sadly, his personality, too—were a pale brown. But he had a winsome, boyish white smile under a broad nose that had been broken more than once in brawls with his boisterous brothers. He had vowed to give up fighting for her. That is, fighting everyone except the British, if it ever came to that. Libby had to

admit that she did at least greatly admire Eddie's dedication and bravery.

Eddie had dressed in his homespun best today, and he offered Libby his cambric handkerchief as if he were the finest gentleman Broad Way Street had to offer. But Eddie and his family lived just up the Amboy Road, near Richmondtown, on Staten Island. They were successful bricklayers, and Eddie was a journeyman in the trade. A brick, Libby thought, as she took the proffered square of cambric and blew her nose. Solid and dependable as a brick—that described Eddie Tiler. She could no doubt do much worse, if it came to having to wed to support her mother and Merry.

"Thank you, Eddie," she managed. "And thank you for coming early today to help cart things for Sally and me in the kitchen."

"Upon my word, no thanks needed," he replied, a concerned look on his pleasant face. "I just wish I had a nice house of my own. I'd hire Sally to be housekeeper, and I'd get me a wife who gets on real well with my housekeeper!"

He smiled sheepishly at the heavy-handed ploy. He often hinted he would propose marriage to Libby if only she would encourage him a bit. But, though she was kind to him, he thought, and really clever and pretty, too, she never encouraged him that way. Still, he had no intention of giving up. 'Specially not now that the Morgan women were all alone in the world.

"I really must go back inside to help Sally," Libby said, and managed a thin smile. "You see, Eddie, you're always coming to my rescue with helpful reminders one way or the other."

As Eddie gazed down adoringly into her face, Libby felt a flash of mingled guilt and anger. She should refuse to let Eddie come calling. She heartily doubted she would ever grow to love him, as Mother said she would. There was not a bit of the sweeping, whirling feeling she and Merry

knew they would experience when it was "the one." Mother had admitted she had felt that way when she had met Father. Mr. Simpson had said he loved his wife "to utter distraction" before she had died of pleurisy last year. Libby knew that such feelings existed, because she read about them in books like Richardson's *Pamela*, which Mr. Simpson had bought from that Philadelphia printer, Mr. Franklin.

But she took Eddie's arm and let him escort her back inside for another conversational round with their guests. Then she excused herself to step out into the kitchen, where, for the past few days, she had spent most of her time helping their girl, Sally Smith, ready this wretchedly festive funeral feast.

The guests departed with final, repeated condolences and promises of "If there is anything we can do...you've but to send over and we'll be here...." Sated, still chatting, they mounted horses and climbed into wagons or walked away as the sun sank below the budding treetops. Their excited talk of viewing the evening fireworks floated back to the exhausted, bereft Morgan women. Libby convinced the hovering Eddie to go, too, and gave him a farewell peck on the cheek. From the kitchen, where she went to help Sally again, she heard him whistling a jaunty tune as he rode his brother's horse away.

The cottage seemed so small and silent now, and Silas's death loomed large. Three days' wages coming from the mill, twenty buckets of honey a year to sell— Whatever would they do? Libby agonized as she furiously cleaned pewter plates with scouring rushes. They were also losing Sally, who was as much friend as servant. Suddenly, long years of endless domestic chores loomed endlessly ahead of Libby. She leaned, stiff armed, on the worn worktable and studied the shadows in the corner.

No more happy afternoons in bustling Manhattan helping

set type, as if it were a thrilling game to make words come
alive with her own nimble fingers. No more watching the
crotchety old journeyman, Josiah Bean, pull the devil's tail
of the press at the gazette. No more books to read from her
godfather's private library. No more listening to the men
talk of free enterprise without England's meddling. No
more being privy to that stirring debate about the God-
given rights of all individuals versus the so-called divine
rights of a king like "Farmer George." No more believing
that some book-learned, clever, kind New Yorker would
stride through the door of the gazette while she was there
helping and want not only an advertisement for his fine
business but a woman to wife who would speak her mind
and love him loyally forever!

"Lib! Lib! You will never guess who just rode up bold
as brass. Mother's invited him in!"

Startled, Libby spun around to face her wide-eyed sister.
"Not Mr. Simpson's son Quentin? I simply could not bear
that dissolute sot today."

"Lib! Eight years ago! What we never told them!"
Merry choked out. Libby's hands flew to her mouth, and
her heart pounded faster. "The younger one—Cameron
Gant! And he's ever so handsome!"

"How dare he set foot here. And on this day!" Libby
spat. "If he has come to apologize about that Gant wreck
of a ferry that killed father and Mr. Simpson," she exploded, "I'll order him out, if Mother won't!"

But Merry had already hurried back down the hall to the
parlor. Libby wiped her wet hands, slowly, deliberately, but
her mind was racing and her pulse was pounding. Nothing
had ever come of that day she had broken the window at
Melrose. She had not laid eyes on Cameron Gant since.
Would he even remember or recognize them now? The
Gants' name-calling and taunts still scarred her as much as
the dog bite on her ankle. She was tempted to snub Cameron Gant by staying right here, but what if he had come

about father's parcels of land, the way Mr. Larchmont had come about those nonexistent shares in the mill? As Father's heir, daughter or not, she was responsible for the family now. Mother was in no state to be bullied and degraded by a Gant.

Her knees began to shake. Her insides twisted and knotted. Now was her chance to tell the man exactly what she thought about him and his crass, cruel, rich-as-Croesus family and the coming war that Tories like him were so certain they would win!

Eight years of dammed-up emotions churning through her, Libby Morgan strode the hallway toward the parlor to face down Cameron Gant.

Two

~~~~~~~~~~~~~~~

Publick Notice:

Liberal Gazette to be reissued soon,
weekly, Wedn. Morns.
12 Shills./Yr
Advertisements 4 Shills./Ea.

Elizabeth Morgan, Printer & Stationer
on Queen Str. east of Hanover Sq.

Libby jolted to a halt, unseen, in the doorway to the parlor. Merry was gazing entranced, saucer eyed, at their unwanted guest, and Mother was chattering away as if she were honored to have that man here. For one moment, Libby just stared.

Cameron Gant towered a good six inches over the two Morgan women, who were neither of them small. The silvered hair she recalled so well still looked torchlit, even in the brash light of the setting sun. He evidently disdained wigs, for he wore his own hair pulled straight back into a four-inch queue tied with a velvet ribbon. His blondeness was slightly lighter than Merry's honey hues, but his skin looked tawny compared to her porcelain complexion. He

must ride or walk out a great deal for such a supposed gentleman. Such striking coloring emphasized his piercing gray eyes. He was turned half away from the doorway, so that she had an excellent view of his patrician profile, and had not yet noticed her, so that she had a chance to study him further.

Broad shoulders, which stretched taut his fashionable cutaway coat and deep blue embroidered satin waistcoat, tapered to narrow hips and strong thighs encased in blue breeches. His mirror-polished riding boots seemed molded to the bulge of his upper calf muscles. She felt a sweeping, whirling feeling. Surely it was only her anger that he had dared to invade the bosom of her family.

But she had pictured Cameron Gant as lanky all these years, a gawky, frowning ogre with a just-broken voice and a nasty temper. Now she heard his voice again, deep-timbred as he answered Mother politely; he looked neither gawky nor frowning. Had the years that had hardened her heart softened his? Yet the elegance of his ruffled cambric shirt and white silk stock emphasized the hint of ruthless, aristocratic power in the angular jaw, high cheekbones, straight nose and taut mouth.

Libby started from her stunned scrutiny when Mother bade him sit down. He acquiesced, bending those long legs, his hands propped on a gold-headed walking stick between them. *That* did it for Libby! Mother had put him in Father's chair!

"I hope Mr. Gant realizes he can never make amends for his family's unseaworthy ferry drowning Father!" she snapped. Her mother gasped and Merry colored as she strode into the room, looking every bit the avenging fury.

Cam Gant turned his head quickly. Libby leveled a bone-chilling stare at him as her mother nervously introduced them. His thick amber eyebrows lifted, then descended as he took her in with a hooded gaze. Libby saw recognition and surprise light those eyes. They hardened from dove

gray to pewter, and his nostrils flared. She held her ground, not offering her hand, despite her mother's fluttering embarrassment and Merry's warning shake of head.

"Mr. Gant has been to visit each of the bereaved families today, my dear," her mother told her pointedly. "You know, of the four men who died in the accident." Georgina Morgan took Libby's elbow and squeezed it. "To offer his condolences and *any help* his family might give, as he so kindly put it. He has been to your godfather Atwood's burial over on Manhattan, and to the funeral feasts of the two Gant hands who sailed the ferry. And he has brought us that lovely ormolu clock on the mantel. Atwood wanted us to have it. It was in his will. Mr. Gant is friends with the Simpson lawyer, you see, and he entrusted Mr. Gant with the clock for us."

Libby did not turn to look at the clock, or her mother. When her mother's flow of words did nothing to change Libby's hostile stare or Cameron Gant's steady perusal of her, Merry stepped in.

"Father's death has been a great blow to us all. Libby, Mother was just telling Mr. Gant our Sally must leave us and asking him about the parcels of land near the pond."

"Yes," Cameron Gant managed at last. He looked as if he were gasping for air after a thorough dousing in icy— if invigorating—water. "You see, ma'am—" he addressed their mother, with an occasional lightning glance Libby's way "—I have been away from home for years. My brother, Charles, who owns Melrose now, and my sister, Catherine, reside in London. I have been to college in Virginia, William and Mary, in Williamsburg. I only returned home ten days since and know nothing of possible small land sales—nor the alleged unfortunate state of the ferry."

"Alleged?" Libby demanded. "You mean to say you never rode it, even when you returned home?" Her voice was as much on edge as her bottom, which was perched precariously on the very end of the bench. She sat at right

angles to the hearth, which Cameron Gant seemed to dwarf as no visitor ever had before. "That ferry desperately needed repairs, sir!"

"You've been riding the ferry over and back to Manhattan?" he countered, those few words weighted with a load of accusing implications. His eyebrows arched again. Georgina Morgan fanned herself, and Merry shifted closer on the bench next to Libby, as if to bridle her.

"I often went over with Father to visit Atwood Simpson, sir, though it is no concern of yours. They were best of friends, and I spent happy days at the print shop there!"

"You? Where all those mutinous rebels gathered to concoct that dangerous publication? That paper's done too much to goad the British, when New York is ill prepared to handle any sort of a military occupation. I don't doubt the British can hardly wait to get their hands on the paper, as well as its city!"

"And I don't doubt you have inside information on that!" she retorted. "Nor that the Gants of Gant London Imports cannot wait to see all the fine and honorable things Atwood Simpson ever worked for ruined. I don't care if you do play the lackey to deliver clocks for his lawyer!"

"Elizabeth, you must apologize at once!" her mother cried, her fan a blur. "Your father would be honored Mr. Gant has come calling to express his condolences. Honored!"

"I am sorry, Mother, but I cannot apologize. I know Father would be honored, but he is gone now, and the things we thought he left us, too," she declared, with a determined toss of flaming curls and lace cap.

At that moment, Cameron Gant felt the strangest, most exhilarating rush of raw feeling that had ever assailed him. The Widow Morgan scolded her eldest girl and adroitly changed the subject, but the younger woman's defiant hazel eyes did not waver. Even when they went on to discuss the

locations of the pieces of land in question, he could not tear his gaze from the slender, ramrod-backed Libby.

It riveted his attention and heated his senses that Libby Morgan seethed with such life and passion, and in this house that was so recently shrouded by death. It might be fury—it was certainly sharp dislike for him—but he found it alarmingly alluring. Though she sat apparently subdued now as he vowed to explore the alleged Morgan purchases of land, he knew that if looks could kill he would surely be dead.

Despite the stretch of time, he had immediately recognized Libby Morgan when she had entered, smoking with resentment, to stand momentarily beside her pretty sister. All of that night, when he had last seen his sister Catherine before she had deserted him for Father and London, was indelibly, painfully stamped on his memory.

Both Morgan girls had changed—filled out in intriguing forms, grown beautiful in their own ways—but this one with the daggers in her eyes made him want to leap up, yank her to her feet and...and he was not certain. He had never felt this violently disturbed before, despite a few dalliances with Virginia ladies and a few brief, hot encounters with another kind of woman. This woman made him want to shake her, hold her, to capture her in his arms and sprint to his horse like some frenzied frontier savage!

Even as the Widow Morgan thanked him for his concern, he glanced back at Libby. Her red hair, with its golden glints, was pulled loosely back from several graceful forehead curls; somehow he was certain it would curl by itself, especially in the rain. A delicate butterfly-lace cap emphasized her vibrant coloring. She seemed to blush now as much from his avid scrutiny as from her own anger. She had an amazingly aloof, classic look, with an oval face, a determined jaw and large, expressive hazel eyes that now looked as green as the pistachio brocade gown she wore. There was a beguiling, girlish sprinkle of freckles across

her nose, and a generous mouth that looked so firm, but would no doubt soften under a masterful kiss.

With that gun-barrel posture, she seemed a bit taller than her more supplely molded sister. But that slender, strong effect was softened by long, graceful limbs. And the silk gauze modesty piece she wore tucked in her low, square neckline did not quite hide the delicious upper curves of her softly rounded breasts. She held her chin ever up— Yes, even as a skinny, dirty hoyden that night the dogs had chased them, her eyes had spit torchlight like that.

The thought of her defiance and anger rocked him to his booted toes, and he shifted his weight on the chair. He longed to see her smile. He ached to melt that stiff, harsh look. But he had responsibilities to fulfill here. He had no time to daydream about his desires for a woman who obviously detested him and his family and blamed them for her father's death.

"There is one more thing besides the clock that Atwood Simpson left in his will that concerns you all," Cameron Gant said in the pause before the Widow Morgan could swoop off again on a new tack. He pulled a vellum envelope with a red wax seal from the inner folds of his coat. "It is addressed to you, his godchild, Mistress Elizabeth, and there is another copy of it with the Simpson lawyer," he continued. His eyes slammed into Libby's again as he leaned forward to extend the letter slowly. She took it, but jerked her hand back when their fingers touched.

Libby felt a jolt of heat rush up her wrist and arm at that mere brushing of skin. Her stomach fluttered with something besides anger.

"And why should you deliver it?" she demanded. Her voice shook. "Why not his lawyer or his son Quentin?"

"His lawyer, whom your mother noted is a friend of mind, has been rather indisposed of late. So he had me bring it over today *because* of Quentin. I tell you quite frankly, Mistress Elizabeth," he went on, his gaze holding

hers captive, "Quentin being a…well, untamed spirit, the way he is, your godfather had the notion that you have better mettle to inherit the gazette. I agree Quentin's habits are not conducive to putting out a paper, but Atwood must have known this bequest would mean his precious paper must be sold." He shrugged his broad shoulders, and a small frown furrowed his high brow. "Quentin's furious and will probably protest, but it is only right that you be forewarned. If you'll just peruse that epistle, you'll see the *Liberal Gazette* has been left to you, lock, stock, land and printing press!"

Merry gasped, and her mother kept repeating, "Oh, Libby. Oh, Libby!" as Libby ran her trembling finger under the fold line to crack the seal. Her quick eyes skimmed the letter. It was true! The two-story print shop on Queen Street, the stationery goods, the press, the paper stock and the precious type were hers to carry on the paper's bold mission with! Hers!

Despite everyone's avid gaze, Libby jumped to her feet and crushed the letter to her breasts in rampant joy. "It's true, it's true!" she exulted. "Atwood Simpson's saved us and given me a life I'd never dared to dream of!"

"Praise Providence, such blessed news you've brought us, Mr. Gant!" Georgina told him as she flipped her fan. "My, my, the sale of the gazette will allow us to—to continue to live in the style to which my dear departed husband had accustomed us."

"Yes, of course," he replied, his gaze still fixed on Libby. Tears had turned her hazel eyes to a shimmering jade and spiked her thick lashes. Her obvious joy was utterly beguiling, yet he still did not approve of Atwood's leaving her the gazette. A spinster of her youth and unbridled spirit and appeal should never live in Manhattan, that seething hotbed of possible rebellion.

He found his voice. "Quite frankly, ladies, I believe another reason Atwood's lawyer made me the bearer of such

news is that he knew the Gants have long wanted to purchase the gazette. Perhaps this is not the time, but since
you mentioned the need for the paper's imminent sale, Mrs.
Morgan, I'd like to make you a handsome offer on it.''

"So very, very kind!" Georgina gushed. Merry, who had
bounced up to hug Libby, applauded. "Of course, we
would be delighted, Mr. Gant, and honored to continue my
husband's previous dealings with your family, so—"

Libby whirled to face her mother. "This paper is our
salvation, Mother," she said, her voice crisp again, "but
not because we will sell it—and never to a Gant. Tory
families have been longing to silence Atwood Simpson's
bold voice for the colonies' rights for years, but I'll not be
a part of that."

"But— If we don't sell it— What—" Georgina faltered.

"I can set type, I have seen it all work. I know the
people," Libby insisted vehemently. "The colonies have
other women printers, some of them quite successful. Of
course, the money we would receive for its sale would be
important to us, but once that money was gone, what would
we have? This will be our trade, our independent livelihood
over the years, Mother, long after Mr. Gant's so-generous
Tory purchase price would be long gone! And what an
honor to carry on in Atwood's tradition and Father's strong
Whig beliefs!"

"Lib!"

"Elizabeth, you cannot—"

"Devil take it!" The male voice drowned the other two.

"Indeed I do mean it!" She faced them all down. "And
I do not believe for one minute Father owns those parcels
of Gant land, any more than he did mill shares or a piece
of this gazette!"

The ensuing hubbub was intense. Sally who had come
in with a candle to light the lamps, stood in the shadows,
her eyes alternately on Mistress Libby and on the handsome
guest, her ears nearly flapping to take it all in.

Mrs. Morgan recovered first. "We will not argue further before our guest, Elizabeth, but I forbid this chuckleheaded notion," she said firmly. "For you to live in Manhattan and unattended by family? Unthinkable! And Meredith is certainly not going with you. I'd still have my reservations even if you were to wed Eddie first! And if you think a fine, upstanding man like that will court a young woman tainted by going into trade in Manhattan, you are quite demented!"

Cameron Gant's brow crushed over his eyes at the mention of a suitor, but he seconded Mrs. Morgan's words. "New York City is no place for a country-bred girl, Mistress Elizabeth. I would never allow my sister to live there." He frowned again as he thought of Catherine, the closest thing to a mother he had ever had, who had bowed to Charles's and his father's orders to return to England without him. "There are certain elements in Manhattan—"

"Certain Tory elements who would like to silence the voice of mankind's rights," Libby said. "Certain wealthy landed folk who have inherited their wealth and mean to use it to sway and humiliate others supposedly beneath them. Such elements always fear the voice of reason over that of privilege!"

"The voice of reason!" he bellowed, losing his hard-controlled temper. He rose to his feet and took one long stride toward her. She stepped back in surprise until her skirts belled out against the bench. "Is it reasonable to set oneself up as a target when the English return? To risk pushing the powers that govern us over the edge of anger and pulling everything else to destruction with it? It is the voice of prideful, stubborn emotion that rules you, mistress, not reason! Good evening to you, ladies. I see my presence here is neither helpful nor comforting."

"Elizabeth, I am mortified to my very soul!" Georgina gasped, rising unsteadily with Merry's aid. "You shall escort Mr. Gant, whom you have greatly insulted, to the door

and apologize this instant. And, sir, I would be honored if you would call on us again tomorrow, when our feelings are not so frayed from the day's events. If you should wish to discuss a price for the paper and its property then, we shall surely listen with a more receptive ear."

Mrs. Morgan sat back down and fanned herself so hard she fluttered her cap ribbons. Merry fetched their guest's tricorn hat. Sally bustled ahead to open the front door. Cameron Gant tucked his walking stick under his arm. Libby stood stock-still and glared. Then she walked stoically to the door ahead of the man and stepped outside on the flagstone stoop with him. She blinked in surprise at the sky. Over the bay, which they could see from the gentle knoll on which the cottage rested, fireworks twinkled in the darkness, and the tiny booms echoed even here.

At last she turned to face him in the sparkling night. "I shall never sell, never," she told him determinedly. "It has long been my dream."

"Some dreams are not what they seem. Harmful when we get them, even. Those fireworks look so pretty in the distant sky, but they could burn one badly at close range."

Libby thought of her father's dreams, of the lies he had told them all because he had wanted things so desperately, things he could not have. She pushed that from her mind. This was different. She could grasp the future now for herself, for her family...and for the cause Atwood had boldly, brilliantly espoused. And this man, of all men, would never again humiliate her, or corner her, or make her feel that she was nothing.

"I do not need your sermonizings, sir. And I am not your sister, to be scolded."

"Thank God for that."

She frowned at him, amazed at the sudden twinkle in his eye and the note of teasing in his voice. "I mean this is not a bit of your affair, Mr. Gant," she retorted icily. "However, there is an old housekeeper there at the gazette.

I shall not be unchaperoned, so do not try to use that to dissuade my mother further.''

He stepped much too close and peered down into her face, just as a spatter of light framed his head like a halo. At that moment she could have fallen into the deep pools of his eyes.

"You pride yourself on logic and the truth, I think, mistress, so let me be blunt with you. If you move to town to run that rebel paper, I shall make it my business. That there is a chaperone there, I am both relieved and chagrined to hear. And, even if you fight me every step of the way, I mean to make amends for the loss of your father, though that was hardly my fault. That is the one fight of several on the horizon that I look forward to with pleasure!'' he added, a bitter tone suddenly sharpening his voice.

Her eyes widened, and her lower lip dropped. Had he meant to give offense, to tease...or to promise? She stepped back when she saw his eyes drop to her breasts, then lift to linger on her lips. The next glittering in the sky etched the angular planes of his face as silver as his hair.

"Until tomorrow, Mistress Liberty,'' he said. She started at his deliberate misuse of her name, but no rejoinder came to her lips. They tingled as if he had done more than touch them with his eyes. He clapped his hat on his head and untied his horse. He stowed his walking stick and swiftly mounted. Her hand, still holding Atwood Simpson's letter, lifted to her pursed lips as he spurred his horse away.

The next morning, after several hours of heated negotiation with her mother, Libby was packing. Her two pairs of sturdy shoes, her one good gown and three day dresses went in the single trunk—hardly a fit wardrobe for stylish, sophisticated New York City. But she would not be stepping out, except for business errands. She would sacrifice one dress for the shop and cover it as best she could with a leather printer's apron.

In return for her mother's permission, she had promised she would send monthly sums for Georgina's and Merry's support and turn a healthy profit within a year—or she would sell the gazette. She had no fear at all that it would ever come to that, and she tried to comfort herself with that thought. Still, she heaved a deep sigh as she gazed at the feather mattress on the high bed under the slant of eaves she had shared so long with Merry. Now she would sleep alone. Somehow that thought brought to mind the unwelcome vision of Cameron Gant. She shook her head and went back to packing.

"Here, Lib, I want you to take this sampler with you and put it on your new bedchamber wall," Merry said as she hurried in. "It's the one you've admired. I just finished it. And tell that old housekeeper Hannah to keep city dust from it, too," she added.

Libby hugged Merry, then held the sampler before her to read aloud:

Though Life is fair
And Pleasure young
And Love on Ev'ry
Young Man's Tongue,
I turn my Thoughts
To Serious Things,
Life is ever on the Wing.

"It's perfect for me, and I will treasure it," Libby vowed as she knelt to close the leather trunk. They heard hoofbeats, and Merry went to peer down into the front yard.

"It's him again, sister! Cameron Gant!" Merry cried, rolling her eyes with a pert, suggestive grin that Libby resented. "I'm going down," she added, and flew for the door.

"I'll be down eventually—if only to keep Mother from

being taken in by his honeyed tongue!'' Libby called as
the door banged.

His honeyed tongue, she mused as she twirled her forehead curls around her index finger and settled her dark blue
skirts over her smaller traveling petticoat. His voice could
be as sweet and thick and golden as the honey the bees
made out back. She shivered involuntarily. She glanced
down at the sampler lying on the bed. There would never
be love on that young man's tongue, she told herself—and
good riddance! There would be only more deceit and prideful, prejudiced Toryism! He was out to shut down her Whig
paper and literally send her packing back home, so he was
still as much her enemy as ever, and for many reasons now!

She ambled slowly down the stairs, though she could
hear his voice in the parlor again. She did not even glance
in, though she realized they had probably all seen her. Unable to resist the deliberate snub, she went out to the
kitchen for Sally, who had her ear pressed to the door. She
and Sally carried the trunk and her other things downstairs
and set them in the hall with a good deal of chatter and
noise. Then Libby turned slowly and glanced into the parlor.

"Oh, Mr. Gant, back again to attempt further amends?''
she asked.

As they had the previous night, their gazes locked.

"Would you accept amends if I offered them, Mistress
Elizabeth?''

"Certainly not.''

"Well, then,'' he said, and he dared to shrug grandiosely.
"Actually, thank you for your avid interest in why I have
returned, but I am here to see your mother and not you.''

"Libby knows that,'' Merry interjected, making a frenzied hand signal pleading for civility behind his back. "But
guess what, sister? Sally, you, too. He's offered our dear
Sally a job at Melrose!''

Libby knew she blanched. She spun to face Sally, who

clasped her hands, beamed and nodded in surprise like a spineless jack-in-the-box. Libby fought the urge to insist Sally go with her to Manhattan. She had no means to support the girl, and Sally's mother, too, would turn sulfurous at the idea of her daughter living in what the minister had termed "Sin City" and "Vanity Fair." She was ashamed of herself that she resented Sally's going to Melrose Manor, as if she were deserting them.

"Of course, you must accept such a kind offer, Sally." She forced the words from her throat and gave the girl's arm a little squeeze. "I'm very happy for you."

"And he's offered to let us lease the land the beehives are on for the merest pittance so that Mother can work them," Merry plunged on.

"Just a pot or so of honey a year will do splendidly for the lease," he said, his eyes straying to Libby again. "I really do favor honey."

"Beekeeping's just my affectation, a hobby," Georgina declared, but she might as well not have spoken, as their guest and Libby did not so much as blink. They glared at each other again.

"Frankly," Cameron Gant said, getting to his feet, "I came most of all to offer you safe passage to the city if you were still determined to go, Mistress Libby. I deeply regret your father's tragic misfortune, and I have my horse with pillion and a safe, closely examined Gant barge at your disposal."

"That won't be necessary," Libby countered quickly. "I have a way."

His obvious anger at her curt dismissal sent a glow of satisfaction through her. At last she had humiliated him as the Gants had humiliated the Morgans! A sharp, heady sense of power swept over her. And yet, she felt the surprising, bitter knife edge of regret.

"Of course," he said curtly. "I should have known you would have a way. In that case, Mrs. Morgan, why don't I

just take Sally over to Melrose and let her meet the staff? I'll send her back by noon, and we will just expect her the first of the month, so that she might spend some more time here with you lovely ladies—Mistress Merry and yourself, that is.''

He had bested her again, Libby fumed. With a sharp nod, he swept by her, the happy women in his wake. Sally ran for her shawl and straw bonnet and giggled when Cameron Gant pulled her up behind him on the wide pillion saddle.

"Oh, bless you, bless you, Mr. Gant!" Libby's mother called to the smirking devil as he shot a last lightning look at Libby. Merry fluttered a hand. Suddenly infuriated beyond words again, Libby turned her back on him, but not before she saw Sally riding off like a rescued damsel behind her conquering knight to the castle Libby herself had dreamed of as a little girl. What galled her most was that, despite her hatred of the Gants and what they stood for in the colonies, she still desperately longed to be that fairytale princess.

"Damn you, damn you, Cameron Gant!" Libby, who never cursed, mouthed silently as she strode back into the house to fetch her cloak and trunk.

By the time she had bidden farewell to her still-disgruntled mother and the weeping Merry and departed Staten Island, Libby was grateful Cameron Gant was nowhere in sight. Her "way" to New York was on a slow barge crowded with firewood that her gruff old neighbor, Clinton Rappaport, was taking to Manhattan. Staring at the city's brick, stone and slate silhouette as they crossed the choppy bay, Libby sat on her tattered trunk, crowded amidst cut cords of wood destined for the hearths of Manhattan.

The pretty seaport of New York City, home to approximately twenty thousand souls, lay before her excited eyes in the crisp April sunlight. Granted, the city was smaller

than Philadelphia and not much larger than Boston or Charleston, but it had always seemed massive to Libby. Today, lofty church steeples tried to snag racing clouds over Manhattan. The cupola and flag of city hall poked at the sky, as did the top of the King's Arms Tavern, the tallest structure in town. She remembered going there with Father and Mr. Simpson to "take the view."

In her mind's eye she saw again the aerial vista of the great, pulsing city laid out before her: the bustling heart of town, with its mostly narrow cobbled streets and its few tree-lined boulevards; the fine Georgian homes on lower Broad Way Street; traffic-choked Wall Street; the distant northern outer wards, all slums and slaughterhouses; and even the faraway green woodlots and rural meadows of the tiny villages of Yonkers and White Plains. In this city they had loved, how much she was going to miss the two dear men in her life, who had opened up so many doors of discovery to her!

She blinked back tears as the barge entered the East River, looking with curiosity at the British warships at anchor in the bay. There were two large ones: the newly arrived *Kingfisher* and the familiar *Asia*, just off the foot of Wall Street. At least General Gage still kept most of the fleet in Boston Harbor. Then the busy wharves and slips studded with British and colonial trading ships leapt before her eyes.

She had almost forgotten! With the tragedy at home, it had even slipped Mother's mind that the London-New York merchant fleet was due in for its biannual colonial delivery of the latest fashions, the newest books, needed and simply longed-for supplies. It caused a business frenzy on Wall and Dock Streets and in all the shops scattered throughout the city the last weeks of every April and October.

Her hand on a corded pile of wood for support, Libby stood to scan the busy wharves. Wholesalers, retailers, draymen, shoppers, gawkers. And on more than one cart

lined up along the ships she saw—proud as you please—
the painted red-and-gold signs touting Gant London Imports.

At that, she felt a strange shiver up her spine and tiny
prickles of heat along her neck and even deep in her belly.
Cameron Gant's stern face, with its piercing gray eyes,
seemed to stare at her. Briefly she heard again the bark of
pursuing dogs and the thunder of horse's hooves as she'd
run. Torches glared at her from the darkness as she turned
to face Cameron Gant, only to see him gazing at her with
desire in his eyes. Her insides churned with a mixture of
anger and longing. She shook her head to thrust the startling
vision from her mind and heart.

"Busy, busy place," the white-haired Clinton Rappaport
observed as the barge was tethered at teeming Murray's
Wharf. "Gonna be a task getting wheelbarrows of my
wood delivered in that mess."

"I cannot thank you enough for the ride over," she told
him. "As the gazette's only three blocks away, I'll be fine.
I will send an apprentice from the shop for my trunk. Now,
don't you take the time to walk me over there today, Mr.
Rappaport."

"Promised your mother," he declared stolidly, and he
would not be dissuaded.

So Libby ended her triumphal entry into Manhattan
walking beside a rickety, bouncing wheelbarrow full of
wood with her hands up to keep her precariously perched
trunk from falling. Still, her heart thundered in her breast
with excitement. Her thoughts bustled faster than the shoppers and cursing drivers bottled up in the narrow streets as
they entered familiar Queen Street, beyond Hanover
Square. Perhaps it was appropriate, she told herself, that
she enter New York today with a load of Staten Island
wood. After all, she intended to set this town afire!

Libby waved Mr. Rappaport on his way at last from the
threshold of the building in which the gazette was housed.

She still had a key, but in fact she found the door unlocked. One of the numerous cats Faith Goodhue kept at the apothecary shop next door was asleep in the splash of sun against the door and didn't budge. The narrow two stories of the printery held a downstairs shop and three cramped upstairs living chambers wedged between a popular wiggery on the right and the Goodhues' on the left.

But, to Libby's surprise and chagrin, the print shop looked deserted. Somehow she had expected to find the head journeyman printer, bald, blustery Josiah Bean, carrying on in Atwood's name. With two journeymen and two apprentices and the master printer, it had been a busy, if small, shop. Frowning, Libby pulled the notice of the death and the closing of the gazette off the front door and shooed the cat away to drag her trunk inside.

"Jos? Henry? Hannah Brewster?" she called to the sadly quiet print shop. "Isn't anyone here?"

She heard a flutter of footsteps above and breathed a relieved sigh. "Who's that?" the scratchy voice overhead called. "Can't you read we be all closed up with the master's death?"

"Hannah! It's Libby Morgan!" Libby called, and met the birdlike, sprightly old lady partway up the steps.

Hannah cried as she hugged Libby to her. "Mercy me! For a moment I was thinking this tragedy be all a bad dream and you was come to stay the day again!"

"I'll be here more than just the day, Hannah! Mr. Simpson's left me the paper, and I am here to stay!"

The rounding of the light blue eyes and the O of the gaptoothed mouth webbed the papery skin of the old face anew. "Mercy me! Did he now? That nasty tosspot son of his will be in a fury, but I can't say I fault Atwood's logic. But if the staff would of knowed it, still can't say they would of stayed, with you being a mere slip of a girl and all."

"You mean they've gone off? But I need them to start things up right away! Where are they?"

"Jos Bean, he's just throwing his savings away in taverns and gazing fondly through the window of the wiggery next door like always. Henry and both 'prentices been hired by Jemmy Rivington, just down the street. Snapped them up like fish bait, he did, the minute he heard the paper went under with the master. And all the stationery trade and readership's gone to Rivington, I wager, though we still got plenty supplies here. I thought Quentin would just sell them off for more rum sooner or later."

"He will not!" Libby cried, and smacked her hands on her skirts. "But I just cannot believe the men and boys went to our rival paper, and a royalist one, too! Whatever has happened to loyalty these days? I know they've got to eat, but I won't grovel at Rivington's to fetch them back! I'll get Jos and hire some new folk! And while there's a breath left in me, this gazette and store are not going under like Father and Mr. Simpson!"

The old woman nodded and pulled her knitted shawl closer. "I never let myself go under neither, my girl. Not when my George died on the ship heading over, and not when my house burned years later to take my second husband and all my earthly goods. Not even when my only living relative, my great-nephew Ben I told you about, up and told me he was joining the British navy. I would have been left on my own then, if Mr. Simpson hadn't offered me this job. But I'm so tickled you're back to stay." Hannah smiled, showing her checkerboard teeth. "No one to talk to for over a week but the Goodhues next door."

"I'm glad I'm here, too, Hannah, but I'm afraid I've much more to do than talk to get this establishment back on its feet."

"But don't you know you're sitting on a real dangerous powder keg here, my girl?" Hannah warned with a shake of a thin finger. "The town's still divided, worse than ever

now with rumors Royal Gov'nor Tryon's coming back from London soon, and who knows with what royal dos and don'ts for all us folks dreaming of freedom. Never did forgive German George for that plaguey Sugar Act that made the price of marzipan and comfits go sky-high!''

"You're a jewel, Hannah!" Libby said, and she hugged her again as they went downstairs. "And I hope I can carry on with just half your fine spirit here!" They stood silent a moment, as if in remembrance, surveying the dim, deserted print shop and stationery desk together. "You know, Hannah, Mother never would have let me come if you weren't here to help look after me," Libby said, her voice quiet now. "So if you'll still oversee the food and turn a hand to clean, together we'll protest against old England if she won't let us speak our free colonial women's minds, won't we? And before I go out to find someone to help me work this press, I'm going to post a new handbill telling this town that the paper's back full-strength under a new owner!"

"Full-strength?" Hannah whispered sadly, and shook her white head behind Libby's back. "You might put out one bill," she muttered under her breath, "but how you ever gonna print a whole paper on your own in this man's city—with all the diff'rent causes everyone's so het up about?"

But, still in her cloak and bonnet as if she didn't notice anything now, Libby Morgan was already pulling type from the many-shelved wooden typecase and sliding it into a composing stick. With another shake of her snowy head that set her mobcap to bouncing, Hannah walked over to the windows and opened the shutters to let in the light.

Three

Morgan Print Shop
Queen Str., east of Hanover Sq.
Elizabeth Morgan, Prop.

This Shop prints: *Church & Lottery Tickets, Deeds on Parchment, Bonds, Advertisements (& provides a Boy for sticking them up), Hand Bills for Sales of Goods or Lands, Shipping & Duty Lists, Almanacs, Hymnbooks, & School Books.*

This Shop sells: *Fine Rag Paper (Larchmont's Mill, St. Is.), Parchment, Ink Powder, Sealing Wax & Wafers, Pounce & Pounce Boxes, Faber's pencils (black & red with India rubbers), Fountain Pens (just arr'd fr. London), Protractors (London made), & Pocket Compasses.*

Remember: *The Choice in this & far more important Things is up to your individual and freely-held Beliefs.*

By late afternoon, Libby had printed twenty handbills announcing that the *Liberal Gazette* was soon to be printed again, and twenty handbills advertising services and goods

at the stationery store. It was imperative she begin to make money soon so she could calm her mother by sending some coins back with Mr. Rappaport by next week. If not, she'd be forced to return part of the four guineas her mother had loaned her for sustenance when she'd left. So she stuck her still-damp handbills up on walls and trees and fences as she went along to find Josiah Bean to offer him his old job back.

Hannah had said she would probably find him in one of four nearby taverns, but he had not been seen all day in the first three she visited. Libby's embarrassment and determination grew with each place she entered. She had refused to bring old Hannah along, despite her urging, but she was beginning to wish for an escort. She shuddered as men's avid or bleary gazes crawled over her. She painfully ignored several rather personal comments and dubious compliments, despite the temptation to refute them. If Mother could see her now, she would be so appalled she would swim the bay to haul her daughter back to rural Brady's Pond Cottage herself.

Libby had saved the Fraunces Tavern at Pearl and Broad for the last, not because it was the farthest away but because it was the gathering place for wealthy businessmen, Whigs and Tories. She had no desire to run into either Jemmy Rivington, who had stolen her print crew, or even the despicable Cameron Gant himself. Besides, she could not quite picture slope-shouldered, bald Josiah Bean among the bewigged Tories or Whigs of the city.

But she was wrong. She heard Jos's distinctive rough voice raised the moment she sidled through the half-open door and stood against the back wall to look around. She squinted through the blue haze of strong Virginia tobacco smoke hovering over the tables and benches. The smell of food and ale hung just as thick in here. Yes, indeed. Josiah Bean, in an argument with some man with an expensive silk puffed and braided periwig in the back corner.

"Gen'ral Washington's not afraid to come here even if the gov'nor does come back, mark my words!" Jos insisted with a swing of his pewter tankard to punctuate his claim.

"When Gov'nor William Tryon comes back from London, we'll have a fine parade for him right up Broad Way Street, you old rumblegut!" his opponent insisted. "You lily-livered Whigs and rabble-rousers think you could match something like that for that Tidewater-bred Virginian? I got ten shillings says you can't, and that's that."

"Ten shillings is a pittance to wager on our gen'ral and those who know his worth!" Jos Bean thundered as he stood, apparently floundering for coins in his pouch. "Damn if I hain't come up a bit short. But we'll raise us a glor'ous parade anyway!"

The Tory's huge wig seemed to smoke with powder and pomatum as he shook his head and snorted a laugh. "You fast-mouthed, addle-brained colonial rumbutts always come up a bit short and always will!" he roared, and others joined in with raucous laughter.

Libby's blood boiled. But Jos looked as if he meant to fight as he wobbled to his feet and shoved the Tory braggart's shoulder. All Jos needed was fisticuffs to land him in city prison, or some patrician challenge to a duel! She hurried to his side.

"Jos, come on back to the shop with me," she said, as she shouldered her way boldly in to take his arm. The other man glared, and a murmuring crowd grew, scenting the high drama of a fight with a woman in the midst of it.

"You his daughter...or something better, woman?" the bewigged Tory asked, and sniggered.

She spun to stare the man down. "Let's just say General Washington has sent me to care for his own," she retorted cheekily. The Tory sputtered, but several others laughed at her wit. Jos let himself be led away, despite a few other taunts that trailed them out. Quickly, Libby tugged him

down Broad Street and up Dock, where he stopped in his tracks and gazed huffily at her.

"Back to the shop?" he said, as if it had taken his ale-sodden brain that long to comprehend her words. "Why? That sot Quentin there ready to have a go at the press? I'd work for you 'fore I'd turn the devil's tail for that no-good legacy to his pa's good name!"

"Fine, Jos, because that's exactly the way it's going to be. Atwood Simpson has left the gazette to me, and I mean for it—and us—to prosper."

"You, missy?" he said, leaning back disbelievingly on a brick wall under a cooper's painted sign of a barrel. He crossed his arms over his chest, ignoring people who passed them on the street. He answered his own question. "Naw! Clever and quick you may be, and good with the type, but not to run the whole blasted thing."

"I've already put up new-printed bills telling the town it's true. And I need your help, Jos. Everyone else has jumped ship for Jemmy Rivington's," she said, and faced him squarely, eye-to-eye.

That bit of news sobered him instantly. "Blast that Tory-toed, Tory-tongued printer!" he declared. "Him and the rest of 'em in the taverns of this town!" He ran his big hand, gnarled and stained from years of presswork, across the smooth pate that embarrassed him so in a world of fashionable wigs he could not afford. Jos had always been too proud and stubborn to settle for a cheap scratch wig such as the poor masses wore. He had saved his money as long as Libby had known him for a fine wig and its expensive upkeep.

"Like to drop by Royal Jemmy's," he went on, "and give 'em all a good ragging for being taken in by money and flash, I would. Just heard tonight Rivington's been named Royal Printer for the province at one hundred pounds a year. One hundred of German George's pounds!

I could get enough ale to swim in and the finest wig in town for life for a fee like that, I could!"

"Then we've got two fine articles for our first issue of the gazette, Jos. We'll tell the city to take everything the King's new messenger boy prints with a large grain of salt, and we'll quote that pompous silk-wigged man back at the Fraunces. We'll tell our readers that he claimed Washington's supporters couldn't even provide a fine parade if our Virginia general comes to town. Are you with me?"

Excitement flared in Jos's pale watery eyes for one moment, then faded. "Naw, missy. Not with the master dead and gone. It's not in me anymore, it hain't."

"What's not in you, Jos Bean? You were going to wager your hard-earned coin and fight that windbag back there for Washington's honor and our right to choose liberty! You do know that bewigged braggart's name for our article, I hope!"

Awe slowly replaced disbelief in his narrow gaze. "Sure, I know the blowhard's name.... Works at City Hall for the mayor, too. But you can't just—"

"Oh, can't I?" she countered, her face alight with excitement at the possibilities. "We'll perk up this city to do more than sponsor fireworks for men who died at Lexington and Concord in Massachusetts. We have to warn our own bold New York patriots before the governor or the full fleet comes back! We've got to attack the Tory forces if they get too bold," she declared, and shoved the picture of Cam Gant from her mind once again. "We've got to make fireworks of another kind, just as Atwood Simpson would have done! Fireworks in people's minds and hearts, Jos!" she insisted, gesturing wildly. "And you mustn't call me missy anymore," she added, her voice subdued now as she glanced about the street at those who stared at her emotional display. "It's Mistress Libby now."

His eyes focused, and he looked into hers at last. She was so young and comely—and so fired-up determined. For

the first time in days he glimpsed something worth living for. "Well, I am almost out of coin anyway."

"But I won't have you ever drinking on the paper's time, or you'll be out. I don't care if you are the finest journeyman printer in the colonies!" she said, scolding and flattering at once. She wagged a finger in his face, but they both exchanged wary smiles.

His beard-stubbled face relaxed, and he heaved his rounded shoulders away from the wall and stood erect. He lifted both spread hands to cover his bare head when he realized he'd left his old tricorne in one of the taverns. "Spent all the money I'd saved for my wig trying to drown myself in ale when the master and your pa went down, missy—Mistress Libby, I mean," he admitted.

"Come to work for me, Jos, and I'll give you a guinea right now toward a fine white peruke I saw in the window of Fanning's Wiggery. But you'll have to vow you'll not wear it turning the devil's tail, or it'll be black in a week. Come on, then, we've a paper to get out on these streets!"

He shook his head in admiration. The day always did have storm warnings flying when the Morgan girl was at the shop, he thought as he walked along with her, faster than his fuzzy head wanted his leaden feet to go. Still, he'd give her only a month or so to make good, he decided. But it did revive his cold, crushed spirit to think this spunky girl would get back at the bigwigs who had laughed at him and Washington's honor at the Fraunces Tavern tonight.

As Libby and Jos passed Rivington's print shop on the corner of Wall and Queen, she had to take his arm to keep him from shouting the curses he had threatened earlier through the front door. Inside, they could see Henry Hamstead and their two former apprentices hard at work with the others at two presses under the glow of bull's-eye lamps. Uncertainty and even the edge of fear nibbled at Libby's resolve. This shop was so well lit, so well staffed,

and it was run now with royal support. How could their dark, little shop ever take on such royalist might and power?

"Come on, Jos. We've work to do!" she insisted. They had just gone by when the door flew open and James Rivington himself filled the doorway. But he had not opened it to order them away. He held a skinny lad by the seat of his breeches and his shirtback. He heaved him out into the street. The boy hit the cobbles hard, then rolled and scrambled to his feet to touch his gashed chin and bruises tenderly. A small crowd spilled from the coffeehouse diagonally across the way as Libby hurried over to the lad.

"That will teach you to sneak food during work!" the plump, immaculately attired Rivington yelled after the boy, smacking his hands together as if they had been sullied. "Apprentices eat what they're told, when they're told!" he shouted, before his deepset eyes took in Libby and Jos.

"Well, I declare," Rivington jeered, shifting his beady gaze to Libby, "if it isn't my formidable new rival come spying. I've seen the bills threatening the imminent return of the *Liberal Gazette* that you've plastered all over town!" His voice dripped sarcasm, just as his brocaded wrists dripped Brussels lace.

Libby helped the lad to his feet, hoping Jos didn't swing on Rivington before she could stop him. She planned to handle her newly inherited rival with ink and paper, not with a hard roll on these cobbles. The chastised apprentice sniffed back his tears. She was amazed at how frail he felt. He was as thin as a broom. It was not unusual for apprentices to be trounced, but fury rose up inside her anyway, quick and sharp. She stood, her hand on the boy's shaking shoulder, and answered Rivington, cutting off the cursing, or worse, that she sensed was coming from the seething Jos.

"I believe you've heard the saying 'Actions speak louder than words,' Mr. Rivington," she retorted. "Let me say

only that you will be seeing our gazette's actions in our words. Good evening!'' Steering the boy along, she hooked Jos's arm to move him, too.

Behind them, Rivington bellowed, ''It'll never work, not from a mere skirt! Not a daughter of that lack-brained liar Silas Morgan that Atwood always kept about him as a charity case!''

In the growing dusk, she spun around to face Rivington. The crowd, which had begun to disperse, came to a halt again. ''They shared a loyal friendship unaffected by class or wealth, not a concept I would expect you to grasp, sir! Especially when the king now as good as buys your associates and advertisers for you. Not since you've become a royal charity case yourself!''

She heard Rivington gasp and cough. Someone in the crowd guffawed. Now it was Jos's turn to pull her away. ''I favor that turn of phrase, Mistress Libby, I really do.'' He chortled. ''Rivington, the royal charity case. You should use it in the article of our first issue,'' he told her as he hustled his new employer and the boy along, one with each hand.

The lad sniffed again and wiped his torn sleeve across his bloody nose. Libby put her hand on his shoulder again. ''So, you were Mr. Rivington's apprentice?'' she asked, her voice gentle now.

''Yesiree, ma'am, one o' five. Run errands. Done good, but, Jupiter, he beat me all the same. My name's Percival Collister, ma'am, called Coll. My family lives down near the docks. I'm gonna be both a printer and a soldier with New York's army when I grow up.''

''Well, Coll, I must say I admire all your ambitions,'' she said with a taut smile at his dirty angel's face. He came barely to her shoulder. ''But I need your help now before you grow up.'' The pale green eyes lit as if a lantern shone within, and he shoved his flaxen hair off his bruised forehead. ''You see, it just so happens I need a boy who can

stick bills up all over Manhattan, and deliver weekly papers, too. But you'd have to work very hard, as you'd be the only apprentice right now.''

"Mr. Rivington said I was no-'count," he admitted when Jos groaned and shook his head.

"But you see, Coll, any no-'count of Mr. Rivington's counts a great deal with Mr. Jos Bean here, and me, too. Isn't that so, Jos?" she asked firmly, getting a stiff acquiescing shake of his bald head. "Come on then, you two," she said, quickening her pace again. Until she found someone else to help her, these two would have to do.

By the next morning, Libby had strained her eyes in wavering candlelight to write the top four articles for their first issue of the gazette. Now she stood at the cases, setting them in type. One talked of Rivington's selling his last shred of independence to the king for one hundred pounds yearly. One detailed the Tory challenge by a city hall official that, if General Washington came to town, his supporters could not even raise a parade. One was a black-banded biography of Atwood Simpson. She portrayed him quite admiringly, yet honestly, she thought, as a common man who had made much of his life through self-education and hard work—and lifelong friendships. The memorial endeavored to inspire others to strive for what they believed in—and not to fear to choose the hard path of daring to speak for freedom. And the fourth article was a condemnation of absentee landowners, such as the Gants of Staten Island, who allowed public conveyances others paid to use to become unsafe and quite deadly.

"Going out to fetch the rest of the lampblack we're owed for ink, Mistress Libby," Jos told her from the door. "I'm taking the lad along to show him the spots we'll want things posted," he groused with a quick glance down at the jumpy lad. "Hannah will be back from market soon, but you'll have to look up long enough from that type to handle the

stationery desk if anyone comes in," he added, amazed anew by her intense concentration.

"I will. You listen well to Jos now, Coll!" she yelled over her shoulder before she turned back to her work.

She heard the door bang. She slid yet another line of type carefully off the stick to the galley and reached for another uppercase letter from the top shelf. The more commonly used smaller type was in the lowercase trays, all painstakingly sorted, so she didn't even have to look when she picked up another letter. She always checked the print rapidly, though she had to read it upside down and backward, before they pulled a proof. She was so intent that she didn't turn at first when she heard the door again.

"So it's really true!" The sharp male voice grated close behind her as she spun to face her customer: Quentin Simpson, Atwood's son! He hardly looked pleased to see her here.

"Oh, Quentin, you startled me!" she said, and put the stick down behind her. She had known him for years, though when he had shown little aptitude for or interest in reading or printing his father had stopped bringing him here and had apprenticed him out to several other trades, none of which had suited him. She wiped her inky hands repeatedly on her leather apron. She took a step forward as he came around the stationery counter and gazed with a proprietary air about the shop. Even from here she could smell rum and tobacco on his breath.

Quentin Simpson looked just enough like his father to unsettle her with the pain of memory. Yet his face was rounder and more flaccid, despite the fact he was only three years older than she. His dark brown eyes were watery and jumpy compared with his father's clear, steady gaze. And his lower teeth were bucked slightly, making him look like a nasty guard dog when he turned his profile. He was dressed very expensively, in a bottle-green brocade cutaway coat with lapels—evidently the new London fashion

the merchant ships had just introduced. He carried a walking stick carved of horn, which he tapped in his beringed left hand.

She did feel sympathy for the man. He had no family now that Atwood was dead. He and some cronies owned a chandler's shop down on the docks but mostly frequented places with sundry available imported drinks, she had overheard Atwood tell her father recently. One of the last things Atwood had ever said of his son shouldered its way through her jumbled thoughts: "The only thing Quentin ever reads these days is bills announcing another new licensed bar opening."

"I want to extend my condolences on your father's death, Quentin," she began. "And I'm sure you were surprised about my inheriting all this," she went on calmly, with a gesture that encompassed the room. "I assure you, I was, too. But you have the fine house on the square, and the rest...his library..."

"His library! Do you think I give a hang for a bunch of musty-smelling books, ones with your greedy fingerprints all over them?" he demanded, shaking his walking stick at her. "I'm selling them off as fast as I can! And I'm not sure I'm so surprised he left you this print shop, you crafty little hussy! I should have seen it coming, the plan you and your father concocted to trick mine!"

"Plan? Trick? Quentin, I did not do any—"

"Especially after my mother died last year, I should have seen it coming! Little Libby always about, always loving his books, always so bright, he said, so sweetly grateful..."

"I resent the tone of your voice and the tenor of your words, Quentin. Now I am telling you I will run this paper as your father would have wished, and I really must ask you to leave."

"I take it we're alone, or you would have summoned someone by now." He smirked when she did not deny his deduction. He fished a flat filigreed-silver flask from his

waistcoat and unscrewed the lid to take a swig. When she tried to edge past him toward the door, he smacked his stick on the countertop to block her way.

"No, no, my dear, you'll hear me out. I intend to contest legally that such a fetching, appealing young woman should so cleverly convince an older, vulnerable man to leave her the livelihood that should go to his son and heir. But I do," he continued, his voice oily now, "really think, since you inherited the shop, I should at least inherit the affection you felt for my father!"

"Get out of my print shop, Quentin!"

He slid his stick along to hem her in as he came closer. "Remember the days we were both here?" he droned on. "You just wanted to read and to see how everything worked. So boring, little Libby. But Libby's all grown up now. Perhaps, you know, if you were kinder, and liked the sort of things I like—" he dropped his heavy gaze down her throat to the top of her apron, as if his gaze could pierce it to her breasts "—I would allow you to work the place for me. We could have little meetings now and then upstairs, hmm?" He tapped his walking stick ominously against her skirts, once, twice, while she gaped, horrified. "Then you could show me how much you're learning, how exciting everything can be here at a paper that specializes in little rebellions, so—"

She kicked his stick away and darted for the door. He yanked her back by one arm; she bounced against the cases, rattling the type.

"You aren't worthy of his name, let alone this paper he loved!" she blurted before she could halt her words. "Get out of here before I scream! Before I print what you are really like for all the city to see and—"

He seemed to explode. He shrieked a curse, swinging his stick at her like a sabre. She took the blow on her lifted arm. He pinned her heavily against the wall, but she clawed at him and yanked away. And then he went quite mad,

swinging at the neatly divided boxes of sorted type, slamming them again and again until some of the boxes splintered and letters jumped out.

"No, Quentin! No!" she shouted, pounding on his back. He shoved the upper case of type; lead letters peppered the floor like bullets. Grabbing her wrists, he held them in a viselike grip while he scuffed and stomped on the type, then swung the stick at her again. She ducked, and it cracked in two on the big platen of the press. Then, before either of them knew someone else was in the room, big hands hauled Quentin away from her and slammed him against the wall.

Cameron Gant! His fist hit Quentin's jaw with a resounding crack. He hoisted Quentin by his armpits up the wall and smacked his head against it. "Devil take you, Simpson, are you demented?" his deep voice demanded. He hit him once more, then let him slide to the floor amidst the scattered piles of type.

"Are you all right, Libby?" Cameron asked, touching her shoulder. She was leaning against the press, gasping for air. She nodded, her arms wrapped tight around her waist, as if to hold herself up. Despite her shock and dismay, the fact Cameron Gant had called her by her given name and touched her shook her. She just leaned there while he hauled the battered Quentin to his feet and shoved him toward the door.

"This time, in honor of your father's memory and this woman's reputation, I shall not challenge you to further justice, man." He gave Quentin another shake. "But the second time I shall have no such qualms. If you have a quarrel with Mistress Morgan, get yourself a lawyer to discuss it with your own father's lawyer, but otherwise keep clear!" He shoved Quentin unceremoniously into the street, where he stumbled, then righted himself. With a quick, angry glance back at Libby through the thick window glass,

which distorted his face to a monster's leer, Quentin brushed himself off and lurched away.

Libby finally moved when Cameron Gant came back in and closed the door behind him. "I see I was none too late to place an advertisement," he said.

If she hadn't been so shaken, she would have laughed at that. "I do thank you—for ridding the place of that display," she said, though it shamed her how hard those words came to her lips. "He was most distraught, and he made some wretched accusations."

Cameron's eyes went slowly over her, as if he wanted to assure himself that she was all in one piece. "I can imagine."

She resisted the temptation to say more. She knelt in the narrow space to scrape piles of type together and placed handfuls on the counter. Cameron straighted his waistcoat and cravat, then leaned his elbows on the other side to watch. "This will set my first issue back," she admitted without looking up. She painfully recalled the strident tone of the article she had been typesetting about the Gants, calling them heedless, British landlords, just like their king, who ran the colonies in the same way. She stood suddenly, meeting his steady gaze and leaning her elbows on the other side of the counter as if to mirror his nonchalance.

"You came to place an advertisement, you said?"

"I thought perhaps you could use one."

She stood erect again. "I don't take charity, sir. Especially not Tory Gant charity."

"Ah, so self-sufficient, so righteously right. You know I am a Tory to my very toes because I am a Gant, is that it? Or because we import London goods? And I wasn't offering charity. You print my advertisement and I pay for it, a mutually beneficial transaction between two fond enemies."

Her eyes sparkled at his subtle fencing, but she could

think of no parrying rejoinder. She needed the funds badly. No one else had been in to buy a thing, and yet—

"You do believe everyone has the right to speak for what they desire, do you not, mistress?" he asked her, his mouth suddenly taut. His disturbing gray gaze had fastened on her lips again.

All of a sudden she realized what a fright she must look. She was ink-stained, and she knew her hair had come loose from its knot in the melee. And when she'd rubbed her inky hands to her face after he'd thrown Quentin out— She felt herself blush hotly as the possible multiple meanings of his words about desire echoed in her brain.

"Yes, I— Of course I believe that. Here, let me write out what you dictate for the advertisement, then." She fetched a piece of rag paper, then poised her quill over it.

"Cam Gant requests... My friends call me Cam," he explained, a hopeful glint in his eye. She tried to ignore it and dragged her eyes back down to her hands. "Cam Gant requests a truce with one Elizabeth Morgan, that they might begin to mend bridges and forge at least a tenuous alliance—"

"Sir!" she said, and banged the tip of the quill so that it spattered ink clear to her wrist. "I will not be mocked!"

"I wasn't mocking, Mistress Liberty," he said, "just gently coercing, and I think you should learn to tell the difference. But I did hope at the *Liberal Gazette* to encounter a more liberal attitude toward a man who tossed out a rather obnoxious fellow before he could harm you more."

His tawny eyebrows lifted in a blatant challenge. To her dismay, she reacted at first like a compass point swinging toward true north. She almost swayed across the counter toward him. This man was dangerous, she told herself, stepping back. She had hated him for years, for all he stood for—for his Tory beliefs, his cruelties and his crassness.

And now she was letting a mere soft, teasing tone and a handsome face—devil take him—almost do her in!

"I assume the real purpose of this advertisement in this busy spring shopping season is for London-imported Gant goods." There, she thought. That sounded much better. She was in control now, despite the trembling deep inside her when he stood as close to her as he did, even with the long wooden countertop between them. "Gant Imports, whose carts that carry only goods off the ships are all newly repaired and prettily painted, while a ferry that carries human souls was allowed to nearly rot!"

He looked as if she'd struck him. "I know you're bereaved and it helps to strike out at someone else, just the way poor, besotted Quentin did today, mistress," he said, his earlier soft tone now as knife-edged as hers. "But I had expected more from a woman who wants to make it on her own in commercial Manhattan."

"Meaning you could buy and sell this paper if you wished?"

"Meaning there will not always be someone rushing in at the right time to save you from the pitfalls I see ahead for someone of your temperament and prickly pride."

"Then I must inform you, sir, however much I admit I need your advertisement, it is best you not buy it. The *Liberal Gazette* is running an article taking your family to task for its shoddy care of the ferry. It is, as I see it, a sign of the times. The king's ministers also run these colonies from afar, in a very Gantlike way."

A frown crumpled his high brow and narrowed his eyes. He startled her by reaching for her wrist before she could draw back. "You know, you've been more coddled and spoiled than I ever was. Best you call this grand endeavor of yours 'Libby's Gazette' if you mean to take out personal grudges in its pages, Mistress Liberty!"

"I— That isn't it at all."

"Then what is it really between us? Just a happenstance

that trapped us both in a bad beginning eight years ago, when you broke a window at Melrose? Just that you happen to heat my blood with this defiant stance of yours? That we may or may not be—your prejudice has not given you time to find out the truth of my politics, of course—on opposite ends of the political spectrum? That you begrudge me my inherited wealth? Perhaps I should begrudge you the fact you had loving parents when I lost mine and my sister left me when yours still cares."

She listened in openmouthed amazement to his spate of accusations, until his voice broke and he paused to bite his lower lip with straight white teeth. "Or are you afraid of this?" he demanded, his voice not his own. He pulled her closer, his strong grip warm on her wrist, and leaned forward to kiss her lips.

The kiss was brief but masterful. Hard, warm, then beseechingly soft. Then he pulled slowly, almost reluctantly, back. She stood upright, too, stunned and yet wanting more. She felt her cheeks stain crimson again, she who never blushed.

He noted that her lower lip had gone slack in surprise. He longed to leap the counter and pull her to him full length for another taste of her. To wet that full, soft mouth, to trace her lips with the tip of his tongue and then dart deeper inside. But he loosed her wrist as she pulled back and leaned his hipbones hard into his side of the counter to gain control of himself. He cleared his throat and straightened his cravat again.

"This is...this could be too much trouble for us both," he said, his voice choked. "Too much between us."

She knew she stood like a mute, limp puppet, a dunce with no voice. But she could not stem the dizzy feeling that came when he merely looked at her like that, let alone captured her wrist and her lips.

"Yes," she whispered. "Trouble between us."

"I'll send someone 'round later if I want an advertise-

ment." He cleared his throat. She saw then that he had smeared his pristine silk cravat with ink. He must have dirtied his hand when he'd grasped her wrist. Some other time, she might have laughed. Instead, she took a step back, and type scuffed under her feet. That brought her back to the real world with a jolt as Cam picked his tricorne and walking stick off the floor, where he must have dropped them when he'd first run in to seize Quentin. He looked back at her once more across the counter. She stood her ground, though she had the oddest urge to run around it toward him.

His eyes swept as much of her as he could see. He pulled the door open and went out. Though she told herself she was glad to see him go, she hurried around to the window to watch him disappear down the street as she heaved a huge, shoulder-lifting sigh.

Then she marched around the counter and scooped up more scattered type as a rush of normal feelings ebbed back to fill the emptiness she had felt when he'd gone out. How dare he call her spoiled? Her, when he lived the way he did in that castle on the Staten Island heights! Call her paper "Libby's Gazette," indeed! But his nickname for her, Liberty, danced through her mind again and again as she spread out the uppercase type and squinted down at it to separate the letters. On the countertop where he had reached over to take her wrist and kiss her she spelled out THE LIBERTY GAZETTE. Yes, that was it, she thought, and really smiled for the first time in days. Well, it was at least subtler and loftier than "Libby's Anti-Gant Gazette," which she would have liked to name it! She laughed aloud, and the rich, mellow sound actually startled her.

Over and over again as she dropped the type back in the proper compartments of the box she hummed the jaunty new tune "Yankee Doodle" that little Coll had sung for her and Jos and Hannah last night after they had stuffed him full of food.

Four

THE LIBERTY GAZETTE
June 25, 1775

Tomorrow, the two looming Forces of our Future come to Town. Not "Yankee Doodle Dandy ariding on a Pony," the British taunt we have adopt'd for our own proud Song, but our admir'd new Commander-in-Chief of the Continental Army, George Washington, riding on a Steed through a fine Display of Support for him. The other Force, London's own long-absent Royal Governor William Tryon, returns via Ship. A Gentleman's tenuous Truce appears to be in order between the Two, but will not some sort of Duel of Honor yet ensue? In the Future, best be prepar'd for more than only two Parades, all brave New Yorkers!

* * *

Finest LONDON Goods available now from Gant Imports of New York: All the newest Fashions, modern Conveniences, & Luxuries for the discerning Eye and perceptive Palette. Retail and Wholesale.

Cam Gant strode down Wall Street amidst the noontide rush of carriages, horses and pedestrians. Shoppers crowded the new open-air market that ran on a platform down the middle of the street from Queen to Dock; strollers packed the coffeehouses and taverns and peered in the windows of the shops. He spoke briefly to many and tipped his tricorne to not a few. But, even as he stopped to stare in the window of a yard goods shop, of all things, he could still not rid his mind of Libby Morgan. Even now, he wondered how her sunset-hued hair would look loosed against that shade of blue satin or how that particular quilted petticoat would swing about her hips when she walked toward him with that defiant step of hers.

His distorted reflection bounced back at him in the glare of the polished, rippling glass. The window flaunted small porcelain and cloth dolls called "fashion babies," dressed in miniatures of the latest London styles, for full-sized garments were seldom shipped to the colonies. Inside, women crowded the narrow shop buying brocades or velvets so that they could copy the babies' gowns or imploring the shopkeeper for the latest "advices" from London. How long, he wondered, would life bustle on like this, with colonials admiring London goods and London tastes. Now, with both Tryon and Washington entering New York City tomorrow, things were really coming to a head. People would have to take a public stand. There could no longer be divided loyalties.

Divided loyalties. The words echoed in his head. The Gants were loyal to England, both economically and morally. And no one wanted to be loyal to his family more than Cameron Gant. But he alone, of the Gants, had been bred in the colonies, had lived here all his life. He had imbibed deeply of the Greek, French—even British—philosophies of freedom during his years in Virginia studying law. But here at home he had seen how shoddily the British

treated men who should be their equals, and he resented it tremendously.

Then, too, he still felt torn about Libby Morgan. He actually wanted to protect and pay court to a staunch, rebellious Whig! She obviously detested him, and partly for his family's undeniable Tory stand. And she was helping fan the flames of brazen, heedless revolt he'd like to stomp out right now!

Still, before he had left town he'd sent several of his business cronies to her to be sure she had advertising money coming in while he was gone. Though he had not dared to place an advertisement for Gant's, he'd instructed his head clerk to purchase stationery supplies from the Morgan Print Shop instead of Rivington's. Since he had returned, he'd visited her mother and sister over on Staten Island. He had inquired after their well-being, but he'd gone primarily to glean information on how Libby was faring.

While he was away, he'd tried to cure himself of the desire to see her. In the hope of forgetting her, he had worked like a demon while in New Haven and Philadelphia to arrange for distribution of increased Gant goods there. If—when war came to the colonies, perhaps the Gants could hope to survive with merely intercolonial trade.

Upon his return, he had read four weeks' worth of Libby Morgan's saber-edged papers. Devil take her, but she wrote defiantly and dangerously! His blood had boiled when he'd seen the attack she had printed on the Gants and how she had dared to use him and his family as a symbol of the way London ruled and maintained the colonies! He'd vowed to be done with her then. The gall of the little witch! Yet his compulsive need to see her, to touch her, to breathe the same air as her, was building inside him like a torrent again.

Still, when he had time to read through this latest issue, he had plans for it, too. After all, a man had to do what he had to do. And he intended to see that, like the other issues

of the newly retitled *Liberty Gazette*, it got to a certain very big, very interested party who needed to be kept informed on rebel sentiments in New York before his parade tomorrow.

Cam Gant tucked her latest gazette tightly under his arm. Surprised to find he was still staring like a spy into the women's shop, he turned away and bumped into a short, wiry man sporting a jaunty cap, a dark blue kilt and bright green stockings, none of which seemed in keeping with the gruff frown crumpling his brow.

They both excused themselves. The man's brogue was as thick as hunter's stew. But then a familiar voice called out a halloo to Cam, and he turned away from the rough-looking rogue.

Cam spun to face Whitehead Hicks, the town's ubiquitous mayor. Hicks slapped him heartily on the back and pulled him away from the Scotsman. "Haven't seen you for days, Gant. Hear you've been out and about to extend your trade in other colonies, eh?"

"That I have, Your Honor. The Gants may be headquartered in London these last years, but we intend to expand on this side of the Atlantic, too."

"Things as tense in other parts as here?" the mayor asked, even as he acknowledged a shouted greeting and waved at a passerby.

"New Jersey and Pennsylvania citizens seemed poised to jump off one side of the fence or other," Cam observed, all too painfully aware of his own fence-sitting lately.

"I tell you, the royal governor's saved my neck here for tomorrow," Hicks admitted. "Tryon's postponed his entry till just after Washington's. Those two parades at the same time would have been a nightmare. Truth is, Tryon thought with all the rabble-rousing in a few of the Whig papers lately—ah, I see you've got one there—that the crowds would flock to Washington's parade out of raw curiosity. The Governor's sitting out in the bay on the *Juliana* al-

ready, but coming ashore at the opposite end of the island after the Virginian's little to-do down Broad Way."

"I'm relieved to hear Tryon's a gentleman yet," Cam said, with a little smirk he could not stem.

"Don't we all hope, man, don't we hope!" Hicks observed, glancing and waving at another passerby. He nodded again at the paper under Cam's arm. "And speaking of that feisty *Liberty Gazette*, I see you're actually advertising in it."

Cam's head snapped up. "No...though I had thought to once."

"You *have* been out of town, my man!" Hicks chortled. "A notice of Gant goods in the last two issues, including the one you have there. Now, don't look so surprised. Maybe one of your clerks just thought it pays to advertise in Whig papers, too. A lot of us have been hedging our bets lately, eh?"

Cam only nodded. Hicks noted that he looked dazed— but strangely happier than he had earlier. "Well, I'm off for now, Gant. Send my best to your brother and that pretty sister of yours. They won't be coming back with all the fussing hereabouts, I wager."

"No," Cam said. "No, they won't. Good day, then, Your Honor." The mayor walked off, almost bumping into the same Scotsman who had been in Cam's way a moment ago. Had the man been hovering about them through their entire talk? With times so tense, he had better learn to be more observant, Cam thought as the Scotsman strolled off nonchalantly, a pack like a peddler's strapped to his back.

But his initial bubble of excitement over Libby's running advertisements for Gant's had been burst by Hicks's mention of Catherine. He still missed his sister bitterly. The pain of loss had never dissipated during the eight years she had lived away at Charles's bidding. She had been Cam's only comforting glimpse of soft, maternal love after their mother had died bearing him. Catherine had been the only

one to make him laugh and tend his scrapes and soothe his fears as a child. But she had not stood up to Charles when he had said she must go home to London with him—almost as if he were jealous of the attention she gave their younger brother. Her almost-monthly letters to Cam were warm and loving. But that was not like having her with him to talk to, to smile at—to understand the dark, lonely corners of his heart.

Cam smacked the *Liberty Gazette* against his palm. Now, at least, he had an excuse to see Libby Morgan. Perhaps she had even run the advertisements because she regretted the brusque way she had treated him. He scanned the clumps of strollers to make certain the lurking Scotsman was nowhere in sight. As soon as he was finished with the shipper he had to see at the coffeehouse, he was off to the *Liberty Gazette*.

Wiping ink off her hands, Libby came around the counter to face a short, wiry Scotsman named Rob Graham. She glanced down again at the note he'd handed her. It was from a printing shop in Edinburgh, and it assured the "Dear Sir" to whom it was addressed that Robert Gordon Graham had learned to typeset, pull a proof, do presswork and make ready impressions.

She smiled at him. The ready impression he made on her was that he was a bit dour and very determined. He was homely, and the homespun shirt stuck in his dark blue kilt was mud-speckled, but he seemed a gift from heaven—one she hoped she could afford. She had absolutely been wearing herself down these past few weeks being both ink-stained typesetter and clean-handed puller of paper at the press.

"Did you find my shop by chance, Mr. Graham?" she inquired.

"No, ma'am. A 'prentice at Rivington's, where I went

first 'cause I heard it was the biggest in town, said try here when I got turned down there."

"Rivington's is our biggest rival, you see, both politically and geographically."

"The master there said he'd ne'er hire a Scotsman anyway," Graham told her, twisting his cap in his hands. "Save for our braw Highland lads they need in the army, folks wi' English ties hate the Scots, an' the feeling's pretty mutual, ma'am. Now the English be looking down their noses at you colonials the way they have us for centuries."

"Yes." Libby tossed head. "I assure you, I do understand your feelings. And your recommendation looks fine. I'd love to offer you a place, but I'm afraid the wages might not be all you'd like right now."

"Can't scare off the likes of a Graham with penury, ma'am. Seen too much where I been to let where I'm going gi' me a fright. 'Sides, I've a bit of a word from the street that the printer I work for should know ri' away—to take advantage of what's coming tomorrow," he said with a shift of his dark eyes.

"What do you mean?" she asked. She admired the glint of cunning charm that shone through the man's rough exterior.

"I tell you, ma'am, we Scots know how to get up early and work late," he told her, with another cryptic look and a turn of his hat.

"Then step right back here to the press and take a turn at helping Josiah Bean, Rob Graham," she declared. She introduced the two men, and Rob dropped his pack in the corner and hastened to work. He had not quite finished telling her and Jos everything he'd overheard from "the Lord Mayor hisself and some fine and fancy braw man on Wall Street" when Cameron Gant came in to hear the last of it himself.

"Is that Scot your man?" Cam demanded of the surprised Libby in a tone he hadn't intended.

"He is now! And what's wrong with a print shop on the rise hiring a new hand? But I'm surprised to see you here. I hear you've been out of town," she blurted, before she remembered she hadn't meant to let him know she had noticed what he did.

"I'm here either to thank you for your donation to Gant Imports' well-being or to pay for two weeks' advertisements I didn't realize I placed," he said, lowering his voice and lifting his brows. He fought to keep from accusing her of sending that wily, kilted pressman out on the street to get her news. She looked tired and a bit ink-smudged, but so tousled and beautiful he could almost picture her waking up all warm and sleepy in bed in the morning. He flushed slightly and hastily lowered his tricorne to hide the ridiculously embarrassing reaction his body always seemed to have to her.

"Ah, indeed, the advertisements," she said, calling him back to reality. "I felt I had been a bit too critical of something you could hardly be expected to oversee during your college days in Virginia. But I can tell you're distraught that your friends will think you have lost your senses and begun to traffic with the likes of the *Liberty Gazette*."

How quickly she shattered new hopes, he fumed. "It never ceases to amaze me how you *think* you read my thoughts at all, mistress. Evidently my initial urge to buy advertisements from you must have been a momentary weakness."

Her heart was still pattering as hard as it had when he'd first stepped in today. She had actually missed the man, and that annoyed and frightened her.

"I am relieved to hear your weakness was only momentary, sir!"

"But the moment's back." He took another step toward her. They had lowered their voices so that they were almost

whispering. The press had halted, and everyone was gawking at them. Yet they just stared mutely into each other's
eyes until she found her voice.

"Well, I needn't ask you which parade you will attend
tomorrow," she blurted, her voice suddenly much too loud.

"No, why ask a Gant?" he countered, his still louder.

"Now that the parades aren't the same time, I shall go
to both—for the gazette."

Cam's eyes lifted accusingly over her shoulder toward
the nosy Scotsman again. "Now that you've had your new
man there out on the street listening in on privileged con-
versations, you obviously know Tryon's kindly postponed
his entry until after George's—Washington's."

"What a gentleman Governor Tryon is!" Libby said
mockingly. "But I believe I heard from some little bird
that our illustrious absentee governor postponed his sad little funeral cortege of a parade because he thought our new
commander-in-chief might draw the larger crowd."

"And to think I came in here to ask you to go with me
to a dinner party at a friend's house tomorrow evening!
You'll obviously be busy as one of your mother's other
little bees preparing a rebellious report of all this for—for
your rabid readership, whom I'm sure await it with bated
breath!"

She almost slapped him. But it wasn't so much his latest
insult that angered her as the fact that he had dangled something she had wanted to hear and then thrown it, denied,
in her face. To go as his guest to a friend's house for dinner! He had actually assumed she would consider such—
that she had a suitable gown and a desire to mingle with
his Tory friends. He had wanted to be with her! She had
put the unpaid advertisements in her paper because she had
hoped he might realize she was sorry for her earlier actions.
That he might come back to see her. He had. And now this.
It was the damned Gants snubbing the downtrodden Morgans all over again. Her voice caught in her throat.

"As you said, I...I'll be busy," she managed.

"I'm relieved to keep this all strictly business," he replied curtly. "I'll send a man 'round with the advertising fees." He turned away, replaced his hat, shoved the door open with his stick as if he couldn't bear to touch the latch and went out without looking back, while she stared dumbstruck after him.

Rob Graham's burr, close behind her, interrupted her agonizings. "Don't mean to poke in, ma'am, but that's the very man I heard on the street, talking wi' the mayor. You should take the man up on that offer. Never know what news you could get at a talkative loyalist gathering tomorrow night, d'you ken?"

She turned on the startled man. "Please just care for pulling and drying the papers, Rob! I will not operate the gazette on overhearing rumors and gossip in the streets or around someone's supper table. Is that understood? Now let's get hopping here, all of you!"

The next afternoon, Libby Morgan dressed in her best gown for George Washington's Broad Way Street parade. She had closed the shop for an hour, and old Hannah, Jos, Rob, and the excited Coll trailed along behind her as they positioned themselves amidst the waiting crowds along the cobbled curb. She had brought some paper tacked to a board and two pencils for taking notes so she wouldn't forget a thing. After this parade, she was sending everyone back to prepare the galleys for an extra edition—with space left for her articles on both parades. It was a gamble that people would want to read about one or both parades they might have seen themselves, but folks seemed hungry for every word about major events. And in times when news was often delayed by bad weather or stale from distance, the major events had come to them today.

Libby had no doubt that the governor's parade would be well attended by the many loyalists in town, who unfortu-

nately included someone she was beginning to know all too
well. To her surprise, though, she noticed Cameron Gant
across the way, waiting for Washington. Indeed, she supposed that even Tories were curious to see this newly-
named commander-in-chief of the Continental Army for the
first time. Word was, Washington and his entourage had
come by ferry from Hoboken to the Lipenard mansion for
a rest before riding south along the Greenwich Road. He
would turn east into the Commons and then south onto
Broad Way Street before marching clear to Hull's Tavern.
She couldn't wait to see him!

But what she saw right now was Cam Gant, apparently
staring at her in the churning, anxious crowd. As if no one
else in the entire town were here, she felt their gazes lock.
Her insides spun madly; she felt the solid ground drop out
from under her. She tingled clear down to the pit of her
stomach—and lower. She blessed the fact that she wore a
ribboned straw hat that kept her face in shadow. If she just
tilted it aside like this, he would not know for certain she
had spotted him at all. But she decided to do more than
just look away. As they heard the rumble of cheers from
many throats coming nearer, Libby shooed her little band
down the street, away from Cam Gant, and wedged them
in again under another tall elm.

As the parade approached, she took rapidly scrawled
notes without looking down. Three Pennsylvania battalions,
with a drum and fife escort, marched in fine ranks in their
blue-and-tan coats. Wild "Huzzas!" split the air. Onlook-
ers cheered themselves hoarse at their approach. People
threw bits of ribbons and flower petals. Children ran along
and had to be pulled back, away from the horses' high-
stepping hooves.

Coll screamed in her ear in the din and jumped up and
down at her side. "Look, look, Mistress Libby! Soldiers,
just like I wanta be! Jupiter, just look at them!"

Tears came to her eyes at this magnificent beginning to

the struggle she was certain must come soon to New York. Let Parliament's Lord North and all the king's ministers send Governor Tryon back to rule over them! she thought proudly. Let General Gage threaten to sail the entire fleet back here from Boston! The crowds loyal to Washington and freedom were three thick along the way! The colonists could raise a greater army behind this man! They would be ready! They would be free!

She cheered wildly, too, but then just stood in awe, for the commander-in-chief himself was coming, riding a white horse, flanked by his newly elected generals, Lee and Schuyler. Washington looked so tall, so straight, in his blue-and-buff uniform, which was inspired by the colors of the Whig party in the British Parliament.

Washington nodded regally but did not wave. He wore a plain white queued wig under his cockaded hat, and his eyes were blue-gray and penetrating. Libby, like everyone else there that day, was certain he looked right at her. With his jaw set squarely and stiffly, he seemed almost over-whelmed by the crowd, but then a taut smile lifted the thin lips, and the stern face softened. He raised a stiff hand to return the waves. Again Libby shouted, whooping and cheering and flapping her arm like a madwoman.

The generals went by all too quickly, trailed by a company of Philadelphia Light Horse and a growing rabble of spectators at the tail of the parade. Before Libby could grab Coll, he was off into the chaos, marching along, beating two twigs on the imaginary drum of his sharply lifted knee. In the sweep of the movement, she herself yearned to chase after the parade, to vow any sacrifice for the cause, to cheer them on and on.

But she stuck to her plan. She sent Hannah back on Jos's arm and sent Rob to fetch Coll. She leaned her shoulder against a tree trunk as the parade marched away, trying to take more notes. When the crowd thinned, she, too, strolled

the way the parade had gone. Then she saw Cam Gant again.

This time he did not see her. He stood talking earnestly with some friends—including several attractive ladies, she noted grimly. Then a man emerged from somewhere and sidled up to him. From behind the man tapped Cam on the shoulder. Cam turned, tilted his head, listened. Then he stepped away to confer more privately with the man. He nodded and scanned the area, as did his informant.

Libby jumped back behind the tree before she even thought to stand her ground. From there she watched Cam and the man weave their way through the remnants of the crowd. Without thinking, she followed, darting across Broad Way as the busy traffic resumed. After scolding Rob Graham today about not getting their news from the streets, she felt somewhat the reckless fool. But she managed to keep them barely in view as they went around the clusters of people hemming Hull's Tavern, then down a tiny lane between two buildings. Her heart hammering, she waited until they disappeared, then hurried after them. She was just in time to see them go in the back door of Hull's, where Washington was staying.

She leaned back against the brick wall, breathing hard. What could it mean? Did Cam Gant mean the new commander good or ill? She grasped her pencil so hard it snapped.

Cam Gant followed his informant up narrow stairs at the back of the tavern and stood there nervously while the man knocked on a door. "Enter," said a voice inside. The man opened the door, and he stepped in. It closed behind him. Yes, it was exactly as the man had said, and yet it was as much a surprise as an honor.

"General Washington," he said, and thrust out his hand.

George Washington rose from a document he was writing and shook his hand heartily. "So good to see you again,

Cam," the tall Virginian said. He was one of the few men Cam had ever had to look up to. "You're surprised I sent for you so privily, I am sure. But I have a favor to beg, and not much time."

"I can certainly understand your hurry today, sir. The city seemed to love you!"

"Seemed, indeed. That is what I need to discuss with you. Yes, I know, the crowds were large and generous. But will they be so when my order goes out tomorrow to raise more troops for the coming bloody battles with the British? And how go your thoughts on that since last we talked? So many families will be torn asunder by this war."

Cam's gaze met Washington's steady stare. "My thoughts are that I must do what I must for my homeland here, General, though my family will be heartily displeased, to say the least."

Washington's arm gripped his shoulder, then dropped away. He sat down wearily once again and motioned for Cam to take the other chair. Though there was no one else in the room, Washington dropped his voice.

"I am asking for your aid in this not only because the Virginian friends we have in common say I can trust you but because of your unique position here in New York City—as a member of one of the prominent loyalist families in the area. To be brief, despite the fine welcome today, I find this big city full of disparate, volatile elements. There are rumors that New York might sue for a private peace. The British fleet may be returning here to their home port soon. If they do, New York City will be a key battleground."

"I'm afraid I agree, sir," Cam said seriously. "It would make sense for the British to try to secure New York City, then sweep up the Hudson. That would cut off the north, which British troops based in Canada could then handle. And more troops would land here to crush the central and southern colonies. And if New York keeps up its present

rebellious uproar it would only encourage the British to accelerate those plans. So what we need desperately is to keep a muzzle on the agitators, to buy time to prepare for all that!''

Washington looked startled, but his gaze took on a new admiration. "My assessment exactly." He smacked his knee with his big hand. "And would you believe these blind city leaders dared to ask me today to swear that if I won a battle here I would resign immediately thereafter? Do they think this war will just take one battle, or that we fight in this so the commander can snatch some sort of American crown?''

"There are so many British loyalists here," Cam said. "Many, even, who are my dearest friends.''

"Exactly. And so I ask you not to join our New York forces openly, even when the call goes out, as it will tomorrow, for four new regiments. I ask you, despite the difficult decision I know you have made to forsake your family's pro-British stance, to stay here as an apparent loyalist. And to keep me informed of how the wind truly blows.''

Cam's jaw dropped. "To spy?" He said when he finally found his voice. "But I do not think I could stomach that. To go against my family and friends is one thing, but then to inform on them...''

"No, I do not ask that you insinuate yourself with them for, shall we say, inside information, unless you think that absolutely necessary. I ask only that you remain a clear-eyed, communicative observer here until the British return in force—which they will do all too soon, I fear. Frankly, it is not so much more than you have begun to do. I was interested when you sent me that Whig gazette—that paper printed by the woman.''

Cam nodded. "Liberty's Lady.''

"Ah, yes, that's good. She's changed the title to the *Liberty Gazette*, hasn't she? Continue to send me that paper, Rivington's loyalist one and any like information that

comes your way by normal channels. Those huge crowds out there, Cam—'' Washington stood again to place a big hand on Cam's shoulder as he, too, jumped to his feet ''—they can be fickle. They are nervous, and torn, and some don't really believe yet we'll have to fight. I'll have to come here with troops soon enough, but with your help I'll know when is the best moment. And when I do return you are free to do whatever you then deem best in the service of your new country. But I should be honored to have you then as one of my top aides.''

''I shall do it, sir. For the future of New York, which hardly seems to know what's good for itself, one way or the other.''

''That's the way to look at it. And, Cam,'' Washington added as he sat back down and picked up his quill again, ''about that Liberty's Lady. I saw your British import company took an advertisement in her last week's issue.''

Somehow Cam felt caught like a boy with his hand in the sugar box. ''I...well, no. Actually, the lady in question placed that herself.''

''Did she?'' His eyes lit, and he almost smiled. ''Quite an independent one, then. That's what we need now, but don't let her overstep if you can help it.''

''Yes, General, if I can help it,'' Cam muttered.

''Separatist papers will push both patriots and the British over the edge of the precipice before we're ready if they are not watched—and perhaps bridled a bit, one way or the other... You know what I mean.'' He lifted an eyebrow. ''What's that Poor Richard says? 'Haste makes waste'?''

''Yes, right'' was all Cam could manage to say. He and Washington shared some friends in Virginia, but he had never dreamed of being on terms of intimacy with this powerful man who had so quickly become America's hero.

''Well, then—'' Washington cleared his throat ''—perhaps it's best no one knows we've had this little talk.''

Cam's eyes met Washington's steady gaze. ''Agreed,

Commander," he said, his hand on the door latch. What a double dilemma he now found himself caught in! Torn not only by political and family loyalties but by his feelings for Libby! He had to stay away from her, yet he had to keep an eye on her. But he couldn't keep his thoughts off her. Or his hands, when he got too close! Their arguments and her snubs and stubbornness seemed only to feed the fires she'd stoked within him.

"Goodbye for now, Cam," Washington said, returning his quill to the order for troops again.

"Until another day when you return triumphant to New York, General Washington," Cam said, and went out.

He left by the back stairs, wondering if there was any way to get Libby to tone down her article on the two parades today. But if he tried to reason with her about restraint, she would only quote him in her paper! Would the Whig and Tory factions he needed to watch then trust or mistrust him?

Perhaps if he could just get a taste of Libby Morgan on a personal level, get her to drop that prickly guard of hers, he'd find her not half so entrancing anyway. Then, too, that might be one way to get her to toe the line a bit more. After all, he assured himself, he'd never had the slightest problem getting his way with the other young women he had known! Yes, he'd take the path of least apparent resistance with her—for duty's sake, of course.

He looked both ways before he stepped out into the street from the narrow lane behind the tavern and headed for Governor Tryon's parade, where he knew he would find Libby.

As the afternoon light slanted giant shadows from buildings and trees across the bowling green, Governor William Tryon's parade disbanded after its march north from the tip of Manhattan. It had not been half so fine as Washington's, Libby mused smugly. Despite two large frigates in the bay,

the governor had no troops in town, and he had had to settle for units of wobbly-legged marines from a warship.

Tryon himself was forty-six, a bluff professional soldier, if a bit vain and pompous. Still, it annoyed her how heartily this smaller crowd had cheered for the man decked out in the bright red uniform that had already moved American patriots to dub British soldiers "lobsterbacks." On the whole, it seemed to her that most New Yorkers would go through the motions of accepting British rule if Tryon did nothing too out of sorts. But she'd do her best to see this issue of the paper made them realize the time to act was *now*, before the British fleet or more troops arrived!

Oblivious to those around her now, Libby slowly headed home across the grassy oval that had been the parade ground for Fort George during the Indian wars. She scribbled notes madly until a sharp command drew her up short. She glanced up, squinting into the sinking sun. It was Jemmy Rivington, flanked by several beady-eyed men she didn't know.

"Just looky here." He blocked her path with legs that were slightly spread. "The little skirt of a printer who has a sword tip on her pen—and stuffings in her head!" His cronies guffawed, and Rivington actually elbowed the man next to him in pure delight.

"The stuff to challenge your sales, I take it, or you would hardly be so bitter, sir," she snapped back. "Excuse me, then, unless you wish to give me an interview so your clever words may be included in tomorrow's gazette."

"Tomorrow's?" he asked, surprised. His mouth gaped like a fish's. "But your paper comes out on Wednesdays!"

"Not when there's such an important story. And another paper to beat to the streets," she added, and stepped back to walk around them.

"But that just isn't done!" Rivington roared.

"Isn't done by whom, sir?" she retorted. "Loyalist presses? Those who always do things by the old ways?

Those who take their bribes straight from the king? Gentlemen like yourself?''

"Now you see here, you little snip!" he bellowed. His circle of friends closed to hem her in. But suddenly there was one more man in the little crowd, a man who was taller than the rest. Her heart leapt to see Cam Gant materialize as if he'd been dropped from the sky.

"There you are, Mistress Morgan!" He strolled nonchalantly closer, twirling his walking stick, to offer her his arm. She took it without hesitation. His face looked composed, she noted, yet she could clearly see the beating of the vein in his neck that signaled that he was very angry to find her taking on Jemmy Rivington.

"The lady and I are old Staten Island neighbors, and I promised her mother I'd get her back before dark," he informed Rivington and his friends. "Good day to you, gentlemen."

With a pert nod, Libby tucked her notes under her arm and turned her back on the men. "What a clever story," she admitted to Cam, trying hard to be pleasant. She at least did not intend to pick an argument until he had walked her clear back to Queen Street.

"It's not a story at all. I promised your mother that when I visited her and Merry three days ago."

"You did?" she asked, again fighting for calm. "Merry's coming over next week with a neighbor, but Mother won't set foot here right now."

"So I heard." To her increased dismay, when they started past a coffeehouse east of the green, he steered her in the door.

"Mr. Gant, I need to go home!"

"Humor me just this once, and you can begin by calling me Cam," he said, and propelled her to a back table with a firm grip on her elbow.

He ordered a pot of coffee and some pecan yeast bread with a simple lift of a finger. She felt somehow relieved

that he had forced her to come in and sit without giving her a real chance to agonize over whether or not to protest further. But she had made two definite decisions about Cameron Gant today. One was that she was done being a coward about the way he fired her senses. The other, unfortunately, was that she must not get close to a blatant Tory who lurked about with strange men and went in Washington's headquarters by the back door.

And yet, be he friend or foe—and he was always a detested Gant—he still made her toes curl so hard under the table in excitement that her feet almost cramped and she had to remind herself to breathe. Perhaps, once she let him get just a little closer, she'd either learn why he seemed to be spying on Washington or, at the very least, learn he wasn't really quite as alluring as forbidden fruit after all!

It was nearly dark when they finally strolled down Wall to Queen Street. They moved at a snail's pace from pool to pool of light under the newly lit oil lamps suspended on their ten foot poles. Few people were out tonight; perhaps they were tired after the day's tumultuous events. Libby could smell the bay from here, could almost hear the lapping of waves on the wharves. The June night was sprinkled with stars and sliced by the sickle of the new moon.

They said little now. She had long ago let Cam tuck her hand under his arm. He carried her paper board and she twirled his walking stick in a lighthearted temporary trade they had made. They had not raised their voices their whole time together. It was as if they had agreed on it as a grand scientific experiment. Her heart had slowed to a mere thunderous clatter now, and she found herself treasuring each step they took, each unimportant thing they chatted about, as if they both knew the spell must end all too soon. Ahead, they saw the print shop windows lit. Their steps dragged even more.

"I'm late," she admitted quietly. "They'll be worried. I'll have to stay up all night to set type now."

He pulled her to a gentle stop between two pale pools of light so that they stood in a fringe of dark. "Can't it wait till morning? I've found there are just a few things worth staying up all night for," he said, his voice slow and low.

"Such as?" she blurted before she realized she should have kept still.

He chuckled. It was a deep, delightful sound she had never heard from him before. She could feel his ribs move where he still held her wrist against them. "I've done it once or twice to read a new book late at night," he admitted. "But that's not what I meant."

"No," she said, amazed at her desire to stand right here with him forever and never go in at all.

The backs of his loosely curled fingers lifted to raise her chin. They skimmed her cheek delicately, then drifted to touch the loosened tendrils of hair before her ear. Then to her earlobe and back down her neck.

"All night, for this and more than this," he whispered, and she could hardly remember what either of them had said before. And then he stepped toward her to move them back into the shadow of the brick walls, and his lips descended.·

She thought at first the ground had dropped away beneath her feet. But he held her to him, one strong arm around her waist. He pulled her even closer, and she came willingly. The walking stick and her paper board slid away and thudded to the ground.

Her will seemed to flow out of her floating body through her lips. His hand skimmed her slender back, and she arched up to him to return the kiss and the caress. When he deepened the kiss, she somehow, crazily, met him halfway, as if she had divined what was coming next.

He slanted his mouth possessively over hers and opened

his in blatant invitation. When she kissed him back that way, she found her mouth sweetly, expertly invaded by his warm, slick tongue. He teased, tantalized, then let her do the same. Her head spun, and she gripped his upper arms. Why had they ever argued? Mouths and tongue...this was what they were for!

He pulled back to stare deep into her wide, dazed eyes, then lowered his head again to outline her pouted lips with his tongue. When she gasped, he forayed deliciously inside again. She moaned deep in her throat, shifted slightly closer to him, so that her skirts belled out on both sides between him and the wall. He dropped kisses on her fluttering eyelids, her cheeks, her chin, down the throat she tilted back to give him access to her ivory flesh. Never, never, had she felt like this! Nothing else mattered when he looked on her and touched her so!

"Libby, Libby," he groaned. He turned them around now to lean back against the wall himself. His hands raced over her back and her trembling arms. She pinned him to her as her nails gripped his big shoulders through the blue coat. She cupped the back of his strong neck and accidently loosed his queue. Her fingers raked through the heavy thickness of his hair; it was silver under the narrow slant of distant lamplight when she slitted her eyes to peek. She knocked his hat off with hers; he only chuckled and pushed hers back off her head. And lifted her up to kiss her harder, his big hands spanning her small waist.

"I knew it, I knew it," he whispered hotly in her ear as he let her slide down against him. "I knew there was all this between us just waiting to be freed!"

How long they stood there, touching, holding, kissing, she was not sure. But his lips were on her throat, and his hand was suddenly more urgent along the low neckline that covered the swells and slants of her breasts. Breathless, she realized that this sweeping sensation, these vaulting emotions, were what she and Merry had been so certain must

be possible with a man! She, whom poor Eddie Tiler was so angry with that he hadn't visited in Manhattan. She, whom Mama trusted grudgingly. She had lost all logic, loving this man she wanted so to hate.

Love— That thought brought her to her senses just as another voice intruded. "Eight of the clock, a clear, warm night!" a voice down the street sang out. She heard a distant dog bark.

"Devil take the man, it's a hot, hot night," Cam rasped, but she was still too stunned to laugh. He held her upper arms to steady her while she stepped back.

A thousand thoughts bombarded her, like fragments of broken glass. She had wanted to know what it would be like to pretend they could be like this...to have him touch her! But what must he think of her now, coming so easily, so wantonly, into his arms? She slanted a glance up at him through thick lashes and was startled by the strained look that drew his skin taut over the angled bones of his face.

"I refuse to say I'm sorry," he told her. "I think we're through with that. I'll take you in now before the watchman comes. We will not be ashamed or argue, though you will promise me here and now that you will not again get yourself in a situation like tonight, out somewhere unattended where Rivington, Quentin Simpson or who knows who else might do you harm. You may have bowled over your sworn enemy Cameron Gant tonight, but if you don't tone that gazette down there will be others out there who wish you ill! Now vow it to me!"

She barely heard his warning. She wanted to tease him, to laugh and lure him on and make him kiss her yet again. Serious, bookish Libby astounded herself by wanting to play the coquette. But, after all, there was surely no harm in such a vow to him. She had no intention of being out anywhere at night alone after this, even if she had no intention, as he put it, of "toning down" the gazette. She

had meant to stay away from this man, but he had rescued her again, and it couldn't be helped tonight!

She sighed. "I promise."

"Your bonnet's tipped, and this modesty piece is all awry," he told her, somewhat gruffly. He found he longed to tuck the gauzy fichu back in her low neckline himself and yanked his hand back. He knew if he didn't control himself now he'd carry her off to his town house! She made something inside him go madder and wilder than he'd ever imagined possible, even when he fought for calm and control.

But he also breathed a sigh of relief. A bit of gentle, sweet coercion and she had promised him to be much more circumspect with the paper. But here he'd meant to make her more pliable and his legs were like blowing stalks of rye and he'd gone rigid as a schoolboy in these too-tight dratted breeches! He stooped almost painfully to recover his stick and her paper board while she fussed over herself.

He escorted her to the front door of the print shop. Blasted reality flooded back over him as he blinked in the candlelight from the open windows. Yet it pleased him how she pointedly ignored the familiar voices and sounds inside.

She stared a moment at him, memorizing the intensity of his gaze, his mussed silver hair, in case this was all a dream or they never got this moment back again.

And just when she opened her mouth to thank him for escorting her back—and more—Coll stuck his head out the window behind her and bellowed, "Here she is, Dame Hannah, with some man! Can I stay up all night, too, Mistress Libby, 'cause my mother, she said it's all right if you need me real bad tonight!"

It was as if her own heart had screamed that last thought at her. She needed Cam Gant tonight, all night. It was pure, perilous folly. Yet she still floated, and she glowed deep within as she went inside to settle the boy down and get to work. And when she looked back toward Cam with another trusting smile and a wave he was gone.

Five

THE LIBERTY GAZETTE
July 8, 1775

New York City is a powder Keg over which our seemingly benign Governor Tryon holds the sulphur Match as he hopes for new Troops from London & the Fleet from Boston. Connecticut Soldiers of our Continental Army have arriv'd, but more homespun Patriots are need'd to swell our four New York colonial Regiments. If we do not raise these soon, who will greet the British when they come calling on our Shores?

* * *

A Call to Women of the City & Province of New York: while we speak of "homespun Patriots," our Continental Army is in dire need of more homespun Bounty Coats. The Provincial Congress has sent out a Call for 13,000 warm Coats for our Boys who enlist for at least eight Months' duration. Let our illustrious Governor sneer at our homespun Boys! We are ever proud of our Coat Roll & the British army will see why if they set Foot in Manhattan again!

The print shop was crowded with fourteen men Libby Morgan considered great patriots. They were some of the most fervid separatists in town, and some were even members of the revered Sons of Liberty. All were men she had inherited as friends from Atwood Simpson. They approved of Libby's gazette enough to drink her weak liberty tea brewed from loosestrife leaves when it was hearty morning coffee they wanted. Still, they mostly ignored her once their weekly meeting began. Gathering here gave them a chance to promote ideas for next week's issue. They argued policy, they offered opinions, they made plans. Big plans. For the future freedom of the city, the province of New York, the entire loose collection of colonies.

It was early, before the shops opened, but the July day was already warm. Libby stood along the wall, guarding the door, which stood ajar to let in some air. The windows were closed and shuttered, as the ever-cautious Garner Brooks, who chaired the rough-and-tumble sessions, always insisted they be. Portly, his face pitted by smallpox, Garner held the floor, sitting in the only chair while everyone else stood. Once again he was gesturing with a rolled copy of the gazette. People watched him, hanging on his every word, all but his younger brother Crispin, who was head tapman at the Fraunces Tavern.

Crispin had eyes only for a boisterous good time—and, lately, for Libby. He was darkly good-looking, and he had a reckless reputation. Libby was polite to him because she admired Garner, but she was as careful to avoid Crispin as she was Quentin Simpson.

"So my conclusion is, gentlemen," Garner Brooks announced grimly, "the whole danged selfish, fence-sitting province of New York is not going to raise even four regiments. Not even to keep the lobsterbacks off our shores. Not even if Washington's recruitment period does go nearly till New Year!"

"Not even," Crispin put in, with a totally inappropriate,

blatant wink at Libby, "if the Continental Congress did post suggestions for recruiting louts in ale houses. Just sign 'em up after they had a few tankards of rum poured down 'em. I say we need patriots to fight, not rumbutts to drink!"

"Don't see you enlisting, Cris," Lawrence Lang pointed out, with an elegant sweep of his brocade-clad arm, "but as for alehouses, you ought to know!"

Lang, a wealthy silversmith, was richly garbed, as usual. His latest tall, powdered white wig probably cost more in upkeep than the entire shop each year, Libby thought as the opinions flew. Lawrence loved theatricality, especially when he was repeating gossip. He delighted in acting out the various parties involved with numerous clever voices. Playacting, gossip and disguises—sometimes Libby thought that Atwood's old friend Lawrence Lang longed for the war to begin in earnest. Then he could become some sort of cloak-and-dagger spy for the colonial cause, though Libby was convinced George Washington would be far above using such low tactics as the British employed.

"As this copy of the gazette says," Eliot Mott shouted over the hubbub, "it's all Governor Tryon's blasted fault. If someone—present company excluded, of course—would wise up and abduct the man, half our problems would be solved!"

"Are you crackbrained?" Crispin banged the stationery counter with a beefy fist. "Then who's gonna abduct the lobsterbacks offa those two warships sitting out there like ducks in the harbor? They're just looking for excuses to come ashore and harass anyone who even looks suspicious, I tell you that!"

"We'll handle those two warships in good time," Garner said, and everyone hushed. "Word is, there's elements in town thinking of, shall we say, 'protesting' the *Asia* and the *Kingfisher*'s unwanted presence here in our waters."

"Indeed!" Libby put in at last. "I just wish we had the backbone to stop sending victuals to the British men-of-

war so we could use the food for our new Continental troops! But first we'd have to steal all their powder reserves from the Turtle Bay warehouse. And saw all their longboats in half so the marines couldn't even provision the ships anymore!''

"Exactly!" said a deep voice from the door. "And all that's impossible right now, unless we want British cannonballs and firebombs shot right up Wall Street."

Heads whipped around to see who spoke, but Libby knew. Cam Gant stood there, one hand on each side of the door frame, as if to block them all inside.

"If New York does refuse to provision the British in our harbor right now, as Mistress Morgan would like to see," he went on with a warning shake of head, "those longboats she wants sawed in half will be armed and foraging for more than just food ashore, that's certain."

Crispin was the first to speak. "It's certain enough you don't belong here, Gant!"

"Nor do you, Brooks," Cam countered without blinking an eye. Several of the men shifted nervously from foot to foot. "You're late for work pulling taps at the tavern, aren't you?"

Crispin stepped around the counter. Libby moved forward and held up both hands, as if to keep the two men apart, though they still stood a good distance from each other.

"It *is* a bit late," she began. "Almost time for work."

Several of the men muttered their agreement. It was obvious that the meeting was now adjourned. Did Cam never come when he was invited? Libby wondered. But then, she realized, she'd never invited him anywhere. He always just came bursting in. The men nodded at Cam in polite, stiff recognition as they got ready to leave, but her eyes met his intense, angry stare and held it. The strange link between them tightened like an unseen chain that threatened to yank them both together.

She tore her gaze away as, behind her, Garner Brooks said, "It's soon going to be too late to protest anything when the Brits invade in force—when they get help from the town's obvious loyalists, like you, Gant. Come on, Crispin. We'll do our fighting with Mr. Gant and his ilk when the time comes, and none too soon."

Following Lawrence Lang, Garner half herded his younger brother toward the door, where Cam still held his ground, blocking their exit. The men stood glaring at him. When Cam spoke it was almost in the men's faces, and his voice was calm and quiet.

"One thing I suggest you realize—all of you—is that in this case long-suffering and patience may be a virtue. Taunting the British lion by hitting his nose with twigs before we even have the island fortified is pure folly, and—"

"What's pure folly—" Crispin shouldered his brother and Lang aside to jab a finger nearly in Cam's face "—is you coming anywhere near here to prate such boot-licking loyalist manure! 'Course, there's obviously another reason why you're here, so—"

"Out, Crispin!" his brother ordered before Libby could protest. Cam moved slightly aside. Garner shoved Crispin a step farther toward the door. Crispin's shoulder bumped Cam's, but it was set like a stone wall. Cam stared Crispin down. The shorter man cursed under his breath and moved huffily out with Garner and Lawrence following.

"I'll be back later to see you, Libby!" Crispin shouted. His words sounded more threat than promise. The room was quickly empty, but for Jos and the ever-watchful Rob, who went busily to work in the corner.

"I must say," Libby observed when Cam only leaned against the door frame again, "you do have a flair for dramatic entries!"

"Only because you're always in the midst of trouble. Next time you and the town rebels have a chitchat, best not

have the door ajar. Next time it might be the British, with your names on a traitor's list. And, Libby—'' he gently turned her to him with one hand on her wrist ''—you do think bootlicking loyalists have a right to speak their piece, don't you? And do you really agree with your friends *not* to trust me?''

She was suddenly very aware of her inky skirts as she stood looking up at him. At least the leather printer's apron hid her gown and her fluttering heart. She was aware of every breath she drew, of how she held her body, how she looked. Warm tendrils of sensation swirled out from where he held her wrist to every part of her. Something wonderful and strange and alluring she could never have named or described uncoiled its liquid warmth deep inside her. Stunned anew at what he did to her just by being here, angry or loud or gentle or quiet or anything, she tugged her hand back.

"Do you mean to tell me you do not love your loyalist family, Cam?" she asked.

"That's not what I said. I love them deeply. More," he added, "than most know."

"You see? You are loyal to them, you are concerned for your British trading ties, you counsel going along with the British policy of provisioning their ships! Yet I'm supposed to believe you're on the side of independence and freedom for us all?"

"Yes! Freedom, eventually. I have wanted to explain this since the first, but you never let me!" He glared over her shoulder at Jos and Rob, who quickly jumped back to work. "New York just can't fight yet," he repeated, looking back at Libby. "We've got to take it on the chin for a while. I've come to show you why."

"What?"

"I want to take you out to see the Connecticut soldiers and New York recruits camped by the Bowery before you traipse out there yourself. You see, I'm helping you keep

your vow to me not to get caught off somewhere by yourself in trouble anymore. I'm riding out there this morning,
and I thought you'd like to go along. I have the pillion
on.''

She squinted past his shoulder into the sunny street. His
big black stallion waited patiently, tethered to a rail. It
seemed everyone but her had been on that fine pillion saddle, with its comfortable leather pillow and its single stir-
rup. Merry had been visiting for the afternoon when Cam
had last come calling. The three of them had strolled along
the bowling green and enjoyed gingerbread and quince
punch before Libby had had to be back at the shop. He had
ended up riding Merry and two other Staten Island women
one at a time on that saddle down to the Gant barge. He'd
been pleasant enough to her in front of Merry. Yet she had
known he was angry about her rousing article lauding the
colonial parade ''marching relentlessly toward liberty.'' If
she went off with him alone today, to visit soldiers, and
Mother ever heard— But what a fine story it would make
for the gazette—

''All right,'' she said. ''I'll get my bonnet and some
writing things.''

The Connecticut regiments were encamped on the west
side of the Bowery, so the ride was only about a mile. But
Libby cherished every bit of it, jogging along in the warm
sun with her hands set as lightly as she could manage on
the narrow waist of Cam's black cutaway coat. She peered
around his shoulder while they chatted. How she wished
she could throw her bonnet off her head and shake her
tresses free. She realized once again how much she missed
her father—the way he had taken her on adventures and
taught her to ride astride before Mother had put an end to
all such freedoms. Well, Mother's rules, a lady's rules, pro-
priety and freckles on her fair skin could all go to the devil!

Despite the serious tenor of their jaunt, she felt happy, excited and free.

And she felt something else. Her right knee, bent forward to allow her to sit sidesaddle, kept brushing Cam's hip and thigh as they rode out along the dirt lane, through fields and woodlots, to where the camp began. The muscles of the powerful horse and her closeness to Cam made her feel almost lightheaded. When he dismounted and reached up for her waist to lift her slowly down, she felt so languorous that she toppled momentarily against his big chest until the world stopped its rocking.

"All right, then?" he asked, his face serious. She nodded as he handed her the writing board. He kept the horse with them, and she soon saw why, as she surveyed the scattered groups of soldiers.

"Oh. They are rather ill equipped. And so young!" she observed.

"You mean," he asked in mock disbelief, "that even though our good neighbor colony has loaned us all these men in case those British ships attack, they aren't ready to hold off the best-trained army in the world?" He nodded and smiled grimly. "I always took you for a bright lady. It would be like a newborn holding off a horde of savage Iroquois!"

He kept his arm on her elbow to steady her as they strolled past tent ropes and piles of random gear, deeper into the heart of the makeshift camp. Her eyes jumped everywhere; she forgot to write down a thing.

"Not even uniforms, Cam."

"Not yet, anyway. Let's just hope those so-called bounty coats they've been issued come in before cold weather, or these lads will all turn into snowmen out here. So now you see what I mean about not jumping the gun, so to speak, with the British."

She stopped and spun to face him. She wanted to believe that was the only reason he advised delay. Or did he, like

the royal governor, want reinforcements to arrive to head
off possible rebellion?

"But why were you out here before today, Cam? You
obviously have been, since you knew what we'd find here!
Why are you so eager to look around out here? Aren't you
moved by their plight, and by your own patriotism, which
you've tried to make me believe in? Not enough to enlist
with Washington, evidently! I hear he needs officers desperately, as pay is much more in the British ranks, or did
you know that, too?"

"Is this some sort of inquisition, Libby? Then which of
those pointed innuendoes shall I answer first? No, I'm not
joining the Continental Army—not yet, at least. And why
have I been out here? My gratitude to you for at least asking. I suppose you some want some cutthroat confession
that I'm out here counting heads and guns so I can send a
messenger pigeon to General Gage in Boston. Or, better
yet, to King George and his ministers, clear across the sea,"
he raged, swinging his arm in a wide arc that took in the
blue-gray Hudson.

"I didn't exactly mean that."

"Of course you did." He pulled her onward, less gently
now, forcing himself to keep his anger in check. "All right,
here's the truth. I've been looking through the regiments
for the son of a business associate from New Haven to tell
him his father's ill. They're a family we hope to begin
trading goods with if the British throw up a blockade,
which I suppose will happen soon— And I don't need that
quoted in 'Libby's gazette.'"

"Then don't say what you don't want printed," she told
him tartly.

"All right. How about this, then? I adore your spirit, but
I'd like to break it sometimes," he began outrageously. "I
love the way you look and smell and feel, especially when
we're holding each other and kissing the way we were the

other night in the dark. And I hope soon to resume that and more. Will you print all that, just because I said it?''

''Cameron Gant!''

''And, though I don't think you knew worth a fig how to kiss the first time I French-kissed you—''

She yanked her elbow free from his hand and stopped dead in her tracks. His horse's head was nearly atop her bonnet before he stopped, too. ''How dare you! The first time you did *what* to me?''

''You mean you want a definition to print, too? I'll bet your patriot friend Crispin Brooks would learn to read if you put that in. French-kissed you, Libby. I hope you recall the darting tongue deep inside, and—''

''Stop it, Cameron Gant!''

''It's just you frustrate the hell—you make me angry sometimes,'' he muttered, suddenly looking every bit the sullen, pouting child.

Ignoring a group of recruits cooking their own food over a large fire where the camps of the Connecticut and the New York regiments merged, Cam and Libby stared defiantly at each other. Of course, she thought, he was put out with her, but she was angry with him for insulting her like this. Unfortunately, the way he was talking and still looking at her made her want to kiss him again, not slap him and stalk away, as she somehow felt she should. He had the most disconcerting habit of treating her apparently politely in the same instant she felt he wanted to seize her and shake her. She could not really like this man, could she? Hadn't he just declared that he was not answering the patriot call for troops? As far as she was concerned, that made it quite clear that he had meant Washington ill the day he had sneaked in the back door of Hull's Tavern!

''I really think I'll just talk to a few of these loyal colonial patriots and then head back,'' she told him. ''I know you want to inquire more for your friend's son, so I don't expect you to wait for me. It's not so far back to town.''

"Absolutely not, Mistress Liberty. I'll be close by and will take you back. Do you understand?"

"Suit yourself," she muttered, with the most nonchalant shrug she could manage. She forced her feet away toward where a fife was shrilling the popular "Yankee Doodle" song while some lads sang, "Father and I went down to camp along with Captain Goodin', and there we saw the men and boys as thick as hasty puddin'...."

Careful not to glance back in case Cam was watching her, she spoke with several of the boys and with one rough-looking officer. She shook her head when a sandy-haired stripling who couldn't have been much over fifteen years asked her for a dance.

"I'm afraid that tune would take a gavotte, and I can only do a slow minuet," she told him with a little smile. "I had—have—a rather strict mother, you see." But, as she watched two young lads quite seriously cut a pattern to the music, she realized it would probably show Cam a thing or two if she did dance with some *true* patriots, for when she had turned down his supper invitation weeks ago she had also told him she almost never danced. But she and the lad had barely started to promenade when Cam cut in and halted them in midstep.

"I assume you did not tell this lad you are permitted to dance only with your guardian, who brought you out here today," Cam intoned.

She turned to face him squarely, while the lad backed off, embarrassed. Devil take Cam Gant, she raged, blushing hot under his intense scrutiny. Of course, he knew full well it wasn't from her exertions or the July sun!

"Don't be ridiculous. I—"

He bowed grandly. "Might I not wait on you in the honor of a dance, Mistress Morgan? It might just buck the lads up."

"No, thank you. I only dance—"

But he took her hand and, ignoring her protest, tugged

her farther onto the beaten grass in the center of the tents where the other lads were already cavorting. Suddenly she was dancing a quickstep minuet to "Yankee Doodle" while the boys clapped, laughed, sang along and even cheered.

"If they think you're the Yankee Doodle Dandy, they are sorely mistaken," she ventured, but she paid for the insult by missing a step and throwing them both off.

He laughed. "No, they think I'm 'with the girls be handy,' though."

"Oh, you—" she said, and then she amazed herself by laughing back. Why could she never stay angry with this man? She had detested him for years, yet still she thrilled to be with him. She loathed his obvious sympathies for the British, for the snide, pompous, arrogant, aloof Gant superiority that had haunted her for years. But now that the real Cam had come to dangerous life in such an appealing, tempting package, she felt so confused and so moved!

She smiled heedlessly up into his silver eyes. They walked, glided, pirouetted. With the sun and wind off the Hudson here, it was almost like sailing with him. "Yankee Doodle keep it up," the lads sang. They sang and they clapped and she went around again, smiling, soaring, holding tightly to his hand while her dizzy gaze drank him in.

A voice pierced her dazed state. "Mistress Libby! Upon my word, it really is you! And him!"

She wished the earth would open up and swallow her. Eddie Tiler! Feeling as if she had been caught in some dreadful sin, she dropped Cam's hand and turned to face her accuser. Eddie Tiler indeed, and with a newly issued bounty coat draped over his arm!

"Eddie! How are you?" she said, her voice faltering. The jaunty music stopped. "You've enlisted."

"Of course I did, soon as I could talk my family into it. Washington sends out for men and I'm ready!"

That simple statement, and his pride in it, shamed her.

She cast a narrow-eyed glance from Eddie to Cam while the two men exchanged stilted introductions. "I'm very, very proud of you, Eddie!" she declared. "It's just what I'd do if I were a man."

"And not be out here dancing with Staten Island's biggest Tory, and don't see he's in either side's uniform yet!" Eddie said. "Say, I got an hour off till I have to muster, Libby. Let me walk you back so I can tell your mother I left you safe at the print shop. Even when I was put out at you for leaving, I've been wanting to see it, though I can't say I approve of it much. 'Cept for the fine things you're printing."

"I thank you for that, Eddie!" she said loudly, with another quick, slanted look at Cam. "Especially coming from someone whose goals, ambitions and dreams I understand and sympathize with fully!"

Cam grabbed his mount's reins and took an almost threatening step toward her before he stopped. He turned away and swung up into the saddle quickly, then sat staring down at them. Eddie and Libby, their backs to a tent, looked up at Cam. The sun glared hot in their faces, making the silhouette of the big horse and its rider shimmer forbiddingly.

Suddenly Libby felt as trapped as she had so long ago, when she and Merry had invaded Melrose. Cam had loomed over her then, too, looking down at her and Merry, thinking she was nothing—that she was wrong and low in what she had done and what she believed.

She took Eddie's arm. The Gants had been traitors then, and they were traitors now.

But it was her heart that turned traitor as she bid a curt farewell to Cam and clung harder to Eddie's arm. They retrieved her writing board and had just started walking back when she heard the thunder of horse's hooves. She tried to attend to Eddie, who was telling her how lovely she was today. But she squinted into the sun anyway as

Cameron Gant charged his black stallion with the bouncing empty pillion saddle down the dusty lane toward town.

Four days later, Libby stood in the alley behind the shops sipping a dish of Mercy Goodhue's raspberry-leaf tea and watching Jos teach Coll to mix ink from lampblack and boiled linseed oil. The process smelled terrible, and she'd been over to her neighbors to apologize. They still could not afford to buy ink already mixed. The gazette was barely earning expenses and keep for Libby's staff of housekeeper, two journeymen and apprentice, not to mention her family, despite a slight increase in advertisements. Circulation was not yet near what Atwood had enjoyed. And just last week she'd heard Jemmy Rivington boast that his orders were at 3,500, giving him the largest newspaper circulation in all the colonies!

She stared over at the swirling, seething ink Jos was stirring. She knew she needed some sort of boiling, stinking mix of bubbling news to boost their numbers! Even the twenty copies she had sent to Staten Island with Merry had been generally rejected on her home loyalist island.

She just hoped her main article in this issue drew more interest. She had quoted a certain well-known, well-connected but unnamed Tory loyalist as saying there would soon be a British blockade. The issue was just out on the streets today.

She hadn't heard from Cam today, but she half expected to. Even if she didn't name him, she had risked his anger by quoting him to stir up a hornet's nest. She hadn't heard from him for four days, but after she'd publicly snubbed him to go off with Eddie Tiler, why should she expect to?

She sighed and reached over to take more newly printed gazettes off the drying poles they set up back here in good weather. She heard Rob's voice inside. He was back from the New York library, hopefully with some fervent patriotic quotations gleaned from great British thinkers, which she

intended to use for filler until more advertisements or news came in.

"Mistress Morgan, a wee word wi' you!" Rob called from the back door. He didn't budge outside, though he well knew he should be out here doing this drying. He had taken to wearing his journeyman's garb of leather breeches and specked shirt lately so as not to draw attention to himself in the kilt.

"Come out here!" she called, but turned to see him gesturing her inside.

"Rob, what in the world is it?" she asked, wiping her hands on the way in.

"It's happened," he whispered. "Just saw Lawrence Lang on the street. He said to tell you on the sly, send a man out to Turtle Bay at first light tomorrow."

"To the king's powder magazine? What's happened?"

"Shh! Naught yet, I take it. Tonight. He said tell you your bold words about sawing longboats in half and borrowing the king's powder and shot is about to come true!"

Libby leaned against the wall and clapped both hands over her mouth as if she could call the words back. With all those rabid Whigs in the room when she'd blurted that out, who knew who had taken the idea to heart! If they succeeded—or if they were caught—what would it mean for New York? What could it mean for the gazette if she was the first to report it? And what would Cam Gant say and do? He had overheard her words that day. She didn't want her words to bring retribution New York couldn't handle yet!

"Mistress Morgan?" Rob's worried voice cut through her agonizing. "You all right, then?"

She heaved a huge sigh and glanced out the window. Soon it would be dark, and some fervent colonial patriots would be on their way to Turtle Bay, perhaps to precipitate a crisis. British troops in the streets against those untrained boys! She shuddered. She had to stop Garner, Lawrence,

even Crispin, whoever it was. Perhaps it *was* wiser to wait just a few more weeks, until Washington had time to send more troops.

"Mistress?"

"I'm all right, Rob." She glanced at him, relieved to find that they were in fact much the same height. "If you don't mind a midnight ramble," she said, "and would put your kilt back on so I could borrow that journeyman's garb, I've got a job for you. But first you'll have to go out ahead of me to hire a sturdy horse for us at the livery stable."

When she saw the leap of light in his dark eyes, she felt she knew Rob Graham for the first time. A man who wanted to best the British at any cost, who reveled in rebellion, large or small. She had to trust him—there was no one else to accompany her—but she didn't intend to tell him she was going to head off the raiding party and not abet it until they were actually there.

"So," he said, seeming to snap to attention before her. "I always thought the rich, clean smell of freedom could blow away the stench of makin' ink anytime." And before she could say more, he gave a strange little whoop and dashed out the door for the stable.

It was after dark, but Cam Gant was determined to see Libby anyway. He'd tried to calm himself with a leisurely dinner with friends, but he was still seething. He'd read today's *Liberty Gazette*. He knew why even Tories were buying it! During his meal, he'd managed to grit his teeth and twist the head of his walking stick as if it were her beautiful neck while his friends tried to guess the identity of the loose-tongued prominent Tory. If the threat of an imminent British blockade didn't panic New Yorkers, which would in turn panic the British, he didn't know what would. He began to walk even faster toward the Morgan Print Shop.

He had asked her not to quote him, he fumed. Did she

think that just meant not attaching his name to it? And he'd thought a little kissing one night had convinced her to tone down the gazette! How wrong he had been to trust her— to want her, damn it! When General Washington read this next issue of her paper he'd really question his judgment in asking the younger Gant son to keep "Liberty's Lady" in line until the Continental troops were prepared to defend this sitting duck of an island! Washington was likely to think Cam had given in to some order from his elder brother, just as Catherine had. Damn, damn the little Morgan witch!

He quickened his steps along Queen Street. He'd like to haul her outside and really have it out with her, but he had to keep control. He'd have to get her away from that old watchdog Hannah Brewster and hope the two journeymen weren't working late tonight. He had never experienced such a violent mingling of passions as those that wracked him when he thought of Libby Morgan. He desired her, and she infuriated him. She lured him, then snubbed him. She was everything he wanted in a woman—and she betrayed him again and again. He longed to protect her and ravish her, caress her and beat her! But for now, if nothing else went wrong, he would try his hardest just to reason with her.

He was relieved to see the shop dark but for a single lamp. He stepped inside. The press was still for once. Both journeymen were gone, and Libby was nowhere in sight. Surprised to find he had twisted the once neatly folded gazette he held in his hands, he slapped it down on the counter. He jumped when the towheaded apprentice sat up on a bench, where he'd evidently been sleeping.

"Oh, sir. Didn't know you was coming. Mistress Morgan didn't say 'fore she left."

"Left for where?"

"Not supposed to say. With Rob, you see."

"The Scotsman? Listen, boy, I have something important

I need to tell her. She didn't go up to some tavern to see that Crispin Brooks or some other friends of hers, did she?''

"No, sir. There's no taverns up at Turtle— I mean…I mean that she likes turtle soup, you know…'' The boy was stammering ludicrously.

"Were you going to say Turtle Bay?'' Cam demanded. His mind raced. She'd mentioned Turtle Bay last week. A guarded magazine and storehouse there held British supplies of sundry types. But it was a few miles up the island on the East River. And if she'd really gone there, and after dark, it could only mean she was taking part in a raid!

He ran around the counter to grab the boy. "It's all right, lad,'' he told him, and hoisted him up so that he could look him in the eye. "It's only that if she's gone to Turtle Bay she might get hurt. And I told her not to, you see.''

"Oh, sure. Well, I knowed you liked her, with the way you look at her and all. That's where she went, all right, with her hair stuck up under a cap. Dressed in Rob's journeyman shirt, and breeches, too. They fit her real good. Rob, he went, too.''

But Cam's mind was way ahead of the boy's chatter. He grabbed a sample piece of stationery from the shelf, along with a quill and some ink. "Listen, boy— What's your name again?''

"Coll, sir.''

"Coll, I'm going to give you a shilling to run this note to my guard at the Gant warehouse down on the wharf, and I want it done full tilt. Understand?''

"A whole shilling? Oh, yes, sir. I'm real fast. And I won't talk nothing more about Mistress Morgan, like she said!''

He sent the boy on his way, then yelled up the steps for the old woman, who took her time coming down. He just hoped and prayed that by morning there would be something left of Libby Morgan to talk about.

Six

This Bill to be post'd forthwith in sundry publick Places by express Order of the New York Provincial Congress July 1775 Yr. of Our Lord

While foreign Warships occupy New York Harbor, the following Activities are bann'd: Theatregoing, Dancing, Gambling, Horse Racing, Bull Baiting, & Cock Fighting. For the duration of any ensuing emergency.

* * *

ADDENDUM: Two willful & unruly Boys spent Monday last in the City Hill Park Cage on display for Failure to properly regard the Sabbath. If there was ever a Time for solemn Sabbath Keeping, surely it is now. Such behavior cannot & will not be condon'd.

By order of Mayor Whitehead Hicks.

Morgan Print Shop, Queen Str.

A thrill sent icy fingers down Libby's backbone as Rob Graham gave her a hand down from their bay mare. Just

over the hill lay Turtle Bay, with the British warehouse and powder magazine on its shore. While Rob tethered the horse, Libby made certain her hair was still secure under Jos's old tricorne. She hitched her breeches up and tucked her shirt in again, cinching her belt tighter around her small waist. How invigorating it felt to dress like a lad and ride astride! But they were here for serious things, she reminded herself, and tried to pierce the thick darkness with her ears when her eyes failed her.

They heard no sound but the hooting of an owl in the dark copse. The half-moon, obscured by scudding clouds, shed such wan light. But it was enough for Libby to see the glint of the gun Rob suddenly produced.

She grabbed his arm. "Rob, no guns!"

"Always take guns where there may be guns," he whispered, and jammed the pistol in the waist of his kilt. "New York be only protesting yet, but rebellion's not far behind! And, more times 'n not, rebellion leads to war."

His warning shook her more than the gun. Events in her life and in the colonies seemed to be hurtling out of control. They climbed the crest of the weedy, scrubby hill to look down over the cove. She murmured silent pieces of prayers that her mother, and not just the authorities, never find out she'd been here. Or Cam Gant! A thousand possibilities raced through her mind. Perhaps the gossipy Lawrence Lang had his information wrong. Or perhaps they were too early or too late for the raid.

But no! Beneath them, on the curve of beach, dark figures were loading rowboats with booty. Libby's heart thrilled. She clasped her hands tightly together. She almost wished she hadn't come to stop them. What did it matter that two warships and a litter of patrolling longboats and sloops bristled with troops just off their shores! A few bold patriots had come to challenge the might of England!

The ground was sandy here, and they half slid, half walked down to join the others. She picked out Crispin

Brooks, though she did not recognize anybody with him. She realized they did not recognize her, either, and if she hadn't come to warn them she'd have been tempted to keep it that way.

Lawrence Lang's voice rang out behind them. "Hold there, you two! I have a gun. Hands in plain sight, now!"

"Plain sight in this dark, Lawrence?" Libby demanded.

Lang gasped when he recognized her voice. "What in all blessed creation—?"

She spun to face him, and Rob went off to help the others. "I see I'm a bit late, but I came to try to stop all this," she told Lawrence earnestly. "Perhaps such provocation *is* dangerous at this time."

"Got your pretty head all turned around by that Tory Gant, eh?"

"It isn't that. I just think it might be too much too soon, when they discover this raid and—"

"Just powder horns, equipment, shot and powder. Our new regiments can use it. And we sawed the two longboats we found in half and clouted three guards on the head, that's all. Now you get on back, however you came. Your place is at the printing press, Libby Morgan. Look, here come some more rowboats in to load up," he told her, squinting toward the shore.

"Lawrence, I just don't want anything to happen to smash all we've built," Libby said.

Yet she really did want to help these men cart off the booty. She longed to shout defiance across the black waters at the hulking *Asia* and *Kingfisher*, there where they hovered like harpies over her city. Excitement coursed through her like wildfire, and at first she thought the new sounds were just her own pounding heart and churning passions.

"What's that?" she whispered as they all craned their necks toward the water.

"Just the new rowboats to pick up goods, I hope,"

Lawrence answered, but his voice and his pistol wavered, and he moved farther away on the sand.

A sharp voice floated to them. A distinctly British voice! One prow, then another, crunched on the sand.

"Halt! Halt in the name of the king!" a voice shouted from the boat, and suddenly all was chaos.

Lawrence yelled in alarm, though he need not have bothered after that pronouncement. Men ran, shouting. A few guns popped. Goods scattered on the sand. The newly landed longboats belched men with crossed white gunbelts and muskets with bayonets. Libby glanced wildly around for Rob, but all was black confusion. She turned and ran.

The raiders darted for the hillside bushes like ants whose nest has been destroyed. They knew better than to shove off in the loaded rowboats with the British putting in. Libby knew instantly that she was being chased. She heard it, felt it. Her feet flung sand, then gravel. Had no other patriots run off this way? She was out of breath, but she tore around the hill, where she was certain Rob had tied the horse. Low bushes raked her breeches and stockings. One of her shoes flew off. She held her hat to keep her hair from spilling free. She could hear her pursuer, closer and closer behind her.

Her entire life flashed before her eyes in those few moments. She would be caught, exposed, arrested, punished. The gazette was gone, all was lost. No one else seemed to be around here; there were only distant shouts in the direction of Turtle Bay now. Desperate, she ducked around a thick tree trunk and grabbed a branch from the ground. She lifted it and swung at her pursuer.

The man ducked and yanked the branch from her grasp, then hauled her hard against him. She tried to kick, to flail, but he pinioned her to him. He pulled her hat off to tumble her hair free and clamped a big hand over her mouth. That voice—as harsh and angry and ragged as it was—she knew that voice!

"Damn you, you stupid little dunce!" Cam Gant gasped out. "I thought it was you, but I could hardly yell out my name or yours down there, could I?"

In all the long years she'd detested Cameron Gant she had never imagined him so angry. She went temporarily limp in his harsh embrace, then gasped in a big breath when he freed her mouth. He turned her to face him, with her hands now held behind her back. The move pressed her body into his. When she tried to wriggle free, he only positioned her closer.

"I suppose you came with the British!" she gasped out.

"I am sick and tired of your pious prejudices! You have overstepped for the last time in planning this raid with your foolhardy cronies! You and I are going to settle everything between us, once and for all!" he muttered, his voice cold and hard. "I'm taking you to Staten Island with me tonight."

"I won't go!" she insisted. But when she tried to kick him again, he only tipped her back so that her lower body tilted harder against him. She could feel his hard thighs and his flat stomach intimately. "No, Cam! I won't just be hauled off like—"

"Like pilfered booty? But that's exactly what you've made yourself tonight. I'm only taking advantage of that before other bastards—British or colonial—do. Now quiet!" He shook her so hard her breasts bounced against his chest. She felt her nipples tighten into taut nubs under the rough shirt.

"Now you see here," she said, despite legs weak as water, "I'm sorry if you're upset, but—"

"Upset? My dear, I don't know if that lunacy back there will push the British over the edge of violence or not, but you've finally done that to me." He pulled her hands in front of her and bound them together with some sort of scarf.

Raw fear surged through her anger for the first time since

she'd realized it was Cam, but she dared not call for help. She tried to kick at him again as he tied his cravat around her mouth to gag her, but he merely threw her over his shoulder. One arm looped around the backs of her thighs and one hand right on her bottom, he strode off quickly into the darkness.

It seemed to Libby that he carried her forever, but at last he found his horse and hoisted her astride. She gripped the saddle tightly with her knees to stop her trembling. She was dizzy, and she was afraid of his anger and of the strength of his hands. He mounted behind her, pulled her back against him and spurred the horse away.

She sat nearly in his lap as he urged this horse—not the black stallion he usually rode—down the lane and straight across the island of Manhattan. Just fields and scattered woodlots belonging to large landowners here, but she recognized where they were as they crossed Bloomingdale Road and plunged on westward, toward the Hudson River. Their bodies seemed to move up and down together, up and down. One hard arm encircled her waist and immobilized her elbows, as if to pin her to him. He shifted his position now and then, bumping her bouncing breasts or resting a big hand temporarily on one of her spread thighs as if to assert his mastery of her.

She felt frozen with fascination at the way her own body responded to the touch of his. The gentleman who had always held himself in check had been replaced by a rough, marauding rogue. But she was as afraid of herself as she was for herself. Finally, on a slope overlooking the water, he reached up to tug down her gag.

"There'll be only my man with a boat here, so don't bother to scream, Libby."

"Hannah will put out a hue and cry for me when I don't return. Rob—"

"Rob will be lucky not to get caught and hanged by that English landing party that arrived just when I did. And I

told Hannah what a fool trick you'd pulled and that I would try to get you to Staten Island to give you an alibi you don't deserve in the morning. But you almost had to get caught on the spot! You need teaching and taming much more than I ever imagined, woman!'' He slid off the horse and hauled her down, then hurried her toward a path that sloped down to the river.

"But how did you know about the raid?" she asked as they skidded on the loose pebbles of the path. "And you can untie me now!" she demanded when they came to a flat, grassy spot on the riverbank.

"Quiet!" He whistled low, once, then again. An echo came back over the water, and a small sloop with a single half-furled sail emerged from the dark like a ghost.

Her head spun. He had everything planned. He had no right to abduct her and keep her prisoner, and yet she had no way to stop him. Devil take the wretch! He had extricated her from an unfortunate situation back there, of course, protecting her when the raid had failed. But this man was a raider, too, she thought, a raider of her reason, her emotions, even her body tonight.

He pushed her onto the narrow prow seat of the small sailboat. There was little other space in it, for it was cluttered with old crates and coils of rope. They put out immediately. The sail bloomed in the balmy breeze, and the sloop dipped and rose in the current.

At least she was going home to Merry and her mother on Staten Island, she thought. But how would she explain arriving in the middle of the night in boy's clothes...and with Cam Gant?

"You haven't told my mother yet, have you?" she asked.

"Hardly," he said curtly, fitting himself in beside her on the seat with one arm behind her back, so that he almost held her in a harsh embrace again. Spray struck the prow

and dusted them with droplets. "She won't know a thing. You're going with me to Melrose for the night."

His brusque, matter-of-fact tone panicked her. Though she was still tied, she struck at him, even though there was nowhere she could run to in the middle of the Hudson. Cursing, he shoved her down within the curved hull of the sloop so that she was wedged between a crate and the side of the boat. He lay beside her, one leg over her to still her, with his arms wrapped tightly around her again to stop her thrashing. Her hands were caught between them. While she gasped in ragged breaths, he tugged her wrists down until her arms were wedged in against his hip and thigh. He shifted his weight to hold her down in the rocking boat. They lay there, both breathing hard. She could hear the sole crewman moving in the dark on the far side of the sail, but the crates obscured all view. For a moment, she thought Cam meant to cuff her. Instead, he fastened his big hand in her wild hair, turned her face to him and kissed her.

It was not a gentle kiss. It commanded, dominated, demanded. Like a madwoman, she answered his passion with a startling raw need of her own. His hands raced over her back, her bottom. When she pressed closer along the curve of hull, he rained kisses down her throat and opened the big man's shirt she wore. Shaken to her very core, she sucked in breaths of air as his lips lavished kisses along her collarbones, then lower, in the curving cleft between her breasts.

She thought she cried, "Cam! Cam!" but it might just have been the slapping of waves.

He didn't stop. He held her, captive and yet willing, in the dark shelter of the prow and cupped her taut-tipped breasts, one after the other, in his spread hand, first through the shirt, then under it, flesh to flesh. While he swept hot, wet kisses down her throat again he moved his palm slowly, gently, over her breasts. The friction there, the sweet ache of it, shot sparkles of sensation to her belly and her thighs.

This was madness, a little voice warned her, but she only caught his lower lip gently in her teeth. His fingers flicked, then squeezed each pert peak. She moaned and moved her legs harder against him. She yearned to be closer, to discover more. And, for the first time in her life, she felt the unmistakable iron thrust of a man's desire against her thigh.

"Fire, always fire between us," he moaned. He sounded as breathless as if he'd swum the river. "I want you so much, my sweetheart, but you're always ruining it all."

Beyond coherent thought, she nodded wildly, and his hot mouth dropped to where his fingers had just been. Though she was stunned by this sweet new assault, she arched her back and thrust herself closer. He licked, he laved, he actually suckled one nipple, then the other.

"Into the narrows, sir," his man called out from the other side of sail. "Melrose landing not far now!"

Libby shuddered with delicious longing as his teasing tongue and pulling lips lifted from her. The night breeze seemed chill now where he had wet her skin in frenzied patterns. She tingled everywhere; the world spun with new possibilities. She trembled as Cam's shaking hands reluctantly pulled her to a sitting position and quickly buttoned her shirt. At last he realized that she was still tied, and, looking sheepish, he unbound her wrists. But his face turned grim again as the sloop nosed into the wooden wharf under the cliff behind Melrose Manor.

When he recalled that she had lost one of her shoes, he carried her up the pebbled path and across the lawn toward the house. Reality hit Libby. She was being carted into this detested place like another Gant possession! And yet her deepest desire was to be in his arms like this, going anywhere, even here.

He entered through a back door to the kitchen, and strode past big, deserted cooking hearths. He walked along a covered walkway, under the window she had broken so long

ago, and in a door of the main house. It was dimly lit inside, and she saw no one. She knew it was very late.

"You can let me go now," she said.

"No. We have things to settle, I said."

He carried her down a softly carpeted hall and elbowed a door inward. She craned her neck. Some sort of library, she thought, though there was a brocade settee, and a leather couch. She stiffened in his arms. He plopped her down on the settee and lit a lamp on a desk. While she sat waiting, saucer-eyed, he turned away to pour two small crystal glasses of amber-hued liquid.

"Madeira. Drink it down," he ordered. When he knocked his back neatly with a toss of his head, she followed suit.

It heated her insides, but not as much as his gaze did. "Before I so much as touch you again, we're going to have this all out," he said. "I pray you'll tell me you didn't really plan or mean to take part in that damned raid. That you only went out to Turtle Bay to poke your busybody little nose into another dangerous rebel story. That's bad enough!" His words came in a torrent. "You know what I saw when I got there—before I figured out which one you were? Two longboats sawed right in half, just as you suggested at that radical meeting the other morning. For an intelligent woman, you are entirely foolish and dangerous at times! Hell, and I thought you'd done your worst when you quoted my words about a blockade in that blasted paper, damn it!"

"Are you quite through?" she blazed. "Your language has deteriorated right along with your character lately, if that's possible!"

His gaze raked her again, and he snatched her glass away. Slamming both glasses on the tray, he stalked back toward her. To avoid being trapped, she rose and sauntered boldly past him to an array of crystal decanters on a silver tray. Taking her time in the hope of stilling her trembling,

she poured herself more Madeira. But her hand shook, and she splashed some out when he came to stand so close behind her that she could feel his body heat. He leaned a loosely balled fist on either side of her against the table to block her in.

She stood her ground defiantly and sipped slowly from the glass, but he was not to be put off. He reached around her, took it from her hands and slammed it back on the tray, spilling the contents. His big hands cupped her shoulders, scalding her through the shirt she wore. Her cheeks flamed at the thought of what they'd done in the sloop and of how she'd wanted more. He turned her to him and slowly tilted her chin upward with his fist. She could tell how hard he was trying to keep from shouting by a telltale little pulse beat at the base of his neck. His words came in piercing jabs.

"Ignore what I'm going to say at your own peril, Mistress Liberty. You're not only going to precipitate a crisis New York's not ready for, you're going to get yourself caught in the process. It was pure luck tonight the marines didn't get you."

"I'll be more careful. Actually, I heard about the raid too late and went to try to head it off, that's all. I swear it."

His deeply furrowed brow softened. "I'd like to believe that. At any rate, things are going to get worse, not better. And I won't have you in the midst of things. I insist I buy the gazette at a good price and return you to your home here on Staten Island. And then, if we can stop fighting long enough, I want to come courting you, and I hope—"

As stunned as she was by his last words, anger boiled up in her. "Courting? Is that part of the payment, or a bribe for selling the gazette? And to you? I didn't sell before! Why should I now?"

"Because things are different between us now," he insisted, giving her shoulders a little shake.

"They certainly are! I've seen you for the meddling loy-alist abductor and seducer that you are! I've always known what the Gants stood for, but now—"

One arm whipped around her waist to anchor her to him, and his fist gently lifted her jaw even more, so she almost seemed to offer him her mouth. "You mean my advice has not been good? You mean you don't feel a bit differently about me than you did the day of your father's funeral? And I believe, Elizabeth Morgan, you have—what shall we say—responded rather *heartily* every time I've so much as touched you."

She couldn't deny his words, but they infuriated her nonetheless. She tried to squirm from his grip, but it was steel and stone.

"You know," he said, his eyes narrowed and his hand-some features stretched taut, "I've tried reason with you. I've tried trusting you. I've tried patience and affection. Since none of those have worked, I'm going to try what's left, and what I've wanted from the first."

She sucked in a little gasp. It shocked her how much she wanted him to say he would try love. Love—with Cam Gant! And at Melrose!

"If this is all there is that we do well between us, so be it." He picked her up in his arms again. "You'll admit to this, at least—in words and deeds!"

He swept her up in his arms again and carried her up a curving sweep of stairs. Family portraits and Roman busts in fluted niches went by. In the carpeted upstairs hall he shouldered a door open, then closed it behind them with his foot. He carried her over to a tall bed that was neatly turned down. Filmy mosquito netting draped it like a big veil. It was as if they could shut out the world here. When he put her down, they just stared deep into each other's eyes for a moment. Then she shoved at his chest and tried to roll away.

He cursed softly and held her tight. She realized then

that she could scream. Sally Smith, the Morgans' old maid-servant, still worked here. Surely others would come running, too! But Cam's hands gentled her as he pulled her shirt free of her breeches. She had thought to yank his hair, but he bent over her and kissed every patch of skin the buttons uncovered. She managed only to rake his hair free of its queue. Then she ran her fingers through its thickness until he looked quite the wild man. She forgot to scream when he lifted over her to take her lips. She just wrapped her arms around his neck.

She knew then that she was doomed. Doomed, doomed to be desperately, stupidly, impossibly in love with Cameron Gant. It was her worst fear, to care for and desire the man she had always hated, the man she wanted so to best. "Oh...oh, no..." she mouthed against his forehead as he divested her of her breeches, her socks and her remaining shoe, but she really didn't mean for him to stop. Once she tried to grab for the linen sheet to cover herself, but his long legs held the covers pinned down. She lay naked, her skin like porcelain, under his gaze and his magic hands.

It was dim in the room, but she watched wide-eyed as his own tawny skin emerged from the clothes he flung away. He paused his quicksilver touching just to look down at her where she lay, tense and waiting and willing but not knowing what to do next.

"So beautiful," he murmured, and skimmed his tantalizing hand up and down her curves. "Strawberries and cream. And red-hot fire and icy snow." He grinned impudently, and his gaze traversed her again. She hardly dared breathe. "Tonight—what's left of it—Libby Morgan, we're going to tell and show each other how much we want to cooperate."

Those were the last words he spoke for a long time. His hands and lips caressed her, and she responded fervently. He stoked all the fires he had talked about. He melted all the snow. She became a woman who found liberty in his

exhilarating touch. She followed his sure lead, learning faster than she ever had at the shop. A flutter of kisses and a few little nibbles on his shoulder and he would stop caressing her to savor it. A petulant tweak of his own nub of male nipple and he would bite his lower lip. A darting tongue in his ear and he would moan. And little yearning circles of her nails on his lower back and—and he rolled her once over him into the depths of the big soft bed and mounted her as if he would ride her.

He kept his weight from her, raised on his knees and elbows. "You didn't think that touching and kisses all over was the end of this, did you?" he asked her teasingly.

"No. I may have been a dolt about being French-kissed, but I'm not totally inexperienced!"

He grinned at the quick retort. How could he ever have been angry with this stunning, seductive, sweet woman? "Mmm…I can see you're not a bit inexperienced," he taunted, skimming his hand over her rosebud nipples and her flat, silken belly again. Suddenly it meant a great deal to him that she offer him total surrender without his demanding it. He wanted her to remember she had wanted him, too, the next time she defied him.

"Oh, what are you doing?" she cried out, stiffening, as his fingers slid lower to dip between her warm thighs and into the moist heat of her. He only chuckled, moving slowly deeper. He showered her with kisses and nips until she moved her lush hips against his hand and he thought he would go mad if he restrained himself any longer.

For Libby, it was the most freedom—even pinioned under him this way—she had ever had. Something mutual and creative that she had never dreamed of sprang to life between them. It made her wild and eager and unashamed. She arched her back and drew her legs apart, welcoming the raider, even rising to meet him. And then he took her up again, to an even higher plane.

"Tell me if it's all right we go on," he whispered against

her throat, unable to wait. "I'll stop now, unless you really want—"

"Oh, I do.... What comes next... I do...."

Although all her limbs felt languid, Libby tensed with the expectation of the ultimate adventure. He settled his knees inside hers and gently nudged them wider. She felt so open, so vulnerable, and yet suddenly unafraid. He lowered himself carefully. She clung to him, her flesh aflame, trusting him, wanting him...yes, loving him. She kissed him back, stroked his shoulders, moved and gave little mewing cries that she could not hold back. He took his hand away and positioned himself over her. And, in the instant that something new flowered ever wilder within her, he took her mouth to still her cries and nudged, then pushed, then thrust, inside her.

"Cam!"

She called his name only in surprise at the sudden wonder of their union, for the pain was only a tiny slice. He gently muffled her cry against his lips. When he moved tentatively, she copied his thrusts. He slid in deeper; she moaned and clung to him to urge him on. And then there was wonder as he set up a steady rhythm against her and in her. It was as if they were still riding the wind across the dark river, and she went with him, on and on and on.

"Steady, steady now, sweetheart, just let it all go, my love." His voice was a hot rasp in her ear. When he rocked hard into her to release them both she knew she would always freely be his captive. She spiraled out of herself, still clasping him tight. Though she felt dizzy and stunned, she had heard the endearments he had called her. *Sweetheart,* he had said. *My love.*

They made love again, sleepily and slowly, in the velvet dark of night. Later Libby shut her eyes against the assault of dawn and cuddled closer to Cam's warmth. How had they ever come to this, that their private little war had be-

come an intimate peace? But he would just have to understand that she could not sell him the gazette. She had a duty to Atwood's memory, to her staff, to her readers, and to the colonies. Surely, after last night, he would learn to compromise, to agree. She could just see that hard, magnificent body in one of Washington's blue-and-buff lieutenant's uniforms.

She blushed again at her nakedness under the sheet, at how natural what they had done together seemed even in the light of the new day. She smiled into her pillow, then raised her head to watch him sleep. He lay on his back, with his side of the sheet twisted about his hard middle. One arm was crooked up over his head to flaunt the golden hair in his armpit. Devil take it, if only this wretched war weren't looming over them all, she thought. And if only she had some decent clothes to go exploring this fabulous manor house in, though she could hardly tell Merry or Mother she'd been here! Her thoughts paraded one after the other, then faded into marching men on horseback and fifers and drummers cavorting to a minuet. Soon, at dawn, in Cameron Gant's bed, she fell asleep again.

The light rapping of knuckles on the bedroom door awakened Cam. He gazed possessively at the beautiful, tousled woman asleep at his side, then got reluctantly out of bed. She looked so stunningly seductive that he longed to climb back in to kiss and stroke her awake. After breakfast he'd have to get her one of Catherine's old dresses. He would send Sally Smith back to Manhattan with her and hope that no one thought a woman who had apparently spent the night at her home on Staten Island had been in a raid. But she wasn't safe yet—not if any of those foolhardy patriots had been caught and questioned by the British.

He sighed deeply as his gaze went over her again, lying there so innocently, with that glorious wreath of hair around her peaceful face and her high, proud breasts, which stays

and corsets usually restricted, in full bloom. He couldn't bear to have this end yet. Silently he cursed the second light knock on the door, wishing with all his heart that he could have hidden away here with Libby for days.

He wrapped his silk dressing gown around his nakedness, tucked in a cravat and opened the door a crack. "The man who comes once a month," the stately butler, Montague, whispered. "I hope you don't mind my waking you, sir, but he's come to the back door downstairs asking to see you."

"Give me a few minutes, then show him into the library." Cam tugged on his discarded breeches and shoved his big feet into morocco slippers. After all, Montague had no idea he had a woman up here. And the liaison between him and Washington was a man to be trusted. He'd meet with him quickly and send him on his way before Libby woke. He ran a hand through his disheveled hair and glanced back at the motionless woman on the bed. He closed the door softly behind him and hurried downstairs to sit at his desk before Montague showed the man in.

Libby woke and stretched luxuriously, then realized something had roused her from her exhaustion. Everything that had happened yesterday, especially last night, flooded back to her. She sat bolt upright in the big bed. Cam was gone. Perhaps he was ordering breakfast, she thought, but when he didn't return she decided to explore just a bit. She slid off the bed and dragged the top sheet around her, as if it were a Roman toga. It was then that she saw crimson evidence on the rumpled bottom sheet of what had happened between them last night.

Her cheeks flushed hot. She covered the stains with a pillow and padded to the door to peek out into the deserted hall. She still felt so hazily happy, and she wanted to be with Cam right now. She'd just tiptoe downstairs to let him know she was awake.

Perhaps it was still too early for the servants to be up. She peered over the edge of the bannister. Yes, Cam must be in the library just below, where they had spoken last night. She'd surprise him at his work. She had to see him, to hold him again, right now! She padded down the steps, then almost turned to flee.

There were voices inside, and she dared not be seen like this! Cam must have some sort of business this morning, that was all. She leaned her shoulder on the wall momentarily and yawned. She really should just go back up and wait for him in bed. But then she caught what the men inside were saying, and she froze like a Roman statue in a toga on the steps.

"Here are the papers for our leader to read," Cam said. "And be sure to give him that note about the Turtle Bay raid and who was in on it."

"Righto. The whole province will be jumpin' with that as soon as the news leaks today. Thanks for your help, as always, Mr. Gant. Hope you don't mind me showin' up so early, but it's quite a ride back."

"I understand."

"Say, Mr. Gant, the leader asked me something else, too. How are you doin' keeping that rabble-rousing little female printer in line, eh? Well, that's not quite how he worded it, but..."

Libby pressed her fists to her mouth when she heard Cam laugh. "Just tell him I'm working on the task, as distasteful as it is."

Her stomach cartwheeled. Stunned, she stood nailed to the carpet. Cam Gant was not only informing on the patriots who had led the raid—her, too, no doubt—he had made love to her, or rather bedded her, just to keep her in line! He was working for someone he called merely "the leader." Would that be the captain of one of the warships in the harbor, the royal governor—or even General Gage himself, in Boston? The messenger had said he had a long

ride ahead, but who knew what that meant? She had to get out of here somehow, not let Cam know what she had heard!

She tore up the stairs and into his bedroom. As she scrambled into her clothes, tears stung her eyes. It was not only that Cam Gant had obviously lied about being on the colonial side and about only cautioning restraint. It was not even that she'd been such a fool as to want him...to think she loved him! It was that all the attentions he had paid her, the visits, the rescues, the—damn him, the pretended loving—had been because she was an assignment to him! And a distasteful one, at that! She could just imagine him recounting all that had passed privately between them as a group of British officers sniggered over the seduction of another stupid, homespun virgin rebel!

She trembled with pain and rage as she stuffed the big, wrinkled shirt in her breeches. And she had been so swept away she had thought she loved him, had thought he actually loved her. She laughed bitterly inside. A Gant love her! Why, he probably still thought of her as a troublesome bitch from her father's Whig litter that might as well have been drowned! Nothing had changed since that first awful day they had met here at Melrose. She'd find a way to destroy him! She'd like to kill him!

His voice interrupted her fury as he came back in. "Hey, sweetheart, you can't go back in those clothes!" He closed the door and leaned against it. She longed to rip his little smile right off his handsome face. "You may have gotten away with being a boy in the dark, but I assure you someone will notice in broad daylight. I'll get a gown you can wear."

She spun to face him, hands on hips.

His smile faded when he saw her face. "Libby?"

"I wouldn't take a thing of yours, ever again, Mr. Gant! I'd much rather be caught and hanged by your British friends!"

"What? Have you been crying? Libby, we promised each other no regrets in the morning," he said, quickly closing the distance between them.

Suddenly she could not hold back. It didn't matter if he derided her to her face or killed her on the spot for what she knew. She had to end this now, any way she could, so that he would never touch her again. If he did, she feared, she would still want him and respond, and she could not risk that anymore. In the war shaping up outside, he was more than ever the enemy within!

"I'll make you a little deal, Mr. Gant." She held up both palms to stop his approach. "I will not print that you've been a British spy all along if you just stay out of my life! And let me out of this horrid place so that I can warn the finest patriots New York can boast that you've betrayed us all!"

She backed away from him, but he stalked her and grasped her elbows. She shook him off.

"Can't you even trust me a little bit, Libby? I'd never do that!" But his eyes widened in realization. "You've been downstairs, haven't you? How much did you overhear?

"I heard, you lying, seducing brute, that you're supplying information to your *leader*. And that, despite how distasteful it's been for you to lie and playact, you've been stringing me along to keep me in line!"

"I'm sorry you heard all that, because it's not what you—"

"Cease the lies, Cameron Gant! Don't worry, I can't print it without telling how I got the information playing whore for you the morning after I was in the raid! Then my reputation and my paper that you've been so eager to sully *would* both be as good as dead. And my country needs that paper!"

"All right, let me explain. I did tell my visitor keeping you in line was distasteful, but it wasn't meant that way—"

"Don't ever touch me again," she shouted when he reached for her. She hit his hands away and stuffed her foot in her single shoe. "Talk about distasteful! I detest the thought of it. Have from the first!"

"Who's lying now?" he demanded. "It takes two to do what we did last night!"

He was furious that this had happened, and he was furious with her. Yet he couldn't bear for her to turn against him again after he'd thought he'd won her over. Yet fate always intervened, and he was forced to look the British lackey while she admired boys like Eddie Tiler and that ruffian Crispin Brooks!

Still, he could not tell her who "the leader" really was. It would be disastrous to even hint to anyone that the commander-in-chief of the infant Continental Army wanted to keep the lid on New York because he didn't even have enough troops to send here yet! Nor could he betray Washington's admission that he didn't trust New Yorkers not to bolt and make a separate peace. Besides, despite how he longed to be with Libby, too many people were beginning to notice the unusual alliance between one of the city's best-known Tories and a radical Whig printer. It might put both of them in danger. He couldn't bear her fiery hatred, but he might have to. Perhaps he should even fan it to make certain she stayed out of his life.

"Let's face it, Libby, you took to what happened between us last night as cleverly as you took to printing. You're a very fast learner. Quick hands and a quick mouth— I like that!"

Before she knew it, her palm had cracked against his left cheek. He didn't move a muscle.

"I may have been a dunce to trust you with my virginity, Mr. Gant, but I'll never trust you again for anything else!" she cried, stamping over to the bed to yank off the bloodstained sheet. She tried to rip it, but it wouldn't tear. She hurled it at him.

"Such lovely, untapped passion," he said, attempting to sound mocking. "I really regret I'm going to have to send you back and be traveling in the next few weeks. Now listen to me, lady! I pulled you out of a bad spot last night." He leveled an arm and finger at her. "You will wait here and do no more damage to the room until I send your family maid Sally in with a gown for you to wear back to town. And you will take Sally back with you for a day or two. It will give you another reason for having come to Staten Island—to accompany Sally over for a visit."

"In case British soldiers are camped on my stoop to arrest and close me down when I get back, you mean!"

At the last moment, he almost changed his mind. He couldn't bear to have her stalk off detesting him. "If they come to your door, I'd put the odds on you! And, Libby, perhaps when they don't arrest all your careless friends you'll understand that what you overheard this morning is not what you believe."

"What I believe is that you are the lowest, foulest excuse for a man I have ever known. And I regret everything that has passed between us!"

To her amazement, he said no more. He let her have the last word. But surely he could not know how bitter that word turned on her tongue, or how it broke her battered heart when she and Sally later walked away from Melrose Manor and mounted a horse, the way she and Merry had done once so long ago.

At the public wharf, the ferry they were waiting for disgorged four British soldiers who started up the lane toward Melrose. Libby hardened her heart again toward the traitor she knew him to be.

Seven

***

THE LIBERTY GAZETTE

The Provincial Congress of New York has resolv'd that for the future Welfare & Safety of Manhattan the British Cannon at Fort George be moved to the Highlands: 21 naval Guns (12 & 18 Pounders) weighing to 1 Ton ea. Patriot Volunteers with ropes sorely need'd tomorrow, 7 in the Evening to assemble at the Fort. New York Regiments to bring Muskets, prim'd & load'd.

Joint Order of Prov. Cong. &
Hon. Mayor Whitehead Hicks

* * *

Patronize Dr. Moses Dunne, Barber and Surgeon. *Cuts, close shaves, wig trims. Bleeding, Blistering, & Cupping. Also enjoy Dr. Dunne's Wonder Drops: cures Gout, Fluxes, Agues, Cholicks, Gripes in the Stomach, Rickets, & all general Pains.*

North of the tanning yards on Princes Str.

Libby's head spun all the way back to Manhattan, and she ignored Sally's protests about having promised her mother

never to set foot in New York City. Cam Gant's degrading, mocking words to that man taunted her. She was grateful that the garments she had borrowed—his sister's—included a white linen complexion mask with a button mouthpiece. It excused her from answering Sally's questions and hid her humiliation at Cam's callous insults.

The fine quality of the borrowed garments themselves were a mocking reminder that she could never hope to be accepted by a Gant. This was only one of Catherine Gant's abandoned day gowns, Sally had said as she had settled the sky-blue satin luxury over Libby's head. It dripped ruffles from the bodice and cascades of fine lace from the tight elbow sleeves. The puffed overgown was looped back with big stiff bows to flaunt an embroidered and quilted petticoat stretched over wide farthingales. It had a tiny pocket for a bosom bottle of flowers, and the white silk hose felt elegant against smooth calfskin shoes with silver buckles. As a final taunting reminder, the straw shepherdess hat was trimmed with silk flowers such as innocent young maidens wore— and she hardly felt that after last night.

"Curse the arrogant wretch!" she muttered, but, luckily, the face mask distorted her words.

"What did you say, Mistress Libby? Is this the street, then?"

Libby only nodded and steered the wide-eyed girl past the Goodhues' apothecary shop, where her friend Faith sat in the doorway, stringing dried poppy heads. Libby didn't need Faith's questions right now, either. She hurried Sally into the print shop before she removed the mask. She heaved a sigh. The place looked only momentarily deserted; she could tell Jos and Rob had just been here. She sent Sally upstairs to introduce herself to Hannah and went into the small storage room at the back. "Rob? Jos?" she called.

The men nearly bumped into each other coming in the

back door. Both lugged armfuls of cut paper. The paper mill's delivery cart stood outside.

Rob looked immensely relieved.

"Mistress! Thank God!" Jos cried.

"I'm fine. I just decided last evening to go over to Staten Island to fetch a friend for a few days' visit," she explained. Her eyes met Rob's. "Jos, don't let me stop you, but I need to speak to Rob."

"Hannah's gone off to Philadelphia on the fast coach!" Jos blurted out. "Word came early this morning, her only living relative took real sick. She said you'd just have to understand."

"There's worse," Rob put in with a warning roll of his eyes before Libby could respond. "For some reason, a troop of redcoats came calling this morning to inquire if you know something about some raid or t'other last night!"

"What do you mean, 'some raid,' Rob!" Jos protested. "You know it's the one everyone's chattering about."

Libby composed her face and clenched her hands in the folds of her dress. "What's this about a raid?" she asked Rob, keeping her voice as steady as she could manage.

"Danged if a newly arrived foreigner would know," Rob said with a shrug. "It seems some London-spawned uppity-up thought the printer of a Whig paper might heard something on the wind. Said he'd be back. A captain named Hector. Seems," Rob added lower as Jos went grumbling back to work, "some lout of a redcoat soldier found a woman's shoe on the raid site at Turtle Bay, wherever that might be. I believe we mentioned to this Captain Hector that you'd just stepped out to do a wee bit of shopping— in both shoes!"

Libby was stricken, but she knew this was no time to panic. But she had to explain to Rob that—

"Mistress Libby—" Sally came skipping down the steps "—there's no one up here at all! Oh!" She caught her lower lip between her teeth when she saw the hairy knees

showing under Rob's kilt. She blushed as she met his surprised, steady stare. Libby noted well the looks between
the two as she explained to Sally that Hannah had taken
the fast coach—which people even called "the flying ma-
chine"—to Philadelphia to nurse her great-nephew.

She introduced Rob and Sally. She could see that she
couldn't keep the girl around here to replace Hannah. She
had no intention of exposing poor Sally to her own sort of
trouble with an avid-eyed man. But what unsettled her even
more was that Rob and Sally reminded her of the way she'd
felt from the first about Cam Gant. Then Jos called from
out in the shop, "Visitors, king's soldiers, and toting arms,
mistress!" and she bridled her feelings.

"Rob, you'd best keep Sally company out here in back,
just for a few moments," she said. "I will handle this."

"With honey, not vinegar!" Rob called after her as she
marched out into the shop's front room.

The soldiers must know something, Libby thought. Perhaps they'd demand to search the place for the shoe that
matched the one they'd found. At least they wouldn't find
it, for it was at Melrose. At that thought her pulse pounded
so loud that she was afraid they would hear. If Cam had
given out the raiders' names, perhaps he had given those
redcoats riding up to Melrose the matching shoe!

"Well, well, and here I had expected an aged widow,"
the thin, stiff captain observed, his sleek eyebrows lifting
at the sight of her. Four other soldiers stood behind him,
the butts of their muskets resting on the floor. A few pas-
sersby on the street peered in the windows at them. They
all seemed to stare suspiciously at Libby in her fine attire.

"*You* are Elizabeth Morgan, printer of that Whig rag?"
the captain demanded, pointing at a copy of the gazette on
the stationery counter.

"No, I am Elizabeth Morgan, printer of that honest and
independent paper, the *Liberty Gazette*," she told him.

His eyes glittered at that, but he introduced himself in a

reasonably polite fashion as Captain Phillip Hector, serving on the *Asia* in the harbor. With his aquiline nose, his sharp dark eyes and his white crest of powdered wig, he seemed an eagle ready to swoop.

"I say, Mistress Morgan, didn't mean to pick a fight unless one's due," he said, backing down a bit. "A blasted bloody insult of a raid was perpetrated last night on the king's storehouse at Turtle Bay. Don't s'pose you'd know aught of that?"

"I know of Turtle Bay. My mother used to make the best snapper soup from turtles my father caught there with a friend of his years ago," Libby retorted with a forced little smile.

Captain Phillip Hector's jaw tightened, and he sniffed. "So you won't be printing a word of the details?"

"A recipe for turtle soup, you mean?" She amazed herself. She was almost enjoying this. Besides, besting the British helped soothe the grinding pain of what Cam Gant had done to her.

"I refer, Mistress Morgan, to the attempted rebel raid on the king's warehouse and powder magazine. Granted, the thieves got away with next to nothing, but we mean to catch them anyway!"

"Why, I admit I'd like to do an article on any raids, if you could just give me some news of them. But I wouldn't expect you to come to town yourself. You would no doubt wish to send one of your lackeys instead," she replied sweetly.

"Don't think Governor Tryon and bigger authorities aren't watching what you do print!" Captain Hector insisted, shaking a finger at her like a stern tutor. "It would be such a shame for a quaint little shop like this to be closed down."

"How dare you threaten me? I am just a woman trying to make my way in a world where freedom used to matter!"

"Used to?" Hector gasped. When he shook his head, fine wig powder dusted his crimson shoulders and his epaulets. "I say, but this pompous town had just better mind its p's and q's, or else!" He turned toward the door, raking her again with his sharp eyes.

"Minding your p's and q's...that's printer's talk, Captain. I'll tell you something that is much more than that." She followed them boldly to the door. She knew she should let him go and be grateful that the British evidently didn't know the raiders' identities for certain. But the anger and hurt seething inside her suddenly exploded. "You've no right, sir, to come here, upsetting my staff and insulting me and my work. And I tell you, the freedom I print about and believe in is not just for the colonies. It's for everyone. I even believe in freedom for Britain."

Captain Hector sputtered at her audacity and daring, and Eddie Tiler picked that moment to arrive in his new uniform. When he looked as if he'd join the fray, Libby tugged him behind her. She stood, trembling inside, with her hand pressed against the edge of the open door. Eddie came to stand beside her. She blessed him for that, but she wished desperately he were another man come to stand up to the British and to help her out. But it was over with Cam Gant, she told herself. Now she had an even bigger score to settle with him for his cruel pride and perfidy.

Captain Hector tapped his long fingers on the hilt of his sword, as if he were weighing whether to go or stay. His suspicious gaze darted from her to Eddie and then back again. "Good day, then—for now, Mistress Morgan," he said curtly after an interminable lull. "But I'm warning you to tell that nasty-faced Scotsman you employ here to buy a suit of English journeyman's clothes. The Crown has outlawed the kilt in Britain, and we don't need to see it in the colonies! Strange that your other journeyman claims the Scotsman has such garb, but he wasn't able to produce it.

I assure you we will be thinking of all you've said—and done. Men!''

The four scarlet-coated soldiers trooped out in his wake. Libby closed the door and leaned against it, her knees suddenly like water. Eddie put his hand on her arm, then pulled her to him, encircling her shoulders. She collapsed against him for a moment. She wanted to feel relief or joy or something in his strong, warm embrace, but she felt nothing. Curse you, curse you always, Cameron Gant, she thought as she pulled gently away from Eddie's arms.

The next five weeks were torment. If she went out during the day, Libby worried that she was being watched. Asleep, she had nightmares of Cam telling the laughing Captain Hector all about their passionate night together—every kiss, every intimate, arousing touch. She lost sleep and weight. It depressed her that, with tensions growing in the city, some families were returning to England. Deserting their homes, betraying the cause, just as Cam had her.

She had been in a sweat when she had missed her monthly flow. What if she carried his child after just one reckless night. But the flux had merely come late. She was immensely relieved to be completely free of him, and yet she wasn't free at all.

She thought the oddest things at the oddest times: about the way one corner of his mouth crooked up before he smiled, about how his laugh vibrated clear in the pit of her stomach when she leaned against his chest, about the erotic blend of roughness and gentleness in his touch. She constantly thought she saw him on the street. She jumped when the shop door opened, thinking it might be him.

Even throwing herself into her work, even visits from dear Merry—who had vowed she would "forget" to tell Mother that there was no chaperone at all living upstairs at the print shop now—failed to really cheer her. She learned from Mayor Hicks, who stopped to ask for an announce-

ment in the gazette, that Cam Gant was traveling to other colonies to expand his business. Good riddance for New York, she thought, wondering if he was really spying for the British elsewhere.

But when Mayor Hicks told her what the announcement should say, she felt her first surge of optimism in weeks. New Yorkers were finally being bold enough to do something about defying the British. They were going to move the old cannons they had to defend the Highlands against the day the British fleet returned en masse.

Libby jammed her feet into her sturdy walking shoes and donned her green sprigged gown to go watch them move the big guns. She did not take a shawl. The August night was hot, and she expected to have to do a great deal of walking along the route to get a good article. Hundreds of patriots, including Rob and Jos, were heading for Fort George to help haul twenty-one cannons. There was nothing the British could dare to do to stop such a bold, united front!

When she arrived at Fort George, men, like beasts of burden, already dragged the guns, which were mounted on creaking wheeled carriages. It was hard going up Broad Way Street toward the Commons, for there was a slight hill. Shouts, orders, grunts, the rattle of drums and fifes, as though this really were a military drill, drowned out her voice as she called and waved to the puffing, straining Rob. No doubt the British could hear the noise from the sloop that had put out from the gunship *Asia* and was now hovering just off the Grand Battery, as if to watch the action closer. Word came back that the sloop was armed to the teeth, so Libby jotted that down on her writing board as she hurried along beside one big gun carriage.

"A lovely evening to move guns!" she called lightheartedly to her friend Lawrence Lang. He was immaculately

attired, as usual, and he was obviously not touching a rope. "Aren't you helping?"

"Just keeping a good eye on our New York musketmen along the Battery. If that blasted sloop fires, I want to be sure they'll have the stomach to fire back!" he said, and stalked off.

She saw others she knew in the crowd. She even felt a stab of pride when Crispin Brooks, who was usually quite a pest, went by, sweating with exertion at the very front of a long rope. But it annoyed her when some of the observers broke into "Yankee Doodle." She had other memories of that tune.

Darkness fell, and now torches lit the strange, blocks-long parade. Libby held a torch aloft and forgot to write. Some women moved among the workers with water buckets when they rested. Everyone felt a communal release in this joint effort. Tonight they would kick England in its ravening lion's teeth and get away with it! Libby thrilled at the sight of the Second New York Regiment, in their brown-and-blue uniforms, with muskets loaded, primed and cocked. She could not spot Eddie Tiler among them.

Hours passed. The crowds swelled and applauded each new gun as it arrived at the midpoint of the Commons. A few hardy souls went back to help with the last guns. Candles flickered in windows to urge on the defiant ones. The only unfortunate occurrences were an occasional cluster of loyalists shouting to them to "stop this madness before something dire happens!" But people just booed or yelled insults back and dragged the cannon on.

Word spread that, offshore, the big-gunned *Asia* had swung inward to anchor in the East River, just a thousand yards off the foot of Wall Street. A ripple spread through the crowd at the news. The lines of men bent over the long ropes halted. People squinted into the torch-speckled darkness down Wall Street, as if they could see the ship hovering in the inky black beyond. Midnight fell, then passed.

"We've gotta go on!" a voice Libby recognized as Lawrence Lang's pierced the night. "We can't stop now. Gotta at least have these last ones as far as the Commons before daybreak, when they'll really see what we're doing."

"They know what we're doing, Lang!" another strident voice countered. "Why else is that armed sloop right on top of our boys down on the shore! We're skating on thin ice, I tell you!"

Libby moved through the crowd toward the dispute, holding her torch up and her writing board tightly to her breast. But at the next voice she almost dropped the torch in surprise. It was a voice that had haunted and tormented her for five weeks, a voice she knew all too well.

"All of you, listen to me! The Commons is as far as these guns should go! Believe me, the British are just looking for a good excuse to fire, and you're handing it to them on a silver platter tonight!"

She elbowed her way to the front and lifted her torch nearly in Cam Gant's face. He stood with one foot up on a long cannon, the other on its bulky wooden carriage.

"If that's true," Libby shouted boldly, "it's because this man has urged them to it! He's a British informer, and a lily-livered coward when it comes to admitting it!"

"That's not true!" he countered in a calm, commanding voice, but she saw that his face had gone taut with fury. "I'm not even a loyalist," he shouted. "Not to England. I'm a realist, and that's what New York needs now, in place of radical, blind and prejudiced rabble-rousers." He pointed a finger at Libby and then swung it toward the sputtering-mad Lawrence Lang. "The great American weakness has always been an excess of optimism, and—"

"That's not true. Nothing he says is!" Libby shouted, thrusting her torch at him like a rapier blade.

He kicked it away, and it dropped under the big gun in a shower of sparks. He reached down to grab her arm, and

she tried to hit him. Lawrence endeavored to pull him away, but he shoved him off and reached for Libby again.

"Can't leave things alone, can't leave well enough alone—or me!" he raged at her.

The crowd pressed forward, arguing, shouting. Then a crackle of distant musketfire froze them all like statues.

"The sloop's firing!" Lawrence Lang declared jubilantly. "We have to fire back. Fire back! Fire back!" he shouted over and over as he clawed his way through the crowd toward the shore.

Then everything exploded. The American musketmen on the shore answered the sloop with a volley. The sloop fled, but the big *Asia* fired one round of solid shot and several rounds of grapeshot. They could hear it pepper the waterfront as people screeched and dived for cover.

"The guns!" someone shouted at those who had thrown themselves down in the street or were cowering behind the big cannon. "Grapeshot can't reach us here! Move these guns!"

Libby found herself hauled off through the crowd by Cam's bruising grip on her upper arm. "Satisfied now?" he yelled into her angry face. "You'll get your fight!"

"I didn't know that you were back!"

"It's touching that you care!"

"I don't, you vile bas—" The rest of that insult was drowned by the rattle of alarm drums and warning bells.

The city had gone mad. People panicked and ran screaming in circles, some in their nightclothes, a few ludicrously wigless, with their burred heads looking as bald as Jos Bean's. Some ran for cellars, some just scurried aimlessly up and down the streets with children or precious household goods in their arms.

"Wait, stop, don't flee now!" Libby shouted futilely at people as they were almost trampled by carts and horses heading for the New Jersey or Brookland ferries. Cam yanked her against the door of a shop and held her there.

"Are you happy now, damn it?" he demanded. "A bunch of green boys to stand up to this!"

"If we had gotten the guns in place before you warned the British we could have stood up to them! This city's been held hostage too long!"

"You are the blindest, most stub—" His words were ripped away by a huge, belching blast. The sky rained fire. Buildings heaved and shook. Terrified for the first time, Libby clung mindlessly to Cam's strength, burying her face against his shoulder as shouts and the noise of ripping wood and breaking glass echoed in the streets.

Cam shook her hard, as if she were a rag doll. She watched, stunned, as his mouth formed words. Jumping white-and-red flames lit his face, making him seem a demon from some nightmare.

"Go back to the print shop and get down in the cellar!" he shouted at her. "For once, do as I say, damn you! People will need help now!"

He shoved her in the direction she should go and lurched off toward the docks, but for a moment she only stood. In the next flare of shellfire she saw a building up the way, its roof scalped and its windows gaping, eyeless. Plaster and brick dust floated in the air to choke her. Sulfur fumes bit at her throat. Pigeons flapped in circles overhead, blasted from their familiar eaves. Disoriented people surged into the streets as the *Asia* fired another broadside, tearing off roofs on the next street.

People will need help. Cam's words echoed in her mind. Squinting into the crackling, firelit night, she stumbled off down Wall Street in the direction he had gone.

It seemed hours later when she saw him, hauling people, soldiers and civilians alike, off the wharves to safety. She helped, too, herding people off the docks, carrying children, helping a pregnant woman get settled in a neighbor's cellar. The wounded she aided first. Once she and Cam bent over

the same old man whose leg was shattered. Their eyes met as they lifted him together back into a cabinetmaker's shop, where a surgeon was working on folks laid out one at a time on a big gateleg table. Cam shook his head in dazed awe when he saw that she had disobeyed him again, but they did not argue.

On her next foray out, she found a deserted wheelbarrow and carried wounded back and forth to the surgeon. She lost sight of Cam again until the clock of a nearby church rang three of the morning and the *Asia* spat shells and lead again, as if to defy the insult of the singing chimes.

That blast threw Libby against a wall. She huddled next to the wheelbarrow, praying, squinting into the blackness at the light that marked the *Asia*, out in the river. Grapeshot followed, with a rattle as it hit. Shop glass tinkled forlornly down the way. More people went down, struck by flying lead. When it was over, she hurried out to help.

And then she saw Cam again. Like a bulky sack, his big form lay very still, just ahead of her in the street.

"No," she said in disbelief. "No!"

She ran to him, stepping over a moaning militiaman. She knelt on hard cobbles and touched his shoulder. Wet! Wet with sticky, warm blood!

"Cam! Cam!" she cried, and turned him over, cradling his big head.

His face looked dirty yet peaceful. No blood there. His eyes were closed, with those long lashes making smudges on his cheeks. She bent her ear to his chest but could not hear his heart over the noise of the wounded and salvaged goods being carted down the street again. She felt for the familiar, telltale pulse at the base of his neck. Yes, it was beating!

She ran for her wheelbarrow and tried futilely to get him up in it. "Help me! Please, help me!" she begged passing people. A woman finally stopped to help her lift him. Such

dead weight! She prayed he wasn't as badly hurt as he seemed.

She labored to get the single-wheeled vehicle over the cobbles without bumping him. His big limbs sprawled over the walls of the makeshift vehicle. Please, dear Lord God, she beseeched, if I did anything to help cause all this havoc, even if I didn't...please don't let him die.

The cruel words they'd exchanged tonight, how furious he had made her feel—all that was nothing now. She had to help him, had to save him. In the cabinetmaker's shop she looked around for the surgeon who had been laboring there for hours.

"Where is he?" she demanded of a man who had been helping. "I need him for this man!"

"Heard his wife was hurt," the man said without looking up. He was wrapping a woman's slick crimson leg. "Had to go."

She knew she had to stop Cam's bleeding, too. She wheeled him off into a corner under a lantern and ripped the ruffles from her last decent gown to make bandages. She wrapped them around his shoulder, arms and leg. If only he'd wake up and talk to her, let her know he was all right. But, if he did, what would he say—that he hated her, that she had caused all this? That he detested her more now than when he'd forced himself to bed her?

The idea, the certainty, of what she must do, hit her with full force then. Faith and Horace Goodhue, next door to the print shop, were clever apothecaries who knew a great deal about medicines and healing. She could put Cam in her bed and care for him. She owed him that much, at least. Sweating and groaning, she managed to bump the wheelbarrow out the door and headed the long distance home through a city turned upside down.

On Queen Street, which had evidently taken no direct hits, she didn't even need to knock on the Goodhues' door.

The elderly couple stood in their dressing gowns in the middle of the street, looking southwest. Libby gasped out what had happened, and they helped her carry Cam into the print shop and up the stairs to her small, slant-eaved bedroom and lay him on the bed.

"Perhaps old Hannah's bed would be better," white-haired Faith observed when she got a good look at the big, handsome man. "After all, this is your bed."

"He's too long for hers," Libby insisted. "I'll sleep there. Please, anything you can do!"

"Here's the reason his lights are out," Horace said, fingering Cam's skull. "No blood here, but something must have hit his head hard. Bump big as a goose's egg. All right, you two try to wash those wounds, and I'll be back soon with the fixin's to patch him up as best I can. He's a big one, with lots of blood to go bad."

"And don't tell that barber down the street, please, Horace!" Libby called after the old man. "He's lost a lot of blood already, and I don't want anyone to know he's here yet!"

She swallowed her last words, realizing how that must sound to Faith. The Goodhues had run the apothecary shop since the old days of the Indian Wars, and she didn't want them to get the wrong idea about her morals because she'd brought Cam here.

But why had she brought him here, her own inner voice asked her. She had lived and breathed revenge and hatred against him for five weeks, but the moment she had seen him hurt—

"Libby, girl, stop staring," Faith ordered her crisply. "Help me get these things off him, and we'll wash that blood away to see what we've got."

By dawn's first light the city had quieted. They had tended to Cam's wounds and bruises, though he still slept heavily on. The wounds in his left shoulder and arm were the worst. Horace said he was glad Cam was unconscious,

because it meant he could dig the grapeshot out of his shoulder muscle without tying him down. He poured hot tallow on the deepest wounds to stanch the bleeding. They wrapped a poultice of boiled spruce on his leg cuts and washed his other surface wounds with thyme water. He lay on her bed, looking whiter than Libby had ever seen him. Even though she had been so intimate with that big body, his nakedness was a shock and an embarrassment to her. She felt the Goodhues must surely be able to read her mind. She felt exhausted, bereft, stunned.

Faith's voice pierced her agonizing. "Libby, girl, listen now, as we're going next door for a bit of sleep." Her glassy gaze met Faith's clear blue eyes. "When he wakes, these sage drops in water will stop any bleeding inside. Make him chew this willow bark to fight the pain."

"Yes...pain."

"Maybe you'd best stay with the girl, Mother," Horace put in.

"No, I'm fine, really," Libby insisted. "Just tired. I thank you so much for all you've done. But, please, until I can send word to his home he's all right, don't tell anyone he's here!"

Horace raised his bushy brows and pursed his thin lips. "All right. We're all exhausted after that peppering the Brits gave us last night. Just remember, if his pulse rate gets fast, it means fever's a-coming, so let us know."

"Yes, I will. I can't thank you enough," she called after them as they went out of the room and down the stairs.

She sat on the single ladder-backed chair in the room— bolt upright at first—watching him in the wan light of the single tin lantern. He breathed deeply. Why didn't he wake? But this way he was hers for a little while, calm and pliable and needy. When he woke there would be all the mistrust again, all the mutual anger, all the mocking insults.

But tonight, her fury had ebbed at the sight of his helplessness, his spilled blood. She slumped against the back

of the chair. She'd have to send for his servants in the morning, she supposed, have to let someone else beside the Goodhues know he was here. She laid her disheveled head back and glanced down at her torn, bloodied gown, which now barely covered her dirty, bruised knees. It was the last thing she recalled seeing before her heavy lids closed and she slept.

She woke with a start when she heard Rob Graham come whistling in below. Daylight flooded the room. She leaned over to touch Cam's forehead. It was cool enough. She fingered his bruised head, and he stirred fitfully. Surely that was a good sign. Sore in every muscle, she threw her dressing gown over her ruined dress and went down the steps.

"What a bonny braw night!" Rob boasted with a grin when he first saw her. "Can't say we gave as good as we got, but we stood up to the redcoated devils at last! Say," he said when she came closer, "you didn't get hurt, did you? We've got to get the paper out, mistress. I been out all night gathering the news," he told her, his voice less cheery now that he could see her exhausted, haunted look. "And best is, the British Guv'nor's put out a hue and cry to have your old friend Gant brought to him for a chitchat. And guess where Tryon is? Out on the newly arrived merchant ship *Duchess of Gordon*, where he's fled, tail between his legs, after last night! Don't that cheer you a wee bit, now?"

Libby leaned her shoulder on the door frame, trying to absorb all he'd said. Governor Tryon had fled and sent word back that Cam be brought to him. To protect him from the crowds after she'd exposed him as a spy last night? To find out what else he knew? Or could it even be that he was angry with Cam for helping the New Yorkers last night when the fighting had begun? And hadn't Cam been right to warn them not to rile the British yet? Still, that didn't settle the problems between them.

"Rob, I've got to trust you with something secret again." He was opening the tympanum of the press, and the tone of her voice made him look up. "Cam Gant—he's badly wounded. I—I have him upstairs. And if the British want him, they're not going to get him, no matter what their reason! He must be working with them somehow, since they went out to see him at Melrose after the Turtle Bay raid, too. If you can help me sneak in things I'll need, he'll be our secret. They can turn the town upside down for him if they want!"

"Your private prisoner?" he asked, with a small, tight smile.

She felt herself color. "He won't be putting up a fuss, not for a while. I'm only doing it to confound the bloody Brits. I'll be down later to put the story together," she said in a rush. "And don't tell Jos, and especially Coll, a thing when they come in!"

She turned and hurried back upstairs. She tiptoed over to stare down at the sleeping, wounded man. She floundered in the jumble of emotions he had always caused in her. She cursed herself once again for wanting to believe what he had said about his political loyalties, but for all that she found she longed to be deceived in every way by the tricky wretch.

"Yes, I guess you are my private prisoner. Gant!" she whispered.

He stirred as if he'd heard her. He groaned. His right hand flexed. One eyelid slitted, then the other, as she bent over him.

"What?" His voice was a harsh rasp. "Libby? What happened? I hurt all over! My head—"

"Just rest. I've got something for the pain if you can chew."

His eyes seemed to dart past her, and then they closed again. "Always was too light in here just after dawn," he murmured. "What happened to me? Last night, what we

shared was...great. I was so ready— You, too." He forced
his eyes open again when he heard her gasp of surprise. "I
was dreaming about it even when I got hurt. Still hurt—
Call my man Montague for me, sweetheart. He won't tell
we've been to bed togeth—" he muttered, and was instantly asleep again.

Eight

THE LIBERTY GAZETTE

The inhumane & savage Attack by the British Warship Asia *on 23 August greatly damag'd the following Edifices, Compensation for which the Provisional Government of New York will petition Governor Tryon from his "new Seat" in the Harbor. To Whit: The Roof of 4 Townhouses; Roof of Fraunces' Tavern; Numerous Buildings on Whitehall Str.; much Damage on the Docks & Wall Str.; many New Yorkers wounded, several still critical.*

* * *

Visit the best Apothecary in Town, est. before the last War, when the British deign'd to be our Friends. Goodhues' offers these fine Imports: Daffy's Elixir, Godfrey's British Oil (it is better than its sullied Name, claims prop. Horace Goodhue); Angelic Pills & Everlasting Pills. Also, the finest Opium Powders. For the Complexion— Hungary Water & La Virginis perfumed Water.

   Queen Str. adjacent to Morgan Print Shop

Cam Gant slept the rest of the day like a dead man. Libby worked feverishly on the gazette, worrying constantly about his loss of memory, and often darting upstairs to observe him. She also went next door to the Goodhues' to ask them if her patient really could have lost his senses.

"Heard of such only twice before," Horace told her sagely. "A blacksmith out in Flatbush got kicked in the head by a horse. Took years for his memory to come back. The other poor soul got attacked by savages on the Mohawk River in the fifties. His whole family got massacred. He was scalped and left for dead. I always thought maybe he wouldn't want his memory back anyway, tragedy like that. Never heard what happened to him. Blows on the head is funny things."

She pondered that as she watched New Yorkers pass the shop all day, heading for the ferries or the more rural reaches of the island in case the British fired again. In a way, they had all been hit in the head, by the reality of war, she mused. And all they really had to be thankful for was that the gunship had shot lead and not fire bombs this time, or the entire city might have gone up in flames.

In the afternoon she sent Rob over on the crowded Staten Island ferry with a note she'd signed Cam's name to, telling Cam's man Montague he was going to be out of town again for a while and needed a change of clothes, some personal items and a nightshirt. Later she dismissed the staff early and waited, pacing, downstairs until Rob came back with food and ale from a nearby tavern. She usually prepared her own cold suppers now that Hannah and Sally were gone, but in case Cam awoke she wanted something hot and hearty for him tonight. She had been pouring cider down him all day, and each time she had raised a cup to his lips she had prayed he would wake. But he hadn't.

She washed her hair in rainwater and brushed it out. Its deep red tendrils curled and bounced below her shoulders. Despite the warmth of the late-August night, she wore her

dressing gown over her old work dress in case he woke. He slept on, breathing deeply and regularly.

She sat in the chair by the bed and watched him, wondering whether, when he did awake, he would recall all that had passed between them. Would he also forget that he had seduced her only because it was his duty? This morning he had seemed so sweet and loving, so sincere, that her heart had gone out to him. Her imagination had run wild at the thought that his memory might not return. And, whether it did or didn't, what should she tell him? She wanted to keep him here as long as she could—but only because the British wanted him to help them again, of course.

She tried to read by lamplight, but she'd been setting print all day, and her eyes hurt. She flopped the book closed and gasped to see his hooded eyes on her.

"Oh! You're awake!"

"And not in my bed at Melrose. I—I thought I was. I thought we had just...been together. Such thoughts and dreams," he admitted, making her cheeks heat as his eyes roamed her tousled hair and *déshabille*. "Where am I? What happened?"

She scooted her chair close to the bed, stalling for time. She must choose her words very carefully so as not to alarm him or make him bolt—not that he was going far. He was plainly weak and bewildered. She was tempted to try to smooth everything over between them, to create the lovely world of her most secret dreams. But she had no way of knowing what he recalled now or would tomorrow. Besides, even though it was still war between them, she owed him the truth—most of it.

"You're here in my rooms above the print shop, Cam. We were together when the British warship fired on the town."

He tried to sit up, but she pushed him gently back against the thick pillows with a hand on his good shoulder. Even at that slight exertion his pale face flushed hot with pain.

"New Yorkers tried to move the big guns from the fort clear up to the Highlands," she went on quietly. "Don't you remember any of that?"

"No. It seems I should, but no. Who else got shot?"

"Too many. No one here dead yet. One British soldier, we hear."

"So, you're going to get your early war, Libby Morgan," he said weakly. "Oh, my head... How long have I been here? I've got to get up...things to do..."

"No!" she said. Then, more quietly: "No. You've lost a lot of blood, and I'm going to take care of you. It only happened last night. My friends next door are apothecaries, and they helped patch you up. Here, this willow bark is for pain. Chew it, and I'll warm up some stew for you. I've sent news to Melrose that you're all right, so don't worry about anything."

He reached weakly for her wrist as she tried to feel his pulse to check for fever. "Then I'm to be duly grateful and utterly cooperative as a guest in your bed, I take it?"

She met his intense stare and decided to ignore the innuendo. "I will take very good care of you, Cam."

"But you obviously haven't told my people at Melrose where I am, or they'd be here. They or the servants from my house in town."

"Your house here? I—I don't even know where it is," she stammered.

"Maybe there's a lot you don't know about me," he said. He sighed and loosed her wrist. "The house is on Broad Way Street, overlooking the Commons. Maybe you could send your boy there for some clothes for me or money if you need it. And tell them where I am."

"They've sent some things from Melrose," she told him, but her mind raced. She had no intention of having anyone, even servants, rush in here to rescue Cam for his British cronies! She broke off a small piece of the willow bark and put it in his mouth to quiet him. His tongue touched her

fingertips as he thrust it back out at her. She annoyed herself by jumping at the merest touch of his mouth to her
skin.

"The Commons...that's where the guns everyone was
moving ended up, isn't it?" he asked, his voice fading, his
eyes closed.

"Yes. Do you remember, then?"

"Only bits and pieces. My whole head hurts, Libby. My
teeth, too. If you could maybe chew that a little first, then
just put it in. I'm so damned exhausted again, and when I
move..."

"You won't have to move. Yes, I can do that," she
assured him with a pat on his good arm. She chewed the
bitter stuff to start the juice flowing. She wondered then if
he was still suspicious enough to want her to taste anything
odd first—as if she were trying to poison him with hem-
lock, the way Socrates's enemies had him. Surely it hadn't
come to that between them! But she needn't have wondered, or even have chewed the bark for him. He was fast
asleep again.

She sighed and spat the bark into a saucer. She went into
the adjoining smaller room and collapsed, exhausted, on
the narrow straw bed. But she couldn't sleep. How to keep
him here, unsuspecting, as he got better, and then get him
out of town so that the British would not have access to
him? How to keep him from wanting to go downstairs?
How to keep him from being spotted at a window as he
got stronger?

Well, she thought, she'd just have to keep him so amused
and entranced that he didn't want to leave for a while. Then
she'd think of something else. Perhaps delaying what he
had to tell the British after his little five-week jaunt to the
other colonies would be enough of a contribution to the
cause of freedom. She had to do something, after all, to
make up for helping rile the Brits into firing on a town that
had only muskets ready to fire back with. How she'd like

to haul some of those big cannon right down to the waterfront and give the *Asia* some of its own medicine!

Medicine. Her thoughts drifted. Cam. She wanted him
well, but as soon as he was recovered he would leave her
for the British. Earlier than that, if he suspected they were
looking for him. She had to keep him happy while he was
in her bed. She moaned and thrashed about on her little
bed of straw, dreaming she was in her own deep feather
bed with him.

Two days later, after he had eaten several meals of soup,
stew and rye bread, Libby decided Cam was strong enough
to sit in the chair while she changed the linens. His memory
had returned in bits and pieces, and she sometimes wasn't
certain what he recalled. She had read to him nearly the
entire gazette but had playfully refused to have Coll fetch
him Jemmy Rivington's latest "loyalist tripe."

They had gotten on very well as nurse and patient, she
thought, relieved. It was much safer and saner than the way
they behaved as adversaries and lovers. But as she stripped
the bloodstained linens from the bed he put the two of them
back on slipperier footing.

"The last sheets I remember seeing had your blood on
them, and now it's mine," he said, taking her unawares.
"Does that make us even somehow?"

Her quick movements halted in midair, then resumed,
even faster now. "No more than it makes us even that the
British came calling on us both the morning after!"

"And you obviously handled them just the way I said
you would. That icy tone of voice implies, I take it, that
you know full well they came to see me—not to question
me, but to share my breakfast and have me tell them all
about the Turtle Bay raid."

She whirled to face him, the crumpled linens clasped in
her arms. "You said it, not I!"

"If you're still going to be as prejudiced and blind as

usual, Mistress Liberty, I don't feel even like speaking to you. But I'll tell you the truth, since you've been honest with me.''

He stared her down, as if he were daring her to make some confession. She clasped the sheets tighter, gripping her hands together under them. She hadn't lied to him about anything that had happened. She simply hadn't told him that he was wanted by the British. But there was surely no way he could know that. "Talk, then," she said.

"The British came to tell me that someone had seen me riding up toward Turtle Bay late the night before. They asked me if I'd seen anything suspicious. If I had supplied them with names—or with the woman's shoe I had in my possession—you and your radical friends would not have gotten off so handily.''

"But, no doubt, they believed you. They didn't believe *me*."

"You are welcome to draw your own conclusions.''

She almost apologized for not having trusted him before. She had to remind herself that this could be just another of his elaborate traps. Still, she felt herself softening toward him, as she had so often these last few days. Her powerful feelings for him made her understand one way people became turncoats, and it scared her.

"Thank you for being honest with me," she said.

"As you have been with me," he countered.

"So, let me get you back in bed. Just settled in to rest, I mean," she added hastily, wishing his merely looking at her that way didn't rattle her so. "The Goodhues gave me some daisy ointment to take the soreness out of your bruised shoulder muscles.''

She smoothed the new sheets and helped him back into bed. "How about my legs?" he said, his voice low. "They're almost as sore.''

"Well, I suppose. All right. But maybe you can reach there yourself.''

"I'd never have taken you for a coward, Libby Morgan."

She surprised herself by laughing. "There are no cowards left in New York, Mr. Gant. They've all fled. You should hear that Vile Governor Tryon's latest threat," she went on, her hands on her waist. "He may have magnanimously granted that the cannon can stay on the Commons, but he also declared if any Crown goods or weapons, big or small, are moved again without his permission, the *Asia* and the *Kingfisher* will fire on the whole town!"

Cam shook his head. "No wonder there's an exodus."

"Let them run!" she cried. "When Washington and his troops get here for the victory, they'll wish they stayed!"

"Libby," he said, taking her hand in his, "I'm starting to remember the night I was hurt. I believe I said then that the greatest American weakness is an excess of optimism. It's dangerous, you see. We've got to be confident but wary. Overly realistic, not overly idealistic. Not in this war."

She stared deep into his silver-gray eyes. This war, he had said. And it was the same for the other war the two of them were waging—no matter how alluring he was or how deeply he moved her woman's heart. She had to remember that he had used and betrayed her before and would again. She had to be strong.

But as she unbuttoned his nightshirt and slid it off his shoulder to stroke the ointment into his bruised muscles, she wavered. She stroked his skin carefully around his shoulder bandage and then—though she knew better and was too stubborn to admit it—moved to his legs, where purple marks discolored his muscular, hair-flecked flesh. His skin radiated warmth clear up through her fingers, along her arm, down to the very pit of her belly and the juncture of her thighs. Little butterflies beat frantic wings in her stomach and tingled her nipples into hard nubs.

"It feels hot and good," he whispered, his head thrown back on the pillow, his eyes slitted to study her face.

She swallowed hard. This sort of rubbing, up and down and around, shook her to her toes. She was afraid she would pitch headlong against him, wrap her arms around his neck and cling to him forever.

"Mmm, so nice," he rasped out, and crooked a knee to uncover more of one big thigh that she had so carefully draped with his nightshirt.

"That's quite enough for now," she told him, her voice clipped. "I've things to tend to downstairs." She knew he had won this skirmish in their war. And he knew she knew it. She rushed from the room and scurried down the steps.

The next few days, though she still worked like a demon, for the first time in her life Libby begrudged the gazette the hours it took her away from Cam. When Eddie Tiler came calling, she almost threw him out the door. Sales were good. This week's issue covered the attack on the city, and she'd included much firsthand observation. Yet for once better sales and higher profits didn't thrill her.

That night marked a week Cam had been here. He was healing fast. She would not be able to hide much longer that the British wanted him, and it was obviously pure foolishness to think she could forcibly detain him. Only Rob and the Goodhues knew she had a man hidden upstairs. But the growing bonds between her and Cam terrified her as much as the fear that the British, the public or someone in authority would find out.

And tonight, dunce that she was, she had let him talk her into celebrating his continued recovery. She had promised to wear his sister's blue satin gown, which he had insisted she keep in exchange for the one she'd shredded to make bandages for him. Though he'd said jokingly that he didn't trust Rob with a razor so close to his throat, the Scotsman had shaved him. Tired of his nightshirt, he was now wear-

ing clothes Montague had sent with Coll from Melrose that first day. So far he had been more than willing to stay in bed. And Libby was absolutely petrified by the implications of all this.

They dined grandly on wine and fowl stuffed with oysters, which he told her teasingly were an aphrodisiac. Before she thought, Libby blurted out cheekily, "But probably not as effective as the Goodhues' secret herbal recipes I've been pouring down you this week. After all, who knows what was in those?"

They shared a warm laugh. He delighted in her enticing blend of shyness and spunk. He had intentionally been putting off getting up from his bed and walking out, as he could have and should have done. He needed to get out of here to see what was really going on. She had seemed very open with him, but she had been so distrustful and spiteful in the street the night he'd been shot that he dared not trust her to tell him everything. That night had eventually come back to him clearly, though he hadn't told her. Dare he think that seeing him wounded like that had brought her around to a reconciliation?

At times her frequent presence had tempted him almost beyond endurance, especially at night, before she went to the other bed. Such sweetness was what he had yearned for from her for so long. Despite his wounds and the weakness of his body, he desired her desperately. But they had hardly spoken of the night they'd made love. It was as if the subject were forbidden. He hadn't even kissed her, though he longed to, especially when she leaned close to plump his pillows and he could smell the alluring scent of her or peek like a guilty schoolboy down her bodice.

She filled his vision when she was in the room. She filled his daydreams—increasingly scalding ones—when she was not. She seemed agreeable and winsome, and yet the tart taste of the old Libby was there in her look and words. Damn, but there was something she was not telling him.

Still, if this was all some sort of trap, it was a wonderful way to go.

"Why are you staring at me that way?" she asked as she took away his tray and untied his big linen napkin.

"Don't I always? I was just thinking how stunning you look in that gown. That sky blue is much better on you than it was on Catherine."

"You loved her a great deal."

"I still do. My mother died bringing me into the world, so Catherine was the only mother I had. She is the dearest to me of all my family."

"Even more than your father was?" she asked, bringing a deck of whist cards over to the bed and standing there, nearly at his knee.

He nodded, but he didn't speak for a moment. "I realize how much you loved your father, Libby. But, you see, when you were just five, you didn't overhear him say he wished you would have died instead of his wife...that you had as good as killed your own mother...."

She stood stunned. He cleared his throat and glared down at his clenched hands.

"Cam, that's terrible. I'm so sorry," she whispered, and perched gently on the edge of the bed to put her hand over his fists. She hadn't sat on the bed all this week, not even when they had played cards to while away the evenings. Her thigh gently brushed his hip with a rustle of satin and crisp petticoats.

He shrugged. "At least he loved my mother."

"My parents were in love, too, despite a lot of differences between them. It helps to know that...looking for someone of one's own...." Her voice trailed off, and she looked away.

"That's right. Listen, I didn't mean to spill all that. It was your gown. I really miss Catherine sometimes."

Libby thought about how much she'd missed her father since his death. She even missed Mother and Merry, and

they were just over on Staten Island. How much harder to know that those you loved had chosen to go back to England, expecting you to stay here to run their business and watch over their estate for them like some hired overseer. How awful to carry the burden of believing your father saw you as the murderer of the mother you had never even known.

Their fingers linked on the bed. Their eyes held until his wandered down her throat to her shoulders and the low square neckline of the gown, then drifted lower.

"To cheer each other up, let's play for a kiss a point tonight," he proposed, with the impudent grin that so evoked the vulnerable boy within the hardened man.

"And here I thought you'd gone all pensive on me!"

"I may yet, if I don't beat you as badly as I have the other nights we've played."

"But not tonight! Not for stakes like that," she countered with a little chuckle.

Their moods swung again. In tandem, she marveled as she shuffled and dealt them each two hands. She relaxed so much that she didn't get up off the bed, and he just scooted over a bit to give them a flat surface. She won the first two hands.

"Will you claim your kisses now or later?" he asked, assessing her anew with his narrowed gaze.

"I'm not the one playing for kisses," she declared archly. "I'd rather have something worthwhile, like dinner at the King's Arms or Hull's in a few weeks, when you're better."

"A few weeks? I really would have to be promised something more exciting than two-handed whist at night to stay that long!"

"Cam Gant! Just deal."

He began to play with a vengeance, not only taking her tricks but flinging cards down. Even one-handed, for his left arm still pained him, he was deadly. Lady Luck tum-

bled so far his way that Libby began to wonder if he might not be cheating in some clever way. He won four points in a row, then six. The smug grin on his face began to annoy, then alarm, her. What had she gotten herself into tonight? Too much wine and good food, perhaps? This dress, and the special way it made her feel? The way they'd shared heartfelt things? His implied threat that he would be leaving soon? When she reached for the cards to deal again, he snared her wrists.

"Eight kisses, lady. Due on demand, and that's right now."

She knew her voice wasn't quite her own as she attempted a bravado she was far beyond feeling. "I should think that with all the free nursing you've received we're more than even, sir."

"A woman who won't pay her promised debts. Next I'll be thinking all sorts of dire things about you."

"All right, but I'm going to stand and just lean over you. Your shoulder, you know."

She jumped up and stacked the cards on the bedside table. Her skin tingled everywhere he looked, even without her watching where he was looking. She stepped closer to the bed; her knees bumped the mattress and bounced her skirts. One hand on the brass headboard, she leaned down slowly, and he tipped his head back against his thick pillows. Obviously she was being overly squeamish and virginal, she told herself. The man was, after all, laid up in bed with bruised legs and a useless left shoulder and arm. And he was her guest here, and he owed her a great deal.

But she had not forgotten the devastation of his kisses. Their mouths met slowly, gently, then pressed a bit as their lips parted. He outlined her mouth tenderly, wetly, with the tip of his tongue. She darted hers inside his slick lower lip to his teeth. Then his hand lifted behind her head to draw her even closer.

The kiss went on and on, until the room began to spin.

She put her free hand on his good shoulder to push herself away, but the hand he had entwined in her thick hair tightened, and his lips slanted harder, wider. She moaned deep in her throat. When she tried to lift her head, he let her.

"One," he said, so close that their breath mingled.

"I don't have the breath for two."

"Then I'll do it all myself. Give your mouth a rest," he told her, wrapping his arm around her waist and pulling her down against him to kiss her throat.

"Cam, your shoulder!" she protested.

"Don't struggle, then!"

His mouth meandered lazily down her ivory flesh to her collarbones. Somehow, one-armed, he slipped one satin shoulder of the gown down and kissed the bare skin he uncovered there. "Delicious," he murmured, nuzzling the swell of her upper breast. "Better aphrodisiac than any oyster!"

"Cam..."

"Kiss two. And now for three!"

He took her lips again, and she was lost. She wanted to be lost, wanted to give him everything and hold nothing back. At that moment he could have been King George himself and she would have been beyond restraint and reason.

She lost count of the kisses, of the places he touched her, even when a rogue hand meandered up under her skirts to skim silk stockings and gently grasp warm flesh above the highest ribbon garter. That same hand soon began to unhook the ruffled stomacher across her bodice. She noted how skilled he was at that, but it didn't matter now. She wanted to be closer to him. She had all week—for five weeks, for her entire life.

She helped him divest her of the bodice. The big puffed skirts and petticoats slid away. In her thin linen chemise she cuddled against him on his good side, molding her

limbs to his. She helped him undress himself. She tugged her chemise away so fast she heard it rip.

He scooted down to lie flat beside her; she shoved the pillows off to give them room. "No," he said, stopping her hand before the last pillow flew. "I want that one behind you."

He settled her against the pillow to prop her on her side. His weight on his good right arm, he half lifted himself over her to ravish her with kisses. Then he pressed her against the pillow and nudged her legs apart with one knee. She found herself pinioned in the pillow's softness with his hardness barely inside her.

"I've been thinking all week how to do this, wanting you...." he rasped in her ear as they merged and moved.

But his skin was so slickly hot from his exertions that she tried to sit up. "Cam," she said. "Your leg. Something is hurting—"

"It's all right. Not hurting as much as another part of me."

"But there's another way. If I just get on top..."

He lay back, panting. "Who the hell have you been experimenting with?" he demanded, his voice gruff. "Not that Tiler lad, or that roughneck Brooks!"

"If you're going to insult me, I'm getting up," she told him. "It's only that I used to ride horses astride...."

He started to laugh. She sputtered angrily, but then she chuckled, too. She could feel his breathing, his laughter, way up inside her when they were joined like this. She smoothed back the wild hair that had come loose from his queue.

"Now we'll throw this pillow on the floor, just as I wanted," she said, and wriggled it away while he groaned and pulsed hotter at her movements. He lay flat and pulled her above him. "Oh!" she said, amazed at how deep he went this way, when no one was moving at all.

"What number kiss were we on?" he asked, and pulled her down to take a budded nipple in his mouth.

She trembled against him. A great longing swept through her, a longing to belong to him, to possess him. Not just his body, like this, but all of him, his past, his future. Even his life today, to share it with him, whoever he was loyal to. The British be damned, she wanted to keep him here forever!

She lifted slightly and settled against him, then again. He moaned and moved his hips to push her on. "Oh, Cam, I can't!" she gasped out. "No more!"

But she did. They did. So much more. And there was only one thing that was not raw rapture that night. When a thousand candles burned with light and melted down to sparks inside her, he only kissed her hard again. In that ultimate moment of their union, she alone cried out, "I love you, love you so!"

Libby moved in a daze of happiness the next morning. It was almost like being wed to Cam, somehow, having been in his arms all night above the shop. Having wakened beside him. Knowing he was upstairs, waiting for her to visit, to chat with him, to eat with him, to sleep with him. Such an aura of radiance surrounded her that she ignored Rob Graham's knowing glare.

She greeted everyone who came in with a smile and waved to folks she knew through the window. And when Lawrence Lang and Garner Brooks entered with a huge order for the shop to print one hundred Oaths of Allegiance, she was beside herself with excitement—until she read it.

"See, at the bottom of every copy—" Garner pointed to the page "—be sure there's lines for twenty signatures. Then, anyone doesn't sign, we'll root them out of their holes and have them rotting in jail 'fore they know what hit them!"

"Arrests just for not signing?" she asked. "But I still think everyone has a right to his own opinions."

"Not if they don't believe in freedom and the rights of all men!" Lawrence Lang put in.

"But don't the rights of all men include the right to dissent? I mean, I really don't think this oath—"

"Whose side are you on, anyway, young woman?" Lawrence demanded. "Are you going to print them or not?"

"Yes, of course I am, but—"

"Well, then, we'll just get them the morning of our weekly meeting here, but we may drop by to see a proof. Word's all over town already, anyway."

As they departed, Libby gazed down at the handwritten Oath of Allegiance in her hand. It demanded compliance with a British goods embargo and complete fidelity to the Continental Congress. Many loyalists would never sign. It would mean more division. And arrests? Cam. She had to warn Cam what he would be facing. This order meant destruction of his family firm and possible imprisonment if he didn't sign! But if she just blurted all that out to him, he would get up and march out of here. And then he'd report this new offensive to the British out in the harbor when he took his other news.

Feeling terribly torn, she handed Rob the Oath and went slowly upstairs. She had to see Cam, had to savor their love, their confidences, their mutual trust. She wanted to kiss him again and cherish the memories of last night, even if he had not said he loved her when she had blurted out her deepest needs to him.

On the small landing, she took off her inky leather printer's apron and hooked it over the banister. She smoothed the petticoatless skirts of her plain brown working gown. It was almost as if that woman in blue satin last night had been someone else. She patted her hair in place and pinched color into her cheeks, though with Cam she

seldom needed such. She'd even taken to using some
scented Hungary water she'd bought from the Goodhues
for her complexion and been rewarded when he'd said she
smelled delicious.

With a little smile of anticipation on her face, she
knocked gently. When he didn't answer, she pushed the
door open, planning to scold the slugabed for still sleeping.
It had been nearly two hours since she'd gone downstairs,
and already she missed him.

The bed was empty. The room was empty. His few
things were gone.

"Cam?"

She ran into the small adjoining chamber where she'd
slept before last night, then peeked into the cramped storage
room. Her heart slammed against her ribs. Gone! But how?
Down the stairs and out the back way?

She tore to the back window that overlooked the delivery
alley. Deserted. She sank down on the narrow straw bed,
her head in her hands. But he hadn't given a hint! Had he?
And after they had shared so much! Drat the man! Had he
gone to his house in town, or to Melrose? To the British?
Had he somehow known she had ulterior motives and been
stringing her along all the while she had thought she was
tricking him?

"Bloody hell!" she swore. The curse would have given
her mother apoplexy. Cursing was something else vile she
had learned from that trickster. But what if his memory had
gone again? What if he was wandering around in New York
City without remembering what had happened?

Her insides twisted with worry. She'd tell Rob and Jos
she had an errand and go out looking for him. Maybe she
should send Rob out, too. She jumped up from bed and
tore to the hall door—and smacked into Cam. He was
garbed in an elegant dark green cutaway coat, matching
breeches and an embroidered waistcoat. In his good hand

he held his lion-headed walking stick, which she had not seen for weeks.

She backed away a few steps as he closed the door with his elbow. "Oh, you're all right," she blurted. "You've been...out."

"Indeed I have. It's been almost as enlightening as last night, though definitely not so much fun." His voice was hard and bitter. His face was stretched so taut it looked as it if might crack.

"I just came up here to see how you were...."

"I'm disappointed, Libby, though I should have known better. And I'm angrier than I've ever been and trying my damnedest to control it. I'd better get rid of this so I'm not tempted to use it on you for your lies and betrayals," he said, and heaved his walking stick across the room onto the unmade bed. He pressed her to the wall, his big hands hard on her shoulders.

"Cam, I haven't betrayed you. How can you say that after last week, last night?"

"Devil take you, last night was almost worth the price. How long would you have used your body to keep me here? I almost wish I had the time to find out. There's a word for women who use their considerable physical attributes to get what they want, you know!"

"Take your hands off me, you brazen bastard! It wasn't like that at all! And if it had been, we'd only be even for the other time you took me on to do your British duty!" Her voice dripped venom. She kicked at him and tried to duck away, but he spun her around and held her in a vise-like grip.

"If you still believe such callousness of me, we're through for good," he told her, his voice low. "Except, of course, maybe you'd trade me a quick tumble now and then for some cloak-and-dagger secrets I could whisper in your little pink ear!"

"You wretched, insulting—"

"But I'm complimenting you, my dear. I can't usually abide deceitful, disloyal hypocrites, but a night in your bed is almost worth it!"

She yanked an arm free and swung a fist at him, but he jumped back, and she only grazed his chin. Tears coursed down her cheeks. She hurt all through her, least of all where he held her upper arms to pin her against the wall again.

"I went to my house and heard there that I'm supposed to be out of town, according to a note I sent to Melrose," he told her. "And my loyal servants tell me that the British—Governor Tryon, no less—have been looking for me since the morning after the attack. You knew that, of course!"

"What if I did? We don't need you reporting all your spying to him!"

His tone was brutal and mocking. "*We* don't, eh? I assume that means your radical cronies know all about your special treats and tricks for keeping me here? Crispin Brooks, or maybe the Tiler boy?"

"He isn't a boy! Stop saying that!"

"But I will admit," he plunged on, ignoring her fury, "I had hoped that at the least you were taking care of me from Christian concern—but that would have meant you would have had to tell me the truth for once."

"*I* tell the truth, you liar!" she choked out, hurt and angry beyond reason. Let him think what he would! "All right! The biggest lie I ever told was that I loved you!"

"Love's the last thing I want from the likes of you!"

She lost control then, jerking in his arms, scratching and kicking until he stilled her. The old nightmare of being caught on the Melrose estate strangled her. He despised her, even after all she'd done and given to him. It was the Gants, with their dogs and horses and torches, chasing her again, only to throw her out when she wanted so much to be part—

She hung breathless in his iron grip, but then she lifted

her chin to defy him as best she could. "There's an Oath of Allegiance that will ruin you Gants and your wealth," she spat. "You'll go to jail. They'll hound you the way you have so many others!"

He loosed her shoulders and stepped back. She locked her knees to keep from crumpling at his feet.

"So I heard in the streets. How long have you been reveling in that thought while we traded hot glances and hotter kisses I won't even consider," he threw back over his shoulder as he turned away. "I'll send money for the week's nursing, Mistress Morgan, and see the Goodhues are compensated, too. As for your other...ah, services...I dare not ask the price."

"But, you—you still won't go to the British!"

He shrugged. "I'm on my way there now. There's nothing to keep me here."

He went out and slammed the door, leaning against it for a moment to catch his breath. That double-edged tirade had wounded him again, as if they'd swung swords at each other. He'd lied to her at the end, for he knew now she would never trust him, and without trust there could be nothing more, no loyalty, no love, however much he longed for it. It was better to crush any remnants of what had been between them. He blinked back tears. Despite her perfidy, he deeply regretted having hurt her. They had declared themselves enemies now, and he would make her pay the price for that if he must. He went down the steps and out the back, as he had done earlier. He strode down the alley to the street, not looking back. When he realized that he'd left his walking stick, he did not consider returning for it.

If he wasn't careful, he'd be absolutely no good to Washington. He wouldn't be able to keep him informed and help him decide when he would have to come to this hornet's nest with what troops he could afford. That time was getting closer and closer. But for now he had no choice but to see what the British brass wanted. If he didn't, he'd get

himself arrested, just as he would if he didn't sign that damn oath.

Governor Tryon had been a close friend of his brother's, but he had no idea whether Tryon was going to reward him for scolding that Whig crowd or chastise him for not taking a stronger Tory stand. Perhaps he'd tell Tryon some of the truth, he mused grimly. He'd say he had lost his memory when he'd been wounded in the British barrage. After all, since Libby Morgan had come into his life, he had almost lost his mind!

Nine

~~~~~~~~~~~~~~~~~~~~~~~~~~

OATH OF ALLEGIANCE

*The Continental Association does hereby declare
& publish the Banning of all English import'd
Goods to New York & other Colonies. The un-
dersigned will swear to obey the Continental
Congress & honor all such Embargoes. Names
of Nonsigners (hereby to be termed Inimicals)
will be printed and posted for Censure & possible
Arrest.*

Provincial Congress of New York

* * *

THE LIBERTY GAZETTE

*Already the Association Ban has caus'd Hard-
ships in our beset City, but we shall overcome.
See specific Information below:*

- —To trade or resell steel Pins & Needles
- —To trade or resell recent Books
- —To use parched Rye & Chestnuts to replace
  Coffee
- —To use Molasses and Pumpkin to replace
  Sugar

> —*To make Gowns from Chair Covers or Stock-*
> *ing Ravelings*
> —*To make Dyes from Walnut, Hickory, & Wil-*
> *low*

Libby had plunged from ecstasy to catastrophe in one short morning. After her bitter separation from Cam, she seemed perpetually short-tempered. Even happy events made her want to cry. The spunk seemed to have gone out of her. Though she signed the Oath of Allegiance her patriotic friends believed in so firmly, she didn't think others should sign it if they didn't want to. But the oath of allegiance her heart and soul seemed to have taken to Cameron Gant caused her far more grief.

She did not see him for endless hours, days and weeks, as Indian summer settled into true, crisp autumn. It was best, she told herself. She never wanted to see him again. Yet she longed for him. Even her thirst for revenge could no longer fuel her hatred.

The exodus of New Yorkers continued. Some fled a few miles away; others returned to England. She feared that Cam might do that some day to be with his beloved sister, especially now that no Gant imports were allowed here. But she'd heard that he was around town, and that he had evidently been applauded by the British governor for trying to stop the movement of cannon to the Highlands. He traveled some, too, she heard, and she tried hard to convince herself that he was just trying to shore up his doomed import business and not spying for Governor Tryon or some other British leader.

Cam had sent her an outrageous sum of money for his week's nursing, every guinea of which she had donated to buy American ammunition. She had made certain the donation was in his name and noted in the gazette. She hoped it made the British suspicious of him.

One mid-November night, after her staff had departed, Libby did not light a lamp. She was always cautious to avoid drawing attention to herself alone in the shop after dark. Mobs of unemployed dockhands too often roamed the streets at night lately, wrecking property in the name of "freedom." Unlike the old-time Sons of Liberty, they were just drunken ruffians looking for an excuse to punish those they thought had caused the embargo.

She sighed as she continued to set type by feel and mere familiarity with the place of the letters in the composing trays. Her mind, as it had been too often lately, was miles away. The lonely, cool dark suited her.

She jumped at the knock on the print shop door.

"Libby? You inside there? It's Eddie!"

She put the stick of type aside and wiped her hands on a rag. Eddie had been gone for over a month on drills to Albany. She hadn't known the Second New York was coming back. She'd have to get a story from that.

She hurried to the door to unbolt and open it. "How good to see you! Come in, Eddie!"

"Upon my word, it's dark in here, Libby!" He stepped in as she fumbled with the tinder wheel and lit a lamp. He squinted at her in the new splash of light, looking rather stiff in his brown uniform with its blue facings. He cradled a tall black bicorne in his free hand. He looked older, leaner, stronger, and she admitted to herself she liked the change.

She smiled as he bent gallantly to kiss her hand, then pecked her on the cheek. "Indeed, you do look fine, soldier boy!" she exclaimed.

"Don't tease, Libby. Look, I know I shouldn't be popping in this late, but we're being sent to camp at the Battery tomorrow, and then who knows where. I had to see you."

"I'll bet you have a lot of adventures to tell," she observed as she watched him lean his polished musket in the corner, then come closer again. "I'm glad to see you look-

ing even more fit than a lobsterback regular!'' She hoped desperately that some of Cameron Gant's money had gone for bullets and powder for Eddie Tiler's gun.

He captured her hand again. They leaned sideways against the back of the stationery counter, facing each other. She would have liked to ask him up to her rooms to give him a dish of tea, but without a chaperone that just wouldn't do. She blushed at the memory of Cam upstairs. She'd given him far more than a dish of tea, and the thought of his presence never gave her peace there anymore.

"I know times are tense and real uncertain, Libby...." Eddie's earnest tone drew her attention back. "There's a fight coming, and we're both gonna be in it in our own ways, and, thank Providence, both on the same side.''

She nodded and forced Cam's face from her mind's eye again. "Libby, you know how I've felt about you for a couple of years now. I know the feeling hasn't been quite mutual.''

"I admire you a great deal, Eddie. Especially lately, I assure you.''

He beamed. "You're the kind of woman patriot that deserves a hero, someone great, like Washington! But I swear I will always do my best to defend you and our homeland. And, Libby, I think you're doing such a fine, fine job here with the gazette that you ought to keep on doing it, though I didn't think so at first.''

Libby sucked in a breath and held it. This was a heartfelt speech, with more maturity and strength than Eddie Tiler had ever shown. It was surprising, and comforting, too. Perhaps it was just what she needed.

"I'm saying that,'' he plunged on, "because I think you ought to consider marrying me. I mean, I'd be willing for us to live here, though I used to hate the city. Not that I'd be here all the time right now to take care of you, with the war coming and all, but I'd get leave sometimes. And after it's all over I'd start my own bricklaying business here in

town and you'd have the paper—till youngsters came along, of course. Why, we'd have the world! Oh, Libby, I really, really love you so!''

How long, she wondered, had he been practicing that speech. It was exactly what she had wanted to hear, but not from him. Her knees wobbled; she grasped his hand hard before she realized he might get the wrong idea and gently tugged it back.

"What an honor," she said, floundering. "A surprise."

"I would of asked your mother first, but there just wasn't time."

"Yes, I understand," she breathed as she turned to the counter to prop both elbows there.

"I don't mean to be real forward, but I want to hold you, Libby. Kiss you!"

She hung her head. Here was an honest and honorable man offering her what any sane woman would want—what any really patriotic woman would value—and her traitor's heart belonged to a traitor! But if she married Eddie that would have to mean the end of her forbidden longing for Cameron Gant. It would show the world, show Cam—and her own foolish heart, too—that it was over. And yet she could not bring herself to use this fine man like that.

"Eddie, I just don't think—"

"I wouldn't need an answer right this minute, of course, springing it on you like this. I mean, I've been thinking this over for months, and it's all new to you."

"It isn't just that, Eddie. My feelings for you…"

"I know I always cared deeper for you than you did me. Love would grow between us, both ways, I know it, Libby!"

"It wouldn't be fair to you," she protested gently with a slight shake of her head. "Believe me…."

"It's just you need a real hero to sweep you off your feet. That's it, isn't it?" he demanded, his pleading voice hardening. "You know, I overheard you and Merry talking

about it once, being swept off your feet. I know I'm not the sort. I'm not like that Gant fellow, rich and handsome!"

"Eddie, please—"

"But I can be someone you'll be proud of and look up to. This private's uniform's not enough, I know that. I'm only earning five dollars private's pay a month, when a colonel gets fifty. But I'm going to do things to make you proud, work my way up to colonel, get you great stories for the gazette, even. We'll work together, you'll see!"

"Honestly, it isn't any of that. Eddie, I'm sorry, but I just cannot accept. The times the way they are, my life's in too much turmoil."

He grabbed her hands and pressed them to his lips. His words came hot between her fingers. "But turmoil's what's gonna make us free, my angel! Just don't say no right now. Give me a chance, just a few days, and you'll see about being swept off your feet, you'll see."

He smacked a quick, hard kiss on her lips and scooped up his hat from the counter. He grabbed his musket and stood looking back at her, silhouetted in the open door, as if he were guarding the place for her against ruffian mobs, hordes of British troops...even Cam Gant.

"Eddie, I just don't want you to plan on—"

"I'm planning on you changing your mind when you see how proud of me you'll be!" he said, and closed the door behind him.

She walked slowly over and shot the bolt. She carried the lamp upstairs. She felt shaken by his energy and assurance. It almost matched the zeal she had felt once for the paper and for the patriotic cause. This had been a new Eddie, strong and appealing, but it had exhausted rather than invigorated her. What sort of special duty, she wondered vaguely, did he intend to volunteer for to turn her head? She smiled for once as she went into her bedroom. Perhaps his visit and his fervent adoration were just what she needed in her desolate, chaotic life.

Then the lamp caught the glint of Cam's gold-headed walking stick, leaning in the corner by the narrow hearth. She should have had Coll take it back to his house, but she couldn't bear to part with it. There it stood, in sharp contrast to the musket Eddie had propped in the corner downstairs tonight.

She sighed. She lit the hearth kindling from the lantern and waited for the flames to take the chill away.

Libby's shop hummed and thumped with the noise of the press, but her ear was always attuned to the front door opening. She sat doing her accounts on her tall stool behind the stationery counter. As usual, when the door widened with a sweep of cold November breeze she looked up instantly with the fierce expectation that it might be Cam. But this time her heart fell, then beat faster, as Quentin Simpson and two slovenly companions entered.

"Quentin," she said warily. "I know it was months ago, but I don't think you should have come back here."

He walked over to her, while his rough-looking companions seemed content to stand back and watch the press in action. Quentin placed three morocco-bound books on the counter, then removed his hat to hold it over his chest, as if he were going to recite a speech.

"That's why I stayed away so long, Libby, hoping you'd find it in your heart to forgive me."

She sighed inwardly, wishing it had been Cam come to speak those very words.

"My behavior was terrible just after Father died," he went on. "But I'm off the poxy liquor now. It took me this long to be willing to face you. I've changed, Libby," he said, his round, flaccid face almost quivering with sincerity. When he was not mocking or enraged, he resembled his father, she thought with a pang at the memory of her late godfather. She felt herself waver.

"I accept the apology, Quentin—for your father's memory."

She thought for a moment that his bulldog look was back, but it passed quickly. "Speaking of my father, I brought you these three books from his library I've been selling off, ones I thought you'd like for old times' sake."

"Quentin, how kind!"

He rattled on, proud as a peacock, as he presented her with *Robinson Crusoe*, *Pilgrim's Progress* and a collection of John Locke's work.

Would wonders never cease? First Eddie's proposal last night, and now this revelation. Yet her heart did not thrill as it would have before Cameron Gant had ruined her happiness.

"And Libby, there's something else I'd like you to consider," Quentin said, lowering his voice with a glance back at Jos and Rob. "Books like these are pure gold right now, with the embargo keeping out new ones, and I've some money to invest in a worthy venture in my father's name. And I'd like it to be in the expansion and improvement of your gazette. No other ties than that," he insisted when he saw her surprised expression, "but I'd like to see that poxy Jemmy Rivington and his blasted gazette ruined. He took the Oath, but he's still printing Tory trash, the hypocrite. But you're my father's heir, too. With my backing and your brains, we could put Rivington out of business together!"

"Quentin, I just don't know. I'm not out to ruin Rivington, though I would love to outdo his rabidly royalist paper! But an investment in your father's name—"

"Look, I apologize for the uncalled-for things I implied about your...your relationship with Father last time," he said quietly. "I was jealous of his good will toward you, that's all, as he had—rightly—little enough toward me. But I regret that sorely!"

Tears came to her eyes. In the past she had hoped she and Quentin could be friends, but when he'd said those

awful things she'd detested him. Now she forgave him and sympathized completely. What deeply agonized and finely expressed things he had admitted today, and at what cost to his pride. Eddie and even Quentin Simpson knew how to be amiable and humble. Why not that pompous, pious Cam Gant?

"Libby, you look angry still," Quentin said. "How about it?"

"I've never intended to take a partner, Quentin, not even a silent one.... That is what you meant? I do intend to keep control."

"Of course that's what I meant. I know you need time to think. Let me take you to a coffeehouse for a quick supper this evening, and we can discuss it further. At least," he said, as if he sensed she would say no and wished to head her off, "for both our fathers' sakes. They were such good friends."

"Quentin, I just don't know. Well, maybe we could have supper, if you'd let me bring Jos along to hear your proposals, too," she said. Surely if there was anything amiss in his intent that would flush it out.

He looked surprised. "Old Jos? Why not? And if our deal goes through, we'll buy him that fine wig he's dreamed about for years!"

"Yes, all right, I'd like to go, then. If you promise not to drink more than a little ale," she added, and met his gaze, which had darted again behind her to where Rob and Jos had the press thumping away.

"No more poxy Jersey lightning or pocket flasks, I swear it," he told her as his gaze met hers. His mouth twisted in a little grin. "I'll meet you and Jos at the coffeehouse diagonally across from Rivington's at eight, then. Enjoy the books."

"I shall, Quentin. Thank you so much. I'll never sell them, no matter what."

He frowned as if she had scolded him, but the look

passed quickly. He gestured with a snap of wrist to his two companions. She came around the counter to walk him to the door, despite the way the two gawked at her, as they had everything else in the shop. Perhaps tonight she'd suggest to Quentin that he change the friends he kept, now that he had changed so much else about himself.

When they had gone, she walked back to the counter and tenderly opened each volume. She stared down at dear Atwood's name, scripted on each flyleaf. At least, despite the hard times in life, there were little victories along the way, she thought. Cam Gant might have turned out to be her enemy, but perhaps poor Quentin could be salvaged, and perhaps he could help the paper, too. She had never quite managed to get it back on the same steady footing as when Atwood had been running it.

"Mistress, what'd you make of those two blockheads with the master's son?" Jos demanded, so close behind her she jumped. "Mark my words, they're trouble! As for Quentin, hain't seen one like him change his stripes yet, neither."

"Perhaps it's only the drink that made him so dreadful, Jos, and he seems to have control of that. I hope you don't mind that I said you'd come along tonight. I felt I needed a chaperon."

From his place at the press, Rob snorted. "Listen, Jos," the distinctive Scottish burr rolled out, "the mistress is sure old enough to know she can't trust men just by what they say and how they look." He gave the devil's tail another double yank to thud the platen to the tympan to punctuate his words.

Libby just glared at Rob, though she didn't say another word as she took the books upstairs. Rob Graham and the Goodhues were the only ones who knew she had spent unchaperoned time with Cam Gant, and she didn't need the wily Scotsman knowing how it had devastated her. Besides,

a man who kept a pistol hidden in a basket of rags in the back room wasn't completely trustworthy, either.

The coffeehouse on Queen Street, just across from Rivington's, smelled of pipe smoke and corned beef and cabbage. Chill drafts swept the floor whenever someone came in the door. From their table near the bowed front window, Libby could see the street. The coffeehouses were only busy at night these days, since the province's financial business had been ravaged by the embargo. She had not been out to eat in a coffeehouse since the day months ago Cam had rescued her from Rivington and his friends. She scolded herself as she forced her mind back to Quentin's words. Why did she always have to think about that blackguard Gant? The first thing she'd done when she'd come in here tonight was to skim the heads, looking for a silver-blond one!

"Admit it, both of you," Quentin was saying. "With my backing—in my father's name, as I said—you can expand enough to challenge Rivington's royalist cause!"

"'Scuse me for putting it this way, Mr. Simpson," Jos observed, "but I always took you for the sort who didn't 'specially have any cause but yourself."

"Jos!" Libby exclaimed. "Can't you see Quentin's really changed his ways?"

"Exactly, Libby!" Quentin said, seizing her hand. Though she didn't like the smug look on his face, she did not pull back. "And you're about to see a demonstration of how well I get things done these days—long-time scores settled, for example."

"What do you mean?" she asked, suddenly wary at his new tone. She tugged her hand free of his with difficulty.

"Well, for example, Rivington always hated my father, so I'm settling that debt tonight in my father's honor. Say, let's drink to that. Tapman, a jug of Jersey lightning!"

"Quentin, you said you wouldn't drink much tonight!" she protested.

Jos cut in, "Let 'im talk, and listen well, mistress."

"Rivington hated my father. He probably hates you, too, but he's doomed!" Quentin said with a strange grin. "And, quite frankly, little Libby, if you don't sign this paper I just happen to have along that gives me half share of the so-called *Liberty Gazette*, I'm going to have to believe you still hate me, and deal with you, too. Ruin your gazette, too, as it were. Ah, the drinks. Thank you, tapman," he said, and tossed a gold guinea down on the table. "See, my dear Libby, money and power to burn these days, so just sign."

"Quentin, you've greatly misled me!" Libby was furious. She bounced to her feet. "I thought you'd really changed!"

"Sit, mistress! You, too, old man! But I *have* changed, my dear. My ways of doing things are completely different now. Ah, yes, for example, just look outside a moment."

"Jos, we're leaving," she said, and started to rise. Quentin seized her arm and yanked her back. Jos leaned over to grab his lapels. Quentin half rose to shove him back and then pointed out the window.

Despite her mingled anger and dismay at having been taken for a fool, Libby squinted through the glass. In front of Rivington's a crowd had gathered, and many of the group had torches reflected in the windows of the darkened print shop.

"What is it?" she asked. "What are they doing?"

"The show—and your lesson, dear Libby—begins!" Quentin crowed.

She and Jos stared as the crowd shattered Rivington's front window and smashed in the door. Whoops and cheers carried even into the coffeehouse.

"Quentin, you knew about this!" she cried. "Stop them!"

"Why should I? It's the answer to your prayers, too! Admit it! And I'd suggest you sign this paper quickly, so the same sort of thing won't happen to the *Liberty Gazette* some night. Or, who knows what the authorities will think tomorrow when they hear Rivington's chief rival and her head journeyman knew ahead of time to come watch the destruction while they enjoyed supper." He lifted a tankard of liquor in a mocking toast.

"You vile liar! You're demented. I'd never sign that," she cried, leaping up and running for the door.

"Then bid farewell to my father's shop. The son of a bitch should have left it to me anyway, you little whore!" he screamed after her.

Horrified at the chaotic scene and at her own stupidity, Libby started across the street. Jos, who had followed, pulled her back. "No, mistress! Don't you see he's right about that? We can't be seen here!"

"I don't care! Someone's got to stop them and warn Rivington. We'll have to run down to his house at least!"

"I'll go. I'll go if you'll head home. I'll send the first fleet-footed lad I meet. Go on, now, and lock yourself in before that demented soul in there comes after you!"

Libby and Jos glanced back at the coffeehouse. Quentin Simpson's silhouette was outlined in the window by the lanterns inside. He had set this up, but he was too craven to join in it, Libby realized. And she had been thoroughly taken in by him, because she had wanted so much to believe he'd changed.

"It's a good lesson for me," she told Jos, though he could not know all she meant by it. She pushed him off in the direction of Rivington's house.

She had one blurred glimpse of the ruination of Rivington's print shop as she fled. They had not burnt it, but the torch light revealed wholesale destruction: the precious imported type being looted; the presses smashed with iron bars; files and paper piled in the street for burning. The

mob seemed like a grotesque blur, but for two individuals who stood out by the freakishness of their silhouettes: a one-armed man and a bulky, black-haired giant.

Tears blinding her, Libby ran. Pain tore at her side; the shrieks of the mob seemed to chase her. She stood, gasping for breath, at her front door, fumbling in her knotted bag for the key. And then she realized that someone was inside when no one should be.

Quentin's threats hit her full force. But this was no mob. Breathing hard, she peered sideways in the front window. A single shuttered lantern that they must have lit sat on the counter. Two forms hunched over her type cases—the two gawking louts who had come with Quentin that day. And they were stuffing handfuls of her irreplaceable type into pillowcases.

She pressed her fists to her mouth, then tore next door to the Goodhues'. The door was locked on a darkened downstairs. They were probably above. She couldn't scream for them, or the thieves might bolt with the type. Holding her side, she ran around into the ink black alley and let herself as quietly as she could in the back door of the print shop.

She slid in slowly, hoping the boards would not creak, but the louts were making a clatter dumping the type into the pillowcases. She heard them begin ripping paper; one man laughed.

She felt for the gun Rob kept in the rag basket, praying he had not taken it since last she'd looked. Her fingers closed around its carved wooden handle. She hadn't shot in years. The gun wavered in her hand as she stepped to the door of the front room. She put both hands on the gun to steady it, and lifted it stiff-armed. She moved slowly into the room behind them.

"Stand, both of you, or I'll blow you to kingdom come!" she ordered, though her voice shook. "I'm going to scream for the neighbors now and if either of you vile

cronies of Quentin Simpson so much as blinks an eye I'll shoot you in his name—for old times' sake!''

Late the next night Cam Gant stood in the shadows across the street from the print shop, feeling every bit the spy. Libby's shop windows were ablaze with light; her entire staff was working late. No doubt she intended to put out a special issue of the paper that would knock the stockings off the city now that Rivington's had been pillaged. But he had come because a friend had told him her shop had been broken into last night, too, and that she had caught the thieves singlehanded.

He shook his head in disbelief and chuckled low at the stupidity of the robbers in taking on bold and plucky Libby Morgan. Yet he had trembled with fear for her when he had heard. The thieves had implicated Quentin Simpson in planning the attack on both print shops. Simpson had been locked up in the city jail. But Cam still wasn't taking any chances on a mob turning up here tonight looking for revenge. Besides, he just couldn't stay away from her. He was, he had finally admitted to himself, at the very least obsessed with Libby Morgan.

The knife-edged wind sliced through his clothes, and he wrapped his cloak tighter around him. He could see Libby's red head wavering through the distortion of the thick windowpanes. She seemed a mirage, a distant vision he could never possess. He had done everything he could think of to stay away from her. But he had failed. And if just hovering close like this to catch a glimpse of her and knowing she was all right was not enough, he wasn't certain what his longings would drive him to. At any rate, she'd probably curse him if she saw him.

The little witch had dared to print a public thanks to him for his donation to the colonial arms fund in the last gazette! Wait until Washington read that. And Governor Tryon, too, for he had intentionally courted the royal gov-

ernor to see what inside news he could pick up. What he'd
gleaned was all bad, at least for New York City, and he
had sent it quickly to Washington. The British fleet was
being sent piecemeal from Boston to see how many of the
ships it would take to squash the rebellion here.

Cam heaved a huge sigh. He had thought about making
Libby's use of his name in the gazette an excuse to see her.
And at least ten times he'd had to talk himself out of calling
on her just to retrieve his gold walking stick. But any talk
between them would no doubt lead to mutual recrimina-
tions again. She didn't trust him, and he didn't trust her.
And, in the long run, things wouldn't change, even if their
meeting precipitated a passionate reconciliation again.

A huge sneeze racked his shoulders, and he fumbled for
his handkerchief to blow his nose. He'd even considered
signing that damned Oath of Allegiance to make her realize
what side he was on, but he didn't believe in such publicly
enforced loyalty vows for either side. Surely people had a
right to their dearly held beliefs. Though he wouldn't be
much good to Washington in jail, if the rumors were true
that people who didn't sign might be arrested. And, for that
matter, what good would he be if he caught an ague out
here, staring in Libby Morgan's window?

A bitter smile curved his hard lips. If he was on his
deathbed with lung fever, perhaps she'd come nurse him
again. Strangely, that week upstairs at the print shop, which
had begun in such pain, had been the happiest of his life
since Catherine had left with Charles for London. He had
missed such feminine companionship. But in New Haven
last week, when he had tried to force himself to enjoy another fetching woman's company, the experiment had left
him cold. He sneezed again and stamped his booted feet to
warm them. Damn Libby Morgan and the day he'd met
her!

His mind drifted back to the first time he'd seen her,
dirty and defiant, caught by the hounds at Melrose. Her

gaze had glared hotter than the torches. Her dignity had put them all to shame. He should have spoken for her then, but he had been firmly under Charles's thumb, trying so hard to earn his trust in his mad rush to make up for his father's hatred.

He supposed that explained his boyhood passion for pleasing his elder brother. Perhaps this longing for a loving father explained in part why he refused to forsake his vow to George Washington, no matter what it cost him. Even if it meant actually sacrificing his happiness with the woman he desired. Desired, and—the thought buffeted him inside as the wind did outside—the woman he *loved*.

He squinted his watery eyes to catch the quick flash of red hair in the lamplight within the print shop again. Yes, loved. He repeated the thought to himself, and it warmed him. But he knew the many things that kept him and Libby Morgan apart would only get worse as times went on.

How he'd love to tear across the street, kick in the door and sweep her up in his embrace. She'd always made him feel the savage. *He loved her!* He'd shout it out loud to her as he carried her upstairs to the bed they'd shared. He'd smother her with kisses and caress her warm flesh right through her gown. He'd lift her skirt and skim his hand up over her stocking to the sweet flesh of her naked thighs. She'd trap his hand there and protest teasingly, "But your hand is so cold, Cam Gant!"

"Warm it for me!" he'd say, and she'd shift those long, silk-skinned legs and moan deep in her throat. She'd toss that thick mane of stunning sunset hair across the pillow, and he'd make her promise—

"Ten of the clock, and a cold, blustery night!" the approaching night watchman sang out down the street.

Cameron Gant shook his head to clear it. He decided then to assign several of the warehouse guards to take shifts here at night to be certain she was safe. He couldn't afford to get caught lurking here. But his mind and heart would

be near her, even if the chances he took risked his very life in the months to come. Even if he never saw her again.

Before the watchman spotted him, he hurried down the windy street and away.

Ten

RIVINGTON'S NEW YORK

James Rivington, Royal Printer for New York, suffer'd a most iniquitous and ruinous Blow after Dark on November 23. His well-known Newspaper was pillag'd & loot'd by a ruffian Mob who know not the Meaning of free Choice & the Right to free Speech.

Articles below include an Interview with James Rivington; Royal Governor Tryon's Warnings; & unfair Treatment of Non-signers of the Oath of Allegiance.

THE LIBERTY GAZETTE

The Gazette is appall'd by the Demise of Rivington's, but proud to print both Whig & Tory News Today. Never let it be said those who believe in their own Freedoms shall rejoice when such is denied to Others.

Articles below include detail'd eye-witness Accounts of wanton mob Destruction which must cease; News of attempt'd Thievery at Morgan's Printshop; & resulting Arrests.

The special double issue of the *Liberty Gazette* sold out, and demands for more kept rolling in. Coll ran out with armfuls of the barely dry copies and returned with empty hands and bulging coin pouch. Late into the next night Jos and Rob turned out more copies Libby dried over poles and lines not only in the shop downstairs but all over her rooms above.

The next morning, a crowd of citizens—both Whig and Tory—formed outside the shop to buy the landmark gazette that spoke boldly for everyone's freedom of speech. Faith Goodhue came over to take the money, and people went away with issues still damp from the press. Horace Goodhue appeared at midafternoon to shove cold meat and hunks of bread into inky hands while they worked on. By afternoon the torrent of demands for the paper had finally become a trickle.

"Our supply of shillings may be up, but I can't believe how low our paper supply is," Libby told her journeymen as they took a short break for cider that Coll had brought back with him. "We'll have to order more from the Staten Island mill. And that reminds me," she said, her mouth full of gingerbread, "I want to take copies of this issue to my home island to sell them. Those Tories over there will buy these for once!"

"The Tories will buy all right, and the moderate Whigs, too," Rob put in as he returned to pulling the devil's tail. "But your staunch Whig friends got a wee bit of a burr under their tails over it, I'd say."

"Blistering mad!" Jos put in as he reinked the type with the mushroom-shaped dabbers. "Free speech only so long as you believe right along with 'em, mark my words."

"The way of the world, man," Rob added with a grunt as he yanked again. "Ne'er did see true freedom or true friendship yet but when I was out in the Highlands once, and that all by myself, wi'out another soul in sight!"

Libby brushed her hands free of crumbs and peeled the

paper from the type. "I only know true friends stick by you when times are hard, and you have done that for me," she told the two men. "I haven't been able to pay either of you what you're worth up to now. But with this big success today you'll both have a bonus."

"For my part of it," Rob said, a twinkle in his eye, "you can invite that bonny lass Sally Smith back for a nice visit."

"She promised her mother never to live in New York, Rob. Because of the too-obvious dangers here," she added pointedly.

"Aye, you might know a thing or two of that," he said. "But she promised me she liked the city much more after she saw my knees under my kilt, you know. Besides, if the lass be banished to Staten Island, I might have to move there myself, and miss all the fun of coming here!"

Libby just rolled her eyes at that. She didn't trust Sally with the wily Scot any more than she trusted herself with Cam Gant. "Jos," she said, to change the subject, "maybe you can buy that wig next door with your bonus. Fannings would sell it to you and let you pay the upkeep fees as you go, I know it."

Jos's bloodshot eyes met hers. He looked exhausted, his brush of overnight beard offsetting his shiny bald pate. "With tougher times a-comin', mistress, just don't know about that. Today success, tomorrow we might all be scrambling to put food in our bellies. I'm squirreling coins away, but I still can't see getting the fine peruke I fancy till I know I've got the money to keep it up. This colony may be jumping into war pay-as-you-go, but it ain't my way to trust for something if it's not right in my own two hands."

They all fell back to work with a vengeance, but Jos's words kept bouncing through Libby's brain. Trusting for the future, believing in something or someone you didn't have under control...

Sometimes you had to risk that. The times she felt most alone without Cam she thought he'd be worth any risk. How desperately she wanted to trust him, to believe the things he said. But he was never under her control; nor were her chaotic feelings for him. It was both awesome and awful. She had never really felt lonely before she had loved and lost Cam Gant, and now, without him, life seemed somehow dulled and muted, even after a victory like today's.

By late afternoon they had a stock of forty extra printed papers, twenty of which Libby hoped to sell on Staten Island. She sent everyone home at last for some much-needed sleep. Half dozing on her high stool behind the stationery desk, she manned the shop herself. When folks came in, she jerked awake. But when they left she'd nod off again, exhausted, propped up on her elbows, her mind drifting. When she looked up and saw Cam Gant in the doorway, she blinked and shook her head. Her insides cartwheeled; her cheeks heated. She sat erect on her stool. It couldn't be!

"Is it really you?"

"Have I changed so much, then?"

"I imagine, unfortunately, that you haven't changed a bit."

"And that welcome tells me you haven't, either."

He came in as if she had invited him. He even took off his cloak and draped it over his arm, and she saw he wore a dashing outfit of pale gray-blue, with a tan embroidered waistcoat and stockings. He closed the door on the chill draft and wiped his boots on the rush rug. He removed his black tricorne. He glanced around, and it hit her then that they were really alone. She felt like a blockhead, just gaping at him. Her voice, the things she'd had in her mind for months to rant at him scattered somewhere, and she couldn't find a one.

"You came for your walking stick."

"I'd appreciate it back, of course," he said, and put his gloved hand on the counter, entirely too near hers, "but I came to congratulate you on a bold and momentous issue of your paper. And not because you objectively printed Tory news for once. I admire the stand you've taken, not for either side, but for what is right."

She cursed herself silently for melting at his compliment and his steady perusal. "It needed to be said, Cam," she managed, as he put his cloak and hat on the counter. Her thoughts settled at last. "The harassment going on over the Oath is as unjust as what happened to Jemmy Rivington. It would be a sad mistake if any of us forgot that this coming battle is not over petty differences, but for larger things, like the individual rights of man."

"And woman," he said, and covered her clenched fists on the counter with his gloved left hand.

She froze. She didn't pull away or respond, but sat staring down at where he touched her. She dangled somewhere between laughing and crying, between ordering him out and jumping over the counter into his arms.

"At any rate, thank you for saying so," she added, her voice a mere whisper again.

"There is something else, Libby. You know you were a magnet for British interest before, especially after the Turtle Bay raid. They may be sitting out there in the harbor like vultures waiting for the kill, but they know what's going on in here. This issue of the gazette may make things worse for you."

Her eyes slammed into his. She drew her hands back to her lap. "I've no doubt you know all about British affairs."

"Don't start that again. I shouldn't even be here, and we both know it. The point is, this issue of yours appears to give something to both sides, but it also exposes the British and the Tories as bigoted, unfair oppressors. Therefore, you have become even more of a danger to them. Meanwhile,

your so-called political friends are probably chewing nails that you printed Tory news at all. Am I right?''

It bothered her that he knew her friends that well. ''They weren't exactly crowing from the rooftops,'' she admitted.

''I know you've never heeded such warnings from me before, but you're going to have to be even more careful in the future.''

''Believe me, I've learned that the hard way!'' she snapped, and jumped off her stool. She was annoyed at how stiff and wobbly her legs felt. She rubbed her hands nervously on the inky print apron she had forgotten to remove earlier.

''Oh, yes,'' she plunged on, ''I've learned to be more careful! You know, I almost fell for Quentin Simpson's friendly line the other day, and I won't mention the other man who, more than once, has taken me in for his own purposes!''

''Taken you in? Is that all it was, Libby?'' He yanked off his gloves, smacked them down on the counter and strode around it. ''You always accuse me of deceit, when you're the one who has lied about how we feel about each other!''

''You must think I'm a dolt to trust anything you say!'' she threw at him, backing up several unsteady steps. ''I know you now for what you are!''

''Do you?'' he demanded, and gently but firmly grasped her wrists. ''Then you know what I am is a poor bastard who can't get you out of my mind, waking or sleeping. You know I have been longing to touch you since I stalked out of here last time because you'd led me on and tricked me. You must think *I'm* the dolt to trust anything *you* say, and yet I'm risking being here, and all for this!''

He half lifted, half gathered her to him. She did not, could not, struggle or protest. She had yearned for his voice and his touch too long. Angry or sweet, rough or tender, it didn't matter. Whether he had actually come to warn her

of the British dangers or was that danger himself, for this one moment she didn't care.

She lifted her hands and flattened them on his chest, then slid them up to clasp his neck. She tilted her head back in surrender. He bowed his to offer the same.

It was as if they breathed intimately together in perfect unison before they kissed. But at the touch of their lips they caught fire. They stepped closer, as if they would merge. His hands caressed her back, and hers grasped the big muscles of his shoulders through his coat. Their tongues teased and darted. He slanted his mouth harder across hers and groaned. Strength seemed to flow from her and then rush back in a dizzying surge of need and churning emotions. When his hard hands pressed her skirts to cup each buttock to hold her tighter, she only pressed willingly against him. She fluttered kisses across his jaw and lowered her hands to his hips, too.

"Cam, Cam, we can't," she whispered raggedly, but she didn't stop.

"I know. Not here," he rasped. "I'll wait. Go upstairs and change, and we'll go to my Manhattan house. Dinner and talk, that's all, I swear it."

She laughed low. Locking her hands behind his neck, she leaned back in his embrace, savoring the feel of his arms without replying for a moment. She had never felt so happy. She hadn't really laughed for weeks...months. He wanted to be with her, to touch her! Then a little frown crushed her brow. He warned her about British and Tory dangers and then dared to invite her to go off with him alone. Ludicrous! And entirely tempting to her heart, no matter what her mouth said.

"Libby, you look tired, and thinner than I remember. Let's just go down the way then, and I'll buy us something to eat. Forget I was foolish enough to propose the other. As for our being together, now that you've put out such a

'pro-Tory' paper, maybe if you're also seen with me it will keep the British dogs at bay.''

"My, but you're a clever one," she said as she stepped reluctantly away from his embrace and leaned unsteadily against the counter. "Calling the British 'vultures' and 'dogs' to sway me, especially when people know you've been out to see Governor Tryon on his ship more than once!"

"That's the pot calling the kettle black," he challenged. "I don't doubt one bit you'd go, too, if you were invited, to get a story for your precious gazette. But don't flatter yourself I'm going to tell you what I have or haven't overheard, no matter what the bribe is this time!"

That annoyed her. But she knew she would hate herself tomorrow and all the long weeks to come if they parted with harsh words again. He might be a British spy, but he was the British spy she loved, she thought hopelessly.

"All right then," she told him. "I'll go out with you for a bite to eat. But I'm a rich woman now," she said lightly, "and I'll not have you spending one Tory shilling for me. Sit in the desk chair if you wish, and I'll be down shortly."

He sat behind the counter in her one good hoopbacked chair and watched her stack the remaining papers on a shelf and take her money box. He was delighted to find her more reasonable. Perhaps with a little shared talk and gently worded advice he could get her to realize he really meant his warning that she might be being watched—and not by the men he'd hired for each night, which he had no intention of telling her about.

Libby felt his eyes on her all the while she was straightening things. Her entire being leapt with life. She had become painfully, exhilaratingly aware of her body again—of the way she moved, the way she breathed. Wondering if she had entirely taken leave of her senses, she turned toward the stairs just as the front door banged open and her sister bounded in.

"Merry, I had no idea—"

"Oh, Lib, wait till you hear! A soldier friend of Eddie's came straight to Staten Island to tell his family! Then Eddie's parents came and told us all about what's going on, and Mother was furious you and Eddie didn't tell her first, about your being betrothed." The words poured out of her in a rush. "But, worse, Eddie told his friend he did it for you."

"Did what? Merry—"

"You haven't heard? Eddie's been caught on a British ship, trying to take some general's private papers for your gazette to print. Lib, he's chained in the brig on the *Asia*, and who knows what they'll do to him? Oh!" she cried as Cam Gant rose from his chair behind the counter. "Oh, Mr. Gant, I didn't know—"

"Obviously, but that happens to the best of us. Doesn't it, Libby?"

Libby's head spun. "Eddie's captured," she repeated dazedly. "And he told them all he did it for me? But I told him no, and I had no idea—"

"Mother says she won't have the banns for your wedding read in church till he's freed, Lib!" Merry added. "Besides, they might even hang him as an example to people sneaking on their ships looking for information!"

Cam's harsh voice cut in. "And here I was joking when I said you'd like a story off the British ships. But you'd already found a way—just send your doting fiancé to risk his life, since worming things out of me doesn't work anymore."

Libby spun back to Cam at last. "You have no right to think I'd do that—any of it! Eddie and I are not affianced, but I think more of his going out there like that than of your parading out there all the time for tea and treason!"

His face a stony mask, Cam shrugged. But he was stung to the quick again by the woman. He'd come to plead for caution and peace, but *she* had spent the days he'd been

longing for her seducing someone else! Someone she was evidently just as willing to sacrifice to her damned obsessive need for news as she was him. He hated himself for being so weak as to risk his mission or to think she wouldn't have plans of her own that ran entirely counter to his.

"Of course, Mistress Liberty," he said mockingly, "you can claim the poor boy's making up whatever stories he tells the British under their rather rough brand of questioning. You can insist the poor dupe obviously told his friends a pack of lies before he went out there for you. You can say all you want that you didn't promise—or already give—yourself to him. I don't know why I ever troubled myself worrying about you. This latest piece of mischief may even get you arrested for questioning, but you'll think of something to say, whether it's true or not."

"They don't dare arrest me! He didn't do it for me!" Libby flared, slamming the money box on the counter. But she knew that Eddie had very definitely done it for her. Still, nobody would understand that it had been because she had turned him down, not the other way around.

"Strange how a man's needs make him lose his senses!" Cam snarled. He strode around the counter, raking up his gloves, tricorne and cape. When he passed Merry, she pressed both gloved hands to her mouth and squeaked.

Then Libby saw it, too. A few heedless moments ago she would have laughed, but now it made her furious, with herself and with him. On Cam's gray-blue back smudged handprints gave clear evidence of the way she had grasped his back, his neck, his hips. When he spun to face their saucer-wide stares, she saw her handprints on his chest, his white shirt and his embroidered waistcoat, as if she had pawed him in her eagerness.

Cam glanced down at his shirt and grasped the situation at a glance. His tawny skin reddened. It was entirely too

obvious to Merry—and would be to anyone he met—what he had been doing with someone with inky hands.

"Who's next in line? You ruin every man you touch!" he threw at her, and stormed out with a resounding slam of the door.

Libby collapsed on her stool, and Merry rushed to her. "Oh, Lib, he was behind the counter when I walked in. I didn't know."

"I didn't know, either—not about Eddie," Libby whispered, and shook her head. Tears for Eddie flooded her eyes. The British could be beating him, even torturing him, and what would he tell them? And she cried for herself. She'd turned Eddie down. In a way, she had sent him out there on that rash, destructive deed. Everyone would believe it of her, just as Cam did.

"Merry, I swear to you—" she grabbed Merry's gloved hand before she realized she'd smudge her, too "—I didn't really send Eddie out there! I'd never do that!"

But she had once thought she'd never speak peaceably to Cam Gant again, either. She'd vowed never to touch him or let him touch her again. Yet today she had been willingly, passionately in his arms again. And now Merry knew.

"I won't tell Mother what I saw," Merry assured her, as if she'd read her mind, just as she often had when they were children. "About his clothes, I mean. Lib, it's so exciting! Cam Gant is so handsome and thrilling! But what about Eddie, then? I mean, Eddie's likely to marry you if the lobsterbacks ever let him go, but Cam Gant surely never would—"

"Oh, Merry!" Libby moaned pitifully through her sobs. "Oh, damn!"

Despite the curse, Merry put her arms around her weeping older sister and held her tight.

Libby's next issue sold almost as well as the last, but with results she couldn't have foreseen. The forty-gun Brit-

ish frigate *Phoenix* had joined the *Asia* and the *Kingfisher* in the East River, and one of her headlines read The British are Coming Back! Her other major story demanded Free Eddie Tiler! Free the Colonies!

That article contained a long list, including Mayor Whitehead Hicks and Cameron Gant, of those who had been calling on the British in New York Harbor for weeks, as if all were rosy. If others were allowed to go out to the ships for news, what had Eddie Tiler done wrong, the gazette demanded? Unless the British considered themselves officially at war with the sovereign province of New York, they had no right to keep a soldier of the Second New York Regiment in the warship's brig! New York citizens were still supplying their ships with food. Perhaps they'd like to trade their next meal for Eddie Tiler!

Other Whig papers took up the cry, and focused on other problems, as well. Trade had slackened off further with only one good result: more displaced dock and shop laborers joined the Continental Army. Private merchant ships trading with other colonies, some secretly, became the saviors of the city. Governor Tryon had deported to London all New York gunsmiths. One refused to go and that bold patriot was lauded as a New York hero second only to Eddie Tiler, lighting another slow-burning fuse. These two smoldering sparks were fanned to flames by the New York papers, with disastrous results.

New Yorkers panicked.

Low carts and high-slung carriages rumbled out of town, loaded with household goods for the packet ships to London. People clogged the roads, and the ferries were jammed. Abandoned property went cheap, though with the shortage of British pounds much of it just stood empty. Libby, who had thought the last exodus after the shelling had cleared out all the timid citizens, was appalled. Despite the first snow of the year, she went down to the Brookland

Ferry to ask people what had made them sacrifice their homes and trades to flee. Their answers both sobered and shocked her.

"Don't plan to wait here till this bay becomes a damned British lake, lady!"

"I'm sick to death of having my windows broken and hens stolen by so-called neighbors just cause I won't sign that blasted Oath!"

"Can't take another day of this town being held hostage for George Washington's good behavior down south!"

"Haven't you heard, woman? The Provincial Congress is gonna print paper money and back it by taxing us. Why, it's the same thing we hate the British for—taxation! No-siree, I can't trust nothing but good, hard, solid British pounds, and I can get them only in London town these days!"

She felt too sad to argue with any of them. As the cold river wind ripped at her skirts and cloak, Libby duly recorded their comments. The silver sky spat fine ice crystals that blurred her ink. She'd run out of imported pencils weeks ago.

She watched the ferry take another load of jostling people out to the waiting packet, which had brought in London supplies, but only for the British ships in the harbor. She glared out at the gunship *Asia*, squatting in the choppy pewter water. Eddie was still a prisoner there. What a mess things were in, and not likely to get better. She started forlornly away and saw the redcoat Captain Hector, who had visited her shop after the Turtle Bay raid. Thin and stiff, his eyes as cold as the wind, he was staring at her.

She glowered back before she remembered Cam's words of warning about being followed. But surely Captain Hector was only here to see citizens depart for his beloved England. She turned and walked away up the slippery cobbles, but he was instantly at her side, touching her elbow. She flinched away.

"I say," he began calmly, as if she'd invited him to stroll with her, "I can't see how you'll get a pro-New York story out of this mad exodus."

"If you've ever read the Bible, sir, which I doubt," she clipped out, "you'd know that after the exodus weaned out the weaklings it was easier to win the battle for the promised land. Good day to you."

He dared to spin her around to face him. "You are a cheeky skirt, my little rebel printer. Back in London you'd be both the scandal and the toast of the town!" he said with grudging admiration as his sharp brown eyes swept her.

"Let me pass."

"Not until we've had a little chat. I just put in after a chilly longboat ride to see you, so you'll not put me off. You know, I've read such passion in your paper for the likes of that wretch Tiler we have in the brig out there, I really thought you'd be much more, ah...warm to me."

She suppressed the insults that came to mind. They began to walk again, their shoulders hunched in the sweep of wind at their backs. "What about Eddie Tiler?" she asked, knowing she was taking his bait but hoping to avoid the hook.

"Why don't you tell me, my dear? And don't bother to deny it's true you're betrothed to him. I know full well he's the little soldier boy who came into your shop when I was there directly after the Turtle Bay raid."

"He actually told you we were betrothed?"

"Let me be both truthful and frank, Elizabeth." He startled her both by turning her to him again and by using her given name. "I hear tell your Eddie Tiler bragged to soldier friends that he was doing something bold for the woman who was his fiancée. Word's evidently all over the rebel camp and Staten Island who that fiancée is. Don't you bother to deny it, even if he does. And here I thought he'd be so proud of you he'd spit right out that you'd sent him

to visit the British fleet for the promise of your hand in marriage. I know I'd promise you about anything for your hand—and more.''

She yearned to rake his smug face with her nails. She walked faster, but he still strode easily at her side. "I resent your mockery and your unjust probing," she clipped out.

"Ah, but the point is, being an honest woman, you'll just have to admit all those things to me yourself."

"You are quite demented." Her shoulders slumped. She was going to cry in front of this demon; she could not carry it off. She felt alone and forsaken. Her vision blurred with tears. Poor Eddie, thinking he could earn her love. They were abusing him in the dank hold of a rocking ship, and still he told them nothing, while Cam Gant played the chatty Tory on the town with his wealthy cronies!

"Ah, tears...how touching. I see Eddie Tiler matters to you very much. How much, I ask myself." His kid-gloved hand lifted to squeeze her shoulder, then tightened when she tried to shrug him off.

"Our families have long been friends," she said.

"I say, cosier and cosier! Whatever you will or won't admit to today, my dear, I'm still pondering how much his life means to a self-sacrificing little patriot like yourself. Enough to settle down a bit with the paper, hmmm? Better yet, enough to show a dashing London officer a bit of hospitality far from home in these long, gray winter months? When we come ashore en masse, as come we will, think how nice it would be to have a friend among the conquerors, eh?"

She blinked back tears and stared him down until his avid gaze wavered. She fought to grasp the implications of his words. Blackmail? More mockery? A veiled threat? A demand she invite him home with her right now? A command she promise to become his mistress? Had Cam Gant boasted to these vile redcoats that she could be enticed and compromised? The thought of that cheapening betrayal of

the intimacies they had shared made her furious and care-less.

Before she thought, she lifted the wooden writing board with the stoppered bottle of ink tied to it and smacked his hand away. Ink spattered the snow at their feet. The board slid down to bounce off his boot.

"Thunder and damnation, you rebel wildcat!" he cracked out, hopping on one foot.

If she had not been so distraught, she would have laughed. She jumped back. "Eddie Tiler's innocent of all but loyalty to his country!" she said. "And if there's a patriotic woman in this city who can stomach being insulted by such ungentlemanly propositions as you have hinted at today, let me know and I'll print her name for the fool she is!" she cried. She stooped to retrieve her writing board and started to walk away.

"We'll be watching you!" he called after her. She was nearly running now, slipping over the occasional slick cobble. "I especially!" His voice swirled into the shriek of wind as she turned the corner and hustled quickly home.

Mid-December loomed dark and gray in Libby's heart. She thought sometimes that she was being followed by Captain Phillip Hector, but when she glanced back she could never see him. Even if there were other people on the street behind her, she recognized no one. Sometimes she was certain there was a man lurking across the street from the print shop at night, but she dared not stare out windows, and she convinced herself it was just her guilty imagination.

She never went out alone if she could avoid it. Unless her staff was staying late, she took most of her evening meals with Faith and Horace Goodhue next door. She both longed for and dreaded her coming holiday visit with her mother and Merry on Staten Island. Eddie Tiler still languished out in the cold harbor, so how could anyone enjoy

hot roasted chestnuts or stuffed guinea fowl or happy toasts to the future? And her mother's angry complaints about her refusing Eddie's proposal would be endless.

Other cares pressed in on her, despite her new prosperity. It was her first Christmas without her father or Atwood. She remembered the generosity of their gifts when what she had cherished had been the men themselves. And Atwood's son Quentin was still in the city jail, no doubt cursing both her and his father's name. Then, too, this would be the first New Year that she'd both detested *and* loved Cam Gant. War loomed. Goods were becoming scarcer. They would have been in even shorter supply if there had not been a few colonial merchant ships—some of which traded in secret, like the one they whispered on the streets about, called simply the Supplier. News from outside the city slowed as the roads became increasingly impassable. The only glimmer of good news was that Isaac Roosevelt, the prominent New Yorker in charge of producing provincial money, had given Morgan's Print Shop the contract for printing two, three and one-eighth dollar bills.

The Continental Congress, strapped for funds already, had refused New York a loan. With the colonists clamoring for solid British pounds, the Provincial Congress was planning to issue one-, two-, three-, five- and ten-dollar bills— with fractional ones to replace coins. Security was very tight to avoid counterfeiting. The printers involved had signed Roosevelt's honor affidavit, and bills would be hand-numbered and signed twice. The city's best silversmiths were engraving the plates, and Libby had just picked hers up this afternoon.

She had been asked to keep secret where she got the plates, so she had gone to the silversmith's alone. The sun had been out on the snow then, but the engravings had not been ready, and she had spent two hours waiting. Then, though the smith had promised he'd escort her home, his wife had taken sick. He'd released his journeyman and his

apprentices earlier to keep the process more private, as Roosevelt had asked.

So, in a sudden swirling snowstorm in the gray late afternoon of December 18, Libby found herself alone with her three precious engraved silver plates, clear across town from the print shop.

She stood a moment under the suspended gold ball of the silversmith's shop, wondering if she should avoid the open bowling green by old Fort George, even if it was a shortcut home. She tensed her shoulders and held her wrapped package tightly to her breast as she plunged into the storm.

Blowing snow swirled to confuse directions and obscure familiar landmarks. Still, she took the shortest way across the oval, grassy bowling green, walking briskly through the gray wall ahead of her. She tried to ignore the slicing cold and the shriek of the wind in the nearby trees. Then a tall shadow loomed ahead of her squinted eyes. She gasped in a throatful of cold air before she realized what it was.

"Only King George's statue," she assured herself in a puff of icy breath. Cloaked in a toga and mounted on a prancing steed, the statue was one third larger than life. Gilded lead on a white marble pedestal with an encircling iron railing, it frowned down at her.

"I hope you freeze!" she called to it, and went on.

It seemed to her that there was someone behind her, but who would be so foolish as to be out in this? Each crunching step in her sturdy walking shoes seemed to echo behind her. She stopped to glance back once, as if she could pierce the smoky white curtain that enveloped her. She was certain there had been a sound of someone else back there, but she saw nothing. She breathed a sigh of relief as she started up Pearl Street. She could walk close to the buildings here, some lit, some deserted. Yet in the sweep of snow it seemed too much a ghost city, as if the British had decimated it already.

The echo of her footsteps sounded louder here among the buildings. Close behind her, someone coughed. Again she spun back, and this time she saw a cloaked form jump between two buildings.

She began to hurry faster, though it seemed that with each step she slipped back. Phillip Hector's threats last week—and Cam's warnings—taunted her. She had made many enemies—even some among the fervent patriots she had always called friends. She nearly ran now through the gray darkness of the storm.

Distances deceived her; nothing looked familiar. Perhaps she should knock on the next lit shop door. Only about five minutes from home now, and yet so far. But what if someone knew she was carrying these engraved silver plates? What if they wanted more than the plates?

Her mind was darting far faster than her feet. Her breath came raggedly; a stitch sliced her side. Her arms clutching the package to her trembled. Her toes stung, and she was shaking with cold.

Yes, she thought as she dared another squinting glance behind her. There *was* someone following her!

She dashed for the first door she saw, but he lunged and pulled her down a dusky, snow-blind alley. Blood pounded in her brain. Red fear and hot panic melted the cold.

"Enough of your damned meddling!" threatened a rough voice she did not know. He wore a hood. A muffler cloaked his face. He shoved her hard against the brick wall. She hit her head and saw whirling stars in the snow. She fell to her knees, but he did not try to pull away the packages she gripped so convulsively as she opened her mouth to scream.

And then her attacker spun away.

"Get up, get home! Now!" another man's voice said close to her. He pulled her up and shoved her away toward the mouth of the alley. "Run!" he commanded. Behind her she heard the smacking sound of someone being thrown against the bricks.

Terrified, gasping, she slipped and stumbled the rest of the way home. The print shop had never looked so good and warm with its lantern spilling yellow squares out the thick windows.

What had happened, who her attacker and rescuer had been, she had no idea. She only knew that for once, no matter what, she would heed at least one piece of advice Cam Gant had given her. Long ago he had warned her against being out anywhere alone. Too cold to fumble for her key, shaking as if she had the ague, she pounded on the door to be let in.

Eleven

THE LIBERTY GAZETTE
February 20, 1776

Many, including our rever'd Leader, General Washington, are still toasting King George's Health at Meals. Some New Yorkers yet believe a Break with England can be avoided.

Now read the stirring Words of Tom Paine, Author of the new Pamphlet Common Sense:

"But where, some say, is the King of America? I'll tell you, Friend. He reigns above, & doth not make Havoc of Mankind like the royal Brute of Great Britain...Everything that is right & natural pleads for Separation...Reconciliation is now a fallacious Dream."

Paine's popular Pamphlet is now on Sale at Morgan's Print Shop, Queen Str.

* * *

A Call to True Patriots! If you are loyal to the Colonial Cause,

    —Ladies, wear your Hair unpil'd & unpowder'd!

    —Ladies, narrow your Skirts!

—*Gentlemen, donate your Coach & Pair to the Army!*
—*Save your Salt & we'll show them we're worth our Salt!*

Just after midnight, Libby Morgan got out of bed and stuffed her cold feet into stockings and shoes. Pulling a quilt from the rumpled bed around her, she shuffled to her bedroom window and wiped a circle clean of frost etchings. Her breath steamed the glass, but she saw that the snow had stopped and the clouds had cleared. She stood there, shivering, staring out across the moonlit snow on Queen Street and the rooftops of New York.

A dream had wakened her. Not a nightmare, but one so real it demanded she ponder it until she found some solution to a puzzle or problem. But using this idea would take a great deal of courage and risk. The lies and pretense she loathed in Cam Gant would become her credo until she got what she wanted from him, faced the British and freed poor Eddie.

In the dream she had gone in the sparkling snow to Melrose and spread a feast of food on a blanket on the ground. She sat among the food as part of the bounteous offering. A snow picnic. Now who would have thought of that awake? Melrose had looked so lovely in its pearly coat of pristine white. Cam had come out the front door, and she had beckoned to him. Arms outstretched, he had smiled and run through the snow, crunching it, making it fly.

Somehow, Mother, Merry and even Father were there then, reaching for the food on the blanket. But Libby asked them to leave, and they fled. She felt bad about that. She loved them all, and it had been wonderful to see Father. But she had to face Cam alone. Then both Eddie and Captain Phillip Hector sat down with her and wouldn't budge.

Rob Graham, with his pistol cocked and his arms crossed, stood a little way off.

Cam stopped in his tracks, frowned, turned and stalked back to Melrose while she called and called for him to come back. But then she awakened with her idea!

As she stood at the window, planning all the details, she unconsciously trailed her fingertip across the cold, frost-laced panes. Afterward, she was startled to see what she had traced on the glass. Eddie's name was circled and re-circled, but Cam's was hemmed in by a jagged heart.

"I have to do it...have to!" she whispered as she scurried back to bed. Outside, the snow lay quiet, but she could not until just before the dawn.

Cam Gant sat the next morning before his blazing hearth, drinking coffee, feet propped on a fire dog. Since dawn he'd been conducting business here. He'd already seen the man from his warehouse who had taken the night shift guarding the print shop. Nothing untoward reported there, except that Mistress Morgan had stood, a ghostly form, in her upstairs chamber window, gazing out after midnight while Cam's man had hunched across the street.

Cam and his accountant had reviewed the books for the remnant of the Gant fleet that had been in the colonies when the embargo had begun—two small packet ships, the *Sparrow* and the *Gull*. Captain Chester, who sailed the larger vessel, the *Gull*, had just left Cam. The *Gull* was anchored off Red Hook until the cargo from New Jersey could be unloaded and sneaked ashore to Manhattan under the noses of the very British who drank tea and gossiped with that trusted Tory Cameron Gant.

Cam sighed and shoved his plate of corned beef and eggs away. What in heaven's name would his brother say if he knew that Cam was using the failing profits of Gant Imports to turn the tide *against* Britain? What would Mistress Liberty say if she knew? Would it soften her ice-cold little

heart toward him—or would she print it, even if it meant exposing him to the British? He frowned at his coffee's bitterness as he downed the rest of it in one gulp.

His butler broke into his thoughts. "Sir, that visitor is here. You know, the one who comes and goes."

"Show him in, Andrews. And send for a plate of food."

Cam's contact with Washington spilled out his news as he ate and warmed himself. "The leader's considerin' sendin' a lot more troops here, but it's gonna be harder now. Half his boys' six-month enlistment term is out, and they've gone home to wait spring plantin'. The leader will come here himself with what he can make of an army if he must—but *when* he must still needs your say-so," he told Cam. "What's the count of Brit ships out there now, Mr. Gant?" he asked, and reached for another piece of buttered toast.

"Three new ones lately, all with big guns, and some Tory bastards spiked all the cannon in the city last month," Cam told him. "The twenty-four-gun frigate *Mercury* and the sloop-of-war *Savage* are new, and that third big warship, *Viper*. I'm trying to keep my eye on everything to decide when it might explode."

"All right, because our leader still needs all the time he can get before it does. That Private Tiler the Brits caught spyin's not helping, either. The leader's been real upset about the rabble-rousing going on in the Whig papers over that. He regrets the lad's predicament, but incidents over individuals have triggered wars before, eh?"

Cam rose and leaned his shoulder on the window frame to survey the street. "Eddie Tiler is no Helen of Troy. Still, I've been laying some groundwork for getting him sprung, though he doesn't deserve it for his stupidity."

He felt a stab of guilt at that. He, along with the rest of the city, had heard that Tiler had been ill out there in his winter captivity. But it was Libby he was angry with. Whether or not she'd gotten herself betrothed to the lad—

devil take her—she was welcome to him, if he was someone she could believe and trust. But she was the one who had, one way or other, sent that troublemaker out there. And Cam was furious with himself. Even with Tiler's life at stake, he still worried that she might marry the man out of patriotism, pity or just plain perversity if he managed to get him freed.

He was starting to think he had too many irons in the fire now: funneling both Whig and Tory news to Washington; avoiding making himself a target for those chasing Nonsigners of the Oath; trying to spring Tiler legally; forcing himself to stay away from Libby, whom he wanted to both soothe and strangle; and now helping to keep the colony on its feet with this secret import business!

But Washington had encouraged that, too, as it fed him information from the other colonies and sustained the city. Except for Captain Chester on the *Gull* and his closest staff at Melrose and the Manhattan house, no New Yorkers knew the Supplier's identity. He intended to keep it that way, and yet sometimes he longed to share that with Libby, if it would only make her think more kindly of him and—

"Well, we all got our own little worries, as well as the big ones," his contact said when Cam just glared out the window. "I'm off, then. Danged if you aren't the luckiest Tory-Whig fence sitter I've ever seen, Mr. Gant."

Cam swung around at last to accompany him to the door. "But the fence keeps getting higher and higher, and sometimes I'm certain I'm going to fall off, my friend. Good day and Godspeed."

He shook the man's hand and went back to the blazing hearth. He propped a boot on the metal fire dog again and leaned his arms on the mantel to stare down into the flames. He had a lot to do today. He found if he pushed himself at breakneck speed and went to his bed at night exhausted, he could sleep—at times—despite the hot, darting thoughts of dangers, destruction and Libby Morgan burning him.

"Sir, a boy just came with a note for you," Andrews said interrupting his musing. He extended a folded, wafer-sealed vellum letter on a small silver tray. All Cam's senses leapt alert. The note smelled distinctly of the sweet stuff Libby had worn the week he had spent in her bed.

"Was the boy towheaded?" he asked. He turned away and broke the seal as Andrews described Coll perfectly. Cam's eyes scanned Libby's scripted lines. He ignored Andrews, who was noisily clearing the table; the entire world receded as he read,

Dear C.G.,

Although we have ofttimes been on opposing Sides of Things, I would like to request that we mend Fences. Indeed, for my Part, I regret some hasty Judgments & overquick Words. Whether or not it does us any Good or Ill to be seen together, let us put aside such concerns & perhaps even avoid them by not being seen at all.

I know a lovely seclud'd Spot for a Picnic; yes, even with the Snow on the Ground. I know you are a busy Man, but with Today's Sun in the Sky, will you not join me at Crown Point in the Meadow overlooking the East River at mid Afternoon?

If not, I shall blame either your Business or my own previous sharp Tongue.

Best Wishes,
L.M.

He stared at her words until they jumped out at him. He read it a second, then a third, time. She wanted to mend fences, when he was afraid of falling off his! He chuckled for the first time in days. "My own previous sharp Tongue," she had written. How well he recalled the havoc that provocative tongue could wreak, both in her paper and

in his mouth! Weak-kneed, he crumpled back on his chair as his mind raced.

It could be a trap, but how? She was not meeting him behind closed doors, but at a secluded spot. He knew the place. It was very open there, so no one could lurk unseen close by or overhear. It would be worth the risk, even if all this was a ploy. Even if she pleaded with him to help Eddie Tiler. Even if he had to anger her by lying and saying that he could not help him, it would be worth another argument, just to be near her for a few hours. And her blatant dotting of perfume on this paper ravished his imagination.

"Andrews," he said as the butler took the laden breakfast tray out, "something's come up."

He almost laughed at that, as if he'd made a poor joke. The merest thought of Libby Morgan being sweet and yielding clamped his groin as if she already pressed against him. He recrossed his legs in the chair.

"I'll be riding out along the river for a while this afternoon. If that Captain Phillip Hector comes here before I return, offer him a drink and try to keep him here."

Andrews nodded. He could tell it was fruitless to ask or say more. His master's head was bent close over the note again, and he was inhaling deeply of its scent and grinning like a scarecrow.

Andrews shook his head and closed the door with his foot as he went out.

"Rob, how clever of you!" Libby told him as she surveyed the little cave of snow he'd cut into the far side of the hill overlooking the river. Here he could be in sight of the smoke from her fire on the adjoining hill and yet not be spotted from the blanket.

"Don't you go thinking it's all a big, braw adventure when you be dealing with Mr. Gant, mistress," he said, and shifted from foot to foot. He lowered his voice, though it was early yet and they could see no one on the distant

road or in the open meadow. "Now let's go over it again, though I don't like a bit of it. The man will be waiting wi' the rowboat to take you out wi' or wi'out Mr. Gant, and then you have to remember to—"

She patted his arm. "I know every step, Rob, and there's no other way. Indeed, I hate the idea of groveling before Captain Hector out on the *Asia* if I must, but I can handle him."

"Don't doubt that," Rob muttered, "but can you handle Mr. Gant? I've seen your face before when—"

"Just never mind! You do your duty, and I'll do mine!"

She hadn't meant to snap at Rob. She was agonizing over parlaying with Cam, but there seemed no other way to get help for Eddie. She felt so wretched that Eddie had gone out to that ship thinking he could earn her love and approval. He was such a patriot; he had adored her for years, and she could not help the fact that she did not love him. She should have demanded to know what he intended that night he'd left the print shop. She should have loved Eddie and not that Tory traitor Cameron Gant. She owed it to Eddie to do everything in her power to help free him.

So she would ask for Cam Gant's aid, even if she had to beg. If he refused at first, she would strive to convince him with encouragements or promises of her admiration and trust—and perhaps even seduce him just a little.

Yet therein lay the greatest danger. She recalled all too well his insulting words when he'd left her rooms above the shop. He'd declared he wanted nothing from her but for a quick tumble in exchange for his British secrets. She had no intention of risking a tumble, however much she longed for his touch. So, should things go completely awry and Cam refuse to help or try to stop her, she would play her last card. If she signaled Rob by putting the fire out, he would run in with a pistol to keep Cam here until she got away to Eddie's prison ship.

"I'm sorry for scolding, Rob, but I'm a bit on edge," she said as she started away.

"Just don't you be forgetting to ask Mr. Gant about having pretty Sally over for the next Sabbath," Rob called after her. She trudged back through the ankle-deep snow, circling far around the back of the hill so that there would be no tracks leading to her blanket from where Rob was waiting.

Her stomach knotted with nerves, she sat down on the black wool blanket and began to unpack the food. What if Cam didn't come? Sweet scent on a note, a picnic in the snow, the promise of as much warmth from her as he cared to read into her written words...what if he detested her so much now that he didn't find her appealing anymore? She blinked back tears in the strong sunlight off the snow and pulled her bonnet ruffles over her ears for warmth. It was poor loyal, patriotic Eddie she had to feel deeply for now, not Cam Gant.

She rearranged the array of food a third time. Sliced pheasant, minced pie, pumpkin bread, and a trifle that had broken apart on the ride out. She rattled pewter plates and tankards together as she placed them. She had water boiling from melted snow for some of Faith Goodhue's raspberry tea. She threw more dried pine branches on the little fire, and they crackled and popped. She would snuff out the flames with snow if she needed Rob to rush in. Now if Cam would only come!

Long minutes later, she heard a horse snort. She stood to see if it was hers. Her heart clanged against her ribs under her dark green cloak and gown. It was Cam, on his big stallion! Cam, coming to her just as she had dreamed and planned! He had always been more than her dream come true.

She fluttered a wave, and he waved back. He sat astride a moment longer, looking all around, then dismounted. He tied his horse to a barren bush close to her hired mount.

He took several things from a saddle pack, and she saw he'd brought a pistol. She shaded her eyes to watch him jam it in his belt under his cloak.

She bit her lower lip in fierce anticipation as he crunched toward her in the snow. Suddenly the day felt as hot as mid-July, and she was tempted to fan herself with a gloved hand.

He stopped a few feet away, and his eyes searched her face. "That's quite a peace offering," he said, with a nod at the spread of food. His voice was as crisp and exhilarating as the wind.

She had hoped to feel calmer. She stood her ground, though she had a powerful urge to run to him and hug him. "It is such a pretty day," she ventured.

"Getting prettier every moment. Oh, here, I brought you something." He came the rest of the way and extended a small box to her.

She opened and gasped. A white cluster of sweet-smelling gardenias stared up at her. "Oh, how lovely! They're real! But in the winter?"

"From the glass house out back at Melrose, where we grow things year round," he explained with a taut grin. "And I have some hot Jamaica spirits to raise ours."

He produced a large silver flask in a woolen wrap from under his cloak. She caught a glimpse of his pistol before the dark blue wool settled back around him. If she had to send for Rob, she'd have to get that pistol somehow, she thought.

"We'll start with a little toast to our private peace, if not to that impossible public one out there," he added with a sweep of his arm that encompassed the distant ships in the southern stretch of river.

Her gaze followed his, and she remembered why she'd done all this today. Eddie was out there, ill and perhaps close to death. She tilted her head and smiled at Cam. His eyes caressed her, but he stood frozen like an ice man for

a moment. Then he scanned the surrounding area while she held her breath. Evidently nothing caught his gaze on the next hill.

"I made the fire for some tea, but this sounds so much better, if you'd be kind enough to pour," she said, lightly touching his arm. She sat on the far side of the big horse blanket to give him plenty of room. But he sat very close to her as he poured tankards half full of the steamy amber stuff.

"How have you been, really, Libby?" he asked as he extended a tankard to her and watched her swirl the liquor.

"All right, considering the embargo. I'm amazed by low supplies and lofty prices, like everyone else. Thank Providence that men like the Supplier keep the city going. If people knew who he was, he'd be a hero."

"But he might also be captured or killed!" he said, more sharply than he'd intended.

"The British aren't stopping import ships or capturing their captains or owners. It would really mean war if they did. Of course," she mused aloud, as if a surprising idea came to her at the vehemence of his tone, "if the Supplier were someone the British think they can trust, then he could be in trouble. If they found that he was playing both sides of things, they might be very angry and want to make an example of him."

"I'm afraid so."

She paused with the tankard halfway to her lips. "You seem very concerned for him—and to know a great deal about him."

"Necessity."

"Cam, you— Who is he? Do you know him?" She stopped, realizing that her questions could be dangerous ones.

He watched raw curiosity burning in her beautiful hazel eyes. He admitted to himself how badly he wanted to earn her trust and confidence. Surely she would never print a

thing about the Supplier's identity, thus endangering the colonies' very lifeline. He gave her a great deal of credit for not blurting out further questions about the Supplier now, even though they were alone. Surely she had changed after all they'd been through.

Before he could halt himself, he nodded, and his lips formed a single word.

Her lower lip quivered, and she bit it. She nodded as if she understood. She could not tell whether he had whispered "Aye" or "I," but whichever it was, her heart overflowed.

"I suppose," he said slowly as he watched her take a sip of the spirits, "the Supplier feels it's worth any risk to serve the same cause you do."

"At any rate," she said, her eyes dewy, "he must be someone fairly well-to-do. He would have to absorb extra expenses and possible losses and be someone who had traveled to places before the embargo to set up supply lines. Don't you think so?"

"I do."

"And maybe he gets away with things because no one would ever suspect him," she concluded.

He watched her smile sparkle like the sun on the snow. His heartbeat accelerated. He longed to tell her more, about how he secretly landed the goods at Red Hook, and how he hoped to sail to New Haven with Captain Chester on the *Gull* tonight. But he could not tell her the rest—about how he was watching New York for George Washington because the general mistrusted the volatile citizens and had a severe shortage of troops. So it was still better to say as little as possible. For the moment, at least.

"Of course," she went on, choosing her words carefully, "it would ruin the Supplier if any hint of his identity ever found its way into the papers, even to advertise or praise his efforts."

"Exactly."

"I, for one, would never let it slip. Of course, I really don't know who he is anyway," she said teasingly, her eyes alight.

She breathed a deep sigh. Could Cam really be the Supplier? She wanted badly to believe it—to trust him fully. Then she could admit to him her desperate need to free Eddie and so free herself from guilt. But she'd been taken in so often, so completely, by men. She hadn't even known of her beloved father's deceits until he'd died. Quentin Simpson had been all smiles and hinted alliances before he'd turned on her. And Cam himself was certainly not to be fully trusted. After all, he still visited his British friends in the harbor. However long, however deeply, she had yearned for them to be on the same side in everything, she had to be very cautious.

"But I suppose, too—" she sat back suddenly for fear she might tumble against him "—the Supplier could be doing it simply to profit his family's British import business in trying times. The things he's imported still cost dearly, if you ask me!"

He looked as if she'd thrown snow in his face. "You know nothing of costs—never have!" he muttered. He glanced away, his narrowed gray eyes suspiciously surveying the scene again. "What did I expect?" he added, his look pure challenge. "That you'd believe me, maybe, but trust? Still, if this is a trap, it's a charming one."

"A trap? It's not— Well, only this kind…" she said, and forced a smile to her pouted lips. "I've missed you. I tell you, I greatly admire the Supplier. And I'm hoping he might supply me with a little kiss today."

She had to smooth things over. She had to move the conversation in the direction she wanted it to go. But, Eddie's plight notwithstanding, her raw need to touch Cam Gant frightened her. She leaned forward slightly to offer him her lips.

He took them faster than he ever had, more determinedly

and more hungrily than she remembered. All her carefully contrived strategies scattered. What was it she had meant to say next? He threw down his tricorne and tipped his head to get in under her bonnet brim. After a breathless, endless kiss, his lips trailed to the tendrils of hair loose before her earlobes.

"The hell with politics today," he rasped. "The sharp tongue your note mentioned seemed deliciously soft just now."

She fully expected to have to do much more convincing and arguing. She had developed a series of questions to be deployed while they ate to test his attitude toward her now. But this...so hot...so compelling and fast...

"Cam, I can't breathe! Aren't you hungry?" She rocked back on her hips a little way.

He caught both of her hands in his and removed her gloves and then his to grasp her, flesh to flesh. "Shall I even admit how starved I am, and for what? And if I did would you print a public thanks in the paper for it?"

He turned her palms over and pressed a warm, wet kiss into each one, loosing dangerous butterflies in her stomach. They fluttered clear down between her thighs. She almost jumped up and ran when she felt her nipples tighten to aching nubs beneath the layers of her garments. She tugged her hands back, and he let her.

"Cam—" she began to pile a plate with food for him "—I do hope it didn't cause you problems with the men you go see out on the ships when I printed you'd donated to the colonial army. I want to apologize for that."

"I think I'm getting very used to being either misunderstood or misquoted, Libby." He reached out to put a hand on her knee. "Perhaps I keep thinking our getting close again will eventually make up for it."

She thrust the plate at him. She hadn't quite expected this sort of capitulation. Holding hands, a few kisses, and

she was so rattled she was ready to get Rob in here already, before she'd even asked for Cam's help.

He removed his hand and took another long, lazy swig of hot spirits while he watched her. "Sweet of you to be concerned how I'm getting along with the British in the harbor," he observed, one tawny eyebrow skewed. "Dare I hope this is a new, solicitous Libby?"

"Yes, in a way. You've been right about so many things before, you see." She took a deep breath and forced herself to slow her words. "Like being followed. I regret I didn't heed your words. I should have trusted you much more.... I see that now. Especially after what you told me today. I can sympathize with those citizens who don't wish to sign the Oath. It's not liberty that they're harassed by that new city commander, General Charles Lee. I hope he hasn't bothered you. Washington sent him to set up city defenses, and instead he's chasing the so-called Inimicals!"

"How nice to know we agree about that, too," he said, and took a bite of mince pie. "Maybe there's real hope for us yet, Libby Morgan."

"And perhaps for you, Mr. Supplier," she threw back at him as he shot her a lopsided grin.

Devil take him, she fumed, how could he look both appealing and forbidding as he sat there cross-legged like an Indian, staring hotly at her even as he stuffed his mouth? But she had to make him want to help her and Eddie. She had to!

"I'm certain we agree about lots of other things, too, Cam. I've always been too concerned with our differences, when we have so much in common!"

"Such as?"

"You've wanted me to tone the gazette down to keep from riling the British sitting out there—like vultures, as I believe you aptly described them. And now I want the same thing, if I have a good reason to do it."

He stopped eating. "Go on."

"I'm determined to go out to the *Asia* and talk them into releasing Eddie, in exchange for a more muted voice in the paper. I want us to work together on this. I need your help. Please, Cam."

"So you can make secret trades with the so-called brutes in the harbor you profess to hate?" he demanded, with a raking look that was almost insulting. He put his plate down and reached for her wrist. She saw all too clearly the set of his jaw and the warning beat of the pulse at the base of his throat. "I'm sure they'd go for that," he told her, his tone mocking. "I know I would."

"I'm serious, and I'll be careful," she said, fighting to keep her temper reined in. "I desperately need your help to know the best way to approach Captain Hector about freeing Eddie. Maybe you'd even be willing to go out with me. I would be grateful. I thought I'd strike a deal with them— Now that I know you're the Supplier, I think the results would please you, too, Cam," she plunged on with a shaky smile.

"Please me, then," he demanded, his voice harsh. He pulled her to him. She tried to stiffen her arms and hold him off, but she slid against him right across the blanket as he wrapped one iron arm around her shoulders. "At last we're down to brass tacks as to why all this cosy sweetness today," he said, frowning. "I do, at least, thank you for spitting it out before dessert."

"That's not the only reason I asked you here. I have missed you, and I did want to apologize. And I thought, since you've so often claimed you were working for our freedom in your own way and your own time, that you would agree to help me free Eddie. Cam, please…I know I've made things a little difficult, but—"

"Difficult? My life has been a disaster since I've known you!"

"But I apologize. And I admit you were right and that I need your help."

"Only to help Eddie."

"Yes."

"No!"

"What? Why? Cam, please hear me out! I thought we could prove to each other that we can work together and trust each other from here on. I'm not going behind your back on this. I did tell you the truth. I'm not betrothed to Eddie, even if I do want to get him out off that blasted ship! Cam, please, I'm willing to return the favor if you'll only—"

"Return the favor? This way, you mean, and strictly to save Eddie Tiler's neck so you can do this with him?"

He pinned her against him, cradling her in his arms as if he held a baby. Her bonnet tumbled off and hung by its ribbons; his head blocked the sun. He kissed her hard, then lifted his big head.

"Even if I did believe all that, Mistress Liberty," he said, so close that his breath scalded her, "I'm not going to fall for this nonsense about a meek, quiet *Liberty Gazette*. And the British won't, either. If you didn't trumpet Eddie's release and all he's overheard out there, those other rabid Whig papers would, and I don't want that!"

She fought to keep her rampant desire for this man at bay. Had Eddie overheard something on a British ship that Cam didn't want her to know?

"Cam, I'll make a deal with Hector, or whoever has jurisdiction over Eddie, if you'll just tell me where he is and who to see. You've gone out to the ships, and I must, too!"

"But *I* haven't attacked them weekly in print, Libby. And I'm not a defiant temptress swishing my hips on a woman-hungry ship!"

He thought of saying he hadn't tried to outfox the wiliest soldiers on earth, but of course he'd been risking his neck doing exactly that. "Libby, they might trade you Eddie for something, all right, but would you be willing to pay the

same price to them you're evidently willing to pay me, like some prostitute?''

"*Their* price? A prostitute? I never meant that! Not with them, and especially not with you!'' she exploded. ''That's what it's always been with you, buying and selling, hasn't it, Mr. Supplier? And you might as well admit that the leader you report to is your friend Governor Tryon. You're trying to farm both sides of the fence!'' She tried in vain to push against his chest.

He laid her flat on her back amidst the spread of half-eaten food and stretched out beside her. Libby tried to catch hold of herself. *Use honey, not vinegar*, Rob had warned. She grasped Cam's shoulders and slid her arms up around his neck.

"Cam, I'm sorry. The price between us has always been my pleasure—and more,'' she admitted, and slanted a look at him through thick lashes. ''Yours, too, I think, so—''

He kissed her so completely her head spun. She dug her shoes into the snow near the fire to lift herself harder into his embrace. She did not realize she had scuffed snow on the signal fire.

"No more distractions for a moment,'' Cam said when he finally lifted his lips from hers. ''Now you listen to me! You'd be way in over your bright, beautiful head on a British ship. I hear Hector's not even in charge of Eddie Tiler, so just stay away from him. Some newly arrived general named Sir Sloan Boyd, on the *Viper*, has him since he's been ill, so there's absolutely nothing you can do. But I think something may happen soon in Eddie's favor if you'll just keep calm and hold down the roar in the gazette. If you'd only trust me a little for once!''

Libby quickly assessed what he had told her. At least she knew what ship Eddie was on and who to see. Cam had refused to help her directly and had tried to put her off with vague promises. But it was the evidence of his still desiring her, still caring, that made her head spin. Perhaps

she should trust Cam on this and wait a bit longer. She could not deny that her need for his approval rivaled her fierce need to rescue Eddie.

She smiled dazedly and nodded. She wet her lips with her tongue. Cam's toes curled in his stiff boots. She was tempting him far beyond his endurance, shifting her body closer to his like that. He leaned over her as her arms went around him. She pressed against him, then delved under his cloak to remove the pistol that stood between them. She was trusting him for once, believing in him!

He pressed her down. She kissed him hard, with her tantalizing tongue thrust in his mouth, until he didn't know or care where he was. Maybe he should tell her that Captain Hector was calling at his house today and that he intended to work further on Eddie's freedom. With this reconciliation, would she still jump to her usual conclusions?

Besotted by her nearness, by the soft feel and sweet scent of her, he reached for her waist, then cupped her bottom through her heavy skirts to clamp her closer. Unknowingly, she scuffed the last bit of snow on the fire. It went out in a dribble of smoke. Cam lowered his head to kiss her breast right through her cloak and gown. He elbowed his pistol aside on the blanket. He put one hand under her and slid one slowly higher between her knees under her warm skirts. Neither of them noticed Rob's stealthy approach with his gun until Cam felt the cold, hard poke of a pistol barrel between his shoulder blades.

"Hands off the lady, Tory! Now!" a distinctly Scottish voice clipped out as a hand snatched Cam's pistol on the blanket.

Cam lifted his head to glare at Libby. Her face was flushed, her mouth swollen with his kisses. She looked as startled as he to see Rob with a gun. Embarrassed, she scooted back away from him.

"Rob, I didn't mean to—"

Cam cut her off. "Damn you, woman! So, this *was* a

trap!'' he roared, getting to his knees and then slowly standing. "Snuggling up close just to get my gun away!"

"But I didn't mean—"

"And I was right that you were bargaining with your wares like a whore—with your procurer hiding just over the hill to stop your poor besotted mark before he could collect what he'd paid you for!"

"That's not fair, not true!" She was shaking in the face of his fury and his insults. They both ignored Rob Graham and the two guns he held.

"You're crazier than I thought if you want me as a hostage to trade for Tiler!"

"At the least, I needed to know where he was being held and by whom. I'm sorry, Cam. When I apologized today—that was heartfelt. But someone has to help Eddie before he dies out there, and your insults are a small price to pay for that. I did ask you here in good faith—"

He snorted derisively. "Good faith! From you? That will be a cold day in hell! And it will be a great help to Tiler when you get yourself in British clutches—the little rebel in skirts they all talk of."

"Talk of with you, is that it?" she said accusingly, her voice rising to match his.

Fury made him see red. She'd had him eating out of her hand in more ways than one. He'd even as good as admitted he was the Supplier. And all to free her fiancé, Eddie Tiler. She'd lied about everything else. She'd probably lied about that, too.

He ducked and lunged. He rolled at the Scotsman's knees, taking him and Libby down. Rob flew back into the snow, and Libby tumbled over him. He heard the breath smack out of her. Food rolled, plates clattered, tankards tipped, as she sprawled across the blanket. Rob fired off one shot over their heads, then scrambled away to point the other pistol at Cam's chest. Cam heard the distinct cock of the hammer of his own gun as he stood stock-still.

Damn the vixen! So she'd told this bastard to shoot him if he must. He'd fallen happily, hungrily, into the worst sort of seductive trap! Cam glared at Libby, despite the gun.

"You've driven me too far too long, woman!"

Stunned by events she had not foreseen, Libby flipped food and snow off her skirts and cloak in an effort to stall for time and find her voice. Her breath came fast through parted lips; her face was scarlet. Obviously, any hope she had of a truce with Cam was shattered now. But she still had to get out to that ship to help Eddie. She was appalled when Cam seemed to read her mind before she spoke.

"If you go out there, with or without me, I only hope I get a crack at you after they do," he said viciously. "Day and night, you couldn't print enough Continental money for what you'll owe me! You've got a big lesson to learn."

She trembled as she retrieved her bonnet and tied it on. "Afraid I'll learn something else dire and traitorous—and true—about you out there?" she snapped. "As for a lesson, Mr. Gant, I've learned I was a fool to expect your help when you offer only your ill will. So I have no choice but to detain you here a while."

She turned to her journeyman. "Rob, he's tricky. You'll have to watch him very closely. Don't trust a thing he says or promises."

"I take it, Mr. Gant, this means you won't be too pleased to have me come courting your housemaid Sally over at Melrose." Rob smirked at his own jest.

"Rob, don't make it worse!" Libby said. Cam ignored Rob, but his eyes burned Libby. Her hands shook so hard she could barely tie her bonnet back on. She knew she would have to face Cam's fury in town after his release, but she intended to sleep over at the Goodhues' and be sure she always had others around. She had to get Eddie freed before those brutes out there in the harbor killed him one way or the other! Her eyes met Cam's stabbing glare.

"Cam, I am sorry."

"Not as sorry as you'll be next time I get my hands on you. And then it will be on my terms, and my way!"

His voice and his expression were so fierce she jumped back as if he'd struck her. "I'll send the oarsman here as soon as I can," she told Rob, who had reloaded and now had both pistols pointed at Cam.

She had the strongest urge to show Cam he had not rattled her, though she felt shaken, as always with him, to her very core. As she started for her horse, she threw back over her shoulder, "If you two get hungry, we've hardly touched a thing!"

Except each other, deeply, deceitfully, too painfully to ever heal now, she thought. Cam's big black stallion whinnied sadly, as if in agreement, as she pulled herself up on the other horse.

Twelve

ROYAL PROHIBITORY ACT AGAINST ALL COLONIAL TRADE
Decreed & Sign'd by King George III & His Ministers

The Sovereign King of England & of the American Colonies does declare & decree that all Trade to & between said Colonies shall henceforth quit or be severely punish'd. Any Vessel large or small breaking this Decree shall be forfeit & those responsible fined, imprisoned, or hanged at the Will of the King's Army or designat'd civil Authorities.

* * *

THE LIBERTY GAZETTE

Fanning's Wiggery does hereby declare that our styles in Men's Wigs shall henceforth be American, not British Fashion. Come to Fannings on Queen Str. for most expert colonial Wigs of sundry fine Materials: human & goat Hair; Linen, Silk & Mohair. Wigs clean'd and recurl'd on hot clay Pipes weekly. Scratch Wigs & Tails available at reasonable Costs, Pounds preferred to

*printed Dollars. Also, for fine colonial Ladies
with their own Hair in American styles: Gauze &
flour Paste, foot-high Pads, head Scratchers, &
wooden neck Blocks for comfortable Sleeping.*

Libby's venture aboard the warship *Viper* went from bad
to worse. She was kept in her cold, rocking rowboat just
off the *Viper*'s hull until Sir Sloan Boyd agreed to see her.
She was hoarse from shouting her business to an officer up
on deck. Aboard, as Cam had predicted, she was ogled and
hooted at, while her British officer escort only eyed her and
smirked. She stood in a dark passageway for an eternity
before being admitted to the captain's cabin to plead her
case. Worse, she felt sick—not so much in trepidation at
this task or fear that she would not get Eddie out as in
raging regret at what she had done to Cam. She wished he
were here now, as this argument with Sir Sloan Boyd was
going nowhere.

Sir Sloan was a big man with an immaculately curled
and powdered wig pulled back in an elaborate ribboned tail.
He kept signing documents as they talked, so he peered at
her through spectacles perched on his ruddy, bulbous nose.
From time to time he tilted his head back to stare at her as
one might some sort of strange specimen. In this light she
could not even see his own eyes behind those fishy goggles.
She felt as if he were literally looking down his nose at
her—and at all her countrymen.

"Free the traitor Tiler? Absolutely out of the question.
The spy will be released when and if we are quite through
with him. As for your gazette, I'd like to knock the whole
thing down, just as the colonial rabble did Rivington's.
Fleas on a fine stallion's back, that's what you Whig papers
are. When the rest of our ships arrive, I'd advise you to
flee to the hills, or at least follow Rivington's lead, young
woman. He had the brains to head home to England."

"You British are entirely disillusioned if you believe most of us consider England home, sir. Indeed, would you in London not do all you could if, say, France or Spain anchored their growing armed fleet in your harbor?"

"Absolutely ridiculous! Not the same at all. They are enemy countries," he snorted. "Now, other than my warnings to you, young woman, you are not to print your nonsense further. Lieutenant!" he bellowed to the man at the door. "Put this rebel under guard in a cubby somewhere until Captain Hector arrives from the *Asia* to fetch her. If I ever catch you near the fleet again, young woman, I shall assume the worst of your intentions—as we did of Tiler. Lieutenant, I have much to do!"

"Please, just let me see Private Tiler, then—even send him a note."

"Absolutely not. Lieutenant—"

She was so furious at Sir Sloan's scolding dismissal that she could not form a protest as the lieutenant marched her up on deck and then down another companionway to the next level. Her heart sank to her feet. It might be only briefly, but she was to be a prisoner, too. And that rude, insulting Sir Sloan Boyd had sent for Captain Hector, as if he were her guardian!

"My rowboat's just off the bow!" she insisted to her escort, who only tightened his iron grip on her arm each time she tried to pull away. "I've done nothing that deserves imprisonment. We're not even at war yet, and you dare—"

"Are we not, mistress?" the angry lieutenant demanded as he shoved her in a small, dim cubicle. "We'll just see, won't we?" He backed out and slammed the door. She heard him shoot the bolt.

Though tempted to beat her fists on the door and scream her frustration, she did neither. She groped her way across the little room, bumping her hip on the small slant-top desk

she'd seen, and unlatched the single small porthole. Tears of regret and grief stung her eyes in the fresh river breeze.

When she poked her head out, she could see the Brookland shore, where some colonial soldiers were stationed to guard the Heights. Five hundred New Jersey boys had been sent east to Queens to disarm the Inimicals. No doubt the rest of the British fleet would be here soon, and then Washington and his army would have to come, too. Wouldn't they? And here, she thought as she pulled her head back in and swiped at tears, one lone woman had thought she could win her own little battle in the face of this big, looming war.

She wondered if Eddie had the same view. Did these brutes allow him any fresh air and sun at all? She mourned that she had failed him. And what had that lieutenant who'd locked her in here meant by implying that they were already at war?

Suddenly exhausted, she sank down on the single rickety chair by the clerk's desk in the tiny room. The ink splattered on the wood, the broken quill pen abandoned here, the crumpled, discarded efforts tossed on the floor, made her miss the print shop.

She bent over and picked up a wad and uncrumpled it. A list of supplies. Another…an order for going ashore to fetch and distribute drinking water. Another…

She gasped as she read. A botched and scribbled copy of an order from the king himself! Something called a Prohibitory Act. She read some of its startling claims aloud in a strangled voice: "All trade, even *between* colonies, to be punished. Ships forfeit…hangings…"

This could chop the colonies to helpless pieces while the British gobbled them up one by one! This would mean certain war—and defeat, if the firepower sitting here in the bay gave chase to the meager colonial vessels and hanged their captains and owners—men like the Supplier!

"Cam! I've got to tell him. I've got to get out *now*."

She smoothed the paper as flat as she could and slid it down her bodice under her cloak. She had just begun to read each discarded piece of paper off the floor when the door bolt grated. She straightened to kick the others behind her.

Captain Hector stooped stiffly to enter. He wore his crisp winter reds and a bearskin bicorne; his sword clanked in its scabbard. She expected raving fury, but, to her amazement, he was smiling like the cat who'd captured the canary.

"And here they put you in a clerk's cubby, where I would have had you waiting somewhere with a bed to earn your way off the ship!"

"I am weary of British insults, sir, and I'll have none of yours. I demand to be released."

To her dismay, he kicked the door shut behind him and crossed to her in two long strides. "You bloody little fool, you are in no position to demand anything!" he snapped, grabbing both her wrists to press her back against the curve of the hull so that her neck and head bent toward him. "Now, usually I favor feisty skirts, but you've overstepped, and badly. If I had you on the *Asia*—"

"But you don't. Loose me or or I'll scream. I assume someone aboard this ship might still belong to that dying breed—the English gentleman!"

He pressed her hands, clenched in his, against her breasts, and she heard the paper she had there crinkle. But he seemed intent on mastering her.

"You will do as I say from here on and stay out of trouble if you ever want to see that traitor Tiler again! Next time I come calling, even though it will be war, you will invite me in and find a civil tone and a sweet demeanor," he spat before he bent down to take her mouth.

Grasping her chin, he ground her lips against her teeth. She kicked and finally bit him.

"Rebel bitch!" he muttered, jumping back to dab at his

lower lip with a lace-encrusted handkerchief. "You've done it now, and—"

A voice sounded through the door. "Captain Hector, sir, your launch is ready!"

Without another word, he dragged her out the door. She went with him gladly, eager to be off this ship, eager to help Cam as she had not helped Eddie. Surely when she showed Cam this note he would forgive her for today. He would say she had done well to go out to the British ship. He would have much to do to save the Supplier's fleet, and she could aid him. She felt strong and sure. Providence had provided her with this paper and would surely protect poor Eddie.

Captain Hector glared at her all the way to shore. "I would be the dying breed of English gentleman and escort you home," he told her icily on the dock, "but your staff is probably awaiting you to print up this fine adventure. I shall call upon you later privily. Good day, my dear," he added, with a stiff bow and a smart snap of his boot heels.

His threats rattled her, but she only turned and walked away, her head high. The paper between her breasts was the ultimate threat from the British, and *she* could do something about it. If things went the way she intended, one lone woman was about to make a difference to the war. She would warn all the colonies before the British began taking ships. And she would become Cam's ally, too!

Libby sent Coll running with a message to Rob, and by the time dusk fell Cam had been freed and her staff was busy printing what the gazette was calling an act of war— King George's Prohibitory Trade Act. Let the British wonder where she got a copy. She was tempted to send a note to Sir Sloan Boyd, threatening to name him as the source of the leak if he didn't free Eddie. But that might bring further retribution. Right now she had to warn Cam.

Just at dusk she went through the alley and in the back

of Fanning's Wiggery next door. Marcella and Thurmond Fanning, who owned the shop, were a bit shocked by her request, but they agreed to it. She emerged disguised as a slender young man in sober, dark garments and a fine wig and tricorne. It was just the sort of wig Jos Bean was always gawking at, but she could not share this moment with him. She had told her staff she'd soon be back after visiting a shop or two.

But instead she took the hired horse the oarsman had returned earlier. She felt awkward but daring to be riding astride in town in breeches like this. She rode out through the alley and looked back several times to see if she was being followed. But there were shoppers in the streets, some mounted, and she could not be sure. She would have to trust the disguise and the horse to throw anyone off, including that bastard Captain Hector.

She began to feel very nervous, almost ill, at the thought of facing Cam. Rob had said he'd ridden away grim and livid when he'd released him. But she had the king's act with her to show him. And she was going to vow not only to keep the Supplier's identity a secret but to help him in any way she could.

She dismounted before his handsome brick Georgian house and banged the knocker on the front door. The butler who answered it seemed quite elderly and a little short-sighted, but she stood in the shadows in case he might guess she was not a young man.

"Need to see Mr. Gant on business," she said. Her voice, roughened from shouting today, sounding quite authentically masculine, she thought.

"Sorry, sir. He's been in briefly, but he went right out again."

"It's very important. I can't wait. Can you tell me where?"

"No, sir. But, since it's urgent, I could send him a note by rider right away."

"No, I— Yes, indeed, that might be helpful."

She stepped into a first-floor sitting room, where the butler provided her with quill and paper. She wrote that she had to see him immediately on vital business about supplies. Her mind leapt far ahead of her quick fingers. She would follow the rider who went to Cam. She hoped he was either still in the city or at Melrose. She had to see him before he heard the news elsewhere. Otherwise, those who told him might also capture and arrest him, despite whatever ties he'd managed to keep with the bloody British.

She tried to warm herself later, as she stood in back of the house, holding her horse's reins and praying a rider would appear soon. It was getting dark, and she'd learned to fear that, though she wouldn't let it stop her tonight. Finally a rider and horse emerged from the mews behind the house. Her spirits lifted. Perhaps everything would go well now.

The messenger on the horse headed for the Brookland Ferry, and she followed. She rode the same craft across the river, keeping her mount between them, and thanking Providence they were not alone. There was only one later ferry these days, so this one was crowded. Her face turned to her horse's withers, she held on to the unfamiliar wig and hat while the wind swirled. She wasn't certain how far she'd have to follow the messenger; she hadn't known Cam ever came to Brookland. If this rider went too far, would she have time to turn around and catch the last ferry back?

When he headed east toward the farms out along the Red Hook Road, she dropped far back. The road followed the river here, but would the sound of the water muffle her hoofbeats? Her stomach knotted tighter as darkness deepened, despite the slice of moon above. She could almost hear Cam berating her for riding out at night, as well as for holding him prisoner, but this paper would prove to him how much she really did care. And if he was the Supplier,

whether he did it out of patriotism or to line his pockets, she could surely still convince him they must bury their past animosity and work together.

She had passed the flickering lights just offshore on Governor's Island when a lantern ahead caught her eye. A two-masted ship was anchored at Red Hook. Could Cam be there? She prayed fervently that it was not a British vessel Cam was visiting, that it was one of the Supplier's fleet. But even if it was the latter, what was she to do now? The messenger had left his horse and gone down to the shore. She dismounted, too, and tied her horse in a cluster of trees. On the wind, she heard hoofbeats on the road behind her.

She squinted to see who galloped into view. There was a scraping sound from the shore like a rowboat putting out, but she didn't dare call out or run to stop the messenger. She held her breath as the cloaked rider slowed his horse to a walk.

She jumped behind a tree, but her mount whinnied, giving her position away. In the moonlight she saw a gun glinting as the cloaked rider moved his horse closer to her. She pressed herself against the far side of the tree. The gun spat fire, and tree bark flew.

She threw herself to the ground as another gunshot echoed. Her horse reared, its flying hooves barely missing her. Yet another shot ripped the air, and then there was a long silence. But when she looked up at last, the rider who had shot at her had toppled off his horse, just a stone's throw away from her.

She scrambled to her feet and pulled on her horse's reins to quiet him. She could hear Cam's messenger rowing the boat back toward the shore, but the voice that spoke came from the direction of the second shot.

"Woman, if you're all right, step out here on this road, and now!"

It was a voice she had heard only once before—in a dark, snowy alley when he'd rescued her, just as he had this time.

The speaker dismounted and rolled his victim over with his foot while she just gaped, her hands pressed to her mouth.

"The British bastard's dead as a doornail. You're this far now, you might as well go aboard, mistress. If the master hadn't said hands off you no matter what, I'd knock your head good for leading this redcoat out here! Come on, then, 'fore the master comes ashore to fetch you hisself."

Libby had never seen a man as furious as Cam was. He strode back and forth across the narrow, low-ceilinged captain's cabin, ranting and gesturing wildly, while Libby sat mutely in the chair he'd shoved her into.

"I hope you realize this is the worst yet. My watchman's had to kill a British soldier because of you, and he'll be missed. There's going to be a lot of killing, but we don't need it yet—and not triggered by a meddling woman! And if that redcoat's task was keeping an eye on you and not me, they'll be after you about his disappearance."

"I can't help that. And how long have you had me followed, anyway?" she shouted back.

She had a good mind not to share the document that would warn him against capture and hanging. She'd almost been killed coming out here to him. And all he did was humiliate her in front of his ship's captain and this—this warehouse guard he'd had on her heels for who knows how long!

"And here," she threw at him, interrupting the angry silence, "I thought you'd be relieved to see me safe, after going aboard the *Viper* today. I was going to tell you that you were right about Eddie, and I—"

"Everybody, leave us!" Cam ordered brusquely, cutting her off. "This bewigged 'boy' and I have much to settle, once and for all! Captain Chester, follow my orders."

"You think you can tell everyone what to do!" Libby fixed her hands on her hips. "I don't want to be alone with

you, and I'm going back directly after I deliver my message if you're going to act like this!''

But, to her growing alarm, his men left, banging the door behind them, as if she hadn't protested. She heard them clomping back and forth on the deck above. Leaning against the door after he shot the bolt, Cam breathed hard as he clenched, then unclenched, his fists.

"You know, you're more foolhardy than I ever dreamed," he told her. His voice was ragged, and his face was grim in the moving shadows from the single hanging lantern. "Maybe I should just do both the British and the Americans a great favor by dropping you over the side at dawn."

His words did not frighten her half as much as his menacing tone and stance. Coward that she was, she reached under her cloak and into her waistcoat pocket for the paper to convince him she'd come for his own good.

"No guns!" he cried, and yanked her toward him. "I'm fed up with your tricks and lies, damn it! 'Cam, I wouldn't lie to you!'" he said, mimicking her words. "'I trust you now, and you can trust me!'"

She felt her control drain away. "Let me go! I have something to show you to make you understand. You're as bad as Hector for putting a man on me. I don't care—''

His hard hands untied and yanked her cloak away. But when he saw she had no gun, he didn't stop. He flung her wig off and pulled her hair free of its ties. Its loosened crimson bounty blinded her as she fought him. But he peeled her coat and waistcoat away, ignoring the popping buttons.

"Cam, Cam, stop! I have to tell you why I came!"

"Quiet! You came because you owe me at least this, and if you say otherwise I don't know what I'll do!"

But he knew exactly what he was doing. The waistcoat with the copy of King George's act was forgotten in the heat of this act. She was terrified by what his hard hands

were making her feel, and yet she helped him divest her of her breeches, her shirt, her cravat, even the bindings around her breasts, and eagerly joined in disrobing him.

Dazed with jumbled fear and desire, she clung to him as he carried her to the narrow, recessed bed and ripped the bedclothes down. But his face was a stranger's still in his rage. And when she saw he meant to tie her hands, she exploded, all kicking feet and pounding fists. But he easily subdued her and, winding their cravats around her wrists, secured her arms above her head.

"How does it feel to be forcibly detained?" he demanded, his gloating face thrust close to hers. "You feel helpless and angry and afraid, don't you, Mistress Liberty? Sorry there's no perfumed, alluring billet-doux or picnic to entice you into my trap!"

"Cam, things went wrong! I'm sorry for all that!"

"I won't let you be sorry, sweetheart. I'll make it worth your time, as well as mine, tonight. And I don't even need a friend hidden nearby with a gun to make you do my bidding, because you'll do it anyway, won't you, Libby?"

"Please, don't—"

But his mouth dropped to a breast, and an aching flame flickered and grew within her. He cupped and molded, and his darting tongue flicked her puckered nipple. His free hand lazily, insolently roamed the length of her, grasping, sliding heavily, as if they had all the time in the world. His mouth covered and invaded hers until she could not breathe, could only want him, no matter how things stood between them. When he freed her lips at last, she made one more grab at sanity, while he rained slick kisses down her belly to the red moss at the juncture of her thighs.

"What will…those men up there think?" she gasped out.

He laughed low in his throat. "All sort of jealous thoughts."

"Oh!" exploded from her as he pushed closer to probe her private warmth with skillful fingers. He reached up,

one-handed, and loosed her wrists. She wrapped her arms around his neck and held tight.

"Oh, Cam, Cam! I want to hate you, but I can't. I'm sorry about today! We're always doing something awful to each other, and—"

But he was kissing her hard again, and his hands were working miracles. Her inner world blazed with light, as if the sky were rocked by fireworks as it had been on the first night they'd met and talked. She forgot why she had come here, forgot about all the dangers beyond this one. She was still feverishly eager to touch this man. However rough his hands or his kisses, she wanted him and loved him more than she had ever known was possible. She was part of him, and she wanted to be, now and always.

"Tell me this is why you drive me mad...why you came here!" he demanded breathlessly as his big knees separated and spread hers. "Then convince me why I should not blame you...."

She wanted to convince him with her love, but she had vowed she would not use the words again unless he said them first. She clasped him to her, grasping the powerful muscles of his taut, lean buttocks. She felt as if they were rolling, dipping and rising on the sea. She lifted to meet his entry and moved her hips in little yearning circles that drove them both wilder. She matched his pounding pace, even quickened it. She pulled them both right off the edge of the burning world into the cooling depths of the sea. And, despite her desperate vow, at that last moment when they both exploded together, she cried out her overwhelming love words to him.

"Mmm... I never...quite...felt so much...like that!" he gasped, as he collapsed, slick-skinned, beside her. He cradled her against him, her bottom pressed into his lap and a hard arm flung over her, as if she might flee. The cool air that blew through the cracks in the hull was nippy, so

she squirmed to pull a blanket up over them on the narrow built-in bed.

"I did come here for a reason, you know, Cam. Something dire."

"Shhh. They say a cat has nine lives, but you've more." He sighed so deeply that his whole big body heaved. "Tell me what happened aboard the *Viper*, then," he murmured.

She spilled it all out in shaky, sometimes angry words. She told him finally about the Prohibitory Act. "It even threatens to hang those caught! Let me up and I'll get it for you out of my waistcoat to read."

"No, I'm not letting you go." He dragged her closer. "The whole world can go to war, but I'm not letting you go."

Deep contentment coursed through her veins. He cared for her deeply, wanted to protect her, even if it was in his own way. She realized with a start that she could be quit of the world right now and yet be very happy.

"You know," she whispered, cuddling closer, "I'd almost swear this ship was moving."

"It is." His voice was muffled against her bare shoulder. "We took your horse on board, and we'll let you go on Staten Island tomorrow. If that redcoat's body's ever found, they'll not figure it out if you're visiting at home. It worked for us the last time you insisted on parading about after dark in man's garb."

She was amazed by how calmly she took this announcement that he was tampering with her life again. Maybe she could get used to it. After all, he didn't sound a bit angry anymore, and he obviously believed her about the king's act without even having read it. Maybe everything could turn out well between them, after all.

"And here I thought that wild rocking of this bed and room was something we did together."

She felt him stir, ready and taut against her hip, even at that tiny tease. "Don't press your luck, Libby. I'm believ-

ing you about the British threat to my ships and my life,
because such an act is overdue. And it means," he said
grimly, realizing he'd have to send for Washington now,
"that war is as good as begun for us here in New York.
But in our own little war, yours and mine, I declare a truce.
I'm going to make hot love to you again, long and slow
this time. Then I'm going to put you ashore before dawn
at Melrose. I'll have to start landing my ships there to ferry
things over."

She'd heard what he'd said about making love, but
hadn't he heeded what she'd said about capture and hang-
ings? "But there are too many Inimicals on Staten Island!"
she protested, and tried to sit up. He refused to budge, so
she settled back against him. "Someone will report you!"

"Not if we move things at night. And not down in the
Melrose cove, if they aren't welcome on the estate. Unless,
of course, they sneak in and break a window or two with
a ladder trying to spy on us."

She was so content in his arms, so amazed at his bold
tone, that she could not summon up her usual bitterness
over her first experience at Melrose. If he could be this
brave, even facing danger and death, she could, too.

"I should have broken your head instead of just a window that night," she told him.

"But you have broken my heart since."

"Don't tease."

"You say you love me, but you only mean you desire
me. Love means trust and loyalty, and I've never had either
from you. Besides, it's not teasing if you intend to do everything you promise, and I do."

She was so shaken by his accusation about her love that
she ignored his marauding hand at first as it cupped, then
circled, one breast. She believed one could love someone
without really trusting him—and maybe without loyalty,
too—didn't she? But she was afraid for them to argue now.
She couldn't bear it if they parted bitterly again.

"Then, in your case, teasing is a threat, Cam Gant!" was all she managed.

"Libby, Libby, Libby," he muttered, and nuzzled her shoulders and neck from behind. "They can try to forbid trade between the colonies, but they'll never stop trades of this kind."

He turned her to kiss her deeply again. His hands roamed her back and bottom. She tensed at his touch, then melted as his sensuous assault spread and deepened. Her flesh flamed everywhere he touched, everywhere he looked. And he looked his fill as he got the lantern to hang it closer so that they could revel in each thing they did together in the next sweet, hot hours of the windy winter night. She felt herself blush often, but she did not hold back. She followed his lead, fulfilled each rasped command, invented excitements and orders of her own. But still, still, he did not say he loved her as sable night raced toward bloody dawn.

"Libby, sweetheart." His voice came to her in the darkness. "The sky's getting gray, and we've got to get you off with the other goods before dawn."

She reached out for him in the warm bed before she realized he stood over her. "The other goods." His words echoed in her brain. Did he even have to tease, waking her up so early, when she felt exhausted and afraid. She wished the night past had never had to end.

"You're even dressed!" was all she said when she squinted at him in the dim glow of the lantern.

"Have been for an hour, much to my regret, seeing you lying there so sweet and supple. Your man's clothes are here, but I want you to go into Melrose with Sally and change into a gown, as you did before."

"All right." She acquiesced trustingly, grateful that he was thinking for her in her softheaded state. When she recalled last night, she flushed hot even in the smack of cold air as she threw the covers back and grabbed her clothes,

which he'd laid on the covers. Amazingly, after all they had shared last night, he turned away like a gentleman and poured two tankards of something.

"Here, hot coffee," he told her as she dangled her legs over the bed to pull on her stockings and shoes. To her utter surprise, he knelt on the floor to do it for her.

"Cam, I can—"

"Quiet. There's a lot you can do for yourself and by yourself. I accept that now. But just drink that and listen."

A rosy glow spread through her as his big hands warmed her bare feet. It made her go all shaky when he smoothed her stockings up to buckle them under her breeches, even though he did it quickly. The feeling of being tenderly touched, of having Cameron Gant at her feet, made it hard for her to concentrate on his words.

"We've come to the beginning of something new and good between us, Libby, and it's about time. Understanding, trust, a certain loyalty...maybe love."

She sucked in a silent breath as he pushed a shoe on one foot, then rested her other, stockinged foot on his rock-hard thigh and gently gripped her ankle. "But times are going to get much worse for both of us. The stakes are high, but so's the prize."

"And we both believe in it, even if not on the rules to win it."

He nodded, shoved her other shoe on, then looked up straight into her eyes. "You've finally learned the world's not all black-and-white—that there are shades of gray in people, in causes, in beliefs. I admire that, Libby, but then, I've always admired you, ever since that time we chased you and Merry with the dogs and you stood up to Charles."

Tears glazed her eyes. She cursed herself for her greed. She wanted his admiration, yes, but she desperately coveted his love! And yet, as Merry had said, a Tiler could and would wed a Morgan, but for a Gant to do so... Never.

"Cam, I just wish…" Her voice trailed off, and her hands flopped helplessly in her lap. She sniffed hard.

"Of course," he said, and covered her hands with his, "I've not yet collected for that broken window, and I intend to. At the same exchange rate as last night."

"Master, sun's almost up!" Captain Chester's voice called on the other side of the door. "We're off for New Haven!"

"Be right up!" he called, then pulled her to her feet and into his arms. "I'm going along this time, Libby. There are some things I have to do."

He didn't tell her he'd already sent a message to Washington that he'd best come as quickly as possible with the rest of his army. Nor did he tell her how tempted he was to take her with him, to establish her in New Haven, out of harm's way, as his mistress. But that last was pure dreaming; Libby Morgan could never be just that for him, not in his wildest dreams, not even if she would agree.

"But you could send your captain and not go along yourself," she protested. "As soon as the word of German George's nasty act is out in the gazette, the Brits have nothing to lose by starting to capture ships. And if they get the *Gull* this trip they'll get you, too!"

"A necessary risk. Just don't print my destination in the paper." He kissed the end of her nose. "I don't often go along," he said comfortingly, lifting her hand to kiss it with a sad little smile.

They heard footsteps overhead, and the anchor chain being winched up. No, she thought. No, she couldn't bear for this to end. She didn't even know when she'd see him again. *If* she'd see him again. They were so close this morning. What if something awful happened and they never reclaimed this precious moment again?

"Don't cry, Libby. I know you're exhausted. But it's not like you," he protested gently. "Pretend something's happened to make you curse my name and want to hit me over

the head with your press while that rebel renegade Rob pokes me with his gun!''

"Cam, don't joke. I'll never curse you again, or be angry or—''

It annoyed her that he laughed, but tears were glimmering in his eyes, too. He tugged her back into his arms to kiss her hard and then, when she clung to him, pushed her gently away. He swirled her man's cloak around her and led her up on deck.

"Look, Libby, there's Sally waiting on the dock. Tell that damned Scotsman he owes me for sending her back to New York with you. You have to have a companion there at the shop at night. Promise me you'll keep Sally with you!''

"Yes, but her mother will be angry—''

"A mother's anger—no one's—has ever stopped you before. Go on, then, and I'll see you when I get back. And we'll talk further about everything.''

She clung to his hand. She couldn't believe she was acting the weak female, but she also couldn't believe she might be losing him for good.

"Cam, you will be careful?''

"Of course. Can't have two of us in a British brig for you to fret over. Go on,'' he added, and patted her bottom through her cloak.

Feeling sad and alone, she walked slowly down the gangplank, only to hear it immediately hauled up behind her. She took Sally's hand and turned back to watch the *Gull* cast off. Cam waved, and she lifted a hand to him, ignoring the hubbub the servants made as they carried the barrels and boxes they'd unloaded into the bushes until they could be covertly ferried to Manhattan.

She blinked into the blush of the eastern dawn as the sails filled to pull the vessel away. It was so hard to believe all that had happened last night, and yet... She only hoped he would be safe. She only hoped that what he felt for her

might blossom into love and that he would know it for what it was someday.

"Come on, then, mistress," Sally urged, pulling her toward the house. "I just knew there was something or t'other between you and the master. I just knew it."

Thirteen

~~~⟳~~~

THE LIBERTY GAZETTE
March 10, 1776

The New York City Committee of Safety requires all able-bodied Men to report to dig Defenses every third Day. See Schedule below. Our Commander-in-Chief & our Army will be here soon. Till then, General Washington challenges us with his stirring Words:

"We fight a Tyrant & his diabolical Ministry...This I would tell them, not under covert, but in Words as clear as the Sun in its meridian Brightness."

* * *

To prepare our children with Discipline for the Future, Dr. Dobson, author of the Pamphlet Proper Deportment and Correct Carriage for Our Youth in These Trying Times *urges all good & loving Parents to do the following:*

—*Let your Child eat standing so he appreciates his Food*

—*For the Youngster who slumps, strapping to Backboards & Harnesses is a great Boon*

—*For correct Posture in the female Child, bal-*

> *ancing Books, metal Stays, & Pins in the*
> *Bodice are most salubrious*
>
> *This Pamphlet now on sale at Morgan's Print*
> *Shop, Queen Str.*

Libby and Sally Smith worked in the line of women toting buckets of water to the men digging defenses along the ramparts of the Grand Battery. Amidst the bent backs scooping and tossing soil, nervous eyes kept turning to the British ships in the harbor. The gunships and support vessels kept shifting positions, as if to warn everyone along the shore of imminent disaster.

"Keep a-going! Don't ya worry!" The overseeing officer's voice rang out from time to time as Libby worked her way along the ditches. "Them lobsterback ships jest trying to miss the ice floes out there. We reckon they're saving their shot till Washington and the rest of his boys get here!"

Shovels, spades, pickaxes, even hatchets, hit into the earth and spat it up again and again. Men of all ages, from young Coll to old Horace Goodhue, were lending a hand. All classes and stations in life, from Jos Bean, who had never yet saved a hundred pounds for his wig, to the Livingtons and the DeLanceys, were here. All persuasions of the political spectrum, too—from the liberal Langs and Brookses to the newly elected Mayor Matthews, one of Governor Tryon's former Tory friends. And Cameron Gant.

Libby made certain to take Cam water every few trips she made. Things were going well between them still, though he had only been back a few days from New Jersey. She smiled down at him again. Only his head and his big, soiled chest and shoulders showed above the long, serpentine trench he shared with nearly twenty others.

"Working up a big thirst again?" she asked, and winked.

"Thirsty and *starved*!" he told her. Their eyes held at

that, for both knew what he was starved for. He drank the dipper dry, then leaned momentarily on his shovel while he watched her water the others.

She glanced back once to see him eyeing her ankles. Unfortunately, he was not the only one. Crispin Brooks, just down the ditch a ways, always took the opportunity to ogle Libby and yell insults at Cam. And every time he did so Libby let the lout go dry.

The too-familiar voice rang out. "Say, Mr. Gant, it's real nice you musta taken your own oath to help the city out today. 'Specially when you didn't believe in the Oath of Loyalty to it!"

"Since you're such a staunch supporter of the Continental Congress, Mr. Brooks," Cam countered, without breaking his swing, "I'm sure you were relieved to hear they recently passed a resolution banning oaths—except the ones we fellow workers swear at each other!"

Libby saw Crispin's face darken with anger at having been bested, but he couldn't think of a quick reply, and he just swore under his breath, as Cam had expected.

"Mr. Gant and his ilk are not one bit worried 'bout helpin' us dig here," another voice put in from down Crispin's way. "He knows as well as his friends out in the harbor that the city's low on powder. What good are these trenches and a bunch of spiked guns along here, anyway?"

"Tha's right!" someone else shouted. "This is a real good way to learn about the city's defenses to pass on to certain friends, I 'spose, Mr. Tory Gant!"

Libby's blood boiled at the way they baited Cam when he was obviously here to help. She was even certain she recognized several of these hecklers from the mob that had attacked Rivington's press. And when she finally strolled down their way with the water bucket, she was certain of it when she spotted that one-armed man standing next to Crispin and a bulky, black-haired giant on his other side in the trench.

"Well, well, it's our old patriotic comrade-in-arms, Mistress Morgan!" Crispin growled up at her. He scowled and added under his breath, "Someone's mistress, that's sure."

"How dare you insult anyone who's here to help—Cam Gant or me!" she cried. "It's just too bad that when the British blasted the roof off the Fraunces Tavern you weren't on it, crowing how great a patriot you and you alone are!"

She was tempted to dump her water bucket into the hole on top of them, but Cam, who had come up behind her, took her arm and pulled her back a step. "If we have something to settle, Brooks," he said curtly, "come find me later. Right now we need every worker we can get to finish this. Even those who work their mouths more than their hands or their heads. Go on, Libby, water some workers who are worth it," he added with a toss of big blond head.

"Taking orders from traitors now, huh?" Crispin called after her. "We'll just see, Gant, how big and brave you are when your time comes! If I didn't have this job to do, I swear I'd—"

Just then the dismissal drum rolled. Men climbed the ladder from the trench or gave each other a boost out. A crowd circled Cam, sensing a fight. He darted a look behind him to see that Libby had, indeed, ignored his orders to go.

When Crispin clambered out, Cam backed him to the edge of the hole. "We dug defenses together today, Brooks!" Cam said quietly. "Let's not let insults make someone dig a grave before the real thing starts! But I'll be in my house on Broad Way Street tonight if you—or some of your associates—want to discuss this further."

He strode away, and Libby hurried by his side across the crowded bowling green. "I'm sorry about that," she said. "I think that ever since that day you showed up at the patriots' meeting Crispin has thought—"

"If you're apologizing for him, I don't want to hear it. It galls me there has to be so much dissension within when

we've got to pull to together against what's out there." He jerked a thumb toward the river.

They slowed their steps as they passed the gilded statue of King George. Although they had argued since he'd been back, they'd always kept it under control, as if they were both fearful of endangering their truce.

"Here, sweetheart, pour that water on my filthy hands so I won't feel so bad about wanting to even touch your arm."

She did as he asked, then flung the rest of the water up in King George's golden face. Several watching cheered and applauded. She took Cam's arm, and they walked across the grass, enjoying the crisp caress of the mild wind on their bodies, warmed and sore from hours of labor.

"Will all this work?" she asked as they paused on Broad Street to look at the wagons and fine carriages some wealthy families had donated to transport tools and workers across town.

"I'm afraid whoever holds the water holds the town. But if we barricade the streets we could make a good stand. Thank God Washington will be here soon!"

"He will for certain? When? What have you heard?"

He shrugged noncommittally and looked away from her fervent face. He was coming to trust her now, but he couldn't tell her that, or how he knew. Not Mistress Liberty of the *Liberty Gazette*. He only hoped that helping to dig these defenses would defuse the rising tension in the town and buy him time and safety until he could openly join Washington's staff. He prayed that his identity as the Supplier would not be disclosed until there was a full army here to at least fire back at the waiting British cannon.

"Cam, come on, a shilling for your thoughts!" she wheedled, pressing a firmly molded breast against his arm to jolt him back to reality.

He felt his resistance to her wavering. Sometimes he knew it would be better for his mission if they were still

estranged. "I do know for sure," he said, evading her question, "that the Committee of Safety's planning a city-wide illumination of thanksgiving when Washington does arrive, and I'd like to escort you to it."

"Oh, how wonderful to have something good to look forward to after all this time just waiting for the worst!" She smiled up at him. She'd never been in the city for an illumination, but her father and Atwood Simpson had described how bonfires lit the streets and candles glowed from every window.

"I thought that would give us a good chance to really talk about where we're going. The two of us, our relationship, even though this war is bound to keep getting in the way..."

They watched only each other as the parade of carriages and wagons rumbled by. Libby felt balanced on the edge of some lovely cliff, some long-dreamed-of desire, as her eyes met his. But he was right about the war getting in the way.

"Cam," she told him quietly. "Those ruffians back there with Crispin...I'm sure at least two of them were in the mob that wrecked Rivington's print shop. Crispin himself may even have been there. You'd best be very careful."

"I will. Don't fret."

She stepped dazedly into the cobbled street in a break between wagons. Cam carried her empty bucket; she held his arm with both hands. But he yanked her back as one last wagon rattled by.

But that sudden rescue did not jolt her half as much as what her eyes beheld on that wagon. She gasped as she saw Quentin Simpson, his soiled, ragged legs dangling over the side and chains on his wrists.

"Oh!" she cried as Quentin's gaze slammed into her. He lifted one manacled wrist to shake a fist at her and shout something she blessedly could not hear over the rattle and

clatter. His chain yanked taut between his wrists, and his face contorted into a grotesque mask.

"They're using prisoners to dig," Cam began to explain before he, too, recognized Quentin. Seeing the hatred on Quentin's face, he stepped in front of her to break the stare. And then Quentin and his seething countenance were gone.

"Sweetheart, you're trembling. Don't worry. You saw he's guarded under lock and key."

She gripped his arm harder. "I know. It's just that his hatred of me is obviously festering in prison. But they did say he's not to be out for several more months, and who knows what will be happening then?"

"Of course. Come on, then, and I'll get us something at a tavern. Not the Fraunces'. It seems we both have enemies there these days."

She walked quickly along at his side. Her legs felt like straw. She darted glances in all directions, as if the British lurked around each bend. Both of Cam's warehouse guards had joined the army, and while she believed Captain Hector had not dared to send a soldier ashore to follow her lately she could not shake the memory of the look of complete contempt she'd seen on Quentin's face. The way his slitted eyes had stabbed her, she would almost rather face the whole British fleet than ever see him again.

The times were terrible, and Libby fought a continual battle with herself about whether to buoy drooping spirits or report reality. Two big British warships, the *Asia* and the *Phoenix*, had stopped numerous colonial merchant ships. So far they had not hanged their captains, but they had imprisoned entire crews. Eddie Tiler, in his sixth month of captivity now, had plenty of company out there. The British were using Governor's Island for an exercise ground and digging their own entrenchments on Bedloe's Island. Although New York was still helping to provision the British fleet, they were making more raids for food and water.

And there were large bands of Tories on Long and Staten Islands just waiting for the British to attack so that they could swarm to their banners. Worse for New York, the British had abandoned Boston, with their entire fleet. Where they might have gone was not yet reported, but new ships were dribbling into New York Harbor daily.

On the other hand, some colonial supply ships, including the Supplier's, were still sneaking through the tightening British net. And, but for a caretaker force in Boston, George Washington had sent the rest of his army here to make a stand—and he had finally come with them!

Although he had been grim faced and full of business when he had arrived with his large official entourage, it had lifted hearts just to know he was there. Despite his victory after the long siege of Boston, there were no proud parades or grand speeches this time. But there was to be an illumination that night in the general's honor, and Libby was going with Cam.

She wore a gold-brocade-and-white lace gown she'd had made from curtains and a tablecloth a Tory family had sold before they'd fled to Canada. The skirts were patriotically narrow, without the usual huge side farthingales. She wore it with an embroidered lace apron to cover a soiled spot on the skirts, but she felt quite elegant. She'd used the last of her Hungary water on her throat and earlobes, though she knew the nighttime April breeze might blow the scent away before Cam could get a whiff.

She trembled at the beauty of the night as she watched Sally light the candles in their own windows on both floors of the print shop. Rob had garbed himself in his Scottish best, with his gun stuck in his kilt, to walk out with Sally. Libby sensed what was between them, but she neither envied nor disapproved. In her own haze of personal joy, she wished all lovers only the best. She felt sorry for Merry, who had been moping about last week at having no one exciting to care one whit for, but even that had not damp-

ened her ardor for Cam, or her nervous expectation at their private time together this special evening.

"I wish Mother and Merry could see this illumination," she admitted to Cam as they strolled through the murmuring crowd toward the nearest bonfire, in Hanover Square. "Merry is forever declaring nothing exciting ever happens to her. And we're not likely to see such a thing for a long, long time again."

His nostrils flared at the sweet scent of her. His gray gaze shimmered silver as they drank her in in the reflected firelight.

"I'm afraid not," he admitted. "Now that Washington's here, the last key player is on the stage. Listen, Libby, I have a great deal I've wanted to tell you, but most of all this. I care deeply for you. I think I have since that night I brought you Atwood's letter about inheriting the gazette. You really knocked me off balance that night, and I can't say I've stopped whirling since. I suppose I've just been afraid to admit it, not to mention the fact we were always fighting."

Oblivious of the shifting, jostling crowd, they faced each other and clasped hands. The leaping flames of the bonfire warmed and gilded them.

"Cam, I love you, too," she admitted before she realized again that he hadn't used that word. "And as for my trust and loyalty, you have all that now. Still, I realize our different stations in life—"

"Shh!" he shouted over the singing and yelling of the citizens cavorting around the bonfire. "New times are coming—a revolution, not just a protest. And, though I'm not going to ask for your hand tonight, I want you to think about it, and all that it would mean."

"But I don't need to think about—"

He gave her shoulders a slight shake. "Yes, you do. When the real trouble starts—if the British come ashore, at least—you won't be safe in Manhattan. And Staten Island

is crawling with Tories. I'm not sure where you and your gazette could survive safely, but definitely not here, and probably not at Melrose. And I intend to join the army in the next few weeks!''

"Oh, Cam!" She launched herself into his arms to give him a hard hug before she realized that meant certain separation. Months, even weeks, ago, she would have icily demanded *which* army he meant to join, but now everything was as clear as the firelit night. "Oh, Cam!" she cried again before he kissed her, right there in the public square.

He held her close, savoring the private moment, despite the public chaos all around. He had originally planned to share everything with her tonight, but he'd seen Washington just a few hours before. The Leader had praised Cam for his help but asked him to keep aloof until actual hostilities began. Cam had agreed, of course, but when the general had seen how downcast he looked he'd asked him why.

Cam had admitted his affection for Libby and how his duties had almost come between them. But surely, he'd declared to Washington, a few days more under wraps would not matter. The general had sympathized, saying he was anxiously awaiting his own reunion with Mrs. Washington, who was coming in with family members to remain until this next siege began.

Cam stared wide-eyed into the flames above Libby's head. His thoughts echoed Washington's words. *Until this next siege begins.*

"Oh, Cam, look what those men have!" Libby cried, pointing. "They've ripped down a tavern sign."

They watched as a clump of shouting men heaved the painted wooden sign of the King's Arms into the flames while everyone cheered. Another sign, marking the George and Crown just down the street, soon followed. And then Cam and Libby spotted Crispin Brooks and his rabble with a stuffed effigy of Governor Tryon dangling from a noose.

"Get us the real thing and we'll tar and feather 'em!" Crispin shouted. "We'll ride 'em out of town on pointed rails so the damned Tories never take another straight step. All Tories! Burn 'em! Burn the lackey bastards!" he chanted, and the crowd took up the shrieking litany.

Cam and Libby noted Sally and Rob in the crowd across the way. Sally clung nervously to Rob's hand while his other fist bounced defiantly in the air in time to the chant.

Libby felt sick. She could not bear to have the night Cam first hinted at marriage marred by hatred and fierce frenzy. "Rob and Sally...they love each other, Cam!" she shouted in his ear in an attempt to think of happier things.

"I still don't trust the Scotsman, but he may prove his mettle yet," he yelled back. "Come on, sweetheart. Let's just walk the streets and look at the quiet candles. I know fighting a war takes passion, but this sickens me."

She was queasy with foreboding herself. Cam had said she would not be safe here much longer, but even to be with him she could not give up the gazette and all it stood for in such perilous times! He would just have to understand that. He intended to fight, and she did, too, in her own way!

His arm around her shoulders, they turned their backs on the blaze and strolled into the dimmer, more deserted streets.

Libby lay awake in bed. She had sat up with Sally when Rob had brought her back, and now she couldn't sleep. Imagine, on this very night Cam had first hinted at marriage, Rob had asked Sally for her hand! The girl had begged Libby to let them both live here, in Sally's little room. Rob was living in a tiny garret now, though Libby didn't ask how Sally could describe it so completely. Now, long after Sally had gone to bed, Libby's thoughts kept her awake.

When she heard the church steeple chime three, she was

still heaving herself about in a sea of rumpled sheets. How desperately she loved Cam, and how far they had come since that first terrible meeting at Melrose. They had broken each other's hearts since, but now was the time of healing. They had come through the harsh words and sad circumstances that had stood between them. Surely—this looming war be damned!—everything would be beautiful and perfect now!

Her heart was beating so hard as she lay there thinking of Cam that she ignored the knocking at first. It blended with the church chimes, or the night watchman's step, or her own thundering thoughts. But when she heard Sally's voice at her chamber door, she sat bolt upright, clutching the bedclothes around her. "Don't you hear it, Mistress Libby? 'Tis a knocking downstairs. It's in the alley, under my back window, but I can't see a thing."

The knocking came again, erratic and forlorn. It definitely was not the wind banging a loose shutter. Libby jammed her feet in shoes and grabbed her dressing gown.

"Don't light a candle yet," she told Sally. "We're going down to peek out the back window first."

Shaking with chill and nerves, they tiptoed down the stairs, holding hands. If it was anyone suspicious, such as Captain Hector, Libby decided, she would not answer the door. But perhaps something had happened to Cam. Perhaps the British had caught a Supplier ship and he needed help....

Gripping Sally's fingers, she shifted the curtain and peered carefully out. A single form, a man slumped against the door. The figure looked hatless and tattered; she could not see clearly or guess his height. Surely not just a beggar this hour of the night!

"Who is it?" she demanded, not opening the window.

"Isn't this the back of Morgan's?" a rough voice called. Then there was a spate of coughing.

Through the thick glass, Libby saw the form hunch over

still more. She should know that voice, and yet— She felt in the rag basket for the gun Rob still kept there. The man sounded like—

Holding the gun down along her hip, she unlatched the door. The bulk of the man toppled in and fell against her feet. Even in the dark, when he rolled over, she knew for certain who it was.

"Eddie! Eddie Tiler!"

Within a half hour, she and Sally had dried Eddie and wrapped him in blankets and had poured some hot broth down him. He looked pasty-white and gaunt—a drowned rat—and even the candlelight seemed to hurt his eyes.

"Held on to a patrol boat rope in the dark till we got near shore, my angel," he told her. "Then swam. Swam in and came here."

"Don't talk now. We've got to hide you somewhere else. They'll look here and take you again! And it would be disaster to try to get him to his family, Sally. If only we could take him to Cameron Gant's house here in town. They'd never suspect. And Washington's troops can rescue him in the morn—"

"What?" Eddie demanded, and choked on his broth. "Him? You can't be still seeing *him*!"

"Yes, Mr. Gant is on the American side, Eddie. Now, don't worry, because—"

"No, no, he isn't!" Eddie insisted. His hands shook so hard that he slopped the broth, and Sally took the tankard from him. He coughed, a hacking, deep-chested fit that left him gasping for breath. Libby silently cursed the British for turning a stalwart man into this withered, sick wretch before her. Anyone involved in this would pay, through the gazette or any other way she could find, she vowed silently.

"Cam Gant," Eddie rasped out when he could talk, "upon my word, he's been meddling in my imprisonment somehow! It was pure chance I got out tonight in the con-

fusion—when they brought in another colonial merchant ship's crew they took. Otherwise, if Gant had his way, I'd be rotting out there still. I thought—'' he hacked into his fist again ''—it was only because he's a dyed-in-the-wool Tory, but it's obviously because he wanted to keep me away from you. But I'd stake my life on it—Cameron Gant's a bloody Tory spy!''

Libby's mind was already spinning possibilities again. That day of the snow picnic Cam had told her he didn't want her or the other Whig presses printing things Eddie Tiler had heard aboard the British ships. Had he meant for her own safety, or because that would expose his double-dealing? Oh, no, she thought, and wrapped her arms around her middle as if she were going to be ill. Oh, no!

"No," she said, voicing her deepest fears. "That can't be. He's—he's been doing certain things to help the colonies. I know it!"

"Like what?" Eddie demanded.

"I—I can't say just now."

"Look, Libby," he cried, seizing her wrist with all his wasted strength. His skin felt leathery and puckered, like an old man's. "I overheard more than once what they said—the officers on the *Asia*, and then on the *Viper*. That Captain Hector, too."

Her head snapped up. She wanted to tear her hand from Eddie's ghostly grip. She wanted to cover both ears with her palms and run screaming upstairs so that she wouldn't have to hear anything he said against Cam.

"Libby, my angel, I thought you'd wait for me when I got caught doing all that for you." Eddie was rambling now, his feverish eyes accusing. "I'm sorry I botched it, but when I heard you came out to the ship to see me, I thought you were waiting—that you would wed me! I lived for that, my angel, you and my soldiering!"

"I told you I couldn't wed you, Eddie. But I was crushed you were taken, and I tried to help in the gazette—"

"I know. I know. They told me—even read an article to me once and asked terrible, vile things about how good you were in the hay— Pardon, Libby, you know what I mean."

She hung her head as his words continued to roll over her. What if her worse fears were true? Had Cam told the British officers how he was keeping her on a leash, however distasteful a task it was to bed her? But no! He'd looked at her with love, he'd touched her so tenderly!

Eddie's awful voice was rolling on. "Cam Gant brought news of the city to those officers. He told things about Washington, too, I just know it, to Captain Hector, I suppose the royal governor, too. I even overheard Hector went to his town house more than once!"

No, no, Libby screamed inside, but she no longer denied his accusations aloud. Perhaps she *should* have demanded of Cam tonight which army he intended to join! Tomorrow was the Sabbath, and she had planned that she and Sally would catch the first ferry to Staten Island and visit Mother and Merry. She had promised Cam she would send Sally to Melrose when they were ready to visit, and he had said he would send a carriage to the cottage to fetch them.

Why hadn't Cam donated that carriage to the Continental Army, if he believed in liberty? she asked herself, covering her face with her hands. Her mind went wild finding double possibilities everywhere. There had been slips in conversation, things she should have asked that might have tripped him up. How had he known Washington was coming? Why had the Supplier's fleet been untouched when other ships had been taken? She loved him so much, but did she know in her deepest soul that things were impossible between them? She couldn't take Eddie to Cam now. What if she found Captain Hector there!

"Sally, I'm going to go to my old Whig friend Lawrence Lang for help to hide Eddie, or at least deliver him to his regiment. But in case soldiers come before I get back, we're

going to have to hide him outside. He can't be here, and I can't endanger the Goodhues or the Fannings this time.''

"I can go with you, Libby!" Eddie said. "I can walk...anywhere with you.''

She cursed herself for it, but at that she began to cry. She should end all her agonizing right here, she told herself. She should love this man, not the other. She should tell this man she would wed him. But she couldn't bring herself to say those words. Not quite yet. Not until she faced Cameron Gant one final time.

She stood up and dashed tears from her cheeks. Sally fetched her cloak, and she wrapped it around her nightclothes. With Eddie leaning heavily on her, she went out into the night.

Libby hadn't slept all night. Just after daybreak, when she was certain Lawrence Lang had Eddie safe with his regiment, she returned to the print shop and made four handwritten copies of Eddie's story. Every detail of his escape was there, and the recounting of his cruel captivity—but not a word of his accusations against Cam. Not yet. Not until she played her hand. She would tell Cam Gant he had a week to leave New York and never return before she had his name emblazoned in the four major Whig papers as a traitor to liberty. With the tar-and-feather-the-Tories mentality sweeping the city, he would be in dire danger here. He wouldn't dare show his face anyway.

She kept one copy for her staff to print on Monday morning, and just after daylight she personally delivered the other messages to the three gazettes that had helped her campaign against Eddie's plight. They deserved the chance to print the news, and besides, if other papers had the story, too, Captain Hector and his friends out on the water could not be certain Eddie had come to her.

She left Sally with a warning not to let Rob go near Cam Gant. But for churchgoers and strollers on this quiet Sab-

bath morning, the streets were quite deserted after the festivities at the illumination late last night. She boarded the first ferry for Staten Island and was ashore by nine.

Her mother and Merry were expecting her, but that wasn't where she was going yet. She walked the Bay Road toward Melrose at such a frenzied clip that she was soon perspiring. Questions, demands, accusations, roiled through her head. Deep anguish sliced through her with each step, but she vowed that no matter what Cam said she would not fall victim to his lies and lures this time. And she was most certainly not going to step inside Melrose Manor. She was as done with that as with her childish dream that Elizabeth Morgan and Cameron Gant might really love and live together for years to come.

She felt the foolish, awkward young girl again as she passed the spot where, so many years before, she and Merry had tied their swaybacked nag so they could take a forbidden peek at Melrose. She recognized the stone fence along which they had run from the Gants. And she passed the very place where the one dog had bitten her ankle. She winced, as if the scar she still bore there were paining her. She nearly jumped straight up in the air when she heard a voice behind her.

"Halt there! No one enters here unbidden! Master's orders!"

That command, too, touched her memory, but she did not recognize the young man upon the horse. She faced him, chin up, but her voice trembled.

"Go tell your master that Elizabeth Morgan has come calling for the last time at Melrose. I will go no farther. Go on then, man!"

At that tone and look, he did as she said, and she watched him thunder up the drive toward the rosy-bricked manor house. She rehearsed what she must say and tried to give herself courage for what she must do. But still she was afraid, of herself as much as Cam. "Devil take you, Mel-

rose!'' she cried aloud, and she shook her fist at the building just before she heard the thud of hoofbeats.

Cam, hatless, rode toward her with his coat flapping and his big black stallion kicking up a cloud of dust. He reined in and shot her a devastating smile.

''I'm sorry about the guard, sweetheart, but I thought we'd agreed you'd send Sally over much later. I've got protection around to keep the supplies safe at the wharf. And what's this about a final visit here? A final visit as an unbetrothed woman, you mean?'' he asked jauntily, and dismounted to stride toward her, his arms outstretched.

She backed up, palms raised, as if he'd thrown dirt in her face.

''Libby? What is it? What's hap—''

''Despite all your attempts otherwise, Eddie Tiler managed to escape on his own. I know the truth about you now.''

His beaming face froze into an expression of stony fury. ''And because I've been out to the ship, he told you I'm some bloody Tory spy, I suppose!'' He seized her upper arms.

''His words exactly! So I'm here to let you deny it once again, only I'm not such a dunce as to believe you this time! Go ahead. Tell me you're not a spy—''

''That's enough, damn you!'' he roared, shaking her hard. ''Eddie Tiler tells you that, and you accept it as gospel truth after all we've shared! So much for your trust, loyalty and love for me. Didn't you promise that just last night? Who's the liar now, Libby?''

''Just take your hands off—''

''Oh, I will, but first I'm going to tell you exactly what you want to hear so that you'll have your hatred to warm you these next years when I'm gone with the army.''

''*Which* army?'' she demanded, speaking the words that had been festering at her since yesterday. ''Go ahead, answer my first question—are you a spy?''

His hard gaze flickered over her scornfully.

"Yes, Libby, I'm a spy, and proud of it, though I've always hated the term. I've been a spy for a year now, and I fancy I'm rather good at it."

He waited for her to answer, to give him even the smallest opening to tell her he was Washington's spy, to show him she believed the best of him. But the words that she spat at him ended everything between them.

"Then, for past favors you had extended—and I don't mean trapped in your bed—I must inform you that you have one week to leave the colonies! Go to your family in London, flee to Canada, take one of your so-called Supplier ships and your fortune and run to the ends of the earth. I don't care. I'm going to do what I should have from the first, and wed Eddie Tiler! As for you, next week the four leading Whig papers in town, including my gazette, will expose you for the Tory spy you are! If you're not gone by then, it will be much too late for you to save yourself!"

His hands, which were still gripping her arms, fell away. "It's already too late, Mistress Liberty. As late for both of us now as for New York City."

He turned and swiftly mounted his horse. His epitaph for their would-be love and the place where it had bloomed echoed in Libby's ears like a dirge. A spy! He'd admitted he was a spy and that he had inside information that New York was doomed!

She stared through a wash of tears as Cam disappeared into a cloud of dust. She hadn't meant to blurt that out about wedding Eddie. She hadn't really decided, but in the pain it had just jumped out amidst all the other terrible but necessary things she'd said. With a leaden heart, she turned to trudge away from Melrose.

Fourteen

❧❧❧

THE LIBERTY GAZETTE
April 18, 1776

Required Reading of the Marriage Banns are
hereby suspend'd for the following couple: Robert Graham, Scotsman, Journeyman Printer, to
Sally Smith, Staten Island, Maidservant, for Marriage at Wall Str. Presbyterian Church, April 20,
1776.

* * *

Citizens of New York, greatly dismay'd by certain Behaviors of Soldiers in our Town, are as-
sur'd of the following by General Washington's
Staff: To Whit: Soldiers tearing Paneling off the
Walls of abandon'd Houses for Firewood shall
forfeit a stiff Fine or submit to the Lash. Quar-
termasters of the Regiments shall require beer
Barrels be henceforth return'd to the Brewery instead of halv'd for washing Tubs. Bawdy Houses
of the "Holy Ground" Area & Taverns in the
city are off Limits except for the House at the
Two Ferries. Soldiers swimming naked in Long
Island Sound in open view of Tory Women with

a Design to insult & wound the Modesty of female Decency shall be subject to the Lash.

Libby stood among the smiling folk at Rob's and Sally's wedding, feeling alone and betrayed. In tears, Sally had finally admitted to Libby that she was pregnant. Did no one ever trust her with the truth of their inner hearts? Libby asked herself. She knew she'd made a fool of herself, ranting at Rob, but she had apologized to him later. She admitted to herself she was reacting to Cam's betrayal, not theirs. She found she almost envied Sally for having conceived a child when she herself had not. Would Cam have felt he had to wed her then? At least Rob and Sally knew how to commit themselves to love.

Libby had suspected Rob of being a flirt, but he obviously truly wanted to wed Sally. When Libby had told Rob that Cam had merely loaned her Sally's services, the Scotsman had put his distrust of Cam aside to ask him to release Sally from her duties. Cam had agreed and had arranged for the banns to be omitted and for the tavern supper after the wedding. Because Sally had desired it, Rob had also asked Cam to stand as his supporter. Unfortunately, Cam had agreed after Libby had said she would stand up with Sally.

Only two days now remained of the week Libby had given Cam to leave New York. And here they stood in church, facing each other, a minister between them, almost as if this were the wedding that might once have been theirs. Today, however grieved she was for herself, Libby vowed to bear up for Rob and Sally.

Libby pulled herself back to the business at hand. In the dim church at midday, the minister's admonitions and blessings rolled over them all. The bridal couple gazed

fondly into each other's eyes. Libby and Cam looked elsewhere.

"If anyone can show just cause why they may not be lawfully joined together," the reverend intoned, "let him do so, or else hereafter hold his peace."

Cam's eyes briefly met Libby's before both looked pointedly away again. Libby's insides lurched each time she even sensed he was watching her. He looked so handsome today in his dove-gray frockcoat and waistcoat and his charcoal breeches, although his snowy-white cravat made his tawny complexion look darkly demonic when he glared at her. Sometimes his narrowed pewter eyes assessed her deliberately, as if he were about to shout some demand or challenge at her.

She was desperate to get away from here, to look anywhere else! Out of the corner of her eye she scanned the wedding guests from Staten Island: Sally's large family, Merry and their mother, two Melrose maidservants. Behind them, in the next row of pews, Jos and Coll, dressed in their questionable best, looked a bit squirmy. Fortunately, Eddie had not come. Somehow, with Cam here, Libby could not have borne that. Everyone looked so happy, so misty eyed, that it shook Libby to her very core to admit again to herself how miserable she was.

"Bless this couple in the gift and care of children, Lord God," the minister was saying, "that their home may be a place of love, security and truth."

Libby dared another slant-eyed glance at Cam. He looked as if he'd like to shake her. His harsh, stony expression, so perfectly, coldly controlled, terrified her more than Quentin Simpson's contorted one a few weeks ago had. She felt regret about Quentin's hatred, yes, but now her life seemed shattered. *Love, security and truth,* the minister had said. She and Cam had never managed to build any of those precious things together.

"I now pronounce that they be man and wife together. Bless and enrich them in joy that they may continually grow in their understanding and support of one another. Amen. Mr. Graham, you may kiss your bride."

Those assembled gathered round to hug and congratulate the couple. Her lower lip quivering, Libby kissed both Rob and Sally. Rob, though never a handsome or a contented man, appeared both pleasant and pleased today. Sally had never looked lovelier, Libby thought, though her gardenia bouquet from Melrose absolutely drenched the air with a heavy, dizzying fragrance. Suddenly Libby had to get some air.

She bumped a hard shoulder as she fought her way through the crush of well-wishers. "Oh, sorry," she said. Then she saw, too late, that it was Cam.

He had the audacity to reply, "I doubt it."

She escaped and stood with the excited Merry and her mother, until her mother's scoldings about not wedding Eddie rubbed her raw again. Then her mother dared to mention Cam.

"And I can tell, Elizabeth, things are quite warm between you and Cameron Gant. You ought to take full advantage of that, my dear. His continued kindnesses to Merry, and me and the way you two have always looked on each other, tell me where there's smoke there's fire."

"Mother, please!" Libby pleaded quietly. "You don't understand! We are not getting on. It has to do with higher things!"

Mrs. Morgan fluttered her fan and her eyes. "Higher things! My, my, at your lofty age of twenty-one, Elizabeth, there's no higher thing than a man and a woman wed and in love."

"And you and Mr. Gant are in love, Lib," Merry chimed in with a pert smile and a prodding elbow in the ribs. "I've seen it. It's what you and I used to talk about. You know,

that the moment you see the one you feel all red-hot inside—a fire, like Mother says."

"Merry, we don't need your two pence worth here!" Mrs. Morgan fanned herself harder.

"Listen, little sister," Libby said. "The red-hot fire Cam Gant and I feel toward each other is intense dislike and disagreement and naught else! Excuse me, please, as there seems to be some disturbance out in the foyer."

She was eager for a chance to escape this painful conversation. It panicked her that the seething feelings between her and Cam were so obvious. It had been sheer folly to deny her longings for Cam to Merry, and she regretted her harsh words to her mother. At least the soldiers she saw peeking in at the entry to the church were a handy excuse to avoid explaining things to her family right now.

Continental soldiers were everywhere in town lately, thicker than mosquitoes in July. Washington's ten thousand men had almost doubled the city's garrison. Manhattan bulged with gawkers in a motley array of uniforms. New Yorkers feared that their own soldiers would wreck the city before the British fired a shot!

When on leave from camping or drilling or digging, boys and men traipsed all over to see the sights of the city. They frequented the prostitutes on Holy Ground, the slum brothel district on land still owned by Trinity Church. And, as was obviously happening here, these country boys, many of whom had never seen a city before, trooped into any public building with a view.

"Excuse me, lads, but we're having a wedding here," she told them, frowning at the tallest boy, who appeared to be their leader. He wore homespun but for a fine blue coat, and he hardly looked old enough to shave.

"Just wanted to climb up in the steeple to take the view, missus," he said. "We been counting lobsterback boats all up and down the island from the high spots, see."

Just then the bell above began to toll loudly, randomly, repeatedly. Libby saw that one of the soldiers had moved to the bell rope and was wildly pulling it. The others laughed and slapped each other on the back. "Playing the bells real good, too," he boasted. "Just let those danged Brits think we're being called to arms!" he crowed as he and his companions all clustered around the bell rope.

Cam's voice rang out behind Libby. "Halt, all of you!" She jumped more than the soldiers did. "That's not a bit smart or funny. You've heard about the boy who cried wolf too many times, I think. You want that to happen when we really toll the bells to bring out the soldiers to face the Brits?"

"You're a fine one—" Libby began, but Cam grabbed her arm and squeezed it to quiet her.

"Well, no, but we're gonna whup them English something awful anyway!" the lad yelled back. But the soldier on the bell rope had halted, and the bell stopped clanging. As Cam faced them down, they trailed sheepishly back outside. Amazed that Cam was still touching her, Libby pulled her arm from his grasp and stalked down the street to the tavern ahead of the rest of them.

The happy toasts, the laughing party, were almost too much for Libby's composure. She breathed a sigh of relief when it was all over. Rob and Sally went off for a night at Cam's town house, of all places. The Staten Island people stood outside the tavern to bid farewell to those staying in Manhattan. Merry blushed as she pretended to ignore passing soldiers who called compliments to her. Mrs. Morgan kept sympathizing with Sally's mother about their daughters living permanently in New York City, where "so much terrible could happen." For once, looking back at her own social, if not business, life here, Libby had to agree with her.

Finally Libby hugged her mother and Merry goodbye and watched them walk away. The streets were full of folk wandering, even shopping, this afternoon. Libby sent Jos and Coll back to reopen the shop and quickly lost herself in the crowds to avoid another possible confrontation with Cam.

She could not believe it, but Cam had publicly declared at the wedding supper that he was not going to leave town. "No," he had said, without so much as lifting an eyebrow, when Rob had asked him if he'd be going now that Washington had come. "Why do you ask?"

"Just wondering a wee bit the lay of the land," Rob had said.

At Cam's denial, Libby had been bursting to pronounce a veiled warning about next week's edition of the gazette to them all. She had typeset the article exposing Cam over and over, but had let no one, including the three other Whig printers, see it yet. But she couldn't face seeing Cam's hatred of her expressed before the entire wedding party if she announced her plans.

Worse, Cam's calm reaction to Rob had made her fear that she might actually have to ruin him publicly. She had thought he would flee. If he did, she'd been considering not printing Eddie's accusations at all. But didn't her reading public have a right to know? Even if they did, she'd almost have thrown it all away to save him, even if he stayed. Her mind spinning possibilities, she ducked down Pearl Street toward home.

She wandered absently along, staring in shop windows. The boom of the new shoppers had revitalized some of the trade, though the shelves were less than half full. At the inflated prices they could charge now, many Whig merchants had hauled out goods they had hidden in fear of a full-scale British occupation.

Libby's reflection stared back at her in the various win-

dowpanes, wavy, distorted, fragile, sometimes transparent. That was the way she had felt today, she told herself. She loved the man despite everything—despite the fact that he now hated her for certain.

Outside one of the elegant shops on William Street, a crowd bulged out into the street. Curious to see what the shop was offering, she edged closer.

"Whatever is it?" she asked a woman she recognized. "Something discounted in price?"

"Oh, no," the woman said with a proud smile and a shake of her bonneted head. "It's General Washington's lady, buying out the shop, and we're all watching!"

Martha Washington! Libby stood on tiptoe and craned her neck like everyone else. She would love to get a good description of the general's lady for the next issue of the gazette! Perhaps if she spoke to her Mrs. Washington would be willing to give a message of hope for the city. The simple fact that the general had sent for his wife and members of her family implied that he believed they were safe here. So how dare that two-faced Cam Gant suggest last week that New York was doomed, Libby thought, seething.

She edged closer, sliding through spaces between gawkers, excusing herself repeatedly. Inside, at the center of all the attention, stood a short, dignified middle-aged lady dressed in blue and accompanied by a pert brunette woman. On the counter between them was a burgeoning pile of packages.

"That young pretty one with her—that's her daughter-in-law, Nelly Custis," someone whispered.

When Mrs. Washington and Nelly emerged from the shop, loud huzzas sprang up. Martha Washington's face was pleasant, plump and very kind, Libby thought as she moved through the crowd in the direction the women walked. Several soldiers loaded with boxes and packages

followed behind. A little down the way was a carriage with a military driver and escort. Libby edged around the crowd and headed there. When Mrs. Washington arrived, trailing her admirers, Libby stood right next to her.

Martha Washington was shorter than Libby, and Libby thought she must look quite mismatched with the six-foot-two-inch general. But none of that mattered. Only truth and trust and loyalty and love made a marriage, Libby thought, clenching her hands nervously.

"I see you're very busy, Mrs. Washington," she said with a nervous smile, "but I just wanted to meet you. I am Elizabeth Morgan, printer of the *Liberty Gazette*, and I wondered—"

"The woman printer. Of course," a mellow voice replied. Libby's lower lip dropped in surprise. "You see, your reputation precedes you, too, Mistress Morgan. In Boston, more than once, I've read your fine gazette!"

"Clear in Boston? But how—"

"Why, someone sent it to my husband," she said, as if that explained everything. "He simply must keep up with places he is not, you see," she whispered, patting Libby's hand.

"I never imagined...didn't know that," Libby floundered, hoping she didn't sound too much the dunce. Nelly Custis climbed into the high green carriage, then reached a hand down to assist Mrs. Washington. "So the general receives papers from all over?" Libby asked.

"I suppose he read yours because New York is strategically important," Mrs. Washington confided with a smile. "Now, I fancied your gazette because it had a woman's view, and yet one couldn't really tell it from a man's. So very clever of you, Mistress Morgan. You know, we're heading back to the Mortier mansion, where they've put us," she said, one foot on the first iron step of the carriage. "Nelly and I would love to have your company, as we

really don't know New York a bit yet, though its shops are better than what the British left us at Boston and Cambridge when they were through!''

"But how kind of you. I would consider that a great honor.''

And as the crowd cheered and huzzahed, Libby followed Martha Washington into the coach.

The chatter with Martha Washington over coffee and cake at the beautiful Mortier mansion in the fine rural northern neighborhood called Lispenard's Meadow was mostly of the day's events—and a new feather bed, bolsters, curtains, crockery and glassware—but Libby already admired the way that this storm-tossed wife clearly strove to make a stable, charming home for her husband wherever they could be together. She maintained her spirits even when faced with the fact that he'd be living all too soon with a single camp bed in an army tent without her. Despite Libby's passion for her printing press, she longed for such a spirit and such a life herself—with Cam.

After about half an hour, Nelly Custis left, and Martha Washington went with her to the door of the room. "It's pure delight to shop again!" she said to Libby when she sat down again.

"Despite those British gunships, we still do have some Manhattan suppliers," was all Libby said. She suddenly wished she could share all her woes with Mrs. Washington, since her own mother would no doubt just scold her for losing Cam.

"So," Martha prodded gently when she saw the young woman blink back tears again, "you say you and Cameron Gant both stood up for your servants in their marriage today. I rather like that—Whig and Tory families joining forces. You know, I'd like to send your servants something

to mark their special occasion. Perhaps a fine piece of pewter or a nice feather pillow for their bed.''

"How very kind. They have little yet, and they would be so grateful.''

"But the point is, Mistress Morgan, I wish a real sort of marriage between the Tory and the Whig side could really happen in the colonies. But with this dreadful Tory spy fever wracking the city, I'm afraid we're far, far beyond that.''

"Yes, I know,'' Libby said, staring morosely at the untouched slice of rum cake on a plate on her lap.

Martha had an urge to take this girl in her arms to comfort her, as she might dear Nelly in a pensive humor, or as she might have her beloved daughter, Patsy, whom she had lost two years before. As they had prepared for bed last night, George had told her about what Cameron Gant had done to help keep him informed and to hold the lid on the overboiling kettle that was New York.

And he had told her of Cameron Gant's admission of what havoc his Tory masquerade was playing with his future with this staunch Whig girl. She would never give away a thing George had confided—or presume to meddle, of course—and yet...

"Elizabeth—may I call you that?—you know, it's interesting you mentioned that Cameron Gant sponsored that wedding party today, for my husband thinks most highly of him.''

Libby's head snapped up. "Cam Gant? But he's a Tory...his whole family, from way back....''

"Well, families, you know how that is. Why, Benjamin Franklin, another freedom-loving friend of my husband's— and a printer, too, my dear—has a son who is a dyed-in-the-wool Tory, and it's split them apart. Wretched business! It happens all the time that people just assume families think the same, you know. Just prejudice and preconcep-

tion," she added as she popped a piece of cake in her mouth.

Libby squirmed on her needlepoint chair seat. Her mind darted back to the day a man had fetched Cam to go into Hull's Tavern, where Washington was staying after his triumphal parade. She had presumed, of course, Cam meant no good toward Washington because of her dislike of the Gants.

"But wherever would General Washington have met Cam?" she inquired.

"Why, I believe they knew each other when Mr. Gant attended William and Mary College in Virginia. Friends and political interests in common, you know, even though Mr. Gant's Whig tendencies angered his elder brother mightily, I'm afraid."

It could not be. General Washington must have been as misled by Cam as she had been. Or could Eddie Tiler have misinterpreted what he'd heard aboard the British ships? Or might poor Eddie even have lied? Before he had fallen on her doorstep, such a pitiful sight, she'd been willing to believe Cam. But now she'd ruined everything. She had to talk to Eddie Tiler. Had to think things out. But she had only two days before the date she had set for exposing Cam. But if General Washington himself—

"Mrs. Washington, could I ask you the great, great favor of trying to obtain a brief interview with the general for me? For the gazette, of course, and—" she met Martha Washington's gentle yet steady gaze "—and for something personal about someone we know in common."

Martha's hand reached out to cover hers. "You know, the general's time is not his own, my dear, but I will try. Trying is all a woman can do in these troubled times, that and tending to her man as best she can."

"Indeed, I think we should be free to speak out and act. We have a right to fight, too!" Libby declared with a de-

cisive bob of her head. "But thank you, Mrs. Washington. Whatever happens, thank you so much!"

Libby learned that Eddie Tiler had recovered enough to be stationed again at the Brookland Heights camp, and she could not get to him there. Washington was busy day and night, and her request for an audience was, understandably, put off, even with Mrs. Washington's request. After all, what was one woman's broken heart in a war-torn land?

Libby rehearsed a thousand imagined visits to Cam, alternately asking his forgiveness and accusing him again. He was back and forth between Melrose and his town house, Rob told her. "He's been damned good to Sal and me, Tory or not," he had admitted once.

She shelved the article she had written exposing Cam as a loyalist spy for another week. After all, until she questioned Eddie under calmer circumstances than the night he'd escaped she could hardly print all that. And, considering what Mrs. Washington had said, until she got to speak with the general she could not print it. If Cameron Gant thought she was being weak and came to see her about it, so much the better.

She threw herself into her work and donated time and money to the building of the defenses around the city. She bent over her type case for hours, until her eyes and back and neck ached with the strain.

Today Sally had gone out to buy precious drinking water, and Rob had whistled at his work until she thought she would scream. His unfailing good humor since his marriage was just too much. Jos had taken his usual break to go next door to inquire at Fanning's if any particularly fine wigs had been resold or reclaimed lately—not that he had the money, for Libby often had to pay her staff with Continental scrip now. One wag had jokingly said it took a cartload of Continental money to buy a cart.

Libby stretched her tired muscles. She heard Coll's quick step as he skidded in the front door. "Coll, I've asked you not to dash about!" Libby told him without looking up. "You could knock a customer right down, darting about like that."

"Jupiter, Mistress Morgan," Coll yelled, "there's a bunch of Whigs grabbed up some Tories on the Commons, and they're tarring and feathering them!"

The hair on the back of her neck rose, and she was already halfway across the room, with Rob right behind her, when the boy choked out, "They've got Mr. Gant! And that friend o' yours, Crispin Brooks, says they're gonna ride him on the rail, too!"

In her inky apron, her hands a blackened mess, Libby ran for the Commons. Rob was right behind, his legs pumping to keep up with her long strides.

"Should of fetched my pistol first!" he grunted between breaths. "No one but Farmer George and his ministers and generals deserves the rail!"

Libby fought back tears of panic. She bounced off a woman, who spilled her basket of onions and shouted insults as Libby tore away. Tarring and feathering had gotten completely out of hand lately, and she'd printed more than one admonition against it in the gazette. But the rail was far worse. It was criminal...unethical...immoral.... Still, the radical rabble of New York had taken many Tories on a rail ride lately, and the painful punishment had sometimes permanently ruined both their ability to walk straight and their manhood.

She gasped huge, ragged breaths as she charged onto the Commons past the row of big old cannon. The Whig crowd was not hard to find. They were bellowing insults, and they had a fire blazing under a pot of tar. Geese being plucked for their feathers set up an awful squawking din.

She clenched Rob's arm as a man she did not recognize

was ridden by on a rail. Four tall men, one of them the black-haired giant she had seen with Crispin, carried the rail on their shoulders. Others ran along beside them, forcing the agonized, bouncing victim to sit erect on the sharp rail. The Tory had been stripped naked and was hardly recognizable with the black tar and random feathers sticking to his flesh everywhere.

"Rob, find Cam!" she cried.

They ran in opposite directions through the milling, shouting crowd. At least she hadn't printed her article about Cam! Why had he stayed when things were so bad? Seeing this rabble here, baying for blood, she felt ashamed to have ever called herself a Whig. But these weren't Whigs. These were scum.

Desperately she searched the line of pitiful Tories awaiting their turns. She saw Cam then, his shirt off, trussed like an animal waiting to be sacrificed. Crispin Brooks was shouting in his face, and two men held his bound arms so that he couldn't move.

"It's the rail for you, Tory bastard. Been out to those ships time after time, he has! And been bedding one Whig woman too many, so we'll just make sure you can't stud another!" Crispin shouted, his face turning livid as he reached for a metal dipper dripping tar.

"No!" Libby screamed, thrusting herself between Cam and Crispin. "You have no right to do this to any of them!" She shoved at his arm, and the ladle dropped.

"Speaking of bedding Whigs, looky who's here!" Crispin roared.

"Libby, get the hell out of here!" Cam yelled behind her. "Brooks, send her away!"

"No," she insisted. "Crispin, your brother and Lawrence Lang would never approve of this barbarity! Cameron Gant has done good things for the Whig cause!"

"Like what?" he shouted, seizing her elbows and nearly slipping in the tar spilled on the grass.

She was tempted to tell them Cam was the Supplier, but then Cam might hate her even more. "Don't you read the gazette?" she demanded, stalling for time. "He's given a great deal of money for Continental arms."

"Ha! Mere smokescreen!" Crispin screeched. "Here, hold this turncoat strumpet, somebody, and let her watch. Now get on with it!"

A man dragged her a few steps back and, despite her kicking and writhing, pinned her arms at her sides. Cam's captors yanked him forward and forced him to his knees next to the kettle of pitch.

"No, no, no!" she screamed.

Her wild eyes searched the crowd for Rob. Where had he gone? She recognized only a few faces, and they all looked demented, demonic. This was not a political protest at all. These men wanted to humiliate and hurt those they envied. She could smell the perverted passion for power that drove this crowd.

Cam's eyes caressed her once, then looked away. Suddenly all she knew was that she loved Cam Gant. Not because of advice from her mother or Mrs. Washington, but because of the way he had always been. No matter what he'd done, no matter if he felt drawn to the Tory cause, whoever his friends were, she loved *him*. How could she have been so blind as to mistrust him so? It was Cam's brother and her own father who had caused her initial feelings against the Gants, not Cam. He had been protective of her from the first. She had to apologize for her prejudice, for the way she'd fought him. Now she wanted only to fight for him here, even if it cost her her life.

Tears blinded her as they ladled the hot, sticky pitch onto Cam's bare muscular shoulders. He gritted his teeth in pain,

and Crispin grunted an obscene laugh. Libby writhed and kicked at her captor.

"Cam!" she called out. "I love you no matter what! I always have...and I always will...."

She thought she would faint as she watched Crispin lift another dripping ladleful. He seized Cam's loosened blond hair with his free hand and yanked his head back so that the ladle was poised over his face. Cam closed his eyes. Shaken to her soul, Libby closed hers, too. And then a shot rang out.

"Loose that man, and all the rest of them. Stand back, or the next bullet won't be over your heads!"

Libby's captor dropped her, and she scrambled to shove Crispin away from Cam. Three mounted officers spurred their horses into the center of the crowd. A pathway opened for them as the rabble hushed. Libby barely noted that the uniforms were the buff and blue of Washington's Virginia regiment before she threw herself on her knees next to Cam and began fumbling with his ropes.

"Just teaching the bloody Tories a lesson," she heard Crispin say, his voice shaky. Cam's ties were sticky with tar.

"Cut those cords!" an authoritative new voice declared. An officer dismounted to use his sabre on Cam's ropes, but Libby looked up and saw that the man who had spoken last was Washington himself!

"We will teach the Tories a lesson on the battlefield. We will fight this war like men, not animals!" Washington said. "What fools you make of yourselves. That man, Cameron Gant, may be from a Tory family, but so were we all once. As Providence is my witness, I tell you he's no more Tory than I."

Cam got to his feet and wiped the hot muck off his bared shoulders and arms. Then one sticky hand gripped Libby's wrist convulsively. She saw that he was trembling. She took

her printer's apron off and draped it around his big, tar-smeared shoulders like a shawl.

"But Gant's been spyin', General," Crispin Brooks protested, and a few faint assenting murmurs rose at last.

"Cameron Gant has been an informant indeed," Washington announced, "but for *me*, and at *my* specific request. And at obvious great cost to himself! Now that the Continental armies hold New York City, I can tell you poor excuses for men that it was to the benefit of all of us that Cameron Gant rubbed shoulders with the redcoats."

Libby gasped aloud. That Cam had been Washington's man all this time was one thing, but she had never imagined that such a fine leader would employ spies, as the tricky Brits did! She knew how naive and foolish she had been.

Washington was still speaking. "Cameron Gant will now become one of my aides-de-camp in the Continental Army. In addition, he has also served this city and province as the importer called the Supplier, who perhaps brought you cowards the very tar and geese you are using here. Unlike you civilians, who have evidently shunned our country's uniform, Cameron Gant has not joined our forces yet because I asked him not to until it was time. It is high time now. Officers, arrest the brazen spokesman of this rabble."

Libby stared speechless, first at Cam, then at Washington, and then at Rob, who had reappeared, rather out of breath. She guessed that Rob had fetched the soldiers, and she nodded her thanks to him. Coll appeared in the crowd to tug on Rob's arm and ask what had happened.

Washington moved his big gray stallion over to Cam and Libby and leaned down toward them. Seeing him up close for the first time, Libby was awed by his calm presence, as well as by his size and his strong features.

"You were right about two things, as always, friend Gant," Washington observed, his sharp blue eyes moving from his face to Libby's and then back again. "One, it was

time for me to come to New York. And two, your Liberty's Lady is worth waiting for, despite the fact that she looks as blackened as you. Are you burned?''

"It's worth it to be freed at last from playing Tory, sir."

"Take Captain Smith's horse and be off, then. Report in when you mend a bit. I can use you just as readily in the brightness of day as I have done covertly in the past. And when the redcoats come calling, the fact that you're a turn-coat to them and their cause won't make any difference. They'll be out to catch us all, Mistress Morgan included."

Libby wanted to declare that she was not afraid, but she was, of course. She was done with overly passionate state-ments. She wanted only truth and trust and loyalty and love with Cam, but she was afraid it was far too late for that.

Rob held the reins of the captain's horse for Cam as Washington tipped his bicorne to them and rode away. Other officers dragged the protesting Crispin Brooks off. The New York jails would now be bulging with criminals cursing her name, Libby thought. The rabble quickly dis-persed, leaving a gaggle of noisy, half-feathered geese to run the Commons.

With a grunt and a glance at his slippery and painful hands, Cam swung himself up on the officer's horse. Rob handed him the reins with a cockeyed salute and a proud grin. Tears of mingled joy and grief washed Libby's cheeks when she looked up at him and their eyes met and held.

Then he frowned, and she knew she was doomed. He would ignore the declaration of love she had shouted to him in front of this horrible crowd. He had decided not to forgive her, despite the fact that Washington had agreed she was worth waiting for. She could not bear it if they parted with anger or hatred between them again, but she knew she had no one to blame but herself, for her long-tended prejudices and her stupid stubbornness!

"I'm getting out of here for a while...over to Melrose,"

Cam told her quietly. "If only you hadn't said you'd never visit there again. I could use someone to hold the reins. Someone who knows something of kindly nursing to tend my burns there."

"Oh, yes, Cam. Please, yes! I don't care what anyone says anymore. I love you and I want to be with you. It's been horrid without you!"

"Give your employer a boost up, if you please, Rob," Cam told the grinning Scotsman. "She'd slip right out of my hands."

"Never! Never again!" she declared as she stepped on Rob's clasped fingers. Sitting sideways, cradled in Cam's lap, she took the reins from his hands. She almost laughed through her tears at the ink-and-tar-blackened mess they both were. But everything would surely be bright and beautiful now, if they could just be together!

Cam clamped the saddle with his legs and pressed his forearms to her waist to keep from toppling off. She flapped the reins and turned the horse toward the Staten Island ferry.

Fifteen

THE LIBERTY GAZETTE

The Water Crisis in Town is as severe as the coming Freedom Crisis. But another Hero has risen to the Fore to take his Place with George Washington, Eddie Tiler, and Cameron Gant (see Articles below.) Christopher Colles plans to provide a public Water System for all of New York City's Inhabitants. We all know the brackish well Water & Price of 3 Pence a Hogshead for imported Pure bought on the Streets is quite outrageous. But Colles has built a roof'd wooden Reservoir & will install 10 Miles of hollow'd pine log Pipes to service 67 Streets & alleys. His secret? A revolutionary Steam Engine Pump. His Problem? Work on Pipes has come to a virtual Halt with Laborers needed for continued Construction of Fortifications.

* * *

Unit'd soon, alive & free,
Firm on this Basis, Liberty.
May Freedom ever bless our Land
Till Time becomes Eternity.

"General Washington actually asked you to keep an eye on me?" Libby demanded. She was carefully rubbing butter on Cam's burns, having already tenderly removed the tar with dabs of mineral spirits. "And here I thought it was the British!"

He laughed, despite the pain of his hands, shoulders and arms where the hot pitch had touched him. "I see I'd best inform our commander-in-chief he has more to fear from you than the British," he declared solemnly, but a grin flickered at the corners of his mouth.

She leaned her shoulder against his hard chest as she soothed his other hand. "Oh, Cam," she said, "I've been such a fool. I revered Washington so much I never admitted he could employ spies or such like our enemies. And I've been so prejudiced against the Gants, from way back. I never recognized all the good you were doing. I've got to learn that this war, as lofty as its purposes may be, is being fought on both sides by men. It's hardly a struggle between devils and angels."

"We've both learned a lot lately, Libby. But, speaking of angels, I hear from a friend in Eddie's regiment that he still calls you his angel and thinks you'll wed him."

"No, Cam. I don't love Eddie. For a long time," she said, her voice shaking, "I've loved someone else—and still do." She turned in his arms. They were both blackened messes, but he had never looked more handsome to her. And she was done with playing games, with disguises and deceptions of all sorts, whatever happened. "I love you, Cam. And I regret that I've made things so hard for you."

To her amazement, he grinned like a boy and scooted closer, though he could not touch her with his hands. "My sweetheart, you can't possibly know the truth of that." He stood and kissed her, long and deep. "I'm tempted to just seal our bargain on that," he whispered in her ear when he

finally lifted his mouth from hers, "but I'd never get clean if I took you upstairs to bathe me. I'll call you a maid, and when we're washed and dressed we'll walk outside. We have, as I believe I'd said before, some things to talk about. I know the perfect place for it."

Libby did as he said in a haze of expectation. A maid filled a large copper hip tub with hot water and helped her wash her hair and skin. She brushed Libby's loosed tresses until they crackled and shone, then helped her slip on a mint-hued sprigged gown and slippers. Libby smiled into the mirror at her reflection. That would teach Cam's sister to desert him for London and her Tory brother. A few more visits to Melrose for Libby and there wouldn't be a stitch left in the woman's wardrobe.

Libby left her hair free in the warmth of the April sun but took a wide-brimmed straw hat. The beauty and grandeur of Melrose awed her again as she went downstairs to meet Cam. How much Father would have loved to be here like this, to pretend even in his deepest thoughts, that it was all his.

"Ready?" Cam's voice broke her reverie. He wore only coffee-brown breeches, a loose-sleeved linen shirt and a loose cravat, for his scalded skin could not have borne more formal clothing, but he looked marvelous. "I'm afraid we'll not be holding hands as we stroll today, Libby. Ah, yes, Montague, our thanks," he said when his butler appeared with a covered basket and extended it to Libby. "I owe you a picnic, I believe," Cam said, straight-faced. "And if you'll carry it I won't bother with someone else to wait on the next hill."

She took the basket readily, blushing at the pointed reminders. Perhaps all would not be so easily patched up between them. Perhaps he had another sort of talk in mind today besides what she longed for.

He led her through the back gardens and across a sloping

lawn into a forest glade. "I've something special to show you, my favorite boyhood place," he said. She followed him around the brow of a hill; they could see the water from here, but not the wharf.

He took her past a natural screen of bushes. "Oh, a little stone grotto," she murmured, charmed by the beauty of it. "It's perfect!"

"For many things," he agreed. "Especially for hiding from stern elder brothers, or even one's father. Here, let's sit."

She flapped the blanket down and laid things out under his steady gaze. He leaned back against a tree before he realized that hurt, too, and sat with his arms propped on his knees.

"You know, Libby Morgan," he said, his voice so serious it scared her, "even before our last picnic I had decided time and again that we were through."

She stopped fussing with the food. She sat back on her heels, her heart thudding. "Oh, Cam, my love just couldn't, wouldn't, end, no matter how hard I tried!"

"But when Eddie escaped you unquestioningly took his word over mine—over what we'd been building. What's going to happen to us next time someone you admire claims I'm still spying for the British?"

"I'm going to believe you, even if you tell me you are King George himself!"

He smiled stiffly at that. "And would a royal command that you do anything I ask avail me?"

"You could try it and see," she murmured, and scooted closer to him.

"I will, but there is one more thing. About Melrose."

"Melrose?"

"The house and the estate...you do understand they're Charles's, not mine? He'll cut me off completely when he hears what I have done. Until then, of course, I consider it

my duty to care for it for him. About Melrose…Libby, I've never been able to figure if you love or hate the place!''

That stunned her. It was true. The way she'd felt about Melrose over the years was much the way she'd felt toward Cam ever since she'd known him. Desire and detestation, love and hate.

"Cam, I admire Melrose. That's why I came here that time. I think the scars of our past will heal." She paused and added inconsequentially, "You know, I actually have a little scar on my leg from that time the dogs chased Merry and me." She remembered the point under discussion and added, "But while my poor father coveted the place, I don't. But I do want the man who lives here—''

"A scar?" he asked. "Still? Let me see it."

When he persisted, she untied her garter and peeled her green silk stocking down. She turned her leg so that he could see the tiny jagged line above her ankle.

"My sweetheart," he said, and bent to kiss it. His lips pecked her leg twice and slid down deliciously to her ankle and then up behind her knee, his tongue darting wickedly, while she held her breath. She felt her limbs go weak, as if they were made of water, even after he sat back to gaze warmly, possessively, at her.

"Damn it, Libby, if only I could hold you and touch you now! But you'll have to do that for both of us until my hands and arms heal. But I can at least kneel and ask you to marry me. You know, when I was on my knees there to be tarred and feathered by those bastards all I could think of was how much I adored and needed you. All I wanted was for you to be safe. And that will still be my fervent prayer when I ride away with Washington to face the British for you."

"You…you did ask me to marry you?"

He frowned. "I did, yes. What now?"

"Only that that is the most wonderful proposal a woman

could hope for, and I say yes with all my heart! And please do not forget, sir, how to kiss behind my knee. I will demand a repeat performance sometime.''

"I won't forget. But shall we go over in the carriage to tell Merry and your mother, or shall I try behind the other knee right now? I'm afraid if I do our picnic will run awfully, awfully long.''

"I'll take both choices, please," she said, and rose to her knees to press herself carefully against him. In a daze of joy, she wrapped her arms around his waist and lifted her pouted lips to his. It was the perfect moment of a lifetime, fit to be enshrined in her mind and heart forever. Surely nothing bad could ever touch them now.

"Congratulations, Lieutenant Gant! Well earned and fully deserved!'' Washington told Cam, shaking his hand heartily, when he reported to the general in uniform for the first time. At Washington's Broad Way Street headquarters, Cam had just signed the papers to become a lieutenant in the Third New York Regiment with a special assignment as aide-de-camp to the commander-in-chief. Cam felt deeply moved that he was finally, after all he'd been through, able to offer his services publicly.

He snapped Washington a smart salute, grateful that he could now use his arms and hands without soreness. He wished Libby could have been here to share this moment with him, but her mother had suddenly been taken ill on Staten Island, and she'd gone over to see her. Washington was sending him to New Jersey for a few weeks, so they had set their wedding date for June 29, when he returned.

"You know, Cam," Washington told him, "Mrs. Washington has been scolding me for sending you away so soon after your betrothal—and for heading for Philadelphia myself for a few weeks. I'm afraid that since becoming ac-

quainted with your Elizabeth Morgan my wife has become
a bit more outspoken.''

Cam grinned. "Let's just say marriage must surely
strengthen one for battle.''

Washington merely nodded, his gaze distant again as it
roamed the papers on his big desk. "Sit, Cam,'' he said.
"There's something else I'd have you see to. I regret you'll
soon think your conversion from abused Tory to Washington aide is like jumping out of the frying pan and into the
fire.''

Cam's tawny eyebrows lifted at that, but he waited to
hear what the general would say. He perched, straight
backed, in the chair, his new blue-and-buff uniform feeling
stiff and scratchy. He clanked his saber as he perched one
hand on the hilt and held his tricorne in the other.

"Although it will be obvious to everyone that you are
my aide, I don't want it to be obvious to them that I'm
going to make you my liaison for dealing with secret matters that come across my desk. I regret the necessities of
this war, but we're going to need a network of spies, some
of them recruited from civilian ranks. I'd like to make you
my secretary and confidant for such—considering all
you've done so well for us in that stead so far.''

Cam immediately acquiesced, though he was not pleased
to be back in the thick of intrigue. He'd have to keep secrets
from his Liberty's Lady, just when he and Libby had promised no secrets from each other. But, of course, Cam assured himself, that promise had hardly meant confidential
army matters.

The evening of June 18 at the Fraunces Tavern was a
wonderful reunion. Cam had returned from New Jersey
with promises of more supplies and a new pattern of trade
contacts and routes to outsmart the British, at least temporarily. Washington had come back from meeting with the

Continental Congress at Philadelphia, ready to face the assault on Manhattan they expected any time now. Even Martha Washington had been away—rumors said to take the highly controversial smallpox vaccination—and had returned.

For Cam and Libby it was a glorious night to be together. Their wedding was a little over a week away, and the marriage banns had been posted. Libby's mother had recovered from her illness, the gazette was doing well, and they were so happy to be together and to have been invited to the elegant dinner the Provincial Congress of New York was giving in Washington's honor.

Libby and Cam lifted their glasses to yet another toast to a prosperous, victorious future for New York and the united colonies. Libby's eyes scanned the tavern's long room, with its three crowded tables in a U shape. Although it was a warm mid-June night, both fireplaces were blazing, reflecting warmth and light in the row of five windows overlooking the handsome piazza just outside. There a boisterous band of citizens had gathered to raise their own toasts to their general and their Congress.

"To loyalty, one to the other! To future happiness!" one of Washington's officers shouted in ringing tones, and everyone huzzahed. In unison, they all downed yet another swig of Washington's favorite Madeira.

Libby felt as if each toast were just for her and Cam. Even with the British still perched out in the harbor, awaiting massive reinforcements, things seemed safe and sure on this night, at least. They knew now that the rest of the fleet that had left Boston, supposedly for Halifax, might well be here soon, but right now that didn't matter. Rumors were rife that the British wanted the town intact for their own strategic base, but folks even dared to shake fists and yell insults at the battleships offshore these days. The batteries to defend New York were ready, and the defenses were

nearly complete. Libby took Cam's hand under the table. Hovering war or not, she had never been happier.

She and Cam had finally reached agreement—compromise, he called it—on everything. If the British should ever take New York, she would go with Jos, Coll, Rob and Sally to Cam's merchant friends in New Haven. There she could continue to put out the gazette and send it back on the Supplier's ships. Since there wasn't enough room in New Haven for everyone and Libby would be very busy, her mother and Merry would go to stay with associates of Cam's in Philadelphia. But until that dire necessity, Libby would live at Cam's town house and continue to work the paper here in Manhattan.

Everyone hushed as General Washington himself stood to raise a toast. He lifted his glass to them all, then said, "There is one essential thing you generous gentlemen have omitted tonight. To the brave ladies of our righteous revolution. With gratitude especially to my dear wife, Mrs. Washington. And to the bold woman we proud rebels affectionately call Liberty's Lady, Elizabeth Morgan, soon to be Mrs. Cameron Gant. Stand, please, my dears. To your health!"

Chairs scraped back and swords clanked. "Health! Your health, ladies!" echoed in the room.

At that their stalwart general took his lady's hand, but Cam kissed Libby full on the mouth before them all.

The week before her wedding went by in a blur for Libby. Nothing could dim her rampant joy. Her mother gloated to simply everyone about the match her daughter had made. Merry bounced back and forth between ecstasy for Libby and grief for herself.

"I have no beau to love, and I never will!" she had confided to Libby. "I'm not likely to find a dashing, daring man immured like some nun on Staten Island when all the

young men have gone to war! Sleepy old Staten Island
never had anyone but Cam Gant to offer with a hint of
danger, anyway! Oh, don't say pooh to me, Lib, you know
the danger in a man is half the fun!''

Despite such domestic scenes, Libby still labored mightily at the gazette. An assassination plot against Washington
was exposed and diffused; the main conspirator was hanged
publicly as a warning. Lookouts watched for the arrival of
the remainder of the massive British fleet. New Yorkers
felt alternately numb and tense, defiant and defeated. They
were literally under the gun.

But June 29 dawned lovely and clear. Nothing could dis-
turb Libby's plans now. Her mother and Merry had spent
the night before at Cam's town house. After the wedding
at Trinity Church, on the bluff, and a reception at the town
house, they would be heading back for Staten Island—
Merry and mother for their home, the newlywed Gants for
a few days at Melrose before returning to take up residence
in Manhattan. Although Sally would go with them to Melrose to act as Libby's maid during the honeymoon, Rob
would remain to work the shop. And on the Gants' return
Rob and Sally would live above the print shop to care for
it.

Libby moved in a haze of happiness. Her gown was a
combination of one of Catherine Gant's cast-offs and Martha Washington's generous donations of ribbons and lace.
It was pale rose, with upswept, gathered ruffles of petal-
pink satin. She wore a cameo of Cam's mother's on a velvet choker around her neck and pearls Cam had given her
in her hair. Their lustrous strands caught and contained her
curled crimson tresses. She was as gloriously fashionable
as his sister had been that night Libby had peered through
the window at Melrose and wondered how it would be to
live that way.

Merry, who was Libby's supporter, wore a peach-hued

gown made from an extra pair of brocade curtains from Melrose. Her golden hair was caught up and studded with Staten Island daisies, and she and Libby together were a feast for the eyes. The scent of the Melrose roses in their bouquets swept Libby's senses as Cam entered in his blue-and-buff uniform to stand stiffly at her side before the congregation and the black-robed minister.

Behind them as they faced the altar, numerous guests, including the Washingtons, stared their way. Yet Libby felt she and Cam were utterly alone in this precious moment of public union. Each breath she took felt rarefied. When Cam held her hand to slip a simple gold band on her finger, his touch sent tingling warmth to every part of her. Three days alone together at Melrose before they had to return here to face the world, she thought excitedly.

She smiled up into his nervous face, her gaze caressing him. She could have fallen into those smoldering silver eyes and lost herself in them forever. Their kiss after the minister pronounced them man and wife was the most wonderful yet. It was more chaste than most they had shared, yet it promised so much. Tears trembling on her lashes, Libby took Cam's arm as they turned to face their guests. And it was then that they saw a stone-faced messenger slip discreetly up the outer aisle to General Washington and bend to whisper in his ear.

"Trouble," Cam murmured as they started down the center aisle.

"Not today. No one would dare!" Libby told him through smiling, parted lips as they walked the aisle together as man and wife.

They greeted people on the front steps and urged them toward Cam's town house. But when Washington came out his manner was brusque and he was without his wife.

He shook Cam's hand, then bent to kiss Libby's cheek. "The British fleet's been spotted by lookouts over on the

northern edge of Staten Island," he told them crisply. "Massive numbers of ships. I'm sorry, you two."

"But they aren't going to Staten Island?" Libby blurted.

"I think we can assume, Mrs. Gant," Washington replied, "that they're coming through the narrows here."

"My three days' leave?" Cam asked.

"Best enjoy your reception and report to me as soon after as you can," the general said with a regretful shrug. "We've all known, through the toasts and the allaying joy, that this is war."

With that he hurried down the steps and mounted a horse a soldier held for him. A cluster of protective aides closed around him as they clattered off down cobbled Broad Way Street. Another aide came out with Mrs. Washington to accompany her to the reception.

"Those blasted British!" Libby hissed to Cam as they greeted guests pleasantly. "I'll have their heads on a platter yet for this!"

He smiled grimly. "Then they're as good as doomed. I'm going to shorten the reception, then take you and your family back to Staten Island for safekeeping. And I'll come back again as soon as I can. I doubt the fleet will sail in on this side of the island. Washington is convinced they'll go around to the East River and not block our access to Staten Island. And the general's right, my sweetheart. This is war. We'll have our wedding night when we can, and lots after that, I swear it!"

When the last guest had departed, Libby and Cam clasped hands and stared deep into each other's eyes on the steps of the church. Finally Rob called to them from the street.

"You two be missing your own party if you don't put a leg to it, and Lady Washington's a-waiting!"

Strangely reluctant to leave this place of sanctuary, they

came down the steps at last to join the misty-eyed Mrs.
Washington in the general's carriage.

Cam took Libby out to Staten Island and then, after many
promises and kisses, returned to duty in Manhattan. Left
alone, Libby fought to keep her spirits up. Mother and
Merry had gone back to the cottage but would be over to
stay with her tomorrow. They would have liked to stay that
night, but Mother's bees still had to be tended in this peak
honey time. It was as if the bees were the only ones whose
schedules had not been disrupted by the looming war.

Time and again Libby gazed out the upstairs windows
at Melrose while Sally helped her unpack some newly pur-
chased things. She cursed the fact she had not insisted on
awaiting the attack at her print shop with her staff. But this
had been her wedding day, and she did not want to begin
her marriage to Cam with an argument.

She toured all the rooms at Melrose and paced the garden
paths. Strange how the lovely place seemed almost a prison
to her now. She thought of the bitter Quentin Simpson and
that bastard Crispin Brooks, both of them in Manhattan's
city prison now. She could only hope and pray they would
either join the army or leave the area when they were eventually released.

She had just started back toward the house when Sally
waved a cloth and shouted at her out an upstairs window.
"Look at the water all around the island, Mistress Libby!
'Tis sprouting ships!"

"Oh, no! No! Washington thought they'd sail past into
the East River! They'll cut us off from Manhattan here!"
Libby dashed in and up the steps to join Sally at her van-
tage point.

It was even worse than Sally had reported. The ships
were dropping sail just off the green, gentle slopes of Staten
Island. The bay had become a forest of barren tree trunks

fluttering signal flags! Within an hour the women counted over one hundred frigates and transports pregnant with red-coated soldiers to be landed.

"Dear God in heaven, protect us!" Libby muttered. "It's got to be Howe's main fleet, and they're obviously going to come ashore." Chewing her lower lip, she stared through the spyglass at tenders stuffed with redcoat soldiers putting out toward shore. "With all the Tories here we'll be pointed out to them and trapped! Cam's made himself their enemy now, and the Brits already here have wanted to stop me for months. We have a lot to do. Come on!"

"Come on where?" Sally demanded, clamping her hands protectively over her barely swollen belly. "Maybe some of them know the master's brother in London and won't do anything to his family or his house!"

"And maybe they'll think that fact is their calling card to visit us!" Libby insisted. "I won't let them get a hand on you, don't worry. I know a good hiding place. But first we've got to bury some of Cam's family silver. He and I have already decided his brother should donate it to the cause. I'm not letting the Brits get it. Come on, then, Sally! I'll tell you what to do, and we'll make Cam and Rob proud!"

Libby stationed the old butler, Montague, with the spyglass in a front upstairs window with two trusted maidservant runners to warn her if redcoated visitors came calling. To be certain that in this household, which had a number of Tory servants, no one would tell the Brits where things were hidden, she and Sally alone dragged tablecloths full of silver out the back and shoved it under the compost heaps in the garden. She went hastily through Cam's desk and removed handfuls of papers she thought important. She sent Sally in to rest and was lugging her third armload of books from his library out to his hidden childhood grotto

when a plump maidservant named Anne ran up to Libby, panting and red-faced.

"Mr. Montague, he says you mustn't come back inside again, Mrs. Gant! The British officers have come to stay at Melrose, and they be searching for both you and Mr. Gant. And Mr. Montague says don't go to your mother's, as they've sent someone there, too. And they've took the whole island without one shot! The militia who promised Washington to defend it just threw their weapons down and joined the redcoats! Oh, mistress, what you gonna do?"

Libby forgot the load of books in her arms and stood stunned in the glade of trees. She had been perspiring, but now a chill of foreboding ran down her backbone. She had been so anxious to save Cam's things that she had no shawl, no food, and no fresh water out here. And no place to lay her head with night coming.

"I—I don't know yet, Anne. But I do know this island. If Montague gets a chance, tell him to set out some food by the compost piles, and not to worry about me. Tell Sally Graham the same. And...have Montague just tell the Brits I'm over on Manhattan with Mr. Gant."

"All right, mistress. But they already found out from someone at Melrose you and Mr. Cameron were here earlier today, so they might be too smart for that," the girl called back over her shoulder as she scurried back out onto the open lawns toward the house.

Too smart for that, indeed. Did she think she was trying to outsmart Jemmy Rivington here, or merely convincing her mother to let her run the paper in Manhattan? That was the British army out there, for heaven's sake, and they were after her and Cam. How could this have happened on their wedding day?

She made it to the grotto with the books before her trembling legs gave way. To be wed to Cam, only to be separated! To stay at Melrose, only to lose it to the British! To

have the colonies and their new, proud people's government beginning to pull together, only to be forced by the might of the trained, professional British army.

She blinked back tears and swallowed hard. She stacked the books with the others, with a rueful memory of how her mother had always scolded her that her books were the most important thing to her when other things should be. Mother had been right. Now Cam and her country mattered, and she would be any sort of loyal soldier she had to be to help them both.

As night fell, she edged out of the glade and peered from behind a tree, feeling very much a frantic fugitive. She was grateful Cam no longer kept the guard dogs that had chased her once. The British were bad enough.

The lights in Melrose's grand windows went on one by one. Oh, Cam, she moaned silently as tears gilded her eyes, we should be up there, celebrating and loving together. She prayed he would not try to come back to be certain she was well. She hoped Sally, who had evidently been trapped inside, would be calm and brave. She prayed for Mother and Merry to stay put, too. Tomorrow, if she was careful, she could walk over there through the woods and try to attract their attention when Mother tended the bees. She would tell them that she was all right and that they should not attract attention to themselves.

From time to time she could see redcoated figures moving past the windows, and would catch a flash of white wigs and X-shaped crossbelts against the red. Cam had said that, after all, Melrose was not his, but it still angered her. How dare this foreign country come ashore in her homeland and make all sort of dire threats? She'd show them somehow.

When no house servants sneaked out with food that night, she quit watching and huddled beneath the pile of books in Cam's little grotto. She fell asleep at last, her head

on Plato's *Republic*, hungry, sore and chilled. She woke in terror from time to time, thinking she heard the redcoats beating the bushes for her, but it was only normal night sounds. How she longed to have Cam here beside her, to comfort her, to caress her—to love her.

Tomorrow, after she visited her family, she'd find some way to cross over to Manhattan, despite the armada of enemy ships between her and Cam. But she should at least wait to see if Sally could slip away to join her before Rob and Cam came tearing over here to rescue them.

At dawn she sat up, stiff and sore and very lonely. She climbed out of the grotto and crept cautiously from tree to tree until she could see Melrose. Still the outsider looking in, she spoke as if to the house itself and raised her fist at its distant vista.

"He promised me my wedding night and a long life together, and I will have it, damn you British!" She turned away, then suddenly bowed her head. "And, my dearest Cam, guard yourself well till then!"

"Have you lost your senses, Lieutenant Gant?"

Everyone with Washington on the Grand Battery jumped to attention. Their general raised his voice so seldom, everyone craned their heads.

"Word is—" Washington spoke lower now, with a wave of his spyglass toward Staten Island "—that Howe himself has taken over your estate. I can't have you going back to rush in on him. You've probably got a bounty on your head, and I'll not have your capture making someone else's career. If they have your lady, I doubt they'll touch a hair on her head. At least they have yet to make war on ladies."

"But she has a talent for riling men, one way or another, sir," Cam argued, struggling to keep his voice controlled. "I'm not planning to go over there looking like Cam Gant

and wearing this uniform. I'll be the lowliest tinker or peddler, in some wretched excuse for a rowboat.''

"But everyone on the island knows you, and most of
them are Tories, man. We saw that clearly enough when
the traitors just laid down their arms without firing a shot.''

Washington was about to order Cam away. But he himself had sent his Martha back to Virginia for her safety,
and Cam Gant had every right to worry for his own wife's
well-being. He remembered Martha's words to him on part-
ing.

"It's so sad, my dearest George, that after fighting and
waiting all that time the poor dears didn't even have a wedding night. And now those British blackguards may ruin
everything for them!''

Washington heard himself capitulate to Cam almost before he knew he would speak. "All right. You do know
the island, and I can use a trustworthy firsthand report of
what's really going on over there. Try to bring her back,
but nothing foolhardy. I can ill afford to lose you—either
of you Gants. I'm grateful the fleet didn't charge straight
through the narrows for the fast attack I was expecting, but
I pity those they've trapped over there.''

Cam saluted and made tracks before the general could
change his mind. Strange, he thought, but while he'd been
playing Tory he'd never needed a disguise of any sort, and
now—

He mounted his stallion and rode quickly for his town
house to borrow some old clothes and some sort of scratch
wig to cover his own blond hair.

He sent his heartfelt thoughts to her on the wind. "Hang
on, Libby. Hang on, my sweetheart, whatever happens.'' In
return, he almost imagined he heard her curse the British
and whisper to him to guard himself well.

Sixteen

THE LIBERTY GAZETTE
July 1, 1776

The Staff of this Gazette wishes to publicly protest the obvious Detainment or Incarceration of our Printer, Mrs. Elizabeth Gant, née Morgan, by the British on Staten Island. In the tradition of Mrs. Gant, we continue this Paper in her absence with General Washington's bold Address to us All:

The Time is now near at Hand which must probably determine whether Americans are to be Freemen or Slaves; whether their Houses & Farms are to be pillag'd & destroy'd. The Fate of unborn Millions will now depend on the Courage & Conduct of this Army. Our cruel & unrelenting Enemy leaves us no Choice but a brave Resistance. We have, therefore, resolv'd to conquer or die.

* * *

We also dedicate this Issue to Mrs. Elizabeth Gant with two Verses from her favorite patriotic Hymn, "The Liberty Song":

   Come join Hand in Hand, brave Americans all,

And rouse your bold Hearts at fair Liberty's call
No tyrannous Acts shall suppress your just
Claim,
Or stain with Dishonor America's Name!

Then join Hand in Hand, brave Americans all,
By uniting we stand, by dividing we fall;
In so righteous a Cause let us hope to succeed,
For Heaven approves of each generous Deed.

Cameron Gant knew full well that for his own safety he should await nightfall. But by then it might be much too late to help Libby. He had to be at Melrose and ready to run with her when night came. He was afraid that if he waited the British might take her to a ship for safekeeping or at the least have more time to prepare for unwanted visitors at Melrose.

Just before noon, his pack full of hastily gathered peddler's trinkets at his feet, he bent low over his oars and rowed toward Staten Island, directly between two big-gunned British frigates. When someone bellowed down to him to board the *Scorpion*, he pretended he was deaf and shook his head stupidly, shouting, "Aye, aye." He had several knives in his pack, but he hadn't dared to bring a firearm, in case he was stopped and searched.

He finally rowed around the north side of the island. The ships' masts looked as thick as winter trees. White tents studded the green slopes below Melrose, and red dots like fire ants infested the shore. But he was relieved to see that none of the ships occupying Staten Island were ones he had visited in the East River. The Tories native to Staten Island, and his own servants, should be the only ones who might possibly recognize him.

Amidst the masses of big ships and brightly uniformed men his little rowboat and tattered garb seemed to make

him almost invisible. When no one paid him heed, he rowed past the Melrose wharf and hid the boat in a willow thicket on the edge of the Gant property far beyond the manor.

Remembering to limp like an old man, he climbed out and shouldered his pack. He had no idea how he would get into Melrose to find Libby and no set plan on how to get her out. But he would manage it somehow, or die trying. At least he knew the house's secrets. Once he managed to get inside in this disguise, he would go straight to the hall behind the kitchen pantry, where there was a rack of long-unused hunting guns that he prayed the British might have overlooked.

He clambered up a winding path from the water, where he had played Indians as a boy. He'd check the grotto first, just in case she'd left him a note or possibly hidden there herself. He edged through the bushes and peered over the little ledge.

Stacks of damned books, but no Libby. Whatever had she been doing out here with these, he fumed. He raked his hair in such frustration that he shoved off the wig he had forgotten he wore. He cursed under his breath as he retrieved and straightened it. He scratched a crude C & L and Wait Here in the ground so that she would know what to do if she came back. He tried to reason out why she had been here and then left.

His heart thudded harder than the pack bouncing against his back as he walked toward Melrose, across the lawn and through the herb garden. He was gambling that the enemy might be more careless about who entered Melrose in broad daylight than at night, when they might double the guard.

Step by step, a strange awareness grew in him of how Libby must have felt that day long ago when she had ventured onto the forbidden estate to peer in the window. She must surely have felt that the enemy was all around. She

must have been curious, afraid, yet exhilarated and driven to do what she did. He had never felt so close to her, as if their minds were linked, and he felt a surge of hope.

He nodded to the first two guards he saw and limped on, heading for the back entrance to the kitchen wing. Amazed to find the door unguarded, he ducked inside. Desperation drove him to an improvised plan. If there were soldiers in the kitchen, he would hide in the pantry with a loaded gun until his way was clear or darkness fell. Otherwise he would try to overhear where they were holding Libby in the main house so that he could sneak in there and get her out after dark.

He heard voices in the kitchen, but the back hall and the pantry looked deserted. He realized he had been holding his breath, and he sucked in air laced with cooking smells. Damn, but these Brits were taking advantage of Gant hospitality.

The old muskets were still mounted on the wall at the end of the hall—just where Charles had left them years before. How perfect his Tory brother's guns should help him free his Whig wife from the British! He grabbed one and the box of shot that lay beneath it, then darted into the pantry and closed the wooden door behind him.

His hands trembled in his haste as he primed the barrel, pricked the venthole and loaded powder and shot. He had no idea if the thing would shoot, but just the fact that he had it gave him hope and courage. He decided to peer out to see who was in the kitchen. He'd feel much better knowing and not just waiting here to be discovered. He slung his pack over his shoulder again to continue his dangerous deception and, musket raised, edged out slowly.

He was in luck! A single soldier stood watching the cooks and the scullery maid prepare a dinner that was obviously meant for the tables of his enemies. His mind raced. He could force this lobsterback to tell him where they had

Libby. Or the kitchen staff might know and help smuggle him into the main house as a servant. He thought that at least some were Whigs, and he could hope they would also feel a measure of personal loyalty to him. With only one soldier here, it was worth the risk.

"Hold. Hold right there! No one moves!" he ordered crisply, and stepped out with his musket pointed at the soldier's chest. Everyone froze. "Over here, redcoat! Now!"

His disguise must be better than he thought. None of the cooks screamed out his name, though if his eyes had not been riveted to the surprised soldier he would have seen the confused, stunned looks when they heard his voice. He grabbed the soldier's shiny Brown Bess musket to replace his own. "Cooks, carry on," he said as he shoved the soldier with his own musket barrel back toward the pantry to question him. With this fine gun and an informant, he felt almost sure of victory now.

Then everything went wrong.

The back door he had come in opened, and a loud ruckus came from outside. He thought he could depend on the cooks not to give him away, but the soldier opened his mouth to shout for help. Cam quickly knocked him cold with the butt of the gun. He'd have to hide again until those approaching passed. He shoved the unconscious soldier and both guns inside the pantry, but he was not yet inside himself when a woman slammed into him and gave a shriek.

Cam spun, praying it was Libby, but it was his housemaid, Janet. And of all the damned luck, it was Captain Phillip Hector chasing her! Could he possibly fool the man, whom he had met with frequently during the Eddie Tiler affair? Damn! What would Hector be doing over here? The *Asia* had been nowhere in sight, and Cam had presumed she was still in the East River.

Janet jumped back and gasped. Cam bent his head and flung his pack over the shoulder nearest Hector and Janet,

hoping to hide behind it. Although his body pulsed with the desire to attack Hector and beat the truth out of him, he turned away, saying, "Sorry, my lord. Sorry!"

But Janet, who had caught a lightning glimpse of him, was neither fooled nor as reticent as the cooks. She gawked, saucer-eyed, with her hands pressed to her mouth. Hector drew a pistol and shoved it against Cam's ribs with the words, "All right, beggar. Let's just see what's in that pack that might please a lady. What would you trade your favors for, my dear?"

Relief shot through him. The disguise might yet outfox Hector. Cam immediately dumped his pack, hoping Hector would bend over it so that he could lunge for the door or a gun. He yearned to get back inside the pantry to one of the muskets, but Hector might see the unconscious soldier. Two cooks came sheepishly out into the back hall, wiping their hands, looking slant-eyed at what was happening.

But when Janet didn't budge Hector squinted at him and gasped. He jammed the muzzle of his pistol even harder into his ribs. Silently, Cam cursed the times he'd met with Hector to try to free Eddie Tiler.

"Well, damn me, if you haven't made my day more than a tumble with this little tart would have!" Hector cried. "I say, turncoat Gant, you've probably just made my career! They sent for me because I'd recognize both you and Mistress Elizabeth if you were here. Thought you'd both given us the slip, and here you've come calling. The commander's over in the main house right now, just itching to find a traitor to hang tomorrow as a warning to others skulking about our new encampment."

"My wife, Hector! Where is she?"

"I regret she's given us the slip for now," he admitted, though the smug smile on his face didn't waver anymore than the cocked gun pointed at Cam's middle did. "But you shan't. Not this time. Not with a nice tight noose

around your rebel neck at dawn. Yes, I believe I'm going to plead for that personally. All right then, Washington's soldier boy, over to your previous house to see your betters! March!''

Cam cursed his luck. He had gambled for Libby's life and forfeited his own. The Brits were smarter than he had thought. They might not have known him from his gardener, but they had sent for someone who did.

As the afternoon wore on, Libby despaired of either her mother or Merry coming out of the Morgan cottage. She had secreted herself behind the thick grapevines, not far from the beehives. She could see both doors of the cottage from here. It was obvious that soldiers had been billeted in the Morgan house, as well as the other homes on the island, for lobsterbacks had come and gone, cocky as you please, through the front door from time to time. What if Mother and Merry weren't even here because they'd been taken off for questioning somewhere?

Libby knew she'd have to head back to Melrose soon. At least Cam's hidden grotto there seemed safe for now. But for a quick dart across the road and through the first field, the path she'd take to Melrose was through thick woodlots.

Her stomach was twisted with hunger and fear—and probably the tart, unripened grapes she'd been eating. How she'd love some of the honey from the hives, but she and Merry had always been very sensitive to bee stings. Even though they could wear the long gloves and veiled hat, Mother usually did the tending.

And then Merry stepped out the back door with that very beekeeping garb in her arms. Libby shook her head to be sure she wasn't dreaming after all this time. Surely, at last, this was a propitious sign. But a soldier stepped out behind

Merry and grabbed at her skirts. Merry swatted his hand away.

"No touching! Your sergeant promised," she said. "Now get back in there and give me a moment's peace to tend these other stingers."

The man laughed, shrugged and stepped back inside. Libby's pride in Merry soared. She waited, watching her sister hop about to draw her feet and ankles into the protective linen boots. She struggled into the long gloves and the heavily veiled hat, then hauled the leather honey buckets over in the wheelbarrow. Obviously disdaining the task, Merry stepped up to the first conical hive on its wooden platform and prepared to lift the lid to draw out some comb. Although she had hoped Merry would move closer, Libby chanced calling to her anyway.

"Merry! Sister! Over here!"

The veiled head jerked up. To her credit, Merry did not run over but immediately moved her bucket and gear to the hive closest to the grapevines. She kept her back to the cottage in case anyone peered out.

"Lib, they're looking for you all over Staten Island! And—"

"How's Mother?"

"Ill. Mostly with worry for you and Cam, I think. That's why I'm doing this. And to get away from those wretches inside—stingers, I call them, worse than the bees!"

"Merry, I need your help, but I don't want you to leave Mother. Don't just stand there, keep working!"

"They said they don't want to be blamed for hurting an old woman just because they want to arrest her daughter, so they've told her she can go to Manhattan. To a doctor. But she won't leave me alone with them, thank heaven, and so she refuses to go."

"And here you wanted men on Staten Island!"

"Lib, how can you joke when they've got Cam?"

Libby almost leapt out of the vines. "Cam? What?"

"Word's all over the island. He came to Melrose looking for you garbed as a peddler earlier today, and they caught him somehow. Oh, Lib, they're going to hang him first thing tomorrow on his own estate!"

Libby pressed open palms over her eyes. Violent colors, spinning, dizzying lights and roaring winds whirled through her brain. But she did not faint.

"Lib, I thought you knew and were coming to get help. I'll do anything, honest, but I don't know what, with those blasted stingers inside with Mother."

Libby jerked alert. Suddenly she knew what she could do—had to do.

"Merry!" Libby said. "I know what we can do. But first you've got to go back inside and convince Mother the only chance for us to all get away is if she agrees—no, insists— they get her to a Manhattan doctor right away. Tell her that for once she has to obey her daughters! Then you get back out here without one of those stingers again. You and I are going to take this wheelbarrow and a beehive and go visiting at Melrose. We'll go the back way through the woods and—"

"Move a hive? But that will make the bees hopping mad!"

"Indeed it will!" Libby agreed. "Now go on and get back here as fast as you can!"

It was a grueling wait before Merry came out to work the hives again and called to Libby that the sergeant inside had promised that Mother would be on her way within the hour.

"But I'm supposed to cook supper for them as soon as I'm done here," Merry told her.

"Let them starve!" Libby settled back amidst the grape leaves until Mother was brought out the front door on a

litter. Libby had an overwhelming urge to run to her, but she watched as Merry did so, then came back to the hives while the soldiers carted Georgina Morgan's litter off toward the civilian ferry.

"At least that stinger who keeps grabbing at me went with Mother," Merry muttered. "Now when are we going to make a run for it?"

"As soon as I judge they've had time to get Mother off the island. Keep looking busy."

While Merry did just that, Libby wriggled out of her petticoat and tossed it to her. "Get ready to cover a hive tightly with that. Then you'll have to lift it into the wheelbarrow. I'll take it and set out. When you think the way looks clear for you, you follow. I'll wait for you across the field in the forest. When we get to Melrose I'll have to wear that beekeeper's garb so the servants don't give me away. Besides, though none of those Brits off the new ships could know me on sight, they could have orders to stop all red-haired women."

"And then we'll sneak in to rescue Cam somehow?" Merry asked, her voice suddenly quivering.

"No," Libby told her. "We're walking boldly in the back door of Melrose and hoping no one stops a pretty girl and her beekeeper mother from delivering some honey to the British!"

It was nearly evening when Libby and Merry entered the gates of Melrose. The guards let them pass with just a little teasing and a peek in the wheelbarrow to be sure they had no guns. Merry pushed the wheelbarrow, with its buckets of fresh honey and its linen-wrapped hive. Libby, swathed in the gloves and the veil—she had discarded the bulky boots as a danger if they had to run—walked along at Merry's side. She pretended to fuss over the wheelbarrow, just the way Mother would have if she had been here. Oc-

casionally they had to move aside as riders thundered along the lane, but no one really harassed them, but for an occasional whistle at Merry.

"Now, remember, you may have to flirt with a few of them at the house to get us in the servants' entrance," Libby told her. "And if worse comes to worst, just leave and try to find that grotto I described. At least it will be dark soon."

"All I know with all you've pumped into me is these British officers must be busy men with all this traffic. Oh, Lib, there's so many redcoats here. And what are we going to do once we get inside?"

The words came to her almost as if Cam's voice were whispering the plan in her ear. "Find out where they're holding Cam and get him out somehow. Grab a gun. Use the bees and the honey as best we can. I don't know, but if you just do as I say we'll make it. We're going to have to use our wits much better than we did last time we invaded Melrose, but I've learned a thing or two since then."

"Pooh!" Merry snorted. "The Gants and their servants were angels compared to this legion of fiends."

"They're all just human beings, Merry, but men fighting men is ugly enough."

At that pronouncement, Libby straightened her back and strode more confidently toward Melrose. The veil magnified her courage. That and the fact she would rather die herself than have them take Cam from her. Despite the enemy that held it, the mansion seemed to beckon to her as never before. At least she knew that even if the British captured Merry they held no grudge against her. She hadn't published a rabble-rousing gazette. They would no doubt let her go. Otherwise Libby never would have brought her. She only hoped her beekeeper's disguise served her better than Cam's peddler's garb evidently had him.

The veil around her head made everything seem hazy

and unreal. But it was real and deadly serious, Libby warned herself. She was relieved that they were ignored by the guards on the front portico. Yet she began to tremble as they wheeled their meager weaponry around to the kitchen entrance.

"Pretend we always take our honey in here," Libby muttered.

"Halt there! What's in the wheelbarrow, you two?" a long-faced guard demanded. He stepped forward and blocked their way with his bayoneted rifle.

Merry smiled prettily up at him. "Just some sweet honey for your generals from two loyalist ladies. Gotta take it into the kitchens, you know."

"Looks like a lot of it."

"I rather thought there were a lot of you here," Merry retorted with a chuckle, though Libby heard her voice tremble. "Here, Lieutenant, open your mouth and take a taste."

Despite their predicament, Libby smiled grimly behind her veil as her comely sister plunged her finger into one of the leather buckets and lifted it, dripping with honey, to the startled man's lips.

"I'm only a private, ma'am," he told her hastily, and leaned his gun butt on the ground. He took Merry's finger into his mouth with a dazed look. Merry, though she'd have loved to choke the wretch, drew her hand back and plunged ahead with the second step she and Libby had rehearsed.

"Mr. Private, sir, you couldn't tell a poor country girl the best place to stand to see that Gant turncoat everyone's talking 'bout hang tomorrow, could you? And I was just wondering if they have him in chains and all. You know, he does deserve it." Merry said, rolling her sky-blue eyes.

"Mmm…" The soldier licked honey from his chin where she'd dribbled it. "The neck-stretching's right at dawn, but they don't want a crowd. O' course, Governor Tryon's coming, and all the brass, especially Captain Hec-

tor, who's getting himself promoted for catching Gant at this very door here.''

Libby gasped behind her veil at Hector's name and silently cursed him for having captured Cam. Her eyes darted to the entrance behind the guard, wondering how Cam had been taken here. Unfortunately, Hector would recognize her the moment he saw her, but she was not turning back.

"But 'tween now and then," the guard rattled on to Merry, "the prisoner's just cooling his heels locked in his own wine cellar down below. Isn't that a good one? Say, who's this silent one in the veils?" he asked as his eyes strayed from Merry for the first time and he squinted at Libby.

"My mother," Merry said hastily. "She really keeps the bees. Sometimes she likes to wear all that in case a bee or two has trailed us, you know—" Libby gave her a little kick behind the wheelbarrow. "Now we'll just get it all unloaded and be back out shortly, all right?" Merry asked in a rush, forcing another smile.

"I guess so, but do it fast. Can't have the hallway cluttered up with maids and honey. We got a lot of guards in the kitchen, too, since Gant's just downstairs. But you sure decorate the place to perfection, ma'am," he said to Merry with a grin.

Just outside the open pantry door, they bent shoulder to shoulder to unload the wheelbarrow and cart their goods in. "You look for Sally, even if you have to go over into the main house," Libby whispered. "If someone stops you, say Sally's the one who knows what to do with the honey. I'm going to take the wrapped hive and a bucket downstairs to the wine cellar to see who's guarding Cam."

"Alone? But—"

"If I have to loose these bees, I've got the protection and you don't. We've both been horribly sick from stings before, and we can't both do it! When you find Sally, get

her out of here somehow and hide in the grotto. And be certain you aren't followed. Now go on!''

With a forlorn glance, Merry did as she was told. Libby grunted as she lifted the hive into her arms. She had had no idea it was that heavy. She could hear and feel the angry buzzing inside when she held it against her. With difficulty, she grasped the rope handle of one leather honey bucket. She started awkwardly for the stairs on the other side of the kitchen, the bucket bumping against her knees.

As she walked across the back of the kitchen, she counted eight soldiers. Perhaps dinner had already been cooked and served, for there were no cooks or hovering footmen.

One young soldier nursing a bandaged head stopped her on her way toward the stairs. But she told him gruffly, ''Honey to be stored over here, lots of it, that's all!'' and went quickly on.

As she left the kitchen she could still hear men's voices, rumbling to mingle with the hum of the trapped bees. If she only had time, she imagined, she'd be able to eavesdrop on their conversation, then flee with Cam to General Washington to report their most secret plans. Yes, she understood now Cam's spying for the country he loved. Not only did she forgive Washington for using covert agents, she would be one herself if he but asked her!

The narrow wooden stairs down scared her. They were dimly lit, and the obscuring veil made it worse. Holding the hive and bucket, she could not see where she was stepping. But a man's voice droned below. Unarmed and alone, praying for more luck than Cam had had was the only strategy she could think of.

She recalled that the door could be locked from both sides. With great difficulty she put the bucket down and fumbled with the iron bolt on the inside. She hoped to grab a gun to force their way out of here. But if those reinforce-

ments came downstairs a locked door might at least discourage them.

She felt her way carefully down each step. How lucky that she had toured the cellars just yesterday. The wine cellar was huge and had a door that locked. A cold cellar with squashes and pumpkins was down here, too, and a general storage area for barrels.

Her shoulder scraped the rough stone wall all the way down. She froze near the bottom of the steps when she heard a voice—one she recognized all too well.

"Enjoy your last night alive, Gant!" said Captain Phillip Hector. "I'll be sending the night guard down now so I can have a good sleep on your hospitality over in the manor house. I suppose some might envy a condemned man a fine cellar full of French wines and Jamaica spirits his last night, but I know what I'd prefer. Not a cool bottle, no, but a warm little vixen like your new wife. But, I say, turncoat, I'll see to her when you're gone. Think of that tonight, then, your willful woman twisting under me while you twist on a rope. I'll take her when the British take New York!"

Libby longed to loose the bees then and there, just to silence that hateful voice. Cam could take his chances getting stung. But reason prevailed. Hector might yell for help, and the hive was still wrapped tightly in her petticoat. She'd have to put it down to free it. Was the key to the wine cellar here? Would Hector shoot her if she startled him? Even from here she could see not one but two pistols stuck in his white military belt.

"I say, who in damnation is that?" Hector demanded, drawing a gun, when he heard her. He started at her shrouded form. She squinted through the veil in the dim light. Yes, the keys still glinted dully against the wall, hanging just where they had been when Cam had shown her the wine cellar that time. Her arms ached and trembled as she knelt to set down the hive.

"Ain't this the cellar to store honey?" she asked in a gruff imitation of the worst country accent she'd ever heard. "Honey, see, sir." She shuffled closer to extend the honey bucket to him. She was tempted to dump it over his immaculate wig, but he had the gun. Her quick gaze took in two more vital pieces of information: Hector appeared to be alone with his prisoner, and Cam had recognized her voice. He pressed his face to the barred opening in the wine cellar door.

She fought to keep herself from running to him, to kiss and comfort him. But that would be the end of them both. Her heart was beating, beating so loud she was certain Hector could hear. If she could just loose the bees somehow and dive for that gun...

"If the honey was ever kept here, woman, it isn't now!" Hector snarled. His voice sounded tense and nervous. "Now get all this tripe back up the steps. But first take off that blasted veil."

"Listen, Hector," Cam's voice rang out, "she's a half-witted neighbor girl who had the pox last year and is a pitiful sight. You've had your amusement today. Just leave the loyalist lasses, especially a poor thing like this one, alone."

"I've had enough of disguises around here!" Hector insisted. He lifted the lantern from the wall and thrust it forward. "Take that hat and veil off, I say!"

"All right, then, sir," Libby said, with an exaggerated sniff, as if she were about to cry. At least Hector had lowered his gun and hung the lantern on the wall above the keys again. She toted her bucket back and sank to her knees behind the hive. With one hand she fussed with her hat and veil; with the other she carefully grasped the petticoat wrapping the hive.

"Now, damn you, girl! I don't have all day!" Hector shouted.

As she flung off the hat and veil, she straightened so that he could see her.

"You, too!" he gasped, jerking the gun upward.

But his shock gave her the extra moment she needed. She gave a terrific rip to the petticoat wrapping to jolt the hive onto its side.

Spilling bees, it rolled at Hector's feet as his gun barked at her.

At the first assault of bees, Hector darted back. Cam's hand snaked through the bars and grabbed him from behind, banging his head once against the door before he yanked away. His spent gun hit the floor. In that same instant a searing pain in Libby's upper left arm surprised her. He had shot her! But it was the noise, Hector's shouting, that worried her. The bees were already thick and stinging. She plunked the veiled hat back on her head and lunged for the keys on the wall.

Hector fought her for the keys, but the bees distracted him. She grabbed for the other gun in his belt, but he smacked it away, and she heard it hit the floor, too. Swatting madly at the bees, he screamed for help, but he need not have. At the gunshot, chaos had broken out above, and fists were already pounding on the door at the top of the stairs which Libby had bolted closed.

Hector won the mad struggle for the keys. She raked his face with her nails and scrambled for the loaded pistol on the floor. When her left arm did not seem to work, she ripped off her right glove with her teeth to hold the gun steadier in that hand. She lifted it, ignoring the pain in her left arm and the warm stream that was running down it. The gun shook, but she cocked it.

"If you don't unlock the door, I'll shoot you and take the keys. This is war, Captain, and I mean it!" Her voice was strong and clear, rising above the buzzing of the bees and the pounding from above.

To her rampant joy, he did as she asked, swinging at the tormenting bees even as he unlocked the door. She only hoped the horde had not found Cam yet. The grating of Cam's lock was drowned in the banging of musket butts breaking down the door above. In the exhilaration of having freed Cam, she had paid no heed to the fact that they were now trapped here, as surrounded and snared by the British as Manhattan was.

Cam leapt out, slammed a fist on Hector's jaw and dragged his crumpled body into the cellar. Sweeping bees away, he crashed the door closed and locked it. "If that's honey in the bucket, pour it on the steps," he said crisply.

"But we're trapped."

"The cold cellar opens outside."

One-handed, she tipped the bucket upside down on a step. He grabbed her left arm and pulled her away. "Oh, Cam—" she cried as pain sliced through her. "My arm!"

"He shot you? I didn't know. I'll help you. Come on!"

Taking her other arm, he hurried her down the little stone-floored hall toward the cold cellar as the door was smashed in above. Someone tumbled down the steps in a clatter of sword and musket. Others howled and swore.

No bees here in the cold cellar. Libby ripped off the hat and the other glove and took a shuddering breath. Cam bolted the door behind them. They stumbled over squash and pumpkins in the dark as he felt for the latch to the slanted wooden door that opened upward. Men's shouts as they found Hector and the bees found them echoed in her brain.

"My sweetheart," he whispered, "I didn't know he'd shot you. The way you fought him, I thought he'd missed. Is the pain bad?"

"No," she lied.

"Good, because I'll have to boost you up. I've got it now. Come on!"

Dusk had deepened in the time she'd been inside. She stared up at the opening, a window into the vast sky overhead, where stars were coming out. Freedom! But there was no time to savor it. Soldiers were pounding on this door, too.

He hiked her up. She extended her right arm to give him leverage as he clambered out behind her. She was drenched with blood and sweat; the night air of Melrose was a cool caress.

"Merry's supposed to meet us at the grotto with Sally," she told him as they darted across the lawn hand in hand.

She felt desperately light-headed but managed to keep her feet running under her until they'd crossed the garden. Then the world started spinning. The horizon tilted. Were dogs after them? Had she broken a window?

Cam lifted her and held her tight against his chest as he ran. He carried her into the glade, surefooted even in the falling dark. She had wrought a miracle in his life, he thought dazedly—more than one of them.

In the grotto, where a frightened Merry awaited them alone, Cam bound Libby's arm. "A surface wound, I think," he assured them, but he felt shaken to the core at what might have happened to her—to both of them. "A lot of blood, but the bullet just grazed you. My sweetheart— Merry, too—you were magnificent! But we're not quite out of here yet. When it gets pitch-black we'll get away in my rowboat, but we'll have to go the long way around."

"If only we had managed to get Sally out," Libby moaned, her good hand grasping Cam's arm as he held her to him.

"But she's already out!" Merry told them, tears shining in her eyes. "The British sent her across to Manhattan earlier today with a note to General Washington that Cam was to be hanged at dawn. And your butler, Montague, said someone named Captain Hector suggested she take the

message. He thought it would be a great joke if she also took a note about Cam's hanging to her own husband, Rob, to print in the *Liberty Gazette*!''

''That vile wretch! We'll print the story,'' Libby vowed through gritted teeth. ''The way it really happened—and with a happy ending!''

''The happy ending's yet to come. We'll have our real wedding night at last now,'' Cam told her. Libby clutched him closer, and Merry smiled despite her fears. At that moment, even with the British fleet between them and that promise, Libby knew it was as good as done.

Seventeen

⸻⟡⟡⸻

THE LIBERTY GAZETTE
July 9, 1776
SPECIAL INDEPENDENCE ISSUE

The Staff of the Gazette is proud to announce the Freedom of our Printer, Mrs. Elizabeth Gant, and her husband, Lieutenant Cameron Gant, Aide-de-Camp to General Washington, from the Enemy encamped on Staten Island. We shall likewise be proud someday soon to announce the Freedom of these Thirteen United States of America.

Today, the New York Provincial Congress meets at White Plains to rename our Province as New York State. Read below in its entirety the Declaration of Independence, newly adopt'd in Philadelphia. Though New York alone abstain'd on both Ballots, we know most good New Yorkers believe in the Truths herein express'd, for:

"We hold these Truths to be self-evident, that all Men are creat'd equal, that they are endow'd by their Creator with certain unalienable Rights,

that among these are Life, Liberty, & the Pursuit
of Happiness..."

It took Cam most of the night to row them around and
through the maze of British ships to safety in Manhattan.
News of their escape was taken immediately to an over-
joyed General Washington. Now, at the Gant town house,
Merry was sitting just down the hall with their mother, who
had been smuggled here by the supposedly loyalist doctor
the British had sent her to. Sally, jabbering like a jay,
helped Libby bathe and put her to bed while Cam was
questioned downstairs by another Washington aide. Still
stunned by the twists of the events since their wedding,
Libby lay in Cam's big, soft bed in the town house, her
arm swathed in bandages, as Sally plumped up her pillows
for the tenth time.

"I'm fine now, Sally, really."

"Rob's downstairs, you know, mistress. Came to see you
were really all right and if you have a story."

Libby smiled. "I have a thousand stories, and more to
come, but not tonight."

"Tonight, mistress? But 'tis midday!" Sally protested.

"Oh, that's right. This war makes everything topsy-
turvy." She glanced over at the thread of sun between the
drawn green velvet draperies. "It's midday, and the dawn
has passed when the enemy was going to hang my husband!
But just tell Rob my stories will have to wait until later.
For once I've something far more important to do."

As if her longings had summoned him, Cam entered, in
dressing gown and leather slippers. Sally went beet-red,
curtsied quickly and hurried out. Cam locked the door behind her and crossed to sit beside Libby. He took her hands
in his big, warm ones. His face looked drawn over his
cheekbones and his square chin, and there were dark circles

under his eyes. Little lines etched the corners of his worried gray eyes, and his lips were pressed tightly together.

"No more bleeding?" he asked.

"No, and I don't want a doctor. I got all the bad blood out on my own, you see."

"Really, Mrs. Gant? All the bad blood that's given us problems in the past, I suppose," he said teasingly, but he sobered instantly. "Libby, my sweetheart, I can't begin to tell you how much I need you. I spent all of what I thought was my last night alive thinking of you, going back in my mind and heart over everything we'd shared. I love you so much, my dearest wife!"

It was the first time he had ever put his love into words. Her heart soared; crystalline tears spiked her thick eyelashes. "Oh, my darling! Let's not dwell on the past, then. Let's make a lovely future for ourselves, no matter what's to come!"

He grinned as he shed his robe in a flourish and kicked his slippers all the way across the room. She smiled up into his eyes as he lifted the covers to join her in the deep feather bed. She scooted over to give him room. Her wide eyes drank him in. His naked, tawny body was muscular and hard and didn't look a bit tired.

They rolled together instantly, but he was careful to keep her left arm untouched. Still, she molded herself to him, sleek and supple as a cat, reveling in the feel of his angles against her yielding softness.

"It seems there's always been something to keep us apart lately, Libby, even when we're together," he whispered into her loosened red hair, marveling at how perfectly they blended, even just pressed together like this. "My burns, your wound, a few bee stings—but bless all the little devils!"

"Stop talking, unless you want to tell me you love me again, Cameron Gant!" she said, tipping her head back to

gaze up at him. "It's midday, you know, and Merry will be knocking on our door wondering how everything's going pretty soon. We may not exactly have a wedding night right now, but we can have a wedding midday."

"Are you sure you're strong enough?"

She grinned impudently. "Are you sure you are?" she countered, and moved her leg along his thigh to the shaft that already pressed against her flesh.

He dipped his head to smother a chuckle against her throat, then kissed her lazily there. "Fine, because I'm in no hurry. Today I've all the time in the world. The general's aide downstairs was quite taken with Merry, so she won't bother us. And, even if the British pick right now to blow the roofs off Manhattan, I've got my orders from the general to stay here today and 'tend to my heroine and wife.'"

She smiled at that, but not from pride at having done something to earn Washington's admiration. Here and here To tend to her...yes, it was soon obvious Cam had his

orders. And he gave her others. Delicious, wonderful, sensual orders, like "Help me get this damned clinging nightgown off you" and "Be more careful of your arm!" But those commands melted into "That's it, my sweetheart, let me touch you there.... Here, lift your leg so I can—ah, yes, that's it, my love...."

Soon raging rapture drowned all memory of pain in her arm. He strewed kisses on her eyelids, her nose, her cheeks. He laved wet caresses down her throat and trailed them around each peaked breast until she quivered exquisitely under his touch before he suckled her. He returned again and again to her taut nipples with skillful fingers and hot lips and tongue. He kissed her lips lightly, then deeply, ravishingly, and finally with a driving, devouring intensity, until they just clung together, their breath rasping.

He went on marauding forays down to her navel, her knees, even the tiny scar on her ankle. He slid his way up heavily to kiss her lips, then went exploring again. His hands and mouth were everywhere. He nudged her knees apart and loved her there. He smiled in sheer delight as she inflamed him with her own kisses and one-handed grasping and stroking. It was a perfectly balanced, equal and free union.

And when she clung to the brink of rapture, her hips made little yearning circles she could not control. She mewed deep in her throat and whirled somewhere outside herself as she clasped him to her.

"Now, please! Cam, now!"

Though he had teasingly said he would give the orders, he instantly obliged. He filled her with his strength and his passion—and his love. They rocked the bed together, rocked the world. No disguises or deceits, no arguments or wars. Only a man and his wife uniting body and soul at last. A moment of heavenly harmony, even in the face of what was yet to come.

Everything bustled at the *Liberty Gazette*. The Declaration of Independence had arrived from Philadelphia but yesterday and was to be publicly read in General Washington's presence on the Commons this afternoon. The newspapers of the town, both loyalist and rebel, had worked all night to put out one-page editions to sell in the square. Libby, however, intended to mark this momentous day by giving her papers away free to rich and poor and telling them why.

"Now listen to me, Coll," she told the boy as he stuffed dry papers just off the line into his canvas shoulder bag. "You're to say the gazette is a gift today so Americans remember the wonderful God-given gift of freedom. But tell them the British don't believe freedom is free, and we

will have to buy it at a dear price. Can you remember all that?''

"Jupiter, 'course I can. But Jos says that's written right here on the first page anyway."

"That's right, but you're to repeat it to them anyway. We've come through a lot to get this far," she said, speaking loudly enough that Jos, Rob and Sally could hear too. "And Mr. Gant and I are grateful for everything you've all done to contribute."

As the press thumped out the last papers and Sally snatched them up to dry them on the lines out back, Jos approached Libby, wiping his hands.

"Done decided myself something just now, mistress," he told her solemnly. He ran a nervous hand across his bald pate, leaving a smear of ink there despite the rag he held.

"What's that, Jos?"

"Since you and Mr. Gant risked so much—I mean, giving so much money for patriot arms and all—and this paper being free today's a risk, too, with hard times a-coming, I'm going next door to get me a wig. A real nice one, like I always wanted. And somehow I'm just gonna trust I'll have the money to keep it up in style, like I always planned. Even with money woes like our new country's got itself in, I just know we're gonna make it!''

Tears flooded Libby's eyes. She had kept herself from crying for too long. Even with the dangers of last week on Staten Island behind her, she had been through another emotional mill when Quentin Simpson had been released from jail last week. But Cam had learned of it and gone to see him. He had bought Quentin's Manhattan house and shares in his waterfront chandlery, though at an exorbitant price, and he had personally put Quentin on one of the Supplier's ships to New Jersey. Crispin Brooks had been released under Washington's general amnesty, too, but his brother, Garner, said he'd convinced Crispin to enlist. Now,

after she'd waded stoically through all that, Jos's simple declaration of his own pursuit of happiness made her dissolve into tears.

"Come on now, Mrs. Libby Gant," Rob said as Jos washed up and went next door to catch the Fannings before they, like everyone else in town, headed for the Commons. Rob handed her a clean rag, and she wiped her eyes and cheeks. "Just think a wee bit of all the other good news of the day. Sal saying if she births a girl it's to be called Elizabeth after you, eh? Or how about that lively way your clever sister described your heroics on the island, too? Why, if you'd let me print it the way that bonny lass told it, we'd have had them rolling on the Commons grass today!"

"I know, Rob." She sniffed. "And here I am crying over nothing."

"Your sister said," he went on, "she 'learned through the grapevine your brilliant plan for salvation of a captured hero.' And 'we sure did learn you can catch more Brits with honey than vinegar!' Merry said. Quite a spirited lass, your sister, eh, mistress?"

Libby blew her nose and nodded. "Too spirited at times. I'd not trust Merry Morgan to write for this gazette, however much I love her. She's so excited to be living in Manhattan she'd turn our political paper to jests and joking. She's yet to learn this war means sacrifice and pain. Go on then, Rob, and take your load to the Commons before you come back for Sally. A little rest before the celebration will do her a world of good. And if you see Coll," she added as Rob hefted his bundle of gazettes on one shoulder, "be sure he's telling folks what I said and not just tossing papers at them!"

While Sally rested upstairs, Libby washed her face and straightened up the shop. No customers had been in all morning, as folks were preparing for the big afternoon. But

she left the door ajar anyway to catch the warm sunlight and the breeze. After today, the gazette staff was taking a brief holiday—unless some catastrophe occurred again.

She should probably get a bit of rest, too, as she'd been up all night typesetting the Declaration. Cam had been with Washington, but he should be here in an hour or so to fetch her. She had plenty of time to change into a clean gown before he arrived. Merry and Mother would meet them at the Commons with the servants from the town house.

Libby closed the wooden tops over her precious trays of type and latched them shut. What a gift her dear godfather Atwood had left her—the richest inheritance of all. The power to make words, to sway people's minds. It was an awesome trust and responsibility. Why, the moment Rob had read the Declaration of Independence he had told Sally he wanted to enlist. Libby would publish the paper with just Jos, Coll and Sally as long as the war lasted, while Cam and Rob and countless others fought for her right to publish it.

Her mind drifted over the old days when she'd hated the Gants, when she'd been so prejudiced against Cam. She relived the happy, if scant, hours they had spent so peacefully together since their escape from Melrose—peaceful but for their wonderful bouts in bed. When she heard the door creak, she turned with a smile on her lips, expecting to see him—and stared into the contorted face of Quentin Simpson.

"You—you went to New Jersey," she floundered as he closed the door behind him with a push of his hips. He had a gun—and it was pointed right at her.

"Couldn't stay there," he told her. "Not with unfinished bus'ness wi' you."

Her insides cartwheeled. He was drunk. And Quentin had always been his meanest when he was drunk. His words

were slurred, as they had been the times she had seen his
father make him leave the premises.

"Ruint me from the first, you have, caused all m' troubles. Been watchin' coupla days for when you'd be alone.
Owe you for so much—and gonna pay! Been holding this
grudge since our youngest days."

His last words taunted her. She had held a grudge against
Cam, but all had ended happily there. Now another bitter
memory might get her killed. Her mind darted for a way
out, but there was none. Sally was asleep upstairs, but if
she summoned her somehow the sodden wretch might
shoot her, too. Rob's gun was in the back room, in the
bottom of the rag basket. Suddenly she knew she would
not escape death from a gun this second time an enemy
held one on her. In the chaos in the cellar at Melrose, Captain Hector had only wounded her arm, but Quentin was
pointing his directly at her heart. She stared at him blankly,
as she might have a viper about to strike, but her heart and
thoughts were all with Cam.

"Your father loved you, Quentin," she heard herself say
quietly. "Don't do this. Cam gave you money. Just go
away."

"I will—af'er this. Af'er I even the score that my father
din't love me at all. Loved you, gave you all this. Your
fault. A pox on you 'n this place I was never good enough
for! Tha's it."

He leaned against the stationery counter and cocked the
gun. She watched his face furrow in concentration as he
prepared to fire it.

The shop door opened so quickly it took both her and
Quentin unawares. Cam! Quentin spun on him even as Cam
hurled himself at the demented man. A gun banged. The
two went down, grappling. Libby screamed and tore around
the counter before she realized that Quentin was no longer
struggling. He lay very still in Cam's arms.

"Cam! You're not hit!" she shrieked.

"But this gun didn't fire—" he began.

And then they saw Sally as she stepped through the door to the back room with Rob's smoking gun in her hand.

Cam got slowly to his feet, gripping Libby's arm. Libby gaped, stunned. Sally dropped the gun as though it burned her.

"Oh, Sally, Sal!" Libby cried, and ran to hug her. "You heard our voices down here!"

"No, no!" she told Libby as she clung to her mistress, wide-eyed and shaking, while Cam came over to comfort them both. "I was asleep and had a dream the British were still after us. 'Twas so real I woke up. But I knew I'd feel better if I could see you. So I just came downstairs—and when I saw Mr. Simpson I knew I needed Rob's gun. And then Mr. Gant came in, but I shot Mr. Simpson. Oh, Mistress Libby," Sally sobbed. "Who says this isn't our war, too!"

"That's right," Cam said as he helped Sally over to Libby's chair. "But maybe it takes a man who has a bold and beautiful woman like you or my Liberty's Lady to know it."

He stood and pulled Libby into his strong embrace and whispered to her, "Quentin's dead. And so is the past for us, my darling. And all our private wars are over now, and we'll face and survive this one, in love, together."

It seemed all brave New York civilians—for that was the only kind left, as all the others had fled by now—ringed the Commons as General Washington rode on his massive gray horse to the middle of the grassy area. Mounted, he surveyed the sea of heads. His brigades had been kept in quarters because an attack might be imminent, but he had brought his honor escort, bold and handsome in their blue and buff. Despite the general's serious demeanor, an air of

festivity and a repressed energy laced the air. Everyone sensed it and responded to it, though Washington did not budge from where he was sitting, stiff backed, on his stallion.

The sky above was a shatteringly clear blue. The Gant-Morgan entourage, without Merry, who was late for some reason, stood together under a large chestnut tree in the shade of the hot day. Georgina Morgan sat listlessly fanning herself on a camp stool Cam had ordered brought for her. Her ill health, the heat, Merry's tardiness and Libby's hair-raising tales of her adventures today had quite taken the starch out of the woman's legs.

Standing behind the family were the servants from the town house and the staff from the *Liberty Gazette*. The print shop folk still held copies of the newspaper they'd been giving out today. Libby, too, had an armful that made her look like a tradeswoman instead of the wife of a Gant, Georgina Morgan thought with a helpless shake of her head. But Libby had insisted on handing them around herself as if she still couldn't afford a maid or even an apprentice. My, my, Georgina thought, if Cam can't control her, at least I am no longer expected to, either!

Jos Bean, prouder and taller than he'd ever looked in his new fine powdered wig, stood with his hand on Coll's shoulders. Rob Graham, in his new gray-and-green private's coat of the Third New York had his arm around his wife's shoulders and, thrust in his new gunbelt, the pistol he had brought all the way from Edinburgh, a pistol that had served his friends so well. Tomorrow he would report to the Grand Battery for his first drills. But today he had come to hear the Declaration that so clearly stated things he'd gladly spend his life for, despite his sweet, brave Sal and the babe that was coming.

The drums of the general's escort rolled, and silence fell. A chaplain read the Eightieth Psalm in a quavering voice,

and then a man's loud voice rang out. "When in the course of human events..."

Everyone listened, nodding from time to time at the listing of the insults of the king and his ministers, insults that touched them especially closely. The enemy had cut off their trade, quartered large bodies of armed troops in private homes, plundered the seas, ravaged the coast and destroyed the lives of people. "We mutually pledge to each other our lives, our fortunes, and our sacred honor," the stentorian voice concluded.

"And I pledge to love and honor you forever," Cam whispered in Libby's ear, and squeezed her arm. Her answering smile dazzled him.

Three loud huzzahs sounded, as if the crowds were cheering Cam's vow. A few hats sailed skyward. Grim faced despite the burgeoning merriment, Washington rode back to his headquarters at Number 1 Broad Way Street while the crowds dispersed to stroll along in the wake of his contingent. Cam sent two maids to help Mrs. Morgan back home, then strolled down Broad Way Street with Libby on his arm.

Along the way, the two of them began to pass out remaining copies of the *Liberty Gazette*. "Remember this day," Libby told a thin, ill-looking old man, pressing a paper into his hand. "Can you read, sir?"

"No," he replied, leaning on his walking stick. "But I'll give it to my boy when he comes home on leave. And thankee."

"Tell your son to keep it," she called back to him. "It tells all about why we have to fight!"

Cam was passing them out beside her, his voice choked with emotion at the thought of all that today meant. "This day's a landmark in our nation's birth!" he told some folks. "Remember it to tell your children and grandchildren. That's what I'm going to do!"

"*Our* children and grandchildren!" Libby added proudly.

"Exactly, and plenty of them!" Cam replied with a wink.

"It's not like Merry to miss all this," Libby told Cam. "Perhaps we'd better go home to see if she's all right?"

"Merry Morgan all right?" Cam teased. "I'd bet either Morgan sister against the British any day. But we'll stroll on back if you want. Besides, I have the strangest urge for a nice, restful afternoon nap."

Libby smiled unabashedly into his eyes and nodded her assent. But as they walked along they saw that the rowdies in the crowd had obviously been putting ale and rum away with their dose of high-minded politics. Three ragged cheers for the general went up just outside Washington's office, and then the crowd surged toward the bowling green by old Fort George.

Coll darted up to them, his papers gone at last. "The king's gold statue, Mistress Gant! Jupiter, they say they're gonna pull it down and make bullets out of its lead insides!"

Cam laughed. "A noble use of it! The king contributes something good to the cause of liberty at last!"

They followed along in the rolling wake. Libby and Cam laughed with excitement and echoed the high spirits of the defiant crowd. More than once the rebel defacers lifted fists and yelled insults at the distant line of ships that still hovered like vultures out over by Staten Island.

Suddenly ropes and crowbars materialized in the crowd. New Yorkers draped nooses around the mounted king's neck and pried at the base of the two-ton statue. At last it tipped and toppled and thundered from its pedestal to the ground in a cloud of choking dust.

People jumped up and down and clapped their hands. The crowd roared. Someone sawed off the king's head and

pried his laurel wreath away. Cam and Libby hugged each other hard. The crowd's cries drowned out their words, but they were lost in each other's presence again.

At last King George's big, gilded head was hoisted aloft and paraded by. At that everyone screamed themselves hoarse in feverish joy.

"I sympathize with the poor statue, losing its head like that," Cam yelled in Libby's ear. "I did the same a long time ago over you, my love!" He pecked her cheek, then turned her to him with both hands cradling her face to kiss her deeply and possessively on the mouth. "Let's go home together."

Amidst America's defiant cheers in the face of the coming war, there was nothing for Cam and Libby Gant in that precious moment but the trust, peace and love they had overcome so much to build.

In the years to come, others would observe and envy that love. Cam himself would treasure it through all the dangerous times to come. And Libby would print it again and again on her heart.

Author's Note

⤷ᴄᴇᴏ⤸

Full-scale war came to New York the next month, when the British swarmed over Long Island. Washington's only victory there was to cleverly retreat to fight again another day. Afterward, Lieutenant Cameron Gant accompanied the Continental Army to New Jersey in the first of Washington's famous retreat-and-regroup maneuvers. Cam served General Washington and the new nation with great distinction during the war.

The conquering British came ashore en masse to take Manhattan on September 15, 1776. To escape them, Libby Gant fled with her *Liberty Gazette* to Cam's friends in New Haven, Connecticut. From there she continued to defy the enemy with her bold newspaper until the British finally withdrew from New York and America in November of 1783.

Although Mrs. Georgina Morgan died just before the British took New York, Merry Morgan, according to Cam and Libby's plan, was also evacuated. She went to live with Cam's merchant associates, the wealthy Shippen family, in the capital city of Philadelphia. The tumultuous years of the War for Independence and the essential role France played in the final victory are part of Merry Morgan's adventures as the "Freedom Flame."

**Everybody in Parish, Mississippi, knows that
come sundown things change....**

Ben Rader was back in town, and, as chief of police, he
intended to use his power to investigate his friend's mysterious
death. He soon realized, though, that he was up against
blackmail, drugs, even murder. And his only key to the truth
was Eve Maitland, a woman he wasn't sure he could trust.

HELEN R.
Come Sundown
MYERS

ALL THAT GLITTERS

by *New York Times* bestselling author

LINDA HOWARD

Greek billionaire Nikolas Constantinos was used to getting what he wanted—in business and in his personal life. Until he met Jessica Stanton. Love hadn't been part of his plan. But love was the one thing he couldn't control.

From *New York Times* bestselling author Linda Howard comes a sensual tale of business and pleasure—of a man who wants both and a woman who wants more.

Available in May!

National bestselling authors

JENNIFER BLAKE
EMILIE RICHARDS

Welcome to the Old South—a place where the finest women
are ladies and the best men are gentlemen. And where men
from the wrong side of town have more honor than all the
blue bloods combined! This is a place where everyone has
their place and no one dares to cross the line. But some
rules are meant to be broken....

Sweeping romance and sizzling passion...
and you will soon discover that
NOT ALL MEN ARE CREATED EQUAL.

Available in May 1998 at your favorite retail outlet.

Look us up on-line at: http://www.romance.net   MANTHSG

bp

AUTHOR NOTE

As the handsome cover of this book suggests,
Liberty's Lady is about two ruling passions: love
and freedom. Although we are not living during the
dangerous days of the American Revolution, we all
must deal with the challenges of love and liberty.

I am very pleased to have this novel re-issued nearly
nine years after it first appeared under my pen name,
Caryn Cameron. And it's exciting to know the book will
be on America's store shelves as we approach the
celebration of America's 222nd Independence Day!

In a way, *Liberty's Lady* is also the timeless Cinderella
story in which so many western women believe.
Dashing aristocrat Cameron Gant seems a dream—
and at times a nightmare—to working-class
Libby Morgan. But, in spite of great odds, it is partly
her independent nature that intrigues him and
provides their happy ending.

I'm also pleased that MIRA will re-issue the companion
book to this novel, *Freedom Flame,* next year. In it,
Libby's younger sister, Merry Morgan, meets her match
and takes the reader the rest of the way through the
War for Independence. For the Morgan sisters, it is also
the battle of the sexes—a woman's war for love.

I enjoy hearing from my readers and answer my
correspondence. You can write me c/o MIRA Books.

Best wishes,

Karen Harper

To my niece and nephews
with love and the wish for liberty always:
Robert, Kristine, Jason, Aaron and Andrew Kurtz

MIRA

ISBN 1-55166-433-X

LIBERTY'S LADY

First published under the name Caryn Cameron.

Printed in U.S.A.

KAREN HARPER

LIBERTY'S LADY

MIRA